Praise for Jill Winters's novels

Raspberry Crush

"Tart yet sweet . . . a long tall drink of entertainment."
—Stephanie Bond, author of *Party Crashers*

"Billie is a cute cookie, and her kooky coworkers make the story even more fun." —*Detroit Free Press*

"Delicious [and] heartwarming." —Barnes & Noble Reviews

"Hilarious . . . one crazy, cool novel." —Book Review Café

"Witty . . . outrageous . . . just plain fun to read."
—Readers and Writers Ink

Blushing Pink

"Fun and sexy, Winters's second novel generates plenty of heat between the two attractive lead characters." —*Booklist*

"Wickedly funny . . . sizzling!" —*Curvy Novels*

"A racy, rompy, and riotously fun tale—a laugh-out-loud page turner." —The Word On Romance Reviews

"A fun and frisky tale. Jill Winters continues her humorous storytelling in this second novel, combining love, lust and laughter into a memorable read." —Escape to Romance Reviews

"An entertaining contemporary romance." —The Best Reviews

"*Blushing Pink* is fun. The main characters are likable [and] the sex is pretty darn hot." —All About Romance

continued . . .

And meet Peach's sister, Lonnie, in Jill Winters's debut novel
Plum Girl
A Finalist for the Dorothy Parker Award of Excellence

"Quirky, sexy, fun!"   —Susan Andersen

"*Plum Girl* just about has it all: great characters, romance, suspense and comedy . . . An intriguing and fun read."
—Romance Reviews Today

"[An] amusing lighthearted romp."   —BookBrowser

"A fun, sexually charged yarn for those who like spicy romance mixed with mystery."   —*Booklist*

"Fans of contemporary romance novels will enjoy Jill Winters's amusing, lighthearted romp."   —*Midwest Book Review*

"[A] fun read . . . very sexy."   —*Affaire de Coeur*

"A vivid debut from an author with a natural voice for humorous romance."   —*The Romance Reader*

"A zany romantic comedy with healthy doses of passion and suspense . . . countless laugh-out-loud moments."
—Escape to Romance Reviews

"I don't know what was more fun, reading about Lonnie's yummy love interest or keeping tabs on her life at work. . . . Fun . . . steamy . . . a great read."   —Curvy Novels

"Newcomer Jill Winters, with her refreshing knack of writing as people speak, has done a first-class job with her first book, *Plum Girl*. . . . Ms. Winters adroitly mixes comedy with mystery and this, together with vibrant characters, witty dialogue, and candid observations, makes *Plum Girl* a must-read."
—Curled Up With a Good Book Reviews

"Lighthearted and witty . . . an interesting blend of romance and suspense."   —*Romantic Times*

Just Peachy

jill winters

 NEW AMERICAN LIBRARY

New American Library
Published by New American Library, a division of
Penguin Group (USA) Inc., 375 Hudson Street,
New York, New York 10014, USA
Penguin Group (Canada), 10 Alcorn Avenue, Toronto,
Ontario M4V 3B2, Canada (a division of Pearson Penguin Canada Inc.)
Penguin Books Ltd., 80 Strand, London WC2R 0RL, England
Penguin Ireland, 25 St. Stephen's Green, Dublin 2,
Ireland (a division of Penguin Books Ltd.)
Penguin Group (Australia), 250 Camberwell Road, Camberwell, Victoria 3124,
Australia (a division of Pearson Australia Group Pty. Ltd.)
Penguin Books India Pvt. Ltd., 11 Community Centre, Panchsheel Park,
New Delhi - 110 017, India
Penguin Group (NZ), cnr Airborne and Rosedale Roads, Albany,
Auckland 1310, New Zealand (a division of Pearson New Zealand Ltd.)
Penguin Books (South Africa) (Pty.) Ltd., 24 Sturdee Avenue,
Rosebank, Johannesburg 2196, South Africa

Penguin Books Ltd., Registered Offices:
80 Strand, London WC2R 0RL, England

First published by New American Library,
a division of Penguin Group (USA) Inc.

First Printing, May 2005

NEW AMERICAN LIBRARY and logo are trademarks of Penguin Group (USA) Inc.

LIBRARY OF CONGRESS CATALOGING-IN-PUBLICATION DATA:
Winters, Jill.
  Just peachy / Jill Winters.
      p.   cm.
   ISBN 0-451-21506-0 (trade pbk.)
   1. Gift basket industry—Fiction.   2. Missing persons—Fiction.   3. Supervisors—
Fiction.   I. Title.
   PS3623.I675J87 2005
   813'.6—dc22

                                                                2004029233

Set in Adobe Garamond
Designed by Daniel Lagin

Printed in the United States of America

PUBLISHER'S NOTE
This is a work of fiction. Names, characters, places, and incidents either are the product of
the author's imagination or are used fictitiously, and any resemblance to actual persons, living
or dead, business establishments, events, or locales is entirely coincidental.

This book is for Amy, a perfect peach.

Acknowledgments

Sincere thanks to Laura Cifelli, my wonderful editor, who can talk business and crack me up in the same phone call, and Annelise Robey, whose patience, enthusiasm, and determination always keep me focused. Much thanks to Meg Ruley and the Jane Rotrosen Agency for all of their support, and thanks to my fabulous family and friends for reading my work. Last but not least, thank you, Peach, for finally cooperating with me, though you could probably stand to gain a few pounds.

Chapter One

"I haven't been this desperate since yesterday."

"Oh, whatever, yes, you have," Peach said, and tugged on her knit cap as long, golden hair blew around her face.

"True," BeBe conceded, grinning. "So remind me again why we're doing this."

"What do you mean? We're serving womankind—it's not our fault people keep crossing the street to get away from us and are desperately avoiding eye contact."

"True," BeBe said again, "but still . . . I don't know . . . why is it no matter what volunteer assignment Tim gives us, I never end up feeling like I'm actually *doing* anything?"

"Don't worry; we're gonna do something," Peach assured her. "I'm determined to sell at least five raffle tickets this morning. I'll buy them myself if I have to."

"You've already bought fifty!" BeBe said. "I think when you exceed our cable bill, you've gone too far."

Hmm . . . she'd never quite thought of it like that.

It was a glistening morning in the beginning of December. Powdery flurries blanketed the cobblestone streets of Downtown Crossing, and Peach was struck by how ethereal the scene was.

As a sea of delicate-looking flakes floated straight toward her, she had the sudden sense of living inside a snow globe. Winters in Boston were always sparklingly pretty, even when they were bitingly cold. Now with Christmas barely a month away, street lamps were wrapped with evergreen garland and trees glittered with little white lights, while bells jingled distantly from street-corner Santas.

A swift, icy breeze suddenly blew across their table, rustling the loosely folded strips of raffle tickets that lay beside the cash box.

Peach hugged herself to fight off the chill that drilled through her red-gold-and-black patchwork coat. The worn velvet jacket harked back to her junior year at NYU, and somehow six years later it was still in one piece—which was good, because Peach planned to wear it until it literally disintegrated off her body.

Just then a big, frosty-wet drop flew right into her eye. With a startled, breathy laugh, Peach tried to blink it away.

"What are you laughing at?" BeBe asked, slanting a look at her.

"Just how pathetic we are right now," Peach replied, smiling. "Sorry I dragged you out of bed for this," she added, shutting the metal cash box that sat impotently in front of them to keep dry whatever puny pittance they *did* have.

"Don't be sorry," BeBe said, pushing the fur-trimmed hood of her puffy winter jacket up over her head. "It's not your fault the financial district is full of cheapskates."

"*Tell* me about it," Peach said. "I was sure catching people right before work would be great. Hmm . . . maybe we aren't being pushy enough."

BeBe held a hand up and warned, "We're selling raffle tickets—"

"Or *not* selling them—"

"Let's not turn it into a pep rally."

"Fine, fine . . . but I still think we should've brought a whistle."

Earlier that morning they'd set up a small folding table on the wide, snow-carpeted patio outside of Borders Books & Music, in a pocket of downtown Boston that was always jumping with people—mostly young professionals bustling their way to work, who apparently weren't interested in entering a raffle for Jet Skis. Why, just because it was December and freezing cold? Sometimes people had no imagination.

The raffle was organized by Boston on Board, a local outreach center where Peach and BeBe sporadically volunteered. Peach had first heard about it a couple of years ago when she'd been working for Iris Mew—a society woman who dabbled full-time in the charity circuit, mostly as a way to legitimize her opulent existence. To Iris Mew, charity had been a means of making social contacts and tax deductions, but Peach liked it because it allowed her to tell herself she was good person. Also, it helped her hone her people skills, and since she viewed herself as something of an amateur psychologist, sharp people skills were crucial.

Meanwhile Boston on Board made it so easy. There was always a slew of new opportunities posted up in the front hall of the out-reach center; volunteers could sign up for whatever projects interested them or fit best into their busy lives. Then Tim, the Boston on Board program coordinator, would contact volunteers with details and instructions. Basically it was sacrifice-at-your-convenience, but Peach had to admit that was better than no sacrifice at all. She and BeBe had met in Harvard Square almost two years ago, when they'd both been working at the same bake sale, handling the cash and, for the most part, resisting the urge to taste-test the inventory.

The two had become fast friends. And six months ago, when BeBe's boyfriend, John, had gotten cold feet about moving in with her, leaving BeBe desperate for someone to share the burden of her new apartment, they'd become roommates, too. Considering it was a gorgeous place in the Back Bay—spacious, freshly painted (by Peach), no blatantly freaky neighbors in sight—Peach had been thrilled to help. Technically there was only one bedroom, so Peach had set her room up in what was supposed to have been the study—which kind of said it all. How many apartments actually came with a study?

Right now, BeBe was probably wishing she were back there, with her head under the covers. While Peach had to be at her office by nine, BeBe's shift didn't start till five. She worked as a bartender at Teddy McMurphy's, a chain restaurant similar to Bennigan's—always replete with lonely hearts at the bar and hyper kids in the booths.

"So finish telling me about this new guy Mindy set you up

with," Peach said, looking over at BeBe, whose face was almost completely shielded by her hood and the fluffy fake fur that was dusted with snow.

"Oh, right . . ." BeBe said, and sat further back in her folding chair, which brought her short legs up enough so that her feet barely touched the ground. "Well, his name's Ken," she said, referring to her blind date tonight. Her hood slipped back a couple inches, revealing a round, soft-looking cheek, and some of her brown pixie cut. With her plump little body and her big brown eyes, BeBe Lydecker was an adorable bundle; she was also Peach's closest friend besides her older sister, Lonnie. "And supposedly, he's not a deviant," she added with half-hearted conviction.

"Good—encouraging," Peach said, nodding supportively.

"Mindy also swears he's not gay, which will be a nice relief."

"Oh, come on, that only happened once. And technically, you don't even know that guy was gay."

"No, I know, you're right," BeBe admitted grudgingly. "Maybe he wasn't gay. He just wore eyeliner, and asked if I knew a good waxing place where he could get 'the full monty,' whatever *that* means."

Peach agreed, "Yeah—gay or not, you don't need a china doll."

"Besides, how would I know a good waxing place? I use cheap disposable razors—if I'm feeling conscientious, and that's a big if."

"Well, he didn't know *that*," Peach said with a giggle.

"True, but still."

"I wonder what Mindy was thinking." Especially if BeBe's exboyfriend, John, was any indication of what she found attractive; he looked perpetually overgrown, with thick scruffy hair, never-say-die five-o'clock shadow, and the only thing remotely lining his eyes was a unibrow.

Still, Peach and BeBe could agree on one thing: Neither of them went for pretty boys. Particularly those with a bad case of shellacked gel-head. Or those with tweezed and sculpted eyebrows. Or those with the contrived "messy" look that required crazy spikes arranged in self-conscious disarray. In other words, the majority of the guys their age. But maybe Peach was kind of picky, and maybe to a fault. Then again, could there really be such a thing? After all, she didn't want to settle, and in the recesses of her mind and body, she was looking for something very specific in the opposite sex. She wanted a man who was more . . . well . . . *genuine* than a lot of the guys out there. Someone unpretentious and unpreening—someone she clicked with, who was smart, sincere, and sensitive, not to mention funny, strong, caring, handsome, unchauvinistic, sexy, and loyal—and it helped if he was close with his family. Surely one of those would be coming around the corner any day now, and in the meantime, Peach was in no particular rush.

BeBe, on the other hand, applied the guerrilla marketing approach to dating. In fact, ever since John had broken up with her, she'd embarked on a string of blind dates, seeming almost urgent to find his replacement. Often lamenting how it sucked to be single—no offense intended, of course—BeBe would vacillate between bright bursts of determination and pessimistic, emotionally charged rants about how no one could measure up to John. It all depended, of course, on how each blind date went, if the guy ever called again, and if BeBe ever *wanted* him to call again—all random factors in a totally precarious equation.

So far none of BeBe's setups had amounted to more than an amusing or bizarre anecdote she could recount to Peach on one of their power walks through Boston Common. *If she would only let herself get over John,* Peach thought now, and not for the first time.

"How does Mindy know this guy?" Peach asked.

"Friend of her brother."

"What does he do for a living?" Not necessarily a deal breaker, but valuable information all the same.

"Um, let me think . . . oh, she claims he's a resident at Beth Israel Hospital."

"What do you mean 'claims'?" Peach asked.

BeBe shrugged and blew on her fists. "You never know with Mindy."

"Well, she wouldn't just *lie*, would she?"

Shaking her head, BeBe brushed some snow off her sleeve and blew on her balled-up hands. "No, but she just doesn't pay attention when people talk to her. It's like she's never really listening. You know, one of those people who's always looking around when you are trying to have a conversation with her."

Sure, Peach knew the type. She'd met Mindy only a handful of times, but she definitely seemed a little flaky. Very petite with artificially pale blond hair, she flitted around McMurphy's with a flirty smile, while BeBe did most of the actual work of bartending. BeBe claimed that Mindy had a true gift for flirting, because she made even the homeliest guys feel cute.

BeBe also claimed that only the dorky losers bothered flirting with *her*—and only if they were drunk. As usual, Peach had difficulty believing her roommate's darkly skewed version of reality, though in this case, if there was any truth to it, BeBe's demeanor at work inevitably played a part. Efficient and all business, BeBe didn't put out much of an available vibe while she was working. Not that she could blame her, but still, Peach hoped BeBe would find a good catch soon—before John launched into another predictable bout of groveling and trying to convince her to give him another chance.

"Well, promise me you'll go into this date tonight with a good attitude," Peach said.

"I will, I will," BeBe said, but her tone was perfunctory. "I'm just trying not to get my hopes up, because so far Mindy's oh for two."

"Two . . . ? Wait, the eyeliner guy, and who else?"

"That married guy, remember?"

"Ohhh," Peach said, nodding as she recalled the guy BeBe went out with last month who had a line on his finger that gave him away. Not a tan line, but a pressure line where his wedding ring had apparently made an indentation in his pudgy flesh. Not exactly the catch of the day. "But I thought your sister set you up with him."

"No, Yvonne set me up with that host at IHOP—who preferred to be called *maître d'*."

Peach laughed and blew some stray hair out of her face that the wind had kicked over. "But back to the great time you're gonna have tonight. You're *not* going to compare everything he says and does to John; you're just going to be devil-may-care *cazh*, right?"

"Yes, master."

Wait . . . was this what BeBe had meant last week when she'd told Peach that she could sometimes be too pushy?

Probably not.

"And my attitude is not the problem. It's the immature guys in this city," BeBe argued. "But this one lives in the suburbs, so maybe he's not as bad. Then again, he probably sponges off his parents and makes his mother do his laundry."

"I see we're getting a jump start on the positive attitude, then?" Peach said dryly.

BeBe just smirked at her. "Anyway, I don't even know why I'm trying to meet a decent guy—it's obviously hopeless. Everyone's got baggage. No one will be as great as John."

"Yeah, real great. He left you high and dry with a new lease and a king-size bed you couldn't afford. BeBe, for*get* about John." BeBe had gotten the new bed only because she knew how much John liked to "sprawl;" apparently he was sprawling out now in his old apartment, with his same deadbeat roommate, as they both stared bug-eyed, and carpal-tunnel-fingered at PlayStation. "John didn't deserve you!" Peach went on. "These things just take time. I mean, look at me."

"I'd rather not; I'll get depressed."

"Oh, please," Peach said, rolling her eyes, unwilling to indulge BeBe when she backslid into an affliction that BeBe herself termed Skinny-Blonde Envy. "Seriously. I know there must be plenty of appealing men in this city who are single," Peach insisted. At the words, they both took a moment to survey their street, through the fluttering swarm of snowflakes, watching as men walked past them on Washington Street and poured down School Street in droves. "Hmm . . . hey, what about that one? In the brown coat?" Peach asked, motioning toward a young man, probably in his late twenties, moving swiftly down the sidewalk opposite from them. Snow fell lightly on his brown hair, and his head was angled down as he used his newspaper to half shield the snow from his glasses.

"Enh," BeBe replied flatly. "I'm not excited."

"Really? I think he's cute," Peach said. A little bookish maybe, but still kind of cute, especially for a random guy on the street.

"Anyway, he probably has a girlfriend," BeBe added with her usual lack of zealous optimism. Although she used to say, "Probably has a girlfriend who's blond and skinny," so in a sick way, this was progress.

"Hey, look!" Peach said excitedly. "Someone's coming toward us!"

Finally! It wasn't an appealing guy—it was even better: someone who'd taken notice of their sign for the raffle ticket sale and was heading straight for their table. This charitable soul was a sturdy if disheveled lady with matted gray hair and a big rolling metal cart filled with newspapers. Okay . . . Peach should've known there would be a catch.

"Hi," she said brightly. "Would you like to enter our raffle? The grand prize is a brand-new pair of Jet Skis, and all the proceeds go to Children's Hospital—"

"Hello . . ." the woman said in a thick, gravelly voice, probably similar to Kathleen Turner's after a night of heavy-metal karaoke. Apparently she was set to ignore Peach's intro. "Can you spare a dollar?" she asked.

"I think that's our line," BeBe said.

Frowning, the bag lady inched closer to the table. "You're such kind souls to listen. You see, I left my wallet on the T this morning, and now I have no way to get home. And if I can't get home, I can't let my kid in when he gets home from school. I just need a couple of dollars so I can get home . . . you know . . . for my kid. I know you kind ladies can understand what I'm going through . . . me and my *kid*."

"Well . . ." Peach began, skeptical of the woman's story, of course, but also a little self-conscious to be sitting behind a big metal cash box—even if its contents at the moment were pretty pathetic.

"Sorry, we're working for a charity here. We can't give the charity's money away," BeBe said firmly.

Peach nodded with a trite look of apology, and suddenly spotted a police car crawling along the snow-covered street. "Oh, why don't you ask that cop for help?" she offered, motioning to the squad car. "He'll help you—at the very least, he'll make sure you get home for your child." She knew there was probably no child, but she was hoping. . . .

The old lady looked over the shoulder of her ratty tweed coat, grimaced, and just like that her demeanor switched from victimized to pissed off. "Forget it, forget it," she snapped. "Thanks for nothing." As she did a quick K-turn with her cart and hunkered off, she muttered, "Rotten bitches."

"O-kay," BeBe said, rolling her eyes and blowing on her cold fists again. "Serving womankind is going better and better. Nothing like getting called a bitch before you've even had a chance to be one. What time is it anyway?"

Peach checked her clunky silver watch. "Eight forty-five," she said. "Oh, shoot, I've gotta get going soon." The Millennium Gift Basket Company, where Peach worked as a creative consultant, was just down the street and around the corner. At this point she'd probably make it to her desk just on time, but only if she skipped her pumpkin-pie latte from the Daily Grind. There was always a long line in the morning; most people seemed pretty desperate, not only for caffeine, but for any way to prolong the inevitability of their desks. Peach rarely dreaded her job, though, and she supposed she could live without her morning shot of pumpkin pie, which was just one of her daily sugar fixes. Slipping out for a flaky frosted pastry from Mackie's Diner was another one, which she'd try to make time for later.

Her mother, Margot, had told her more than once that her sugar habit would cease being cute when Peach hit thirty. Obviously there was only one way to find out.

BeBe covered her mouth to yawn again.

Suddenly, like a thunderbolt, Peach remembered something

crucial. "Hey, what's going on with the puppy?" Eagerly, she searched BeBe's profile, what she could see of it behind her hood, and noticed the vibrant pinkness of her cheek, which was probably ice-cold to the touch. "Did you talk to your mom's friend about bringing it over tonight?"

Ellen Weinberg—friends with Ramona Lydecker, who shared her affluent, tennis-playing, country-club-dwelling, sidecar-sipping way of life—was a prominent dog breeder. Specifically, she bred bichon frise and Pekingese show dogs. As an animal lover, Peach couldn't even fathom taking care of a cute, sweet little puppy and then, after several weeks, selling it off to someone else without emotion. Well, for the most part, anyway. Shamefully, she had to confess that even after working in an animal hospital when she was in college, she still found Pekingese dogs a little creepy. Besides looking like mutantly large tarantulas, they hobbled around like limping rodents with avaricious mouths that were full of jagged teeth. What could she say? She couldn't warm up to *every* living thing that crossed her path.

But not the bichons, which were always fluffy and adorable, known for their natural smiling expression and spunk.

According to BeBe's mom, when Ellen Weinberg discovered that her bichon's ears were too long to make for a "best in show" dog, she'd decided to sell it to a pet store, but BeBe had intercepted first. She'd begged her mom's friend to let her have the puppy instead, so she could save it from its cruel fate of a smelly, slipshod pet store where the air was stagnant but germs were in constant circulation. Weinberg had acquiesced, but it wasn't as though she needed the money anyway.

"Right, I've gotta call her this afternoon," BeBe said. "The sooner I get her, the better. I've always wanted a dog. And thanks for agreeing to help me."

"No problem," Peach said, and rose to her feet because she really had to get to work.

BeBe stood, too. So the great raffle ticket experiment had winded to an anticlimactic close. After zipping up her winter coat till the collar partially covered her mouth, BeBe turned to look at Peach, and in a moment of quiet seriousness, she said, "So . . . just to recap . . . you really think if I keep going on dates, I'll find someone better than John?"

"Of *course*," Peach assured her, squeezing her in a friendly one-armed hug. Hell, she could probably find someone better than John if she went to the DMV and picked at random. But BeBe didn't need to hear that. What she needed was to think positively, especially since she had a blind date tonight with Ken, the supposed resident at Beth Israel Hospital.

"Maybe I should be more laid-back, like you," BeBe said as she set the cash box on the ground and helped Peach fold up the table. "Maybe instead of trying to date, I should just sit back and wait for things to happen naturally—"

"Nope," Peach said swiftly, noting that it had sounded more like an order than she'd intended it to. As she took a wrapped block of gum out of her pocket, she said, "Look, you can't sit back and wait because you don't *really* want to. You want to be out there—you want to be proactive. And anyway, you have fun on the dates."

BeBe slanted her a look that said, *Puh*-lease.

"Well . . . *most* of the time," Peach amended. "Plus, if you don't go out with other guys, you'll just sit around obsessing over John even more than you usually do."

BeBe grimaced, but didn't bother denying it.

Snow continued to float around them as Peach reached inside her patchwork coat for some money. "What are you doing?" BeBe asked.

"I'm gonna buy five tickets so today's not a total loss."

"Oh. Okay, me too—by the way, can I borrow five bucks?"

Peach shook her head and laughed.

Chapter Two

The Millennium Gift Basket Company was on the eighth floor of a tall stone building; it sat on a busy street corner right between Au Bon Pain and the Daily Grind coffeehouse. The company had moved to the financial district about two months ago because it was rapidly expanding and in need of a larger space. What Peach couldn't get over was that Millennium's recent explosion in popularity was something that could never have been predicted, but which had sprung completely from fate and circumstance.

Millennium had launched onto the online retail scene in 2000, enjoying moderate success, until six months ago, when one of Peach's creations—the Ethan Eckers doll—had taken off like a rocket.

Now Millennium was officially on the map, with all the other hype that went with that. While Peach was extremely flattered—and still a bit awestruck—that her simple little rag doll had become an overnight sensation, she considered Ethan Eckers just one of a hundred ideas she'd conceived while working for Millennium—many of which had either fizzled or barely eked by in terms of sales. She wasn't about to let this one fluky success go to her head. Besides, she'd already moved on to other ideas, untapped creative juices, new possibilities.

Now she nudged her way through the revolving doors of her office building, hauling the folding table and chairs she and BeBe had used along with her, trying not to slip in her wet high heels. BeBe had offered to help her carry the table and chairs back, but Peach had insisted they were really light. Okay, her mistake. Apparently they *were* light, but only for the first three seconds; after that, her arms strained and ached nearly right out of their sockets.

As always, the bright, airy lobby was frenetically busy. People streamed through the doors, heels clicking, coats swishing, as they crossed the salmon-colored marble floor in different directions.

To the left of the elevators was a long desk where the building security guard sat; to the right was an elegant paisley couch, which rested against the glass that doubled as a wall for Starbucks. Rather than heading toward the elevators in the center, Peach hooked a left, past Thomas, the daytime security guard, who smiled broadly at her and rose from his seat. "Here, let me help you with that!" he said, coming toward her.

"Oh, thank you so much," Peach said with relief, having no problem revealing her naked desperation. "You're such a doll," she added, as Thomas took the table and one of the chairs out of her weak, nearly numb hands. It only took a second for her stiff fingers to relax and declaw.

"So where's this going? Upstairs to your office?" Thomas asked.

"No, to the assembly room," Peach replied, then realized. "Oh, but I guess you probably shouldn't leave your post, huh?" Thomas just chuckled, his smile creasing his dark, pudgy face, as he told her not worry about it—as if he left his post *all* the time and considered it no biggie—which probably should've made her worry.

They both turned down a long, carpeted hallway off the lobby. When they got to the end, Peach thanked Thomas again for his help. "I can take it from here," she said, smiling, and pushed open the door with her shoulder. Thomas winked at her in his warm, paternal way and headed back to his post (at least she hoped that was where he was headed).

The assembly room was the place where the Millennium gift items were kept, and where the gift baskets that customers ordered online were actually put together.

"Hey, Peach! Need some help?" It was Marge, one of the employees who assembled the gift baskets for shipping. Her cohorts, Lizzie and Ron, turned to say hi.

"Hi, guys," Peach said brightly, as she dragged the stuff over to the supply closet, wincing as the chair made a shrill screech against the tile floor. "Thanks, but I've got it; I'm just putting these back."

The assembly room was filled with boxes, bows, and baskets of all sizes. Wall-to-wall shelves were stocked with supplies like cellophane, doilies, and gift cards. In the far right corner were a temperature-controlled pantry and a massive yellow refrigerator that stored the various edible treats included in many of the baskets.

Peach spent a lot of time in the assembly room putting together mock baskets and experimenting with new ideas. As Millennium's creative consultant, she was the one who designed most of the gift packages, from the color scheme to the contents to the choice of ribbon. She'd been working at Millennium for about a year. She'd stumbled upon the job by answering an ad in the paper, but she'd just had a feeling about it, and for the most part her instincts had been right. The creativity and the autonomy she had at work made her job seem much less corporate than it really was. The only down-side was the occasional boredom that settled in on her after she finished her work early and caught up with all her personal e-mails, phone calls, text messages, and IMs.

After chatting briefly with Marge, Lizzie, and Ron, Peach headed back to the lobby, tossing her gum, which she'd already chewed to tastelessness, into the sleek, reflective trash bin by the elevators. Darting forward, she held her hand out to stop the elevator doors midway to closing, and they sprang back open—revealing a middle-aged man with an electric-blue golf shirt visible beneath his winter jacket. (On a side note, the rampant male obsession of wearing golf shirts even when it was snowing out was an irrational pet peeve of hers.)

He smiled briefly, and stared down at the floor.

"Hi," Peach said amiably, and pressed "8." Then she reached into her coat pocket to pull out her date book. It was a little smaller than a paperback, with a velvety powder-blue cover, and a loop that secured a pint-size pen with a troll on top. She flipped open the book and scanned today's happenings. Sometimes it was hard to read her own writing, and she got sloppier the more she wrote, which her mother always said had to do with being left-handed. Plus, Peach sometimes abbreviated things in ways she couldn't remember, and in her haste, underlines often turned into cross-outs.

From what she could decipher, the only things written for to-day's agenda were: *return mom's vacuum* and *get haircut*. Usually Peach went to Francine's, a swanky salon five minutes from her office, where they plied her with Chablis and talked her into highlights. Then again, could someone really be talked into something she didn't want to do?

Okay, that settled it. Haircut after work with possible highlights, stop home, then take the D line to her parents' house in Brookline.

The elevator *ding*ed as Peach set her date book back in her pocket. "Have a nice day," the man beside her said.

"Thanks, you, too," she said, feeling a little bad for thinking he looked foolish in that golf shirt a few minutes ago. She stepped off the elevator onto the shimmery honey-colored carpet and hooked a right. The wide hallway overlooked the lobby below, and ultimately led to a set of glass double doors with embossed gold lettering that read: *Millennium Gifts*. Because of the expansion, Robert Walsh had changed the company name to drop the "baskets," because he planned to transition the inventory from just baskets to a much more comprehensive selection of gift items. Peach didn't really get too involved with Millennium's future plans, though.

She didn't know how much longer she'd be there. She liked her job, but she wasn't planning to make a career out of it. Which begged the question: What *did* she envision as her career? Hell if she knew—*yet*—but then again, what was the rush?

The funny thing was that ever since Peach's Ethan Eckers doll—which she'd created out of some random fabrics, cotton stuffing, and funky, mismatched buttons one rainy night at home—had become an overnight sensation, Robert Walsh and Millennium's VP, Brenda Perhune, had begun treating her like the queen bee. So far she'd gotten a raise—which made her feel inexplicably guilty for Scott West, the other creative consultant, who hadn't gotten one—and rather than simply getting Robert's cordial charm or Brenda's efficient camaraderie, now Peach got their respect. They never pestered her, as if she were some elusive genius whose creative process must never be questioned. A few times Robert had actually referred to her at staff meetings as "the golden child." Thank God he'd finally stopped doing that.

BeBe had claimed that this was so typical, more evidence that Peach led a charmed life, but Peach never saw it that way. There was so much that she hadn't experienced yet, so in her mind, it was way too soon to say it was charmed. *Unspoiled*, maybe.

As soon as Peach walked through the Millennium doors, she was greeted by Ethan Eckers. He sat in a huge gift basket wrapped in cellophane and a big green bow, on top of the shiny black table that fit nicely beside a large bonsai tree, rising up from an enclosed bed of lacquered rocks. Was it just Peach or did nerdy little Ethan not particularly go with Robert's fondness for Asian décor? But she couldn't deny a sense of pride that still fluttered through her chest when she thought about how popular that particular basket had become. *It just goes to show,* she thought, *deep down, most people relate to the nerds of this world.*

Here was Ethan's deal: He was a cute, pudgy doll with deeply indented dimples and a squiggly little mouth. Marketed as a lonely scientist, he wore clunky, oversize goggles and a white lab coat. There were a variety of baskets that centered around him—an Ethan Eckers basket for every occasion—and, of course, there was a gimmick. Any Eckers doll wearing a square gold button underneath his lab coat was worth five thousand dollars. Of course, there were very few of these in circulation. All Peach had done was make the doll; Brenda Perhune was the one to come up with this way to capitalize on Ethan Eckers's sudden popularity.

Another life lesson: *Not so deep down, people like money.*

Several of the cubicles Peach passed on her way to her desk were vacant because, though Millennium was on the verge of expansion, at present it was staffed by only eight people. Besides president and vice president, Robert and Brenda, there was Nelson Perhune, Millennium's advertising coordinator as well as Brenda's husband; Scott West, creative consultant; and Rachel Latham, data processor and resident FOC (Fresh Outta College).

Also among the staff was Grace Gomez, Robert's executive assistant, and Dennis Emberson, the office accountant, who on some days could pass for Pigpen's father.

The small group was dispersed throughout the new office, which was like a spacious and elaborate maze. Bonsai trees and bamboo shoots sprouted from every corner, while subdued Asian silk screens lined the honey-colored walls.

Peach had reached the threshold of her cubicle when she heard pounding footsteps, getting closer. *Grace.* After she slid her coat off her shoulders and tossed it onto the L of her desk, she turned to face her expected guest. "Hi, Grace," she said, smiling pleasantly. Hey, one of them had to; Grace looked perpetually pissed off and beaten down by life.

"Good morning . . ." she said, dragging out the words like she didn't believe them. Still, her face brightened for a fleeting moment, which Peach considered a compliment, since Grace's default expression was sourpuss. Unless she was around Robert, of course. Then, magically, she turned into a corny, operatic Goody Two-shoes—the jovial helper who sings in a high-pitched, almost grandmotherly tone, "Right-*ooo!*" and answers requests with a chipper, "You *bet*cha!" or "*Yip*pers!" Think junior high drama teacher in a former life. That was the act, anyway. And you could almost buy it— especially if you were around her for only short spurts of time, which Robert was.

It wasn't that Grace was rude to people's faces; it was just that she deeply enjoyed being the martyr-in-residence, griping about anything and everything, and basically sneering about what a tired work-mule she was. Basically, she loved to vent, and anyone with ears would do.

"I have a feeling this is gonna be a long day," Grace said. Laying her hand on top of the high partition wall, she pulled on the front of her shirt to keep it from riding up. She was a broad-shouldered woman, probably in her late forties, obviously big on blouses with prints of ropes and anchors.

Twisting her lips in disgust with whatever was today's crisis—it was only nine fifteen, but fine—she said, "I'm going to the kitchen. Feel like taking a walk?"

"Sure," Peach said, and tossed her knit cap and gloves over toward her coat. After straightening out her swirly pale-pink-and-burgundy sweater and smoothing a hand over her long, fitted burgundy skirt, she crossed over to the far end of her desk to plug in the chili-pepper lights that were strung around her cube. They glowed warm red and green, which was especially festive now that Christmas was coming up, but Peach kept the lights up all year anyway. And Robert and Brenda never seemed to have a problem with it—the elusive-genius thing again. She grabbed her dark-red ceramic mug, which was emblazoned with the translated Italian saying, *Where rosemary grows, women rule,* and then fell into step with Grace.

"So how was your weekend?" Peach asked, as they headed down the hall together.

"Too short," Grace said. "Sometimes I can't *stand* this place." By *sometimes* Grace must have meant Eastern, Central, and Pacific.

"What happened?" Peach asked with as much sympathy as she could find within her at this hour. She pulled on the heavy glass door that opened slowly to the kitchen, and let Grace pass first. The room was huge and designed in contrasts. The floor and countertop were both shiny black, while the circular tables were bright white, the chairs were checkered, and the refrigerator was a silvery stainless steel.

Now Grace leaned her elbow on the countertop while she filled her own mug with hot water. The whispering began. "So did you hear Brenda's coming in this afternoon?"

"She is? Oh, I hope she brings the baby!" Peach said, and clapped her hands together excitedly, which made her three silver rings clink. Brenda Perhune had been on maternity leave for the past few months, and though she was still working from home, she occasionally stopped by the office to pick up files or just to say hello. She usually brought her baby, Annie, with her, which for the most part was wonderful. Sweet and soft, Annie smelled like baby powder and grape juice, and she lit everyone up with that shared wonder that came with being in the presence of someone so small and innocent.

The only downside to seeing the baby had nothing to do with stinky diapers, baby throw-up, or relentless wailing. It was the shameless, gag-worthy baby talk that Brenda and Nelson forced everyone else to listen to; in the presence of their progeny, both were compulsively cooing and cutesy, and that was putting it mildly. In fact, it was honestly hard to say what was worse: the nasally baby talk Nelson displayed with his wife and child, or the lame jokes he subjected others to every other minute of the day.

"She's coming in between three and four o'clock," Grace continued with a sneer. "*El Asshole* just springs it on me that Brenda's birthday's coming up, so I should get her a cake today." Absently, Grace bobbed her tea bag up and down in her mug, sloshing Earl Grey against the rim, and splashing some onto her ropes-and-anchors blouse du jour. "Can you *believe* that jerkoff?" she hissed, and rolled her eyes.

"Hey, if you want, I'll get the cake for her," Peach offered. It wasn't a big deal; after all, they got a cake every time an employee had a birthday—usually just something from the display case at Mackie's Diner. But Peach knew how little patience Grace had for, well, life.

"No, no," she said, shaking her head, "I'll *do* it. I'll get the cake just like I do *everything* around this place." Hmm . . . should Peach be insulted? "It just ticks me off that Robert just drops things on me when I've already got fifty other things on my desk—unh! The man's got his head up his ass!"

Unfortunately, since Peach was an artistic person, that image was way too vivid for her liking. Grace always made Robert Walsh sound like a marauding buffoon, when in reality he was a smooth and very polished boss—a well-dressed, attractive man in his forties, with short salt-and-pepper hair. Articulate and calm, Robert never lost his temper, and always presented himself with professional aplomb. But then, didn't people usually vilify their boss? It was the law of the urban jungle.

Peach filled her dark-red sister-power mug halfway with the Holiday Spice decaf that had already been brewed (probably by Rachel Latham, who was still an eager beaver).

"Wonder what'll happen if Claire ever decides to sell the company," Grace whispered, referring to Robert's wife, who owned Millennium Gifts. "Robert's gravy train will be up then," Grace added snidely.

It wasn't the first time Grace had gotten Peach thinking and speculating about Robert's position as the president of his wife's company—and, more interestingly, the state of their marriage. It was all conjecture, of course, but Peach couldn't help wonder—with the help of Grace planting seeds—if Claire and Robert were headed for divorce, and what it would mean to his job security if they were. Apparently Claire lived in Baltimore, where she owned and ran a large cosmetics company. Rumor had it that she was too busy with that to get involved in the hands-on management of Millennium. She left that to Robert.

Seemed reasonable. *Yet . . .*

You had to wonder about the dynamics of a long-distance marriage. Maybe it was a mutually beneficial arrangement for both of them. Or maybe Claire had simply lost interest in Millennium . . . or Robert . . . or both. And if she ever got rid of *either*, chances were excellent that Robert would be out of a job. *Pretty shitty,* Peach thought, considering that Millennium had just been catapulted into the big time with the sweeping popularity of the Ethan Eckers doll. It had all happened under Robert's helm.

Without him running Claire's company, maybe VP Brenda Perhune would take over?

Now Grace ambled alongside Peach back to Peach's desk, where everything was right where she left it—all over the place: different-colored folders scattered, papers strewn, and photos lined up in silver and wooden frames—photos of her parents, Margot and Jack, her older sister, Lonnie, her good friends from college, April and Stephanie, who now lived in San Francisco, and a photo of BeBe, of course. There was a stuffed Santa in the far corner of Peach's desk, leaning against the partition wall. If you squeezed its stomach, it would play Eartha Kitt's version of "Santa Baby."

While Peach sat down at her desk, Grace plopped down in the chair opposite her and set her mug of tea down on the L-shaped desk with a thud.

The chili-pepper lights overhead gave a warm, orangy glow to Peach's cube, adding a kind of depth to the smooth black desk and tightly cushioned black chairs.

Peach switched on her computer and watched it boot up, while she heard Grace whisper something about Brenda's residual baby weight. *Whoa.* "Wait, *what*?" she said, ready to draw the line right there. It was one thing to let Grace vent about her workload; it was another for her to slander Brenda.

"Brenda's supposed to be on Weight Watchers," Grace explained, "yet she can have *cake*?" Her lips twisted into a smirk.

"I think Brenda looks good," Peach said truthfully. Brenda had a simple, natural look that was very attractive. A tall woman in her mid-thirties, she was half-Chinese, half-Japanese, with shiny, straight hair that came to her shoulders. Her pleasant demeanor complemented her sharp business savvy, and no, Peach had never noticed any baby-weight problems. In fact, the only problem she *had* noticed was Brenda's questionable taste in men—or more specifically, ugly white guys.

Hey, it wasn't slander if it was true, right? And if Peach never uttered these thoughts out loud?

"Well, I'm not saying she's *fat* or anything," Grace qualified quickly, "but she has gotten kind of chunky in the rear end."

Unlike Grace, who remained consistent in her look, which included a short square-cut, hairstyle so she could have not only the body of Frankenmonster, but also the head shape. In fact, all that was missing was the tattered blazer, but probably it was hard to find one with ropes and anchors on it.

Peach hoped she wasn't being too hard on Grace, though. She knew it was all a classic case of projection. Most people were chaotic manifestations of their own insecurities—a compilation of sides, really. With Grace, yes, there were cattiness and carping, but there were also diligence and responsibility, for despite her constant complaining, she was very competent at her job and always got her work done.

And there was also something else in Grace that Peach perceived—an innate loneliness. That needed to be accounted for, too. She'd never been married, lived alone, and her closest friend seemed to be her sister, Midge, who lived in Boca Raton.

"You know, I'll bet Nelson *loves* Brenda working from home," Grace said without transition, then let out a little snort. "Probably never wants her to come back to the office. Think about it. She's a big cheese around here—men like that can't handle when their wives are more successful than they are."

Peach didn't bother asking, "Men like what?" because she had a feeling she knew the answer: men who were loud, attention-craving, and short—i.e., Nelson. Still, Peach had never seen any indication that Nelson was threatened by his wife's success, and she considered herself a pretty good judge of people. If anything, Nelson was too busy trying desperately to be cool to notice much else besides how his attempts failed constantly.

"Little *shithead*," Grace added. Clamping her hand over her mouth, she whispered, "He barely makes half of what Brenda makes. I saw it in the personnel files; she makes sixty-five and he only makes thirty-four."

Peach blinked, surprised that Grace had just told her that; those files were confidential. Stunned, Peach didn't get a chance to respond, though, because Grace blurted, "I think he's got little-man's complex—ha, ha—*little Napoleon!*"

A shocked laugh burst from Peach's throat, and her mouth dropped open. *"Grace!"* She felt like such a hypocrite for laughing like that, but honestly, it'd just spilled out of her.

Grace just chuckled at her surprise. "I only speak the truth," she said smugly.

Peach's phone rang. Usually the only people who called her were friends, family, or clumsy headhunters on fishing expeditions.

"Let me get that . . ." Peach said, reaching back to pick up her receiver as Grace rose to her feet. "Hello?"

"Hi," a pleasantly familiar voice said.

"Oh, hey!" Peach said enthusiastically, then covered the mouthpiece with her hand and said softly, "It's my sister."

Grace nodded and took her mug of tea off the desktop. "See ya later," she said with a wave, and left Peach's cube.

Leaning back in her chair, Peach crossed her legs and absently tapped her high heel against the bottom drawer pull. "So what's up? You're calling early."

"I've been up since six," Lonnie said, not sounding particularly tired, though. Knowing Lonnie, she'd probably had her requisite two to three café mochas by now.

"How come so early?" Peach asked, as she twisted the phone cord around her finger.

"I've been trying to do some work on my dissertation. So far I've adjusted the margins . . . and I spent half an hour trying to download a font that would be perfect for my header."

"That's so pathetic," Peach said with a laugh.

"Oh, and I also wrote the word 'the,' " Lonnie added.

"Much better."

With a lighthearted sigh, Lonnie admitted, "I am so screwed. Papers have exploded all over my living room . . . and bedroom . . . and dining room. How can I concentrate in this mess?"

"So work in Dominick's office," Peach suggested, recalling her sister's cute house in Maine and the cozy unused room on the first floor that she and her husband had flipped for.

"Well, I would, but I use his office for all my other stuff—I don't want to get confused. Besides . . . I've already made a mess of that, too."

"Jeez," Peach mumbled, rolling her eyes. Though she supposed, in her sister's defense, that as a full-time instructor at Maine Bay College as well as a Ph.D. student, Lonnie was pretty much drowning in paperwork. This past semester she'd had to teach Women's Studies, Women in Literature, and Freshman English, while completing the last of her doctoral courses at night. Now, in terms of her Ph.D., she just had her dissertation to finish. Or to *do*, as the case may be. "Last time we talked you were working on your title page," Peach recalled. "How did that go?"

"Good. I forgot to tell you: I have a title now. I'm calling it, 'Feeding the Hand that Bites You.' "

"Oh, I like that," Peach said, knowing Lonnie's topic dealt with patriarchal brainwashing, contemporary literature, and female empowerment, but not certain of the exact details.

"Thanks," Lonnie said brightly. "Now I just have to write the fucking thing and I'll be in heaven."

Peach tugged open her top drawer and rooted around past Post-it pads and pens to find a Blow Pop. Palming one from deep inside the drawer, she pulled it out. "So how's Dominick?" she asked as she tore the wrapper open with her teeth. The sticky-sweet scent of strawberry was already drifting to her nose.

"He's fine." Lonnie paused. "But I feel guilty. . . . I've been so moody lately."

"Moody? How?"

"Lately I've been snapping at him—then I feel so guilty about it. I don't know; lately I just feel like I'm in a funk."

"*Interesting . . .*"

"*That's* interesting?" Lonnie said sarcastically. "That I'm in a moody-bitch funk?"

"Hey . . ." Suddenly Peach had a thought. "Do you think you might be PG?"

"Postgrad?" Lonnie asked, confused.

Scrunching her face up, Peach shook her head. "You are turning into such a dork."

"What?" Lonnie said with a laugh. "Oh, *wait* . . . you mean am I *pregnant*?"

"Yes. Do you think maybe—"

"No way. I'm definitely not," Lonnie said.

"Oh," Peach said, suddenly feeling disappointed. Maybe thinking of Brenda's baby earlier was making Peach wish for a little niece or nephew. A fragile little being, pure and uncomplicated, someone Peach could snuggle and love . . . and eventually teach how to draw.

"Well, just think, you have winter break coming up soon," Peach reminded Lonnie. "You can work on your dissertation then, get up to speed."

"Valid. I can't wait. I won't have to teach for an entire month! And I really shouldn't complain, because I have the best mentor ever—Dan has been so great."

"Who's Dan?"

"You know, Professor Connelly. My dissertation adviser. I mentioned him to you before."

"Oh, right . . . so it's *Dan*, now, huh?"

"Please," Lonnie said, "you sound like Dominick."

"How old is this Dan?"

"Thirty-three, I think."

"Is he married?" Peach asked probingly.

"No."

Peach whistled, then said, "Dominick must be going crazy by now."

"No, no," Lonnie insisted. "He just teases me about spending time with Dan. It's not like Dominick's really the jealous type anyway."

Hello? Where the hell was her sister living that she couldn't see that Dominick was very much the jealous type? Even-tempered, yes. Sweet and caring, no question. Devoted husband, definitely. And did he let Lonnie have her way 95 percent of the time? Absolutely. But still—it was patently obvious to Peach that Dominick was profoundly possessive of her sister.

"Oh! I just remembered why else I called," Lonnie said suddenly. "I mean, besides to whine. There's a new guy starting at your company today who sort of knows Dominick."

"Really? What's his name?"

"I'm not sure."

With a smirk, Peach said, "Okay, I take it 'Dominick sort of knows' means that they're not too close."

"Well, Dominick doesn't *know* him, know him. It's a friend of one of his employees. I guess he saw the gift basket you sent to Dominick's office last week and that's when it came up." Lonnie's husband ran a software development company not far from their home in Seabring, Maine. Wait . . . Suddenly Peach remembered—the new network administrator was starting today. Vaguely she recalled Robert saying something about it at last week's staff meeting. The last network administrator had quit three months ago. In the interim, Robert had hired consultants to fill in occasionally.

Since Millennium was such a small company—though presumably not for much longer—the network admin had traditionally manned the intraoffice computer network, as well as Millennium's Web site. Though crucial to Millennium's business, the Web site wasn't something Peach got too involved with—unlike Nelson Perhune, who bought and sold online advertising, and Rachel Latham, who processed all the orders placed on the site.

"Okay, I'll go over and say hi," Peach said. She'd do that anyway, of course—provided she remembered that a new employee was starting at the company.

"All right, but feel free to call me later," Lonnie said. "I'll just be here, working on my dissertation . . . so *definitely* call me."

"Later," Peach said. "Love ya."

"Love you, too."

After Peach hung up the phone, she swiveled in her chair to face her monitor, then dragged and clicked to check her e-mail. A new message from her friend, Cheryl! Peach had met Cheryl three years ago, back when she was working for Cheryl's mother, Iris Mew. Since then Cheryl had been living a whirlwind life—she'd broken up with her serious boyfriend, Jean-Paul, to move to Atlanta and attend culinary school. A while back Peach had convinced Cheryl to maximize her fabulous cooking skills, so she could one day start the big catering business she'd always fantasized about.

In culinary school, Cheryl had met a really nice guy named Ralph. And it was truly, unapologetically *Ralph*—not one of these Ralphs who tried to pretend his name was pronounced "Rafe."

At twenty-seven, Ralph was eleven years younger than Cheryl, but he was one of those mature-for-his-age, ready-to-be-a-monagomous-man-of-the-house-since-he-was-sixteen kind of guys, someone who clearly adored her. Last Peach had checked, the two of them had been talking about moving in together, possibly getting engaged, and Cheryl had been ecstatic to finish her degree and look for some restaurant experience that would give her the exposure and credibility she wanted before she started her catering business.

Now Peach scanned the e-mail message, which had the subject header: *Question* . . .

Cheryl was asking her advice, which made Peach feel flattered and special—that her once painfully shy friend still needed her. Torn between two jobs, Cheryl didn't know if she should take a position at a small, quaint restaurant in the suburbs, or one at a trendy, fast-paced new hot spot in downtown Atlanta. One was safer, more traditional, slower . . . the other was more exciting but definitely scarier.

Immediately, Peach hit REPLY, changed the subject header to: *Fake the funk*, and told her friend the choice was clear; in the end, the scarier job would probably make her stronger.

Since she was still waiting to hear back from the distributor about the lacy ribbons she wanted for her new Sweethearts' Basket, Peach figured it was as good a time as any to go say hello to the new guy.

She hopped up, twirling her Blow Pop in her mouth, and

hooked a right out of her cube. Looping around, she passed the entrance and kept going, then turned left, following the wall to the big network admin cube that was isolated in a corner of the office.

As she approached, Peach heard something. Soft and smooth, it was a rich, masculine voice she'd never heard before. *He must be on the phone,* she thought, as she heard the new guy say, "I know, I know. . . ."

Tentatively, Peach inched closer and ducked her head in, just enough to get a look—she'd always had a curious nature—but he had his back to her. Facing his computer, with his phone pressed against his ear, he was nodding into the phone, as if waiting for his opportunity to speak again. He had dark brown hair and a nice build—at least, his shoulders looked broad and strong—he was wearing a white shirt, and when he turned slightly to rest his forehead in his hand, she saw that he was also wearing a dark blue tie and glasses.

Well, it was obvious he was in the middle of something, and curiosity was one thing, but she was about to tip over, so she would just come back later—

"Okay—look, I'll talk to you later," she heard him say, and froze in her tracks. "Dad, look, I'm sorry, I gotta go. I'm at work. Yeah, I'll call you later."

So he was getting *off* the phone. . . .

She lingered outside his cube. Hmm, to stay or to go? She wasn't normally this indecisive. As she wavered, her sharp heels dug into the carpet, and suddenly she heard him hang up the phone. With a sigh, he leaned back in his chair.

"Hi."

Startled, he turned. "Oh," he said, his eyes widening behind his glasses. "Hello." She'd just seen his profile before, but now she was looking at him dead-on. He looked as though he'd been caught off-guard, but then so had she. Peach was silent for a second, studying his face.

Where had she seen him before?

Of course! It was the guy from the street earlier! *Whoa . . .* Now this was weird. Peach couldn't help thinking that this was somehow the work of destiny. Or maybe the work of meaningless coincidence, but either way, her Monday morning was getting more interesting.

Chapter Three

Adam was a little startled when he heard someone say hello—but even more startled when he saw who it was. A knockout with long dark-blonde hair and bright blue eyes. Jesus, she was pretty—did she actually work here?

When she extended her hand, Adam glanced down and saw a wet pink lollipop already in it. "Oh!" she said, obviously just realizing herself, and palmed the lollipop off into her left hand. Then they shook. "Hi, I'm Peach," she said, smiling.

Wow—killer smile, too.

"Hi," Adam said, quickly standing up to greet her properly.

"What's your name?" she asked, releasing his hand. Automatically he stepped back several inches, not wanting to crowd her space. For some reason he felt a little awkward, so he stuck his hands in his pockets, looking for something to do with them. He wasn't the most talkative person, especially when he first met someone—especially if that someone was a gorgeous woman who'd simply appeared in front of him.

"I'm Adam," he said. "Adam Quinlan."

"Nice to meet you," she said, giving him another smile; then she surveyed his cube. "So . . . you getting all settled in?"

"Yeah, I suppose," he replied simply, as Peach hopped up to sit on his desk, which was bare except for the three computers there, spaced far apart, and his phone. Since it was his first day, Adam had gotten to the office early, about an hour ago, but then his dad had called his cell and the time had gotten sucked up.

"So where's your kitsch?"

"Excuse me?" he said, confused.

"You know . . . the personal touches," Peach said, looking around the bare-bones cubicle again. "Photographs, a stress ball, maybe a calendar with pictures of golden retrievers, that kind of thing."

Taken a little off guard, Adam half grinned. "This is it, I guess," he said, and motioned with his head to the mug of pens and the small ceramic soccer ball that sat unassumingly beside his main monitor. The mug dated back to his college days, while the soccer-ball paperweight went back almost twenty years, to when Adam was nine—not that he ever truly used it to keep papers in place.

"Oh, I see," she said approvingly, then crossed her legs. He couldn't help but notice, eyes darting down but quickly back up so she wouldn't think he was ogling her calves. "Where did you work before here?" she asked as she tossed her lollipop stick into his trash bin before she'd gotten to the gum.

"A pharmaceutical company in Chicago," he answered.

"And what did you do there?" she asked. "Same kind of job you'll be doing here?"

"Um, no. Somewhat different," he said without elaboration.

She nodded as she recrossed her legs, and then crossed her arms over her chest. Adam couldn't help noticing the way the movement pushed her breasts up more firmly against her soft-looking sweater.

"Well, have you always been into computers?" she asked.

A little shyly, he smiled and said, "I guess so, yeah."

"Was that what you studied in school?"

"Yes."

"What school did you go to?"

"Northwestern." Hell, what was next, the school mascot? It was time to deflect attention off himself and onto Peach, who made him feel like he was being interviewed again. Quickly he said, "What do you do here?"

"Creative consultant. I come up with designs for new baskets," she answered simply. "So are you from Chicago originally?"

Apparently she was in no frame of mind to be deflected. Adam took a seat in his chair again. "No, I'm originally from New Hampshire," he explained, figuring the one-word answers were only making her ask more questions. "Manchester. My family still lives there." Actually his mom had moved out of the house nearly a month ago, and was now living in Portsmouth with her sister, Emily, until she found her own place. That is, unless she changed her mind about divorcing Adam's dad, who was as pathetically helpless without her as he was staid and stubborn *with* her. But Adam quickly pushed these thoughts aside. They'd taken up enough of his morning already, with his dad calling him first thing, and his sister, Sonny, leaving a pissy voice mail about how unfair the divorce was—to her.

Peach uncrossed her legs, then recrossed, this time bringing her right over her left, which drew his attention to the sleek curve of her calf that led up to the teasing beginnings of her thigh. Her legs were sexy and slim, and she wore black sheer stockings and high heels. He felt an unexpected stab of lust, like a rush of hot blood to his groin.

"So your family must be happy that you're in Boston, huh? It's much closer to New Hampshire than Chicago, that's for sure," she said, but it was more like a question—*another freaking question.* Granted, Peach's friendly, animated demeanor was kind of charming, but still, Adam felt bombarded. He guessed she was trying to be nice, but he was reserved by nature. *Nice* to him was saying a polite hello when you passed your coworkers in the hall, making chitchat occasionally in a shared space like the kitchen or elevator. Not babbling about his degree and experience, or discussing his personal background. What did she expect him to say? *Yes, my family's thrilled I'm closer so they can all pull me in fifty different directions, and when they call me to complain, we'll be in the same time zone.*

"Do you have any sisters and brothers?" Peach asked, still pursuing the family stuff.

He swallowed an irritated sigh. "Yes, one sister, one brother."

"Older or younger?"

Christ, what was it with her already? "My brother's older," he replied tersely, but Peach still looked expectant. "I'm in the middle. Anyway—"

"What are their names?"

"*Why?*" Adam blurted with an impatient sigh, then realized it made him sound overly defensive.

"Just wondering," Peach said with a shrug, adding, "Adam, really, don't be alarmed; these are all routine questions. Any information you share will be used only for the in-depth psychological profile I'm building—which will later be submitted to the FBI. All my records are kept strictly confidential—unless I deem something amusing or freaky, and feel like sharing it with others."

He paused, just blinking at her for a couple seconds; then he looked down at the floor and chuckled. So she was recognizing that she was interrogating him . . . yet he had to admit he was overreacting to her nosiness. In a moment his eyes darted back to hers, and she smiled at him. Another jolt of lust shot through his veins—animal attraction, pure and simple. It was that smile—warm and inviting and, like everything else about her, so damn pretty.

"Hey, I forgot," she said then, snapping her fingers and breaking the moment. "I think you have a friend who works for my brother-in-law—in Maine."

"Oh, really?" Adam said, surprised, and nodded. "Oh, right, must be my friend Chris." Chris was the only friend he could think of who lived in Maine. But since Adam hadn't talked to him in a while, except to exchange brief e-mails the week before, there seemed little else to say on that subject.

"Well . . ." Peach began, looking around Adam's cubicle again, nodding, and restlessly turning the ring on her middle finger. "How do you like it here so far?"

"So far, so good," Adam said, nodding back. "I hope it doesn't get any harder."

A little laugh slipped out of her, and she shifted on the desk, accidentally hip-checking Adam's cup of pens and sending them rolling. "Oh!" she said, startled, and hopped up as a dozen blue pens did successive dive-bombs over the edge of the desk. "Jeez, sorry about that," she added with a crooked smile, and bent to the floor to pick up the mess she'd made.

Adam knelt down, too, which brought their bodies much closer—and their faces mere inches apart.

It was a closeness that seemed almost too intimate; he felt a wisp of her breath on his cheek, which for some reason rekindled that animal attraction. Scalding heat washed through his body, thickening his dick and making him catch his breath. He swallowed hard.

Then he caught a glimpse of Peach's thigh, because her skirt had ridden up when she'd leaned over to scoop up the last of the stray pens. Adam's mouth ran dry as desire swelled in his cock. He was just so close to her, and he knew damn well that his eyes had trailed up much higher than they should have.

When he glanced up into her face, though, his arousal didn't subside; it only raged on. Something about those long eyelashes . . . the faint trail of freckles across the bridge of her nose. Up close, her skin looked so soft and smooth; her mouth was ripe, her lips dark and shiny, probably from the lollipop. Or maybe it was her tangy-sweet smell. . . .

Just as quickly as he'd experienced the sharp stab of lust, he felt the dull ache of guilt. Or was it frustration? Uncertainty? He wasn't sure; he only knew it had to do with Robin, his girlfriend of five years, who'd moved to Europe almost two months ago.

Adam knew it was wrong to be thinking such intensely sexual thoughts about another girl, even if his relationship with Robin was rapidly dying. Wasn't it?

Of course it was . . . especially since he'd just met this girl, Peach, who was nice but borderline annoying, and especially considering he was still involved. Even though Robin had left Chicago—and him—to take a job in Europe—one that was a purely lateral move within her company, by the way. And even though she'd done it just to test him, to hurt him.

Even, even, even.

Peach stepped back, and Adam followed suit, grateful to her for breaking the tension, which he would just have to chalk up to the fact that he was a man and she was a pretty, sexy woman. He just prayed she hadn't noticed him checking out her legs. Talk about inappropriate. The last thing Adam would want was to alienate someone at work, especially on his very first day!

When she leaned against the desk, crossing her arms, she took more careful notice of Adam's pen cup, which was a souvenir from the state soccer championship in 1996. His nickname was printed across it.

"Quin?" she said, arching a questioning eyebrow.

"Yeah. That was my nickname in college. Actually, my friends in Chicago always call me that."

"Oh," she said. "Should I call you that, too?"

He squinted at her, registering what he considered a particularly weird question. Then, a little uneasily, he said, "Uh, sure . . . if you want to . . ."

"Well," she said, smiling, and straightened up. "It's nice to meet you, but I don't want to overstay my welcome," she added as she edged toward the entrance to his cube.

"No, no, you're not," he said, trying to compensate in case he'd been rude.

"I was just joking," she said. "I realize that's *impossible*."

Grinning, Adam ducked his head down for a second, then looked up at her. She was grinning back.

"See you later, Quin," Peach said with wave, but when she left, she was still kind of there.

Back at his desk, Adam fell into his chair, and his phone rang. When he answered it, he was disheartened to realize it was his dad again, asking if he knew where Adam's mom kept the laundry detergent. Adam suggested the obvious—laundry room—then suggested the even more obvious—to go to the store and get some more. Adam's mom, Liz, had moved out of the house last month, after a major health scare, which had changed her perspective on life—or more specifically, on her marriage.

She'd told Adam's dad, Martin, that she wanted a divorce, and his reaction had been predictably stoic, stymied, and uncomprehending. She'd told him that she needed to breathe—to find out what else life had to offer, because she'd been so young when she'd married him—she'd said he wasn't "emotionally available," and he asked her what on earth that even *meant* . . . then didn't listen to her answer.

Most of this Adam had heard from his younger sister, Sonny, who'd heard it from their dad. There was no chance she'd heard it from their mom, because apparently Sonny wasn't talking to their mom. She figured if she gave her the silent treatment long enough, Liz would give in and forget this whole divorce idea. But Liz wasn't budging. Adam had to admit, he'd never known his mother could be so willful and determined.

Liz let Martin stay in their house in Manchester, while she went to stay with her sister, Emily, who lived about forty minutes away. That had Martin in a tizzy, too, because compared to Liz, Aunt Emily was a swinging single. She'd been divorced twice, and Martin was convinced she was going to poison Liz's mind against him and their entire marriage.

Very predictably, Adam was torn. He understood his mom's perspective: after thirty-two years together, she was tired of Martin forgetting their anniversary, forgetting Valentine's Day, forgetting that Liz was allergic to yellow gold and buying her generic gold jewelry anyway. At the same time, Adam felt sorry for his dad, who'd come to rely so heavily on his wife that without her he was rendered almost helpless. A brilliant mechanical engineer, who was compulsively conscientious when it came to his ingenious little toys, and who sometimes exhibited the sensitivity of a robot, Martin was flummoxed by everyday things like cooking, cleaning, and conversation. Still, Adam grappled to understand how his mom could really make a break from Martin after so long together. Sure, his parents had seemed to drift apart to the point of barely communicating, but wasn't that ultimately what happened in all marriages?

Thinking about that now made him think of Robin again, and

the tightening around his throat he'd been getting whenever the concept of marriage and Robin arose simultaneously in his muddled mind. There was a time when he thought they would end up together; he'd been so taken with her initially because she loved computers as much as he did, and she was bright and had a witty, deadpan sense of humor that was appealing. But after five years of dating, their relationship had dwindled into a lot of bickering over the dumbest shit, and then her dropping the bomb that she was moving to Europe.

Yet she'd still wanted to continue their relationship. That had been the real bomb. According to Robin, she would stay in Prague for a year or so—it would be a "good experience"—and then she'd come back and everything would be like it was before she left. *What bullshit.* Oh, he knew she'd come back—probably within the next few months, judging by how lonely and homesick she was already. But the bullshit part was that it could ever be like it used to. It had probably been too late for that even before she'd left, but now . . .

It was hard to feel more connected when you were even farther apart.

Things had changed drastically for Adam within these last two months. He'd accepted a job in Boston, working at Millennium, which was rapidly growing. In fact, it was currently one of the top retail outfits on the Internet, especially with all the exposure it had gotten from its overnight sensation, the Ethan Eckers doll. For Adam to get in now, as the sole network administrator, was a major coup—one that justified leaving behind Chicago, where he'd lived for the past ten years, and moving to a new city where he had no friends, and his batty, dysfunctional family was only a ninety-minute drive away.

Chapter Four

When Peach called her sister later that morning, Lonnie picked up on the first ring. "Hello?" she said, sounding eager.

"Hi—a little desperate?" Peach said teasingly. "You must've known it was me."

"Oh, hey. Sorry, I thought you might be Dominick."

"Is everything okay?"

"Yeah, I just started a stupid fight this morning, that's all." Stupid fights—her favorite kind to start with Dominick. "It's dumb," Lonnie went on. "I don't even feel like getting into it." Peach waited. "Basically he was being all cold and distant, so I snapped at him about it, and I just text-messaged him and asked if he was still mad, and he wrote back, 'Ask me later.'"

"So he's not mad then—he's hurt," Peach said, decoding the obvious for her sister.

"But if he wasn't mad, he would've just written 'no.'"

"No, if he were really mad, he would've just written 'yes'," Peach offered, as she opened up the spreadsheet on her screen that kept a count of the specific contents and colors that had been used in gift baskets in the past year. Hmm . . . so fire-engine red was already in too many of the Valentine's baskets to be the theme color for the Getting in Touch with Your Womanhood basket Peach was currently noodling with . . .

"What was the fight about?" Peach asked as she scrolled down her screen, looking for another color that jumped out at her. "Look, let's just get it all on the table so I can solve it, work my magic, and then we can move on. Why was he being cold and distant? Obviously there was a reason."

"Well . . ." Lonnie said, then went on to explain how Dominick had planned a romantic evening—came home early from work, rented a DVD, brought dinner—and then Lonnie had to call and cancel on him, because her mentor, Dan, had moved their meeting to that night. He'd said he was going to be on campus attending a lecture anyway, so that evening would be more convenient for him. After hearing her whole spiel, Peach shrugged and said, "Well, honestly, that doesn't sound so bad. So you had to cancel one time—"

"Well, three," Lonnie said tentatively.

"Three?" Peach echoed. "You mean, the DVD, the dinner, the whole bag?"

"I know . . ." Lonnie said, her voice drenched with guilt. "I feel so terrible about it, but I didn't know what to do. Lately Dan always has to move our meetings at the last minute."

Hmm . . . Peach couldn't help wondering. Maybe Professor Dan Connelly, Lonnie's dissertation adviser, had sincere, albeit self-absorbed, reasons for scheduling his meetings with Lonnie after dark. But then again . . .

Normally Peach might write off Dominick's jealousy, but this Dan character . . . well, what did Peach really know about him? This was the problem with living so far away from her sister; she couldn't give her the hands-on guidance she so clearly needed.

From what Peach had gathered so far, Professor Dan was thirty-three—a year younger than Dominick—and single. Meanwhile Lonnie was extremely intelligent and strikingly pretty—not to mention married, which made her the proverbial forbidden fruit. It was a classic case, and it only stood to reason that Professor Dan might have some designs on her.

"When I finally got home, I was so tired," Lonnie added, releasing another guilty little sigh.

"Too tired for sex," Peach supplied candidly.

"Oh, no, of course not," Lonnie said. "No, it was *him*. He was being all cold and hard-to-get. I tried to put the moves on, but he wasn't interested."

"So he was sulking," Peach remarked. "Did you apologize for canceling on him?"

"Of course!" Lonnie said. "I mean, I know he'll get over it, but I *hate* when there's tension between us."

"Hmm . . ." After a moment's contemplation, Peach realized what her sister needed to do. It was the simplest, most efficient way to combat the situation. "You're gonna have to let Dominick know—"

"—how much he means to me."

"—how ugly Professor Dan is."

"Wait, *what*? That's ridiculous," Lonnie said.

"No, no, it's perfect—but you've got to be subtle. You know, just slip it into conversation—like how he's a real troll with onion breath and a microwiener."

"What!"

"You're right—leave out the microwiener part. Dominick will wonder how you know. But if you can, definitely mention how short and ugly he is. And balding—definitely balding."

"That's absurd," Lonnie commented. "First of all, Dan's none of those things—what if they meet one day?"

"Obviously you can't let that happen."

"And *second*—even if Dan was hideous, why would that make Dominick feel better about us not getting enough time together?"

"Trust me," Peach said. "But just make sure they never meet." With a small, breezy sigh, Peach thought, What would her sister do without her?

They chatted briefly about what was new with Peach, which included meeting Adam. "He's nice, seems kind of quiet," she said. Yet . . . in the brief time they'd interacted, there was something distinctly charming and intriguing about Adam Quinlan—*Quin*.

No more than a minute had passed after Peach hung up her phone than it rang again. BeBe calling, bearing puppy news.

"We're getting her today!" BeBe said excitedly.

"Omigod, that's great," Peach gushed; she loved life's sporadic bursts of the unexpected—so long as they were good.

"I know," BeBe continued. "Ellen Weinberg just called, and she said she's flying out to Michigan tomorrow morning, so she's gonna try to drop off the puppy tonight. She said to consider it a 'trial period.' If we find it's too much for us to handle, she'll take her back and find her another home." Another home meaning a smelly, over-populated pet store, Peach figured, but not that it mattered, because it was never going to happen.

Ellen Weinberg's husband had died under mysterious circumstances several years ago. According to BeBe, various stories still lingered through the halls of the country club, ranging from a freak golfing accident to a mauling by a pack of his wife's dogs. Whatever had happened to the late Mr. Weinberg, his sprawling home in Newton was now solely Ellen's, and it was the center of all of her doggy pursuits. Surely if she weren't such good friends with BeBe's mom, the Weinster would never freely give away one of her puppies, so BeBe and Peach were truly grateful.

Now Peach clapped her hands together enthusiastically and said, "This is fabulous! Yay, I can't wait!" She'd never had a dog, but when she was a junior at NYU, she'd worked in an animal hospital on Staten Island. More than anything, she remembered the bichon frise for its thick, velvety white coat. Even when a bichon was groomed traditionally—namely, to look like a canine android with an electrocuted-cauliflower head—its indelible cuteness was instantly disarming.

They talked a little more about the puppy supplies that they would need, which BeBe said she would pick up that day. Then Peach asked, "By the way, do you know what you're gonna wear on your date tonight?"

"No . . . something that fits . . . Maybe I'll stop over at my aunt Lynn's house and borrow a muumuu."

"Hmm, you should probably call first," Peach said glibly, as she scanned her spreadsheet, looking at the column labeled "winter col-ors" to see where Millennium stood on buttercup yellow.

"Seriously—do I have time to get my pants let out?"

"Please," Peach said, rolling her eyes. "You have a distorted body image." Which, tragically, applied to 95 percent of women in America.

"Distorted body image," BeBe echoed. "Doesn't sound like me . . ."

"Uh-huh . . ."

"Meanwhile, I can't even go to the beach this summer because I might be harpooned by mistake."

With a laugh, Peach said, "Do I *need* this?"

"Fine, sorry," BeBe said, sounding more amused than sorry.

"Seriously, you're gonna look fabulous tonight. You always look adorable; why don't you ever believe me?"

"Adorable. Okay." Her voice dropped as she mumbled, "For a turkey"—and Peach thought, *Damn, how does she slip them in like that?*

Turkey as in Butterball. Could BeBe just pick an animal and stick with it?

After Peach hung up with BeBe, she hopped up from her seat and headed to the kitchen. When she got there, she saw the office accountant, Dennis Emberson, through the glass doors. He was hunkered down by the open refrigerator door. Peach entered the room and crossed over toward him. "Hi, Dennis, what's up?" she said brightly.

He turned and gave her a crooked, almost weary smile. "Heya, Peach," he said as he pulled a carton of creamer out of the fridge. As he walked a few steps over to the counter, he swept back the wisps of his receding hair that had flown forward, and set down his jelly doughnut.

Dennis always looked tired and a bit out of sorts—with his bedraggled countenance and slow-moving gait, his rumpled clothes and furrowed brows. But he was a sweetheart. As with Grace, Peach often wondered if Dennis was lonely. He'd been divorced for a

few years now, and from what Peach had gleaned, had experienced
practically zero romance since then. Interestingly, he'd gone on one
or two dates with Grace soon after his divorce, but according to
what Brenda had told Peach, Grace and Dennis had hardly classi-
fied as an office romance. They'd fizzled without fanfare before
they'd even begun, and it'd seemed a mutual thing. Hardly startling
news to Peach, of course, who could never picture Dennis and Grace
as a lasting couple. Anyone could see they weren't love-connection
material—Grace was too bombastic and Dennis was too much of a
sad sack.

He had a daughter named Nan, who'd just turned eighteen.
Coincidentally, Nan was in the same high school class as Rachel
Latham's sister Alice. According to Rachel, Nan and Alice had been
best friends until a recent falling-out. Rachel said that she didn't
know what their fight was about, but whatever it was, it seemed to
have ruptured their friendship completely.

Ironically, Dennis's paternal appearance—his paunchy physique,
his semi-droopy eyes, his sloppy hair—also made him seem kid-like.
Like a lost little boy who needed help—*Peach's* help, a unique brand
of tough love and timeless wisdom, with some guesswork thrown
in. Really all she wanted to was cheer Dennis up, and bring a glint
of laughter to his eyes.

Wait, was this what BeBe had meant once when she'd said she
was too nosy? Or was it melodramatic? Either way . . . probably not.

Recently, Peach had been toying with the idea of fixing Dennis up. He needed to find love—or to have it found for him—
whichever came first. But who would be the right match for
Dennis?

She'd already considered the women she knew from the outreach center, but most of the volunteers who were in their forties
like Dennis were already married. And Peach sincerely doubted that
a younger woman would have much patience with Dennis and his
general lack of energy. Sometimes *she* could barely stand it, and she
was his friend.

"How was your weekend?" he asked now, as he poured cream

into his tea and accidentally splashed some onto the countertop. Then he crossed to the fridge to put the carton back, and left another milky puddle on his way.

Grace was definitely not going to like that. She frequently lamented to Peach that people in the office must've thought she was the "goddamn maid" by the messes they left in the kitchen. So Peach tore off a piece of paper towel and wiped up Dennis's spills. "How are things going, Dennis?" she said, tilting her head and looking thoughtfully at him. *Stop it,* she told herself. Somehow whenever she asked Dennis how he was, it always came out in a deeply concerned, psychiatrist-like way. She honestly didn't mean to do it; she just never caught herself before the patronizing tone of voice oozed out of her mouth.

"Oh, I'm fine," he said, sounding almost wistful. Peach gave him a more careful glance. His shirt was only two-thirds tucked in, and his frayed belt looked like it had seen better days (like maybe the Bicentennial). Right now he went to take a bite of his jelly doughnut and some dark red jam dripped out and landed on his shirt. The stain was symmetrical with the ink stain on his pocket—if only his pen had been red, both splats would match.

Peach shook her head and thought, *He needs a woman*—now.

"How's Nan?" she asked, as she opened the fridge and grabbed a bottle of water.

"Good," he said, brightening up a bit. "Hey, guess what? She came in third for that poetry contest I was telling you about last week."

"Wow, that's great! Which poem was it?"

"Um, I think it was 'Down with the Barbie Bitch,' " he said.

Nodding supportively, Peach again said, "Wow, that's great," though she couldn't help feeling like it was a minor victory for bad poets everywhere. Dennis had shown her a sample of Nan's poetry once, and from what Peach could tell, Nan was big on rhyming pentameter and shock language—her sentences were filled with over-the-top angst and the basic teenage emoting about how the world owed her a favor. Still . . . as someone who liked to be creative, Peach had to admire Nan's diligence about expressing her feelings.

According to Dennis, Nan had handled her parents' divorce really well, and was still close to both of them—even though they were definitely not close to each other. In fact, this week she was going on a two-week trip with her mother. Dennis had mentioned something about a cruise, followed by a hiking trip through the wilderness.

"By the way, do you know if Rachel's here yet? I really need to speak to her about something." Peach told him she had no clue. "Well . . . better get back to my desk," Dennis said, waving his mug in a cheers motion and predictably spilling some tea on the black tile floor. Cluelessly, he turned and went on his way. As he slunk out of the kitchen, Peach watched jelly drop in globs whenever Dennis brought his doughnut to his mouth for a bite. More tea splashed onto the floor, and Peach just watched, as if it were happening in slow motion, then shook her head. Luckily Dennis's back was to her, because she could feel a pitying expression taking over her face, and she couldn't seem to stop it.

Jeez, there had to be a woman out there—somewhere in this city—who would wake Dennis up—shake him out of his weary little world, put the proverbial bounce in his skulk. He might not be depressed, but he was depress*ing*, even if he couldn't see that.

So what *did* Dennis have to offer a woman? Well, he seemed like a genuinely sweet guy with a big heart. That made up for a lot, as far as Peach was concerned.

Maybe it was her fascination with people and their basic psychology, but Peach loved to see others *excited* about something. She firmly believed that near-euphoria was something everyone could tap into, even if just briefly, but it often required a push.

She glanced down at the bottle of water in her hand, and only then noticed the "Do Not Touch" Post-it note stuck to it. Peach opened the fridge again to put it back and grab another one, and, still lost in thought about Dennis Emberson's love life, she stepped backward to shut the refrigerator door and accidentally smacked right into someone else. "Oh!" she yelped, startled. Whipping around, she grinned as soon as she saw who it was. "It's you."

"Sorry about that," Adam Quinlan said, smiling a little shyly, and stepping back to give her more space than she needed. "Hi . . . Yes, it's me." A short but awkward pause followed; he had to know as well as she did that the fleeting contact of bumping into each other just now had been . . . intimate. In fact, Peach was still processing what it was she'd just felt against her lower back. A hard bulge, that was what. Okay, so much for processing it. And she could've sworn that she still felt the sensation of it, the impression of it against her body.

Instantly, as if driven by their own power, her eyes shot to Adam's crotch. It appeared perfectly normal. This was good—it meant that he wasn't some kind of deviant, aroused in the middle of the day for no reason. Yet, she was sure she had felt *it* . . . which could mean only that Adam was . . . well . . . *big*.

She swallowed hard, suddenly feeling a little flushed. Her breath quickened, and her mouth ran dry. When she licked her lips, she found Adam swallowing, too, and avoiding her direct gaze. *He's shy*, was her first thought. Her second thought was, *So he felt it, too*. Shyness was extremely cute in a guy and not something Peach saw too often. Many guys her age were brimming with what they hoped passed for confidence (but was obviously desperation with the need to be accepted and to attain some veneer of "masculinity" and all its contrivances—who needed it?).

She held back a smile, realizing how immature she was being about the whole thing. "That's okay, Quin," she said brightly, eager to break the tension of the moment, to lighten up the weirdness, to settle that unfinished feeling hovering between them, reminding them there had been a kind of connection there, even if only for a passing moment.

After she left the kitchen, heading back to her desk, Peach pondered that connection. First she had seen Adam on the street that morning. Then she'd found out he not only worked in her office but, in a roundabout way, knew Dominick. And now this—a kitchen craving at the exact same time, plus the accidental brushing of Adam's (substantial) package against Peach's body. She didn't want to get too mystical here, but really—if that wasn't fate telling her something, what was?

Chapter Five

Later that afternoon, everyone had filtered into the conference room for a staff meeting/cake party. When Peach got there, she found Brenda and Nelson standing at one end of the long, oval black table. Brenda wore jeans and a sweatshirt, and cradled their baby, Annie, in her arms, as Nelson looked on—or *up*, as was the case.

The conference room was another tribute to Robert's fondness for Asian décor. In the center was a long, sleek black table with tightly cushioned black chairs around it. There were gold, red, and black silk screens framed and hanging around the room, and the cabinets along the back wall were elegantly adorned with gold-lettered kanji.

Peach really didn't mind the staff meetings too much, probably because her part in them was always fairly small, mostly just show-and-tell. She would share her newest basket innovations, get some feedback, and that was pretty much it. Grace was always on her best Mary Poppins behavior by the time Robert got there. Before he entered the conference room, she'd try to get in as much grumbling and snide comments as she could about keeping the kitchen clean. Most of it was directed at Nelson, who, despite his health-food obsession, had the table manners of a potbellied pig.

"Brenda!" Peach said brightly, and came closer. "Oh, hi, little Annie!" She reached out to pet the baby's soft skull with her open palm. Smiling warmly, Peach mused out loud, "*God*, she's cute." Annie had sparse wisps of dark hair and almond-shaped brown eyes.

Her cheeks were pudgy and velvety-smooth. It was impossible not to cuddle her.

"Hi, Peach," Brenda said, smiling as she rocked her baby gently in her arms. Annie reached out and grabbed Peach's finger, her tiny fingers barely closing all the way around, and her chubby cheeks creasing as she giggled—or gurgled with a smile on her face, whatever the case might be. "Wanna hold her?" Brenda asked.

"Okay," Peach said, gingerly taking Annie in her arms. She squirmed a little, but then adjusted to Peach, who touched her cheek to Annie's smooth forehead.

Nelson stood beside his wife, and a good five inches below. What he lacked in height, he overcompensated for in width, with a bulky, muscled upper body that tapered triangularly down to his narrow waist. He had kind of an intimidating look with his most distinct features being his large flared nostrils. Right down to his short blond hair, he seemed to be a glaring contrast to his wife.

"It wouldn't be Monday without a staff meeting to put us all to sleep, eh?" Nelson said to Peach, and snickered. She agreed, knowing that the cake part was a secret—Brenda had no idea they were going to celebrate her birthday this afternoon.

Just then Rachel entered the conference room. A pleasant-looking girl, she had curly black hair that sprang just above her shoulders. She usually wore a glossy dark pink lip shade that offset her bright smile—which was in blazing full effect most of the time. Rachel was an avid people pleaser, big on compliments and positive energy, and she usually waited to hear others' opinions before voicing her own. But Peach liked her and definitely saw potential. After all, she'd graduated from college just a few months ago; give her a little longer in the so-called real world and she'd be less maniacally bubbly in no time.

"Great sweater, Peach," Rachel said now, smiling brightly. "Where'd you get it?"

"Thanks," Peach said, and gently passed Annie back to her mom's expectant arms. "My sister got it for me. Birthday present."

Okay . . . she wasn't perfect. She knew damn well the store Lonnie had bought it from was right on Arlington Street, but she was afraid that if she divulged, Rachel would come in next week with the same exact one. Believe it or not, that had happened once before. It shouldn't have been annoying, but it was. As much as Peach liked Rachel, she didn't need a clone.

Peach and Brenda took seats at the table; Rachel and Nelson quickly followed suit.

Next Scott West strolled in. At twenty-six, he had a Midwestern kind of cuteness, with sandy brown hair, light blue eyes, and an affable grin. He was about six-one and slim—definitely a nice-looking guy, though not Peach's type. At this point, Peach wasn't really sure what her type was; she'd managed only to figure out what it *wasn't*. In Scott's case, besides the fact that he seemed to enjoy hanging out with his friends too much to be stellar boyfriend material, there was just no spark there. And as long as he hovered in that hazy place between being a guy and becoming a man, Peach figured she wouldn't even bother trying to set him up with anyone. "Hey everyone," he said, smiling, pulling up a chair next to Peach. "The baby's here. Nice." After exchanging pleasantries with Brenda, he asked, "Does she get you up a lot in the night?"

"Does she get me up?" Brenda echoed with a laugh. Glancing at her husband, she said, "*All* the time. Right, babe?"

"Right, babe," Nelson replied. "Hey, what's the deal with newborns anyway? If they're not getting up, they're *spitting* up—do they *ever* quit?"

Peach forced a smile, and Brenda did the same.

Soon Nelson and Brenda got immersed in gooey baby talk amongst themselves, and Scott swiveled back and forth in his chair with childlike impatience. "When do we get a little cake action?" he said quietly.

"I know—I've been looking forward to it all day!" Rachel agreed enthusiastically, which wasn't exactly a surprise. One, because this was Rachel, and two, because this was *cake*.

"Are you a good widdle baby?" Brenda crooned to Annie, her

voice about five sugary octaves above her normal pitch. "You're a good widdle schweetie pie, aren't you?" Rocking Annie back and forth in her arms, she cooed on, "Are you Mommy's good widdle baby?"

"Sure she is," Nelson answered. "She takes after her old man." Meaning that Nelson was a good widdle baby, too? Peach wondered. "Don't you, little schweetie?" he added, using his own nasally enhanced infant-speak. "Dontcha, widdle monkey face—widdle schweetie monkey face?"

Okay, granted, Annie and monkeys were equally cute; in fact, monkeys had nothing on her. But still—why did Brenda and Nelson always have to gush in this insipid manner? Not to be a bitch, but come on—baby talk was just plain annoying even if you *were* talking to a baby. And what was up with the deliberate lisp? Should parents be encouraging that?

Peach shuddered to think what it must be like in the Perhunes' house, though she had to admit, she'd always wondered what Brenda and Nelson had in common, and the grating goo-goo-ga-ga bit was at least one thing.

"Babe, will you hold her for me?" Brenda asked her husband, her voice back to normal, as she used the pet name she and Nelson called each other at work (ad nauseam). "I have to run to the ladies' room."

"Sure, babe," Nelson said.

"Thanks, babe."

Peach stifled an eye roll. After Brenda darted out of the conference room, Nelson held little Annie up high in the air and blew loud farting noises on her stomach, which was showing beneath the hem of her ruffled pink shirt.

"Um, Scott . . . how was your weekend?" Rachel asked, eyes bright with interest.

With a brief yawn, he shrugged. "It was okay, just hung out, watched some football. Went to a hockey game Friday night. What about you?"

"I went out with my friends to this really fun sushi place. You like sushi, right?"

"Sure, who doesn't?" he said casually.

"You said it, brother," Nelson piped up. "There's nothing in this world like salmon rolls with a little home-brewed sake," he added, pronouncing *sake* "sock-*ay*." Like he'd ever home-brewed that or anything else in his life—and was there some reason he needed to start picking between his teeth with the corner of his folder?

Peach tapped her heel silently on the carpet, looking at the door. Where was the new guy—Quin? Granted, they were still waiting on Robert, Grace, and Dennis, but she just hoped that Quin knew about the cake party.

There was something . . . interesting about him. She supposed she was intrigued by his shyness, his reservation before speaking, those quiet pauses followed by nonelaborative answers. But then, anyone who was that different from her was bound to intrigue her. She recalled Adam's rich brown eyes, blinking back from behind his glasses. . . . Yes, there was definitely something offbeat and cute about him.

"Peach, you look deep in thought," Scott commented.

"Oh . . . I was just wondering if Quin knows about the meeting," she said, leaving out her further contemplation of his cuteness.

"Who?"

"Adam," she clarified. "Adam Quinlan, the new network administrator."

"Oh, I haven't met him yet," Rachel said.

"I'd better go get him," Peach said, rising out of her chair, suddenly overwhelmed by the urge to go find Quin—to pull him along into the conference room, to extend her own brand of friendship, premature as it might be, to this enigmatic new recluse. (Too dramatic?)

She was just about to hip-check one of the glass doors open when Robert came through it. Tall and lean, he had a clean-cut kind of middle-aged appeal, with neatly trimmed salt-and-pepper hair and a discreet wedding ring on his left hand. Peach took that to mean that Robert's wife, Claire, was still in the picture, even if she hadn't visited Boston—or Millennium, anyway—in nearly a year. "Oh, pardon me, Peach," he said, smiling politely. "I didn't mean to get in your way." He held his arm out in a chivalrous after-you gesture.

"Oh, thanks, Robert. I was just going to go get Adam. I don't think he knows about the meeting."

"No, don't worry; he knows," Robert assured her smoothly. "I made sure to mention it to him this afternoon."

"Oh." With a pang of disappointment, Peach returned to her seat.

A few moments later Brenda returned from the bathroom, and on her heels came Grace Gomez with the cake. "Finally," Scott said, smiling and rubbing his hands together, just as Brenda turned back, looking confused. And again Peach wondered, Where was Quin?

"Comin' through!" Grace chirped, Mary Poppins game face on, as Robert gallantly rose to his feet to hold the door wide-open for her.

"What is this?" Brenda asked, scrunching her eyebrows.

"Happy birthday, babe!" Nelson said, leaning over the arm of his chair to give his wife a kiss on the cheek, which was blushing with surprise. A laugh burst from Brenda's throat then, as a warm smile broke out across her face.

"Oh, my gosh! This is for me?" she said, pressing a hand to her chest. "I had no idea. My birthday's not for another week. You knew about this, babe?" she asked, turning to Nelson.

"Of course, babe. And you say I can't keep a secret, babe."

"I'll cut the cake so we can all dig in," Grace offered in that cheery "right-o," the-hills-are-alive tone of voice she used only in Robert's presence. For all Grace's tough talk behind her boss's back, she kissed his ass relentlessly.

"Hey, Brenda, how old are you now?" Scott asked, as Grace sliced the cake while humming loudly.

"I'd rather not say," Brenda said with an affable smile, though she couldn't have been more than thirty-five.

Suddenly Nelson let out a juicy belch that shattered Peach's concentration. (Luckily her appetite was still intact.) He gripped his stomach and groaned, as if to indicate exactly where the belch had

come from. Peach tried not to grimace, not that Nelson would notice anyway. He was a very dichotomous individual. It seemed like
he consumed health shakes, protein bars, and other GNC goodies
religiously. Yet, on the flip side, he exhibited a grotesque lack of eti-
quette in most public settings, not to mention questionable personal hygiene. Definitely not averse to picking or scratching in
other people's company, he usually went for any handy office tool
that would alleviate the itch. Most common offenses included biting his fingers down to gnarled pink stumps, and cleaning his ears
with a pen cap (not always his own).

Just then the conference room phone rang. It could only be for
Robert, whose phones were forwarded to the conference rooms
whenever he had a meeting. Grace set the knife down and hurried
over to grab it off the wall.

"Hell-ooo," she sang merrily. "Robert Walsh's office. Oh, yes,
please hold." She pressed the hold button, and said to Robert, "It's
Nicholas Easterbrook for you."

With a nod, he rose from his chair. "Right, I've been expecting
his call. I'll take that in my office. Thanks, Grace," he said, as he
stood from the table. "Please, everyone, enjoy the cake; don't wait
on me. Oh, and Grace? That reminds me—could you get me a
work contract for him as soon as possible? He's going to be doing
some consulting work for us again."

Once Robert stepped out of the conference room, he unwittingly left a tense, charged silence in his wake. It hovered over the
table like a thick, heavy cloud. Everyone knew that Brenda had had
an affair with Nicholas Easterbrook a few years back. It had been
before she'd married Nelson, during a brief time when they'd been
broken up. In fact, for a while people had speculated that if Easterbrook hadn't ended the relationship, Brenda might never have gone
back to Nelson—making their marriage more of a rebound than
anything else. ("People" meaning Grace, who'd been the one to fill
Peach in on all the intraoffice scandals predating her employment
there.)

Now at the mere mention of Easterbrook's name, Nelson compressed his lips into a thin, tight line, while his large nostrils expanded and contracted with suppressed emotion. Understandably, the subject was still a sore point.

Meanwhile Peach was thinking she could dwell on any of this only so much, when a wedge of German chocolate cake landed at her place. *Yum, yum, yum.*

"Thanks, all, so much," Brenda said again, breaking into her cake with a pink plastic fork. "This is so nice. . . ."

"But Brenda," Grace said once she sat down with her own slice, "what about your diet? Aren't you on Weight Watchers?"

Brenda froze with her mouth open and her fork in midair. "Oh, right, well . . . I know, I probably shouldn't, but . . ."

With a lopsided shrug, Grace said, "Okaaay. Don't say I didn't waaarn you. . . ."

"I know, I know," Brenda said guiltily, nodding. "You're right, I shouldn't, but . . . actually I think I've saved up enough points for this."

Grace's brows arched incredulously. "Really? How many points is chocolate cake?"

"Um . . . well . . ." Brenda floundered.

"Grace, jeez, give her a break," Peach intervened. "It's her *birthday*. I'm sure Weight Watchers would understand."

"Okay, I'm just trying to help," Grace remarked, waving a hand loosely through the air.

Not to mention trying to release a little bitchiness before Robert returns to the room.

"The diet starts tomorrow," Brenda offered lightheartedly.

"Famous last words . . ." Grace said.

"No more diet talk, please," Peach said, more to get Brenda off the defensive and back onto the birthday pedestal, which seemed only fair.

"Yeah, what's the deal with diets anyway?" Nelson asked, talking with his mouth full of cake. "Didja ever notice those people who go to a fast-food restaurant, and order two cheeseburgers, a huge thing of fries, and then a *diet* soda?"

He waited for laughter that didn't come, and then Scott shrugged and said, "I order diet soda sometimes."

"You *do*?" Nelson said, surprised.

"Sure," Scott replied unself-consciously, and ate another big forkful of his cake.

Chuckling, Nelson looked around the room as he teased Scott, "Oh, so what, do you order a *salad*, too?"

"Sometimes," Scott said. Then he grinned boyishly and patted his flat stomach. "Hey, gotta look good for the ladies," he added.

A laugh slipped out of Peach, and Rachel beamed a smile when she said, "I think Scott's a player."

"No, no," he said, still grinning. "I'm looking for the right woman. I just like to look *very* thoroughly."

"What's the deal with salads these days, anyway?" Nelson said, apparently still trying to latch onto that limited subject. "Like now they've got mandarin oranges in them, pears, raisins—it's like, hey, did I order a salad or a *fruit* salad?"

Rachel let out a nervous giggle, and Brenda patted Nelson's knee, which was her way to what? Tell him to shut up or encourage him to continue?

"You know the ladies who should be eating salads," he went on, as Peach thought, *Okay, clearly the latter.* "The ones who try on an outfit and it's too tight—and then they find out it's a *maternity* outfit—and they're not even pregnant!" Another expectant pause. "And then they find out—they're wearing it *backward*!"

Most of the table looked confused. Meanwhile Peach got the joke but wasn't sure if she should laugh or cry. How did Nelson *live*?

Glancing at his wife for supportive laughter, he found her pre-occupied at the moment—affecting a lisp and similar speech impediments for her baby daughter, who was apparently drifting off to "shweep" in her arms. It was a crying shame, really. She liked Brenda, and she hated to see her become one of those annoying parents who encouraged their kids to say "punkin" and "pasghetti."

A few minutes later Robert returned to the conference room,

and he brought someone with him. "For those of you, who haven't met him, this is Adam Quinlan, our new network administrator."

With a brief smile, Adam said hello and apologized for being late; he had been on the phone with Millennium's hosting company. After Robert made all the introductions, Peach blurted out, "Quin, come sit over here—I saved you a seat!"

Chapter Six

Throughout the meeting, Adam found it increasingly difficult to focus. He was listening to Robert speak about the company's goals and objectives over the next fiscal year, but kept having his attention diverted by his physical awareness of Peach . . . breathing in her sultry scent. . . . It was subtle but kind of tangy, like a sweet, citrusy perfume. There was just something inexplicably intoxicating about it.

A strong sexual reaction stirred in his body. Jesus, that was twice now: once when he'd been eyeing her thigh earlier, and now as he was breathing her in—palpably feeling her presence and her body heat. A hot wave of desire flooded his groin, and he shifted just slightly in his seat, trying to ignore it and focus back on the meeting.

But the air around him suddenly felt thick and heavy, charged with the electrifying awareness of another person and the self-consciousness of it—did she have any idea? Could she tell how attracted he was to her? Sucking in a breath, he stole a look at her. She was eating a piece of her chocolate cake, licking it from her fork, and he zeroed in immediately on how ripe and soft her lips looked, how lusciously wet. . . .

Just then Peach shifted her legs to cross the right over the left, and suddenly her calf brushed against his knee. A jolt of lust spiked up his leg to his groin at the contact, even though it was really innocent. Tell that to his body, to the blood rushing to his cock, making him hot and hard. . . . Peach didn't even notice that their legs were still barely touching, because she didn't move away, and when Adam glanced down, he realized that, in fact, their legs weren't still touching. Rather, he was still feeling the *zing*—the sensation of Peach touching him. His body was still savoring it. Jesus . . . he needed to get a grip.

Here he was, trying to figure out how to make a break from one relationship; the last thing he needed to contemplate was a relationship with someone new. Or a romance of any kind. Especially with his family strife, moving to a new city, starting a new job—no, he definitely did not need the aggravation of getting preoccupied with an infatuation. Even if it had been a really long time since he'd felt such a strong, fierce physical attraction . . .

Peach switched legs again, brushing Adam's knee once more. It was a fleeting caress—the contact of her stockings against his pants barely perceptible—yet he felt more sexual awareness strum to life, quickening his breath and thickening in his groin. And then he felt himself blush, just a little, but he was embarrassed, even though no one knew what he was thinking. He still felt like an idiot. All this raw animal lust coursing through him over something as innocuous as a leg brushing up against him, and for a beautiful girl he'd just met, who was oblivious to him. It was fucking ridiculous.

Just then Adam zoned in on Robert Walsh's voice. He was asking him something. "Um, what was that?" Adam asked, straightening up a little in his seat and adjusting his glasses, which weren't the least bit crooked.

"I asked if you had any questions so far," Robert said.

Yeah, what the hell had he said this whole meeting? And what arousing perfume was Peach wearing right now that was turning him on and making him totally lose his focus, which wasn't even like him to do? "Uh, no, I can't think of any questions at the moment," Adam said.

"Well, if you do have any—" Robert began.

"You can ask me," Peach piped up brightly, smiling her warm, adorable smile, and looking at him with sparkling blue-eyed innocence. Yet . . . the thin dark lining under her eyes gave her a hint of dark sensuality. He wanted to bite her luscious lower lip.

Instead he smiled briefly, nodded, and said thanks. But if she only knew what he'd been thinking . . .

Later that night Peach was settled in at her apartment. It was on the third and top floor of an ivy-covered building, in a row of brown-brick houses that elegantly lined Commonwealth Avenue. Right now she was working on a collage that had spilled all over the living room. She sat on the soft, caramel-colored area rug, with her back leaning against one of the red paisley couches that overflowed the room. And she waited for BeBe, who was frenetically changing outfits.

The wide wall opposite Peach had a lush mural spanning across it; it looked as though you were stepping into the woods, with lots of greens and muted blues. She called it "Sparkle Forest." The opposite wall was pale pink with vibrant streaks of color slashing through it, and amorphous images that were almost iridescent with their many shades of blue and violet. Peach called that mural "Anticipation."

Now she had scattered pictures covering the oak coffee table and filling her lap. A collage was a relaxing way to release some creative energy, and more important, it was something to work on besides Peach's never-ending kitchen-ceiling mural—a picture of angels that looked more like Kewpie dolls, but did anyone really look up that often?

"How about this?" BeBe said, trotting out of her bedroom for the fifth time. She was getting ready for her blind date with Ken, the resident at Beth Israel Hospital, and so far she'd settled on black boot-cut pants and skinny black heels—per Peach's advice—even though BeBe had said she looked like a cow on stilts, which Peach had ignored, of course.

Now she was settling on a top to wear. Her heels clicked down the shiny hardwood hallway and paused at the wide archway to the living room. "Okay, what do you think?" BeBe said, holding out her hands, modeling a melon-colored cardigan.

"Um . . . too motherly," Peach said. "I liked the other thing better."

Glancing down, BeBe said, "I could see that. Wait here; I'll try something else."

"I'm not going anywhere."

BeBe turned and scurried back to her bedroom, while Peach arranged her pictures on the floor, tilted her head to assess them, then rearranged. "Hey, did I tell you I made a friend today?" she called out.

"So what else is new?" BeBe called back.

Smiling, Peach added, "His name's Adam; he's the new computer guy."

"Uh-huh . . ." BeBe said, and Peach could hear the frantic swishing of fabric as she changed yet again. "Is he cute?" she asked when she came back out.

Peach stopped to think about that for a second. "Yeah, actually . . ." She was about to tell BeBe that he was the guy they'd seen on the street that morning, when BeBe stopped to pose right in front of her.

"All right, what about this one?"

"Yes," Peach said firmly, standing up to get a better look. "Definitely that one. *Very* sultry." It was a deep vee-neck sweater, pale blue—a potentially meek color but not when it was covering a pair of big, pillowy breasts. BeBe looked sexy, soft, and huggable.

"Really?" BeBe looked unsure, to say the least, her dark brows squinching up and her mouth twisting into a skeptical grimace. To an objective observer, Peach's fashion advice might seem questionable; she had on silky red pajama pants and her standard-issue "ugly" sweater, which was a mess of greens, oranges, and yellows, with bright red along the collar and hem. It was her absolute favorite thing to wear, besides her patchwork coat. Her dark gold hair was tossed up in a makeshift bun, secured with two pencils.

"Okay, this one," she agreed. "Thanks for your help." She turned to scoot back to her bedroom, to strip out of the outfit before taking her shower. On her way, she called back, "Hey, so I can't believe I still haven't heard from Ellen Weinberg!"

"I know, she's killing us," Peach said. Here BeBe had gotten tons of stuff from Pet Emporium: a crate, a dog bed, toys, food, water dish, and rawhide sticks for puppies. But no word from Weinberg. Peach hated waiting. Also, she'd gotten home that night to find a message from her mom on the answering machine, because Peach had forgotten, yet again, to return the vacuum she'd borrowed two weeks ago. (In fairness, maybe her mother hated waiting, too.)

Brushing her collage stuff aside, Peach hopped up to go to the kitchen. It was around the bend from the living room—a warm, cozy nook with chocolate-brown cabinets and a high round table with tall upholstered stools. The table sat next to the kitchen window, which overlooked a small enclosed garden down below. During the afternoon, coppery sunlight spilled through the curtains—but now, at night, the sheer lace curtains appeared to be coolly tinted blue.

Above her was her mural in progress, angels in a haze of gold and blushing pink. She'd have to get back to that one of these days—preferably before BeBe lost patience with the pile of painting supplies clogging up half of the counter space. After grabbing a can of cherry 7UP from the fridge, Peach hopped up to sit on the countertop. She could hear BeBe start the water running in their big, old claw-foot tub. In a house that was nearly fifty years old, the pipes took several minutes to warm up.

BeBe came back out wearing her white terry-cloth robe and leaned against the doorjamb of the kitchen, killing time while the bathwater ran. "So tell me more about your new friend," she said. Peach told her that he was the guy they'd spotted on the street that morning. BeBe's eyes squinted quizzically. "I don't remember."

Peach twisted her lips knowingly. "Well, you weren't paying much attention. You were too preoccupied romanticizing John."

"Remembering."

"Re*vis*ing."

"Remi*nisc*ing," BeBe insisted.

"All right, fine," Peach said, smiling and relenting on her point. "Just remember that John doesn't deserve you." Okay—*now* she'd relent on her point.

"I know, you're right," BeBe mumbled.

"So does this mean you're gonna give Ken a real chance tonight?" Peach asked, referring to BeBe's latest prospect.

Eyes wide with utter innocence, BeBe held out her hands and said, "Of *course*."

"Uh-huh . . ." Peach said, grinning a little skeptically, and hopped off the counter to go back into the living room to work on her collage. BeBe followed. "And speaking of setups, I really wish I could find someone for Dennis."

At this point, she refreshed BeBe on the situation with the sweet, hapless office accountant who obviously needed some direction in his life—some *love*. Today's jelly doughnut debacle had only confirmed it. Now Peach was on a mission.

BeBe scrunched her face doubtfully. "I don't know, Peach. I wouldn't bother trying to set him up unless he asks. A person has to be ready, I think."

"He's forty-four, single, and can barely dress himself. I think that qualifies him as 'ready.' "

"Yeah, but who knows? Maybe he's not over his ex-wife yet. Or, hey, he could be gay, for all you know."

Rolling her eyes, Peach dropped her head back dramatically. "You're completely obsessed with how every guy's gay. That only happened once!"

"That we know about . . ."

"Anyway, Dennis is not gay. He's just a boring, run-of-the-mill, middle-aged white guy—basically an ineffectual male who needs a woman's touch."

"Hmm . . . and is that how you're going to talk him up to the girls?" BeBe asked with a laugh, then held up her hands with mock defensiveness. "Just curious."

Glibly, Peach said, "I'll keep you posted."

Adam found himself in a plaintive state of discontent. Leftover buffalo wings and an ice-cold can of Coke had left him with a slight stomachache—reminding him that with each passing year he couldn't eat exactly as he had when he was in college. Jesus, was he turning into an old man already?

Now he sat at the computer in his living room with his TV set on, a hockey game in progress, some scrambled code on his monitor, and his mind elsewhere altogether.

He'd just gotten off the phone with Robin, and she'd told him how much she loved and missed him. Maybe he was getting cynical, but her words just didn't hold the same sincerity they once had. There was a desperation to them now, a threadiness, as though she were reaching out to cling to him, as though she realized that moving on to other, bigger things was scary, so she was trying to reestablish the intimacy they'd once shared.

Unfortunately, it wasn't that easy. He honestly didn't know *why* it wasn't that easy, but it just wasn't. At this point he was finding it nearly impossible just to parse out exactly what was love and what was nostalgia and residual attachment.

Suddenly his phone rang and jerked him back to the present. "Hello?"

"Hi, baby!" Speaking of nostalgia . . . it was his newly single mother with her familiarly frothy voice.

"Hi, Mom, how are you doing?"

"Hanging in there," she said, sounding upbeat and lively despite her words. He got the feeling that his mom had built a whole world around trying to stay positive enough that no one would notice when life was in disarray. "But let's talk about you," she coaxed.

"Okay," he said with an awkward laugh. "What about me?"

"Well, how's your new job?"

"It's good. It was only my first day, but the people seem nice."

"Uh-huh, that's good. And have you talked to Robin lately?"

Instinctively, Adam's jaw tightened. "Yeah, I just spoke to her, actually."

"Oh, no, what's wrong?"

"Nothing."

"I can tell by your voice there's something. What is it, sweetie? Did she change her mind about moving back soon?"

"No, she's still thinking about it," was all he said.

"Well, whatever happens, I know it will be for the best," she said supportively. "And whatever you decide to do about your relationship, you know that I'm behind you a hundred percent, and that I love you more than life."

He half grinned at that bizarre non sequitur, though that type of thing no longer surprised him. For the past month, his mom had become even more expressive and affectionate with him and Sonny than usual, often relying on over-the-top declarations of her maternal devotion, undoubtedly as a way to mitigate her guilt about the divorce. Or *impending* divorce; Adam still had a hard time picturing his parents going through with it.

"I know, Mom," Adam said, then switched gears. "So how's Aunt Emily?"

"She's fine." Tentatively, Liz added, "Which reminds me . . . are you still going to help me look for my own apartment this weekend?"

"Of course I am," Adam said, his voice softening. "I told you I would."

"Oh, good. Thanks," she said, and instantly Adam's chest tightened. One, because he could just see the relieved little smile on his mom's face right now, and two, because his mom shouldn't have to feel so grateful; helping her out was the least he could do.

Not that that logic carried much weight with his older brother, Derek, the token family fuckup, who mostly drifted into their parents' lives when he needed money. Derek Quinlan was the proverbial black sheep—the rebel without a checking account. Last Adam had heard, his brother was living in California after a brief stint working in a casino in Vegas, and was still deluding himself—and anyone else who'd listen—that he was a musician.

Adam had always felt inexplicably guilty growing up, because Derek had been terrible in school—first his grades, then his behavior—while Adam, who was two years behind him, had excelled in most of his classes, especially math. He'd been in AP calculus his junior year, while Derek, who'd barely squeaked by with his diploma, had been crashing at their parents' house when it was convenient, then disappearing for days at a time.

Adam supposed it was only normal that he was the one his parents counted on to be responsible; he was the one they'd turn to for help. For all intents and purposes, he was the oldest. And Derek was just the perennially lost adolescent.

"You know you're the reason I live," Liz was saying now. "You know my kids are the reasons I get up in the morning. Your happiness is paramount to my concerns, and I really hope that you can own that."

Furrowing his brows, Adam said, "Mom, what the hell are you talking about?"

"What?"

"All these things you've been saying lately . . ."

"Well, I'm just trying to . . . See, I've been reading in this book how important it is for parents to let their children know that a divorce isn't their fault. And to make sure their kids know how much they're loved and cherished every day."

"Believe me, you don't have to do that," Adam said flatly. He didn't need the touchy-feely reminders that his mom loved him; of course he knew she did. Besides, he'd never been one to saturate himself in emotions. Not that he didn't feel things deeply like anyone else, but he rarely let his feelings rule him. Logic and reason, like the empirical nature of math and science, were much more consistent tenets to live by. "And we're not kids anymore; we're adults." Though the words, once out of his mouth, didn't sound right. Derek and Sonny adults? *No fucking way.*

"Yeah . . . it's not working with Sonny either," Liz admitted with a defeated sigh.

"She'll get over it," Adam said, with little sympathy for his spoiled younger sister.

"But she's my baby," Liz lamented, "and she's not even speaking to me!"

"Did you say *your* baby or *a* baby?" Adam muttered.

"Don't start—"

"Sorry," he said halfheartedly, as he double-clicked on his mouse to open a program he'd started writing last night, when he hadn't been able to sleep, lying awake in his new, barely decorated, all-too-quiet new apartment. He'd almost wished for neighbors clanking pots and pans, or the sound of a dog barking . . . something to take him out of the blaring silence of his blackened bedroom and the vacuum of his mind. . . .

"I guess she's still mad at me because I'm not going to be able to buy her that car I promised. Not until I get a job."

Rolling his eyes, Adam said, "Jesus, Mom, *another* car? What the hell's wrong with the one you bought her two years ago?" He hadn't meant to snap, but Jesus Christ—his sister wasn't just spoiled; she was shameless. Twenty-four years old and still subsidized by her parents. Okay, that was one thing; she'd graduated college three years ago, so he supposed there was a grace period. Of course, *he'd* been working all through college and immediately after, but fine. Sonny had tried temping, but then decided she didn't want to work in an office. (Who did?) Then she'd tried waitressing, but quit after less than a month because she "wasn't enjoying it." (Did anyone deeply *enjoy* waitressing? It was a hard, tiring job, like most other occupations.) Then she'd decided to travel with her friends (on her parents' dime, of course), and now she was back in New Hampshire, set up in her own apartment (see *parents' dime*), and still loosely contemplating what to do with her communications degree.

Ordinarily none of this would affect or even bother Adam; in truth, he never would've thought much about it. But now things were different. With his parents now separated and their money situation ambiguous, at best—frozen and earmarked for lawyers, at worst—there was simply no place for Sonny's overblown sense of entitlement. Why couldn't she see that? More important, why couldn't their mom see that? Why did Adam have to field one infuriating phone call after another from his whole family (except Derek, who was God knew where right now)?

Now, to think of his mom scrapping to support Sonny, combing the want ads to get a job to keep "the baby" happy . . .

Sometimes it just annoyed the shit out of him.

"Well, the car is almost three years old now," Liz explained, "and it's a two-door, which your sister's never been crazy about." The two-door had been a graduation gift to Sonny, and call him unconventional, but since when did one need to be rewarded simply for not flunking out of school?

God, what's with me lately? he thought, shaking his head, ashamed at his own thoughts as he heard them reverberate in his mind. Suddenly he was ashamed of his attitude, his anger. It wasn't right. He'd always been the one his family turned to for help, so why should that change now? If his mom wanted to vent about Sonny's latest tantrum, he should try to be supportive. And since when did he feel such animosity toward his siblings anyway? He loved his family more than anything, so what had changed now to make him irritable when it came to family business as usual?

Here Sonny had already left three messages on his cell phone and Adam hadn't even gotten back to her. He hadn't called only because he knew if he did, he would lose his patience and tell Sonny to fucking *grow up* already.

Then again . . . maybe he should take his own advice.

"So, we'll go on Saturday, okay? To look at apartments?" Liz said now, breaking his train of thought.

"Sure, that sounds fine," he said.

"Are you going to tell your father?"

"No, why would I? I don't want to get him upset."

"Well, he's not the only one who's upset, you know," Liz said with mild defensiveness. "And he didn't mind making *me* upset for the past thirty years."

"Okay, I know," Adam said, anxious to end the conversation before his mom tried to reexplain how her health scare had prompted her decision to leave, and there was nothing Adam hated discussing more. Thinking about how close his mom had come— what one doctor had thought was pancreatic cancer, but turned out to be a terrible pancreatic infection that was now fully treated . . . well, Adam hated reliving the terror he'd felt for his mother, the acute sense that he had to be calm and reassuring, that he shouldn't cry—he wasn't sure why exactly, but he just shouldn't. And so he absolutely *hated* revisiting that topic, which inevitably came up whenever Liz felt she needed to justify her new outlook on life. He honestly did understand it—pretty much—but yet . . . why did he still feel a little annoyed with her for leaving?

Soon they said good-bye. Adam dropped his phone on its hook, and instantly he heard the silence descend on him again. Scrolling his mouse across his computer screen, he clicked on his e-mail in box. No new messages. Suddenly he'd never felt so lonely.

Chapter Seven

Peach had just drifted off to sleep when she heard someone enter her room. In that hazy, foggy place between dream and reality, she wasn't fully awake or processing, and then she felt someone say her name, a sharp whisper, and she jumped.

"Oh!"

"Oh, I'm sorry, I'm sorry," BeBe whispered quickly. "I just got home."

"Hey," Peach said, slowly coming awake and sitting up in her satiny bed. "Did you have fun?"

"Enh," BeBe said with a shrug, and sat down on the bed. "It was okay."

"Well, was he cute?"

"Yeah, he was okay." Two okays—so she definitely wasn't bowled over.

"And?" Peach pressed, waiting for some details.

"And nothing," BeBe said, then paused, and added, "Well . . ."

"What?" Peach said, sitting more upright, waiting impatiently.

"He's cheap," BeBe finished.

"What, was he one of those 'you can get the tip' guys?" Peach asked.

"No, one of those 'you can get the snacks at the movies' guys."

"Ech, I *hate* that," Peach said.

"I didn't even *want* snacks at the movies, but then I felt all this pressure." BeBe kicked off her heels, and Peach heard them hit her floor with a thud. "These things are *killing* me."

"How was the movie?"

"Stupid. It was some action movie; I can't even remember the name of it now."

"Where did you go for dinner?" Peach asked.

"Olive Garden," BeBe replied. "I ate to the point of pain."

"Lovely. So there were no sparks at all?"

"Let's just say the highlight of my night was the bread sticks."

A laugh slipped from Peach's lips as her head flopped back down on her pillow—a second wave of sleepiness was hitting—and then, suddenly, she remembered something *huge*. Her eyes shot open, and she darted back up into the sitting position. "Omigod! Where's my head?"

"What?" BeBe said, sounding confused, as Peach threw her covers off her and hopped out of bed.

"I have major news," she explained, then tugged on BeBe's sleeve to get her up off the bed and into the living room. "Follow me."

"Why, where are we going?"

"Just trust me; this is better than bread sticks."

"What is it?" BeBe asked impatiently, as they navigated through the darkened living room, around the furniture, and over to the bay window. A stream of illumination from a streetlight sliced across the side of the shiny, metal dog crate that BeBe had purchased that afternoon—and inside it was a little ball of white fur.

"Oh, my God . . ." BeBe said, her face breaking into a smile as she glanced back at Peach. "The *puppy*?"

"Isn't it great!" Peach yelped, then lowered her voice, which just seemed like the thing to do in the dark. "It was a total surprise."

Earlier that night Peach had been stepping out of a steaming shower when the phone rang. It had been Ellen Weinberg calling on her cell phone, five minutes away from their apartment with the dog in its carrier. She was on the way to Logan Airport and wanted to drop the puppy off before she left for her trip. Apparently the Weinster wasn't big on notice. Not that Peach had minded. Please— she'd been elated, racing around the apartment naked, her body damp and filmy, hair wet and tangled, as she tried to puppy-proof the apartment. She'd put plastic blockers in the outlets and spritzed all their electrical cords with this nasty stuff that was supposed to deter dogs from chewing the wires.

Finally Peach had folded fresh towels and laid them neatly inside the crate BeBe had bought, so the little sweetie pie would be comfortable.

Her heart had turned over when she saw her, no bigger than a football, with a bright pink bow pushing up through her fluffy white fur. Peach's first thought had been, *Yes, a girl!* Her next had been, *Wow . . .*

How could something so tiny and innocent even exist?

"She looks just like a powdered munchkin!" Peach had said when the Weinster's limo driver had brought her up.

"Not even three pounds," he'd said with a smile. "Half of it's probably her fur." Then he'd tipped his hat and headed toward the elevator, and Peach had leaned against the door, cradling the puppy in her arms.

"I can't believe it—you're *literally* a powdered munchkin," she'd said. But the munchkin was fast asleep, and had been zonked out ever since.

Even now she was curled up in the fetal position, snuggling in between the soft folds of the towel in her crate. "Oh, my God," BeBe whispered again, wonder filling her voice as she knelt down to get a closer look. "I can't believe it's really ours."

Gingerly BeBe opened the wire door of the crate, which squeaked slightly on its hinge. But the puppy didn't stir. In the shaft of light cutting across the living room, Peach could just make out the little slits that were her eyes, squeezed shut, mostly buried underneath her paws. Her heart lurched.

Kneeling beside BeBe, Peach leaned down and stroked the dog's fluffy white fur gently. Just then the puppy's nose started twitching; maybe she was dreaming. What did dogs dream about anyway? Steaks? Running free? Slippers?

"Now . . ." Peach said, getting to other business, "there's the matter of her name."

"Why, what is it?" BeBe asked.

Pausing for effect, Peach pursed her lips and said, "Well . . . apparently the Weinster couldn't decide between Rochelle and Giselle, so she'd kind of been calling her both."

BeBe just looked at her, then scrunched her face and said, "So basically what you're telling me is that her name is Rochelle Giselle Weinberg." When she reiterated the three names in such a deadpan, staccato fashion, Peach had to laugh.

"Pretty much," she replied with a giggle.

"Ech."

"I know—okay, first things first: The name's gotta go," Peach said. "And we want something with a little spunk."

BeBe nodded. "I agree. But wait . . . what if she's used to it by now? I don't want to confuse her."

"No way, she's only two months old," Peach countered.

"We could always keep her name as is, but make a nickname out of it. Um . . . how about . . . Rochy?" Peach tilted her head and waited for BeBe to come to her senses. "Yeah, I guess that's kind of weird."

"Look, if you're even *contemplating* Rochy you might as well just give her a whole new name," Peach said.

"Let me think. . . ." While BeBe was thinking, Peach sat down on the floor; she leaned back and rested her weight on her hands. "Oh, I know!" BeBe said suddenly. "How about Buster? That was the name of my imaginary dog when I was little; I just remembered."

Interesting . . . BeBe had mentioned once that as a child she'd had an imaginary dog, but she'd never mentioned his name. (Apparently she'd also had an imaginary cat, an imaginary best friend, and an imaginary mother. The amateur psychologist in Peach would love to sit down with BeBe and her mom to delve more deeply.)

"Buster," Peach echoed, then clapped her hands together. "That's so cute!"

"Yes, you're definitely a Buster," BeBe said, slowly opening the crate door and reaching in to pet her new dog on her small rounded belly. Buster rolled over and revealed a rounded pinkish belly. "It feels like velvet," BeBe said softly.

For a few moments Peach just marveled at how perfectly peaceful Buster looked, how pristinely innocent, how utterly angelic.

Except, little did she know, Buster wasn't the angel she appeared to be—and this was just the beginning.

The next day at work Peach was on the phone with Lonnie, who was about to lament her marital strife—if you could even call it that, and then whine about her dissertation—if you could even call it *that*—but first she asked about the puppy. "So how do you like being a mom?"

Hmm . . . one would think that since Peach and BeBe had gotten their third roommate only twelve hours ago, Peach would still be in euphoria stage, but actually Buster had already showed some of her—forgive the euphemism—*spunk* that morning at around four thirty that morning. She'd woken up whining to go pee, but felt the need to lurch out of the crate and frantically bite Peach's feet and ankles and tug on her kimono until it tore at the hem. But then, how could it not tear? Buster was holding on to it by needle-like teeth the whole way down to the street.

BeBe had trailed sleepily behind, but Peach didn't hold it against her, because BeBe had always been a legendarily heavy sleeper; it usually took her a full half hour to make coherent sense in the morning. Afterward, they'd both tried to pacify Buster, feeling sorry for her that she was in a strange place and scared. They'd tried to cuddle her, but she wasn't having any of it. And it wasn't like the few teeth she had even hurt that much, but she literally went in and out of spastic frenzy from four thirty to six thirty, before passing out in a final exhausted stupor. Peach and BeBe did the same, but only for about half an hour in Peach's case. She had to jump in the shower and get to work.

"Well?" Lonnie said now, breaking Peach's reverie about Buster's early-morning rampage.

"It's great," Peach said, realizing that Buster was just scared. It was sweet . . . a little sad. "How's Dominick?"

"Fine," Lonnie said without total conviction.

"Anything wrong?"

"Nope."

"Well . . . how's the feminist opus?"

"Treatise," Lonnie amended, "which is one page long."

"Right."

"Okay, I guess . . . if you're into abject failure and professional ruin."

"Sure, who isn't?"

"Seriously—I'm dead meat."

Peach grinned and rolled her eyes, because only her sister would say "dead meat," and then she told her, "I know you'll get through it."

"Thanks. Luckily Dan is meeting with me later to go over what I have so far."

Peach opened her top desk drawer and rooted around for a Blow Pop. "Professor Dan is coming between you and Dominick," she stated simply, pulling out a cherry one and tugging on the wrapper with her teeth.

"No, no. It's not Dan; it's just that I'm so swamped with work, and these deadlines are killing me. I have to put on a mock oral defense next week, and I'm so not even ready."

"What are you defending? Correct me if I'm wrong, but doesn't something have to exist before you can defend it?"

"Semantics," Lonnie said sarcastically, then threw in, "and for your information, yesterday I wrote a page."

"Yeah, you told me," Peach remarked with lackluster enthusiasm. She turned her attention to her computer, which had been sitting untouched for the past half hour, because Peach had been downstairs in the assembly room, trying something with lace doilies and confetti that didn't really pan out. "Oh, shoot," she said, as she typed in her user name and password. The computers automatically locked when they were left unattended; it was a security setting from the old network administrator. But Peach changed her password all the time, just like she changed her screen saver and screen background, out of boredom, a desire to keep things interesting—relatively speaking, of course—and now her mind was drawing a blank. She typed in a few possibilities, but none of them were working. The screen kept saying, *Password denied.*

"What's wrong?" Lonnie said.

"Oh . . . nothing. Look, I've got to go here. I locked myself out of my computer," Peach explained. "It locks if you leave it idle for more than thirty minutes."

"Busy at work, I see," Lonnie said dryly.

"Oh, whatever, shut up," Peach said, giggling, and typed in *daffodil.* Denied. *Pinklily.* Denied. *Cherryblossom.* Nope—so much for flowers. "I'll call you later."

After she hung up, Peach racked her brain for a few more seconds, then realized this was silly. She would just go to the network administrator for help. After all . . . maybe Quin was lonely over in his faraway corner cube all by himself. She picked up her phone and looked at the extension list hanging tacked up to her partition wall. His number was 3335, only one number off from hers, which was 3334.

"Adam Quinlan," he said, answering on the second ring. His voice poured through the line like honey; there was something so natural, so unconscious of its sensual quality. *Whoa . . .* That had just hit her out of nowhere. A shiver prickled at the back of her neck, and her lower body fluttered at the sound.

"Hi, Quin," she said, "it's Peach—you know, from around the corner?"

He chuckled briefly. "Hello."

"Hey, we're practically twins," she said.

"What do you mean?" She explained about their matching phone extensions. "Oh, I see," he said lightly. "So can I help you with something?"

"Yes—we've got a situation here." She told him what it was.

"Oh, no," he said warmly. "Okay, I'll be over in a second."

While she waited for him, she crossed her legs and tapped her foot against the inside of her desk. Absently she licked her lollipop, but managed to stop herself just in time before she attacked the encrusted gum nucleus like a savage. Somehow the thought of pink lollipop shards stuck in her teeth while she talked to Quin didn't seem too appealing.

"Hey," he said, appearing at the entrance to her cube.

"Hi!" she said brightly, and hopped up from her chair. "Thanks for helping me."

"Well, it's my job," he said with a grin as Peach walked a few steps closer to him. He glanced down at the mutilated lollipop still in her hand, and Peach's gaze followed his.

"Oh, I forgot," she said, smiling, and promptly chucked it into the wastebasket.

As he stepped farther into Peach's cube, Adam was struck by the red and green lights strung all around, glowing above them, and the glimmering green garland slung over her filing cabinet. Then he noticed all the clutter on her desk—folders, pens, a slew of picture frames, a Santa bear in the corner, and a little heart-shaped stress ball with legs. *Okay.*

Then, idly, he wondered: Had the bear been a gift from her boyfriend?

"Excuse the kitsch," Peach said.

Adam walked closer, toward her computer, and Peach followed behind him. There was something about being so close to her, in such a small, intimate space—*her* space. It smelled alluringly of her, that sweet, light citrusy scent he'd already come to associate with Peach.

"Sit down," she commanded, pulling out her chair. With a backward glance, he quirked his mouth at her bossiness, then took a seat. She stood behind him, leaning over him; damn, she was definitely too close to him if he could pick up a hint of lollipop on her breath, which was barely brushing across his neck in warm little puffs.

"Okay," she said softly, "this is the problem," and she reached over to grab the mouse. Adam swallowed hard, unable to deny the stirring of desire at the sultry sound of her voice this close to his ear, and the magnetic heat of her body so close to his. She jiggled the mouse, which cleared the screen saver, and brought up the box that was up, asking for her user name and password. "See? I'm lost; I'm drawing a complete blank here," she said, and let go of her mouse . . . but still didn't move away. Instead she let her palm rest on the edge of her desk, so she was still half enveloping him.

Speaking of drawing a blank . . . Adam swallowed again, took in a shallow breath, and told himself to concentrate. He really had to stop getting so aroused around Peach, who was obviously one of those gorgeous, confident girls who could have any guy she wanted. Hell, it was only his second day and he could already see that Scott had a thing for her, too. It wasn't like she'd be interested in Adam, anyway—not that he was looking to get involved with anyone right now. In fact, he was decidedly looking to be *un*involved, and to uncomplicate his life.

"I've tried a few different passwords, but I'm still locked out," she said, turning her head to make eye contact, which drew their mouths only inches apart. *Finally* she seemed to realize the proximity of her position, pulled back, and moved to lean against her desk, beside her monitor. Facing him, she crossed her arms; the movement was so casual, so unintentionally sexy, as it lifted her breasts up and together, but still Adam had to face her monitor. Being almost eye level with Peach's breasts right now was only making them more enticingly blatant to him, only making him itch to touch her. . . .

"Quin?"

Right. That's me. Snap back into focus. Jesus, you'd think he hadn't had sex in ten years. More like two months, although . . . it felt like a lot longer than that since he and Robin had actually made love—since they'd really connected on a significant level. The memories seemed more distant all the time.

"Okay," he said, clearing his throat now, and focusing on the issue at hand—which was a two-second no-brainer anyway. "So we'll just reset your password; that's easy."

"Oh . . ." Peach said, sounding troubled . . . or disappointed? "Well, I was kind of hoping I could keep my old one."

Adam squinted, baffled by that one. "But if you can't remember it—"

"Maybe you could help me try to remember it," she suggested. "You know, before I just give up on it."

Give up on it? Never in his life had he heard someone put their PC password in such a context. She was proving stranger by the minute. "Let's just reset it," he said, and reached for her mouse, but her warm palm cupped his wrist before he got a chance. A zing shot up his arm, and down much lower.

"Wait, just a few guesses before I give up, okay? I'd hate to think that I'm really such a dizzybat that my password has blitzed right out of my mind for all eternity. Surely you can understand that."

"Not really."

Ignoring that, Peach pressed a slim hand to her forehead, squinting her eyes as though deep in thought. Finally, she spoke. "Try 'carrot cake.' That sounds familiar."

Adam slanted her a sideways look, because it was a strange password, but then, he supposed it was better than "cat," which, believe it or not, was all too common. What he didn't get was why she needed him there to do this. Unless . . . was she just trying to chat again?

"Nope," he said after he typed in "carrot cake" without the space, but it got denied.

"Hmm . . ." Peach said, squinting again, rapping her fingers on the desk. "How about 'lemon pie'?"

He punched it in. "No. That's not it, either," he said, grinning in spite of what a waste of his time this was. Hell, what kinds of passwords were these? Between the Blow Pops and this, this girl had to have the biggest sweet tooth he'd ever seen.

"What about 'cherry pie'? Or maybe 'lemon coconut cake'—no, too long. Or maybe 'peach cobbler'? No, no—that would be too much, even for me," she said.

"Peach puns are beneath you, huh?" he asked.

"Totally—oh, I know, try 'magic elbows.' "

That threw him. But he wasn't even going to ask; he just typed. "No . . . wait, you said 'elbows,' right? Not 'elmos'? Just making sure I typed it correctly."

"Elmos?" Peach echoed, squinting as though he were crazy. "What does that even *mean*?"

"You're right, sorry," Adam said dryly—as if her suggestion had a very clear meaning. Jesus, Peach was so pretty . . . but so damn *odd*. And he really didn't know why he was going along with any of this, except that she was sort of fun to be around. "Okay, well, like I said, I'll just reset your password."

"Thanks, Quin. Hey, we tried," Peach said with a shrug, then added, "You're a doll." He swallowed, feeling heat rise to his face at the compliment. Meanwhile Peach reached over to grab the black scarf that was draped over her partition wall. The movement brought her breasts back to his eye level; he swallowed again. As she straightened and coiled the scarf around her neck, she said, "Whew, well, I'm drained. I think I'm gonna go get something to eat."

Adam looked at this watch. Only ten fifteen—too early for lunch.

As though reading his mind, Peach said, "Breakfast. I'm going to Mackie's, down the street. Ever been there?"

"No. I'm really not too familiar with the city yet," he explained. "I just moved here a month ago, so . . ."

"Wanna come with me?" Peach asked, sounding hopeful. (*Could that be right?* he wondered.) "Come on; it won't take long."

"No, no, I can't," Adam said.

"Are you sure? They have the best Danishes there—sticky and messy." She said that as if it would be the deal maker.

"You're way into this sweets thing, huh?"

"Sugar and spice, that's me," Peach said glibly. "Come on; it'll be a nice break from being shackled to our desks."

Honestly, he was tempted.

"I wish I could, but I really have too much work," he said, then rose from her desk chair and stood up, which brought his body up next to hers—barely a foot away. He looked down at her, then cleared his throat, suddenly feeling self-conscious about the scant space between them—and stepped back to let her pass. "After you," he said, and Peach smiled at him, but didn't move at first. She stayed close to him, looking at him, for only a few seconds, but they were heated seconds. Adam's breath hitched in his throat, and he found himself focusing on her ripe, flushed lips.

He pictured leaning down and kissing her right then and there . . . not a gentle kiss, but a possessive one, a deep, wet, fiercely carnal one that would end with both of them on top of the desk, and Peach's skirt pushed up—

"Well . . . see you later," she said, finally breaking the moment, combing some errant strands of her bronze-colored hair behind her ears and smiling quickly at him as she ducked by. Inadvertently, his eyes dropped down to her butt as she headed out past him—he couldn't help himself. He swallowed hard, watching her sexy, graceful body move.

For the first time, he thought he'd felt a rise of sexual tension between them—a mutual crackle—a spark coming from her, too. No, he told himself, he must have imagined it.

Chapter Eight

Mackie's Diner was one of Peach's favorite spots. It wasn't trendy. It had never heard of "low-carb," and it didn't scream "self-consciously fifties!" Instead, it was a pink-and-chrome anachronism nestled among the tall buildings and busy shops on Federal Street. In the springtime it was half-shielded from view by drooping branches bursting with bright green leaves and frilly white blossoms. Now, in early December, the tree's limbs looked like fine-boned skeletons, slim and bare, threading together and reaching up toward the light blue sky.

The interior looked like something out of *Back to the Future* (well, what other frame of reference did Peach have?); when you entered, you either veered to your left to grab a booth, or you went straight to the tail end of the Formica counter for the express bakery line.

Now Peach pushed open the door and heard the jingling bell above her. "Holly Jolly Christmas" was playing on the jukebox in the far left corner of the restaurant, and the whole place was gleaming with silver tinsel and shiny green ornament balls. Despite the seasonal festivity, the express line was business as usual: a bustling crowd, pushing and shoving, clearly wanting their pastries, and wanting them *now*.

Just as Peach wedged in at the very end of the line, the chime above the door sounded again. Peach glanced back and saw Joan, one of the regular waitresses who often worked the express counter when Peach was there. When their eyes met briefly, Peach gave her a little wave; Joan, in her typical no-nonsense manner, nodded once, and slipped off her gloves. They caught Peach's attention because they were bright red and crocheted, with long tassels with balls on the end of them. Joan slid them into the pocket of her coat, which was one of those dated black-and-white tweed deals with crinkled shoulders shaped like muffin tops. (Peach hadn't understood that style back when she was ten, and she was equally mystified today.)

She watched as Joan hung up her coat by the door, preparing to start her shift.

Probably around forty, she was skinny with a long, drawn face. Her frizzy hair was always pulled up, and lines of age framed her mouth like half-moons. She usually wore ankle-length dresses with high-top Reebok sneakers (which, admittedly, complimented the eighties tweed coat). "Hey, how ya doin'?" Joan said, pausing at the end of the line to make small talk with Peach before heading up front.

Today she was wearing an oatmeal-colored cardigan, which hung loosely over her tan-and-white-checked dress. Inconspicuously, Peach shot a glance downward, and saw thick wool socks snuggling Joan's ankles.

"I'm good, how are you?" Peach said, smiling.

Joan was always pleasant to Peach, who was a certified regular there, though she tended to be curt with many of the customers. But Peach had the feeling that other customers didn't really "get" Joan. Her gruff exterior was undoubtedly just a way to protect herself emotionally—it was a classic case. In fact, Peach would bet that Joan was a big marshmallow inside, only craving some level of acceptance like everyone else.

Suddenly Peach had an idea. It hit her like a thunderbolt, yet was so damn obvious. *Of course!* Why hadn't she seen it sooner?

Dennis Emberson—the hapless office accountant, the unhappy divorcé, the nice guy who could occasionally stand a good hosedown. Peach might have just found the perfect woman for him!

As with Dennis, Peach sensed a vulnerability in Joan. But she also had a toughness and a kind of leadership quality that would complement Dennis so well.

Now Peach's mind came alive at a frenzied pace; she always got like this when she had a new (fabulous) idea. A burst of energy in her chest, anticipation, a need to make it—whatever *it* was—happen as soon as possible.

She absolutely *hated* waiting—had she mentioned that?

Now she just had to figure out how to proceed here—i.e., how to broach the subject of a blind date, and how to make it actually sound appealing, all while Joan was on the way to the counter to start her shift.

Better move fast . . .

Since she didn't really know Joan, it was hard to figure out how to break the ice. All Peach knew was her first name, which was printed on her plastic name tag, and what her people instincts had assessed so far: that this was a warmhearted woman underneath the emotional armor (just as Dennis was a decent, loving man underneath a befuddled, jelly-coated veneer).

Of course, Peach needed to find out if Joan was single. She didn't wear a wedding ring, but she still might be involved. So back to the initial question: How to proceed?

Well, first things first: Don't let her leave. "Wait, um . . ." Peach floundered. "I know you have to start your shift, but . . . Hey, that's a pretty sweater," she said quickly, motioning to the bland-looking cardigan sagging down from Joan's narrow shoulders.

With a short, startled laugh, Joan looked down. "Really?" she said, surprised. Then she shrugged. "Thanks, I've had it for years."

Hmm, not exactly breaking news. Nodding, Peach fished some more. "Umm . . . was it a gift from someone special?"

"Uh, yeah," Joan said dryly, "a guy named Marshall—he lives down the street."

It took a moment for Peach to realize that she meant Marshall's, the store. Smiling, Peach said, "Oh, I see."

Suddenly she was body-checked by the hefty woman behind

her in line. Her shoulder was pitched forward, which knocked Peach smack into two other ladies. "I'm so sorry," Peach managed halfheartedly, because right now she was way more preoccupied with Joan, and the possibility that Peach might lose her in the shuffle.

Instead, Joan tapped her arm and motioned for Peach to follow her to the counter. "C'mon," she said, "I'll sneak you up to the front." Ordinarily Peach would've felt a little guilty because of all the other people who'd been waiting ahead of her, but these were obviously special circumstances. If she lost Joan now, she'd have to wait for her next opportunity to talk to her. Waiting—enough said.

So Peach followed Joan past the throngs of people crunching together in line, and over to the far side of the Formica counter. "Jingle Bells" started playing on the jukebox, and somewhere in the background a platter crashed against the tile floor. "So what can I get ya today?" Joan said.

Peach scanned the counter. There were no lemon Danishes left, so she picked a raspberry one with powdered sugar on top. "And an oatmeal cookie," she added, because it sounded just tame enough to appeal to Quin.

"Here ya go." Joan rolled up two crinkly white pastry bags and handed them to Peach, who gave her three dollars in return.

"Keep the change," Peach said, trying to butter her up, then seized the moment before Joan could turn her attention to the next customer in line. "Wait!" she blurted. "I have a question for you. . . ."

When she got back to the office, Peach stopped at the rack of mail bins that were on the wall opposite of Robert's office. Grace wasn't there right now, but she'd kindly left some boiled eggs out on her desk, peeled and stinking up the joint. She had obviously stepped away from her lunch, which she almost always ate at her desk.

Peach tucked her treats under her arm and grabbed her mail from the bin marked *Just Peachy*. (That peach pun had been Brenda's doing—honestly.) She flipped through the stack as she walked to her cube. Mostly catalogs from suppliers, along with the usual deluge of ads. Included was the daily hot yellow flier advertising Monkeyville, the new comedy club on Arlington Street. For the past few weeks the whole office had been getting fliers plugging Monkeyville's grand opening and amateur night.

The last item in the stack wasn't for her. It was a plain white envelope addressed to "Richard West." *Richard?*

Once at her desk, Peach shrugged off her patchwork coat, slung it over the partition wall, and tossed her mail on top of a pile of multicolored folders. Then she sat down and leaned over to brush some still-clinging chunks of hardened snow off her high-heeled boots.

"Hey, there."

Startled, Peach turned and saw Scott standing at the entrance to her cubicle. "Hey, what's up?" she said, then stomped her boots on the floor to shake the last ice crystals off.

"Man, I love this new setup," he remarked, looking around the hallway. "It's like a maze—it's so easy to act busy." It would be that way until more staffers were hired to fill up most of the cubes. The expansion and transition would probably be complete within the next six months. For now, though, people were very spaced out among the empty cubicles and Asian accoutrements filling the office.

"Oh, I got a piece of junk mail that I guess is supposed to be for you?" Peach said, handing Scott the envelope addressed to Richard West.

After studying it briefly, he said, "Oh, right, it's this headhunter who won't stop bothering me."

"He can't even get your name right?" Peach said. "That's so typical."

"No, no . . . Richard *is* my name; I just go by Scott. Scott's actually my middle name."

"Really?" Peach said, surprised. "I never knew that."

"Yeah. I can't stand Richard."

"Oh, I see . . . too many opportunities for people to call you Dick?" she said kiddingly.

"Exactly," Scott said, giving that cute, flirty smile of his that came so naturally. When Scott turned to go, he nearly collided with someone else. "Oh, hey, man, what's up?" he said as he stepped past Adam and headed down the hallway. And just like that, Peach's pulse kicked up. *Quin . . .*

It was insane, he knew it, but for some reason the sight of Scott talking to Peach irritated him. His chest tightened and he'd almost turned and retreated, but how fucking cowardly, he reasoned, as he swallowed down a distasteful lump of . . . competition? Jealousy?

"Hey!" Peach said, immediately lighting up for him. Instantly Adam felt a rush of warmth spread throughout his chest, and his face broke into a smile.

"Hi," he said, "I um . . . oh, right, I just came to tell you your PC's all set. Just enter one-two-three-A-B-C, and then you can change the password to whatever you want. But you might want to write it down this time."

"Okay, great," Peach said, picking up one of the white bags sitting by her keyboard and rising to her feet. "Here, this is for you."

"For me?" Adam asked, surprised.

Before he unfolded the bag, Peach said, "Oatmeal cookie. Do you like those?"

"Yes, *definitely*," he said, smiling at her. "Thanks . . . that was nice." Unfortunately, he couldn't think of anything less banal to say at the moment, even though he honestly was touched.

"Please, it was nothing," she replied with a breezy wave of her hand. Just then he noticed the thick silver watch she wore on her right hand. It had to be heavy on her slim, delicate arm. Without thinking, he imagined running his open palm down Peach's bare arm, which he'd bet was smooth and supple.

His eyes met hers for a long moment. So she wasn't only pretty and odd, she was sweet, too. "Anyway . . . uh . . ." he said, scraping for conversation, "how was the Danish? Sticky and sloppy and everything you hoped for?"

"I don't know; it's right here," she said, motioning to the other bag. "It was so crowded in there, and— Oh, that reminds me!" Her pale blue eyes widened and then she paused as if she were about to say something but didn't know if she should. Then she bit her lower lip—it was full and vivid, a flushed pink color, he couldn't help but notice—and she tilted her head at him. "How do you feel about setups?" His face fell. Stunned, all his defenses went on alert until Peach said, "Oh, no, no! I don't mean for *you*."

"Oh," he said, relaxing his shoulders and unclenching his jaw.

"Okay, you can't say anything—I mean, not that you would, or even that you'd *care*, but—"

"I won't say anything," he said simply.

"Well . . . you know Dennis?"

"Yeah," he said with a nod, "the accountant, right? Robert introduced me to him yesterday."

"See, he's such a great guy, I was thinking of trying to set him up on a blind date." She hopped up on her desk, which Adam was beginning to recognize as her favorite place to perch herself instead of her chair. Then she told him about some waitress at Mackie's Diner, how she seemed like the perfect match for Dennis, how Dennis needed love, whether he knew it or not. When she was finished, Adam was still processing all of it, and Peach said again, "But don't tell anyone yet. I don't want to put Dennis on the spot or to jinx anything."

"Oh, I won't," Adam assured her, not really sure why she'd felt comfortable enough to tell *him*.

"What?" Peach asked after a pause.

"What, what?" he said.

"You look . . . troubled," she said, tilting her head as though studying him.

"No. I'm not."

"Come on, Quin, tell me, what are you thinking?"

"No, really . . . it's just . . ." Should he say anything? Why get involved? What did he care what Peach did anyway? "Do you think it's a good idea to set up a coworker?" he asked.

"How do you mean?"

"I just mean . . . well, I guess I would feel awkward doing something like that. You know, just interfering in someone's personal life who I work with."

Again she looked profoundly confused by the concept, and Adam regretted sharing it. Hell, it was none of his business if she wanted to butt into Dennis's private life. It was only his second day on the job; for all he knew, this was a normal thing for her to do for Dennis.

"But if you thought two people might be good together, wouldn't you want them to meet and see what happens?"

Adam paused, then said, "I just wouldn't want someone to blame you if it didn't work out. I mean, what if it were the other way around and someone set *you* up— Oh." He stopped himself abruptly. "Not that you're . . . I mean, you probably have a boyfriend or something already, but I was just giving an example—"

"I don't have a boyfriend," she said. Adam swallowed, suddenly feeling awkward and inexplicably embarrassed. "I'm too much woman for most men," Peach added, presumably by way of explanation.

"I see," Adam said, half grinning. He had to admit she was not only good at putting him on edge, but also at ease. Grinning back at him, damn, she was cute. Her face was natural with a pink glow on the cheeks, and her lips were so . . . *ripe.* A little wet. Succulent and full . . . Some blood rushed to his groin, inadvertently stimulating his cock. *Not this again . . .*

Peach's phone rang. *Thankfully.* With so much work to focus on, getting turned on whenever he was near her wasn't doing much for his job performance. "Well, I'll let you get that," he said, smiling, and turned to go. "Oh, and thanks . . . for this," he added, turning back and holding up his cookie.

"Sure . . . well, bye, Quin. See ya later."

On his way down the hall, he heard her answer her phone, and he couldn't help but smile at the warmly sultry yet bubbly sound of her voice. And vaguely he realized, in the back of his mind, that Peach had him smiling again.

Chapter Nine

Peach got home that evening to find BeBe embroiled in conflict with Buster. She was running through the apartment yelling, "Come back, come *back*!" while Buster raced past her, darting through her legs, nearly tripping her in the process, as she dragged a bra between her teeth.

"Oh, my God." Peach laughed. "This is too funny."

"No, it's not—that bra's actually expensive," BeBe said, spinning around, confused. "Where did she go? Hey!" she yelped when she spotted her, then called out, "Peach, catch her—catch her!"

Lurching down, Peach almost got her, but Buster sideswiped her and zipped by in a white blaze of glory, sprinting into BeBe's room with a lacy black bra flying behind her. "How did she get your bra?" Peach asked with a giggle.

"I don't know; I guess I dropped it when I was folding my laundry," BeBe replied, sounding a little out of breath. Then she flopped down on the sofa. "Oh, I give up; let her eat it. So what's new?"

"Not much," Peach said, still distracted by Buster, who was ominously out of sight at the moment. "Are you sure about the bra?"

BeBe waved her hand through the air. "Don't worry; there's no underwire in it. Buster ate it already—just kidding. So how was your day?"

Peach filled her in on finding a potential love match for Dennis, who unfortunately had left for the day by the time she returned from Mackie's, so she'd have to tell him about Joan tomorrow. BeBe nodded, but stayed noncommittal on the subject. "And how's your new friend?" she asked, putting her size-five feet up on the coffee table, revealing light blue socks with skiing penguins.

"Good," Peach said simply. "He's nice—I like him." She didn't get into the specifics of how fundamentally *sweet* and decent Quin seemed . . . nor did she mention the spark of sexual attraction she'd felt for him earlier today when she'd overheard his smooth, rich voice over the telephone, or when he'd been next to her in her cube.

"So . . . John e-mailed me today," BeBe said.

"Really?" Peach said, not the least bit surprised. "What did he say?" she asked as she tossed off her black patchwork coat, and sank into the armchair across from BeBe.

" 'I love you more than life; just thought you should know.' "

Peach rolled her eyes. "God, he's so dramatic."

"I know."

"So did you write back?"

"No. There's nothing to say anymore."

Hallelujah—at least for the moment.

"By the way, were there any messages?" Peach asked, feeling too lazy to check the machine.

"One from your mom—"

"Shoot! I forgot to return the vacuum again!" Peach said, hitting her palm to her forehead, feeling the icy chill of her silver rings against her skin. They were still cold from the biting night air.

"And one for me—from Ken."

"Hey, the doctor from last night?" she said, eyes wide.

"I don't know why he's even calling me. Our date was a dud."

"He *likes* you."

"Whatever," BeBe said.

Buster came racing back down the hallway, this time with a red sock in her mouth. When she hit the living room she picked up speed. A *lot* of speed. In fact, Peach had never seen anything like it! With a low, constant growl that sounded like a revved motor, Buster started doing laps around the coffee table. She ran faster with each one, and even started tipping to the side a little, she was going so fast. She looked like a windup toy that was totally out of control, and BeBe and Peach stopped talking for several moments just to watch her go.

"Holy shit, what's wrong with her?" Peach asked, concerned.

"I don't know," BeBe said, clearly stunned as Buster kept sprinting around the room looking like a cross between a motorcycle and a manic bunny. (Yet she was still so cute!) "Hold on; let me check something. I bought this today." She reached for a book on the end table called *The Bichon Frise Mystique*. BeBe started flipping pages, and by the time she found something relevant, Buster had abruptly stopped her run and flopped down in the corner, panting, winded, and still totally mystifying. "Okay, that was called a 'bichon buzz'— it's when they run around like maniacs and nobody knows why."

"You mean that was normal?" Peach said, because what did she really know about dogs anyway?

"Yes," BeBe said, skimming her book. "They say just wait it out; it usually only lasts a couple minutes. Oh, do you want me to take the leftover raffle tickets down to the outreach center?"

"No, it's okay; I have to go there this week anyway. I'm gonna help organize the singles' charity dance next month—which you're going to, by the way."

An incredulous laugh burst from BeBe's mouth, but Peach remained firm. "I'll find a way to get you there. Just you wait."

"God, you're pushy."

"Thank you," Peach said glibly, as Buster picked herself up from the floor and walked toward them. The panting had subsided, though she still had a big, open smile on her face. Trotting casually, she stopped right by the sofa, and quite unceremoniously peed on the floor.

When Peach got to work the following day, she found two Blow Pops on her desk, grape and strawberry, right beside her monitor. *Who . . . ?*

Then she saw the yellow Post It note that simply read: *A.*

Quin. She smiled to herself, thinking it was sweet and oddly touching that he'd noticed her Blow Pop habit. Immediately she went to thank him, winding through the office and its maze of empty cubicles, passing two bonsai trees on her way, and several rectangular floor lamps that looked like tall black buildings with all the windows lit up. As she turned a corner, she abruptly intersected with Scott. "Oh! You startled me," she said, pressing a hand to her heart.

"Sorry about that," he replied affably. "Hey, have you seen Dennis? I wanted to talk to him about something."

"No, but I just got here," Peach said, noting that *she* wanted to talk to Dennis, too—about his love life, an undoubtedly more pressing matter than whatever Scott was bringing to the table. As soon as Scott passed, Peach caught a glimpse of Rachel Latham about ten feet ahead, entering her cubicle with a paper cup in one hand. That reminded her—Dennis had said something yesterday about needing to talk to Rachel, though he hadn't said why. Jeez, Scott was looking for Dennis, while Dennis was looking for Rachel; you'd think they worked in a huge corporation rather than an eight-person company. Then again, the labyrinthine new office was so damn big, it was easy to lose yourself in the freedom of it, and to hole up in your own space for big portions of the day.

"Hi, Rachel," Peach said when she got closer.

"Oh, hi, Peach!" she said excitedly, plopping down in her desk chair. "Love your outfit!" Pausing, Peach looked down; it was a stretchy black blouse and a tea-length shimmery blue skirt that flared at the hem.

"Thanks," she said, then like a shot, "By the way, did you ever talk to Dennis? I think he was looking for you yesterday."

"Um . . . uh . . . no, I haven't," Rachel said, brows knitting as though she were troubled by something. "Um . . . I'll stop by his desk later," she added, and then tacked on a smile.

Okay, that was weird. But hey, whatever.

As Peach neared Adam's cube, her stomach tightened at the sound of his voice. It was low and smooth, like he was speaking to someone on the phone.

As she ducked her head in, she heard him say, "Look, nobody's blaming you, okay?"

Sounded like a personal conversation; she'd better come back later. With thanking Adam for the candy on hold, Peach veered around toward Dennis's desk for her next mission.

"Hey, Dennis—got a minute?"

Dennis turned around at the sound of Peach's voice, and in doing so accidentally spilled some of the coffee in his mug onto his lap. "Oh . . . whoops . . ." he said, lifting his hands up in a gesture of defeat, as he watched the dark brown liquid seep into the fabric of his pants.

"Oh, gosh!" Peach exclaimed. "Is it still hot?"

"No, no . . ." he said, looking around for something to dry himself with, and ineffectually at that, since there was a tissue box right next to his printer.

"Here you go," Peach said, handing him a few tissues and hearing her voice accidentally slip into that concerned-guidance-counselor tone. "By the way, Scott was just looking for you," she remarked.

"Oh . . . gee . . . yeah, I was supposed to talk to him yesterday afternoon, but I didn't get the time," he said. Heaving a sigh, he pushed some wisps of thin hair back with the palm of his hand. "I think he's kind of upset about some stock I recommended to him. I was following a tip from my cousin in New York, but it's not doing so well." Slowly, he kept dabbing with the already saturated tissues on his wet lap. "By the way, have you seen Rachel around? I never got to see her yesterday, and I really need to talk to her about something."

Suddenly Peach recalled that Dennis hadn't come to Brenda's cake party yesterday, which she supposed would've been a good opportunity to talk to Rachel. She asked him why he'd missed it, and he shrugged and said he'd had too many expense reports to go through. Apparently, with the impending expansion of the company, there were a lot of accounting issues for Dennis to tend to, not that Peach had any clue when it came to the fine-tuned minutae of good business sense.

"If you need to talk to Rachel, why don't you just give her a buzz and tell her to stop by your desk?"

"I tried that," he said, more to himself, "I left her a message to call me or come talk to me, but she never did. And I've been so swamped here."

That was weird. Why would Rachel avoid Dennis?

But Peach had bigger fish to fry right now, like love, which brought her to her point. "Dennis, there's something I want to run by you, and you have to keep an open mind," Peach began, and went on to tell him all about Joan—how she seemed like the perfect woman for him and how she'd agreed to let Peach pass along her number. When Peach finished hyping up Joan, she realized she'd succeeded only in building her own excitement. Dennis, on the other hand, squinched his face in pained perplexity.

"I don't know, Peach," he said, scratching his head and letting the flat of his hand rest there. "I don't know if I feel comfortable. It probably won't end up working out anyway, and . . . well, I guess I'm just leery of that sort of thing." Leery and weary—was it just her or did Dennis desperately need a new shtick?

"Come *on*, Dennis," Peach said with a touch of frustration, "it's only one date. For Pete's sake, take a bite out of life!" Then she softened her tone, giving him an encouraging smile, which was somewhere between plastic-cheerleader and concerned-guidance-counselor again. "*Trust* me," she coaxed. "What have you got to lose?"

If only she'd known then the twisted answer to the question.

Adam had just hung up with his dad when his phone rang again. "Adam Quinlan."

"Hi, it's me," Robin said, her voice crackling through a staticky connection.

"Hey," he replied. "What's up?" She answered, but the words didn't make it to the other line. "What was that? Robin, I can't hear a word you're saying."

"Forget it . . . not important . . . just . . . say hello . . . you busy?"

"Um . . . kind of, but nothing major," he said.

She paused—at least, he thought it was a pause; she might have just been cutting out again—and then he heard her say, "I'll let you go then." The good news was that the connection was clearer; the bad news was that now she was pissed. Man, it really didn't take much to bring out her defensiveness. She'd always been like that—always had to hang up first and say, "I love you" second, always had to protect herself from some phantom sense of rejection. It was odd how the things he had loved so much for the first half of their relationship—her low-key sense of humor, her serious side, her interest in computers—didn't seem all that important anymore. Right now he could just picture her with her face all pruned up and sulky.

Christ, listen to him—he was a fucking hypocrite. Sometimes he had to be the least expressive person in the world; he knew that. Probably too often he retreated into himself, especially when he was upset (though he was reluctant to use the term "sulky," which didn't sound particularly manly).

"Well, is everything okay?" he asked now, feeling guilty that he'd told her he was busy.

"Everything's fine," she said in a clipped tone. "God, I just called to say hi."

"And I appreciate it," Adam offered lamely. "So let's talk."

"No, forget it. I've got stuff to do anyway." It was a blatant lie, and he knew she wanted him to know it. Wanted him to know that *she* was the one opting not to talk to him. Had to make sure that they were "even," Adam noted to himself, rolling his eyes and bracing himself for a pissy hang-up any second.

"Okay, well, I'll just talk to you later then," he said. That wasn't going to make her happy. He knew this game; he was supposed to try to implore her to stay on the line, and then she got to cut him off at the pass. Too bad he just didn't have the energy for it at the moment.

"Fine," Robin said curtly, and banged the phone down.

Adam just looked at his phone, then shook his head as he set it back on its cradle.

"Hey, you."

Abruptly he swiveled around in his chair and found Peach standing in the entrance to his cube. She was sucking on a Blow Pop. He assumed it was one that he'd picked up for her at CVS early that morning. She slid it out of her mouth, then licked her darkly stained lips. With a smile, she held up her lollipop, still wet from her tongue, and thanked him.

Chapter Ten

A few hours later Peach and Adam were having lunch in the kitchen, after making a pizza run through the snow. He'd wanted sausage pizza, but Peach was a vegetarian, so instead they were splitting her favorite: ricotta and carmelized onions. Now they had the box sitting in the center of their table, along with two icy cups of Coke dripping with condensation, and a bunch of brown paper napkins spread across the table, accordion-style. The rest of the airy black-and-white kitchen was empty.

"So what happened with your whole matchmaking scheme?" Adam asked casually as he reached for his cup. His hands were strong-looking, smooth but masculine.

"Oh, great news—Dennis is going through with it!" she replied, smiling.

"Really?" Adam said, raising an eyebrow, but then he realized, *Wait, why am I surprised? I barely know these people.* Shrugging, he said, "Well, I guess you were right then—he does want to be set up."

"Wellll . . . I wouldn't exactly say that he *wants* to be, but . . ." Adam quirked his mouth at that and waited. "Don't get me wrong; he agreed," Peach explained, sounding a bit defensive.

"Let me guess: He very *reluctantly* agreed."

"Still, he agreed."

"Of course he did," Adam remarked as he reached for another slice. "You're kind of hard to refuse."

"I am?" Peach asked, clearly surprised by the comment. "Like I have some kind of mystical powers of persuasion?" She sounded half-kidding, half-hopeful.

Grinning, Adam said, "More like mystical powers of relentlessness."

"Ohh," Peach said, nodding. "Well, yeah, sure, of course I have *that*." Adam chuckled, shaking his head. "Sometimes I see that people are afraid to go after what they need so I just try to, you know, give them a little push."

Shove was more like it, but of course he didn't say that.

"I'm just more cautious, I guess," Adam explained. "I mean, like this whole blind-date thing. Now you said this is some lady who works at the coffee shop down the street?"

"Right. Joan. The misunderstood waitress from Mackie's. Continue."

"Okay, Joan what?" Adam asked.

"Um . . . hey, you know, I'm not sure what her last name is."

"Where does she live?"

"Hmm . . . I'm not quite sure. Boston, I'm assuming."

Adam shook his head. "Exactly my point. What do you even know about this woman? She could be a homicidal maniac."

Peach scoffed. "C'mon, Quin, that sounds pretty far-fetched—especially for you. She's just a nice lady, around Dennis's age, but her face is missing that softness, that radiance, that blooming *something* that comes with being in love."

"Oh, Jesus," he muttered.

"What?" Peach said. "Too much?"

"I'm eating here," he said sarcastically, and she laughed.

"Seriously, though—I know what I'm talking about."

"What, are you some kind of expert on being in love?" Adam said. And the minute he did, he wished he hadn't. Christ, her love life was none of his business, and now it looked like he was flirting. Which he wasn't—*really*.

Peach paused, biting her lower lip as she studied him. Adam reached for his Coke again to busy his hand. "I just know people," she said finally.

Hell, he hoped not. Otherwise she'd sense his potent sexual attraction to her, the arousal stirring him whenever she was close. Clearing his throat, he continued, "So why is Joan single? I mean, is she divorced? Widowed?"

"Well, jeez, I didn't want to *pry* . . ." Peach said, rolling her eyes.

"Okay, fine. But what if she's single because she just got out of prison for murdering the last blind date she went on?"

"Quin, you are so paranoid!"

Then she lightly tapped his shoulder, not counting on the sensation that sparked from the contact. It was like an electric shock—she wondered if it was mutual—a heated sensation that startled her, seeped into her skin. It might sound crazy, but from the fleeting touch of his shoulder, the solid muscle and bone, the hard strength, heat swept up Peach's neck, flushing her face, but could any of it be the sunlight pouring through the windows? She didn't know what she'd expected Quin's body to feel like. She supposed she hadn't even thought of it, but now it was hard to think of anything else. Hard not to speculate about the rest of it. His shoulders and upper arms were powerful . . . what about his stomach? His back? His legs? Then she recalled his soccer championship mug. If he played soccer, his legs were probably killer . . . fiercely strong, devastatingly sexy. Peach bit her lip just thinking about it.

Just then Grace pushed open the door to the kitchen. Happily, it broke Peach's reverie about Adam's bod and snapped her back into focus. Carrying a crunched-up plastic bag, Grace approached their table. "Hi, mind if I join you?"

"No, of course not," Adam said, and stood to pull a chair out for her.

"Not eating at your desk today?" Peach said conversationally, as she shifted her chair over to give Grace more room.

"No, I have an hour to enjoy my lunch today, and I'm gonna take advantage of it. Normally Robert hangs around my desk asking me for a million things while I'm trying to eat." Systematically, she took out the contents of her lunch bag: a small Tupperware container with white stuff inside (mayo, Peach knew from past experience), a long baguette, and some grisly, reddish cold cuts with multicolored flecks in it.

"Where's Robert now?" Peach asked, making a conscious effort not to wince at both the smell and the aesthetics of Grace's lunch.

"Out to lunch with Easterbrook," Grace replied.

"Who's Easterbrook?" Adam asked.

"He's one of the consultants we use from time to time on different projects," she said. "And speaking of Easterbrook, I wonder if he still wears that bad toupee. It always made him look like he was wearing a big hairnet."

Peach ignored the comment, though inwardly she agreed. She'd met Nicholas Easterbrook only once or twice several months back, but yes, his full, Elvis-twirled black coif definitely made him the poster for shockingly ill-fitting faux hair. Again, you had to wonder what had ever attracted Brenda to him. "What's Robert hiring him for?" Peach asked. "Is it related to Ethan Eckers, or those spin-off dolls Robert has talked about doing?"

"I'm not sure. I know Robert's got several business lunches scheduled with him over the next week. In fact, he just bought Easterbrook a new laptop so he could work at home." She dipped her baguette into her Tupperware container, covering the tip with a generous slathering of mayonnaise. Poising to bite into it, she added in a whisper, "If you ask me, Robert's trying to keep the whole thing kinda hush-hush."

Tilting her head, Peach said, "Why would he do that?"

Grace looked from side to side even though the kitchen was empty; then she said, "I think some people might be losing their jobs."

Whoa . . . Peach hadn't seen that coming. She exchanged looks with Adam, who joked, "Well, if it's me, I should probably find another line of work." Considering it was his third day, he had a point.

Meanwhile, Grace snorted a laugh and said, "Yeah, and we know it can't be Peach; otherwise they can kiss the golden goose good-bye."

"Oh, please," Peach said, sloughing off the comment with a wave of her hand.

"What does that mean?" Adam asked, confused, looking at Peach for clarification.

"Ethan Eckers, my little brainchild," she said dryly.

"Wait . . ." Adam said, his jaw dropping for a moment. "Do you mean that *you* were the one who invented Ethan Eckers?"

"She made the whole doll herself," Grace interjected. "Then came up with the whole concept, all the different baskets, everything. Well, except the sweepstakes gimmick. That was either Brenda or Robert."

"It was no big deal, really," Peach said, not wanting to deprecate herself, but feeling a little embarrassed by the praise.

"Wow, that's incredible," Adam said, smiling at her. "I'm really impressed."

Swallowing deeply, Peach felt warm color drift to her cheeks. Was he a sweetie, or what?

"Don't say anything to anyone," Grace said now. "I don't want people freaking out about losing their jobs; it's just a hunch 'cause Robert keeps talking about 'streamlining'—you know, now that the company is growing there are big changes ahead. There's gonna be a lot of new staff, and there's no law you've got to keep the old ones, right?"

Interesting point . . . Peach couldn't deny there was a certain logic to it.

With her voice dipping to a low whisper again, Grace added, "And if you ask me, Nelson ought to be pretty worried. If anyone gets canned, believe me, he'll be the first to go."

"Really?" Peach said, though she supposed it wasn't much of a surprise, since Nelson was supposed to be the sales guy, the hunter, the one who made deals happen, the one who wheedled the company's way into corporate accounts, but it seemed none of Millennium's financial successes could be traced even in a roundabout way to any of his efforts.

"Sure," Grace continued. "I can tell Robert thinks he's a classic a-hole." (Was there any other kind? And on a side note, Peach noticed that Adam was fixing his attention on his pizza, not getting engaged in the conversation at all. It was obvious that catty chitchat like this made him uncomfortable. Were her instincts honed or what? What a sweetheart!)

"Anyway, it just burns me up how nobody around here does *anything* except for me," Grace groused—tactlessly, Peach might add, considering that was a direct insult to both her and Adam. But then how offended could Adam get on his third day, and how seriously could Peach take it when they'd just been lauding the sleeper success of Ethan Eckers? Still, would it kill Grace to learn even a modicum of tact?

"Like the other day, when Scott was in Dennis's cube talking for almost an hour—*an hour*, just talking away while I'm working like a dog." Peach never quite understood that expression, since dogs seemed to sleep and eat more than they worked, but then, look at Buster. She worked overtime to drive BeBe and her crazy, dragging as much clean underwear across the floor as she could find, and hey, that had to be somewhat tiring.

Suddenly Peach recalled what Dennis had said about recommending a stock investment to Scott, which now seemed to be tanking. Maybe that had been what they were talking about for so long at Dennis's desk the other day.

"And I still don't even understand what the hell's going on with Robert and *Claire*," Grace added, peeling back the plastic wrap on her cold cuts. "Claire called him the other day, and she sounded *pretty* frosty when he got on the line." Peach didn't bother asking Grace why she'd stayed on the line to assess said frostiness.

Several minutes later, Grace packed it in. After wiping her mouth with a coarse brown napkin, she burped her Tupperware container and stood to go. "Well, back to my desk. See ya later." As she ambled out of the kitchen, Peach checked her watch, disappointed to learn that Grace was right—lunch was over—and here she and Adam were not nearly finished talking.

On the way back to their desks, Peach tried to keep the convo going. "Quin . . . Tell me more about you."

Slanting her an almost wary glance, he said, "What do you want to know?"

"Rel*ax*," she said with a smile. "It's not like I'm gonna ask you your most embarrassing moment. . . ."

"Thank God."

"Yet," she finished. Adam just looked at her, bemused, or maybe at a loss, and she continued, "Right now I'm just interested in the basics. You know, family history, likes, dislikes, dreams, darkest fears—you know, small talk."

"Didn't we pretty much cover all that when we first met?" he asked, half grinning. "Remember that little interview you gave me at my desk?"

She had to think for a second. Then she scrunched her face, recalling their all-too-brief first conversation. "What, *that*? Please! We barely touched on anything remotely interesting."

"I'm flattered," he muttered dryly.

"So let's hear it."

"How about you start?" he said, then held his hands out—*wow, really great hands*—and insisted, "It's just better if you start. That way I can use your information as a prototype." Less than a second passed before he shut his eyes, shook his head, and said, "God, I can't believe I just said that."

"It's okay, Quin," Peach said with a giggle. "So you're a little dorky; it's nothing to be ashamed of."

"Thanks."

"I'm just teasing you; you're not really a dork, I swear." Shyly, he cleared his throat—again. "You're smart . . . and quiet. It's really charming." With a downward glance, faint color came to Adam's cheeks; then he looked back up. *Make that extremely charming.* "Hey, when's your birthday?" Peach asked, which seemed to take him by surprise.

"November fourth, why?"

"Scorpio," she said.

"Why, are you into astrology and all that?"

"No, not at all, just people and their different characteristics, personality traits, you know," she replied. "So . . . a Scorpio . . . *interesting*."

"Why?"

"No reason." Hey, she wasn't about to tell him that Scorpio men were not only a bit moody; they were notoriously sexy and mysterious. He'd just get all embarrassed again. "So your birthday was just last month then. How old?"

"Twenty-nine," he replied. "What about you?"

"Twenty-five," she said, "till August. I'm a Leo . . . you know, as in a lioness."

His mouth quirked up. "Go on," he said, "we're talking about you first, remember?"

"Okay, let's see. Here's some basic four-one-one. I have one sister, Lonnie. She's married, lives in Maine. My parents live in Brookline. I'm starting to think my mom's a little obsessive about her vacuum, but that's a whole other story. I'm into drawing, painting, and basically touching the lives of those who know me, and in my spare time I like long walks on the beach, candlelit dinners, and honesty." She figured she'd finish her spiel with a mock personal ad. Adam laughed. "Okay, your turn."

"Whoa, wait a minute," he said as they turned the corner, both on the way to her desk. "How is it my turn already? You forgot your dislikes, aspirations, and darkest fears."

With an impatient sigh, because she didn't feel like talking about herself, Peach said, "Fine. Dislikes . . . that's tough. I'd say I have more pet peeves than genuine dislikes, and too many of those to name."

"Just give me one," he said when they reached her cubicle. Both of them lingered at the entrance, several inches apart from each other.

"Just one . . ." Peach said. "Let me see . . ." She went to sit at her desk, but Adam stayed at the entrance as Peach crossed her legs and tapped her high heel against her bottom drawer. "Oh, I know. I hate it in talent shows when people lip synch. That's a real pet peeve of mine. I'm sorry, but lip synching is not a talent," she stated flatly.

Furrowing his eyebrows, Adam said, "You go to a lot of talent shows?"

"Well, no. I mean, you know, like back in high school or something."

"Yeah, but shouldn't a pet peeve be something that's happened at least once in the last five years?" he asked.

Mouth curved open, Peach blinked, surprised and amused—so he was sarcastic. "Well, I feel this one's timeless," she replied with reciprocal sarcasm.

"Oh, I see."

Peach could see the sparkle of Adam's eyes behind his glasses, and for the first time that day she noticed the faint hint of darkness along his jaw, where he'd shaved. It was by no means a Fred Flintstone look—in fact his shadow was subtle—yet Peach found herself focusing on it for another moment or two anyway.

"Now you're up," she said finally.

"Right. Which do you want first, likes or dislikes?"

"Surprise me."

He started with his likes (she knew he would; it seemed like the more orderly, rational way to go about it). Included among them were computers (obviously), soccer (knew that one already), and snowboarding (definitely hadn't seen that coming). Then he hit the dislikes—snakes, crowded buses, and double meanings (all to be analyzed at a later time). "I should get back to my desk now," he said then, and it was hard to argue, because from the time they'd left for pizza to now, almost two hours had gone by.

"Wait, wait," Peach protested, coming to her feet, coming closer to him. "We haven't even gotten to your darkest fears yet."

"Yeah, that's too bad. . . ." he said, edging his way out into the aisle. "Is there anything real quick you want to know? Before I go back to my desk?"

"Um . . . let me think. . . ." Peach said, tilting her head and scrutinizing him very carefully.

"Is it possible for you to think without squinting?" he said.

That stopped her short, and she laughed. "You know, for someone who's shy, you're kind of a smart-ass."

The next day was Thursday, and according to Dennis his blind date with Joan was set for that evening. Adam had summed it up best by saying, "Jesus, that was fast," and Peach had agreed, but she'd taken the optimistic view. Obviously Dennis and Joan had clicked on the phone.

Which, ahem, not to brag, but let's not forgot who's ultimately responsible for all this. . . .

Over lunch Peach continued to feed her intrigue over Adam. Why did he seem so fascinating to her? Maybe it was the all-too-brief answers to an endless barrage of questions that left a girl wanting more. Or maybe it was the way that he would smile at her sometimes—affably, warmly, like he was inviting her in, even if only for a few seconds.

Peach supposed she had a lot of friends, but how many were truly close to her? Besides Lonnie and BeBe, probably not too many. Basically she knew lots of people, but couldn't help feeling that very few knew *her*.

She'd talked him into Chinese food today, and by the time they got around to their fortune cookies, Peach had learned extremely briefly about Adam's parents' separation, and the fact that his older brother, Derek, was for all intents and purposes absent from the family. There was something in Adam's tone when he spoke about his family. He was more than just guarded about his privacy; she could tell there were unresolved issues there—things bothering him he didn't want to discuss.

Of course, it wasn't Peach's place to pry. But then, there was a fine line between prying and helping, and she'd just be careful not to cross it. "So who are you closer to, your mom or your dad?" she asked.

"I don't know. Both the same, I guess."

"Are you close to your sister?"

"Yeah, I guess." No elaboration.

"What does she do for a living?"

He shrugged. "Used to temp, had been waitressing for a while . . . I don't know—now she shops and whines, mostly. Oh, and leaves me messages about how unfair life is." Then he smirked and said, "No, I'm exaggerating. She's okay, just a little spoiled."

So far, all normal. In fact, the youngest was always spoiled, with Peach being the exception, of course. "And what does Derek do?" Peach asked, trying to sound casual. Really, she was very curious, especially since he sounded like the quintessential black sheep—the older son who'd always gotten into trouble, had never done well in school, and, in frustration and even envy for his younger brother, had rebelled, turned against the family, and eventually drifted away. Meanwhile, Adam had probably become the surrogate eldest, unconsciously identifying with his parents, viewing his sister as "a good kid," and feeling responsible for looking out for everyone else. How did Peach get all this? Classic case—more or less—of some dynamics she recalled learning about in her Family Psych class back in college.

"I don't know; it depends on the week," Adam said, referring to Derek's profession. "He kind of floats around. I really don't talk to him much, to tell you the truth."

"Well, will you see him over Christmas?" she asked.

Adam's jaw tightened a little, and he said, "Peach, I really don't know. I mean, what's the difference?"

"Nothing, just trying to get to know you better," she replied. "What do Sonny and Derek think about your parents' divorce?"

"I don't know. They're fine with it, I guess," he lied, feeling raked over the coals. Jesus, why did she always have to take her cute inquisitiveness too far? "Can we change the subject? My life is boring. My family is boring. I'd much rather talk about you."

"Okay, sorry if I'm being pushy. I mean, it's really none of my business."

"New concept," he said, grinning, but there was tension belying his smile.

Chapter Eleven

On Friday Adam got a big, showy box of Godiva chocolates delivered to him at work. From his *mother*. Not exactly the most masculine thing he'd ever heard of, but oh, well.

He called Aunt Emily's house to say thank-you.

"I'm so happy they got to you okay, and you like them?" Liz said hopefully.

"Yeah, Mom, but why did you send them? You didn't have to do that."

"Oh, I just wanted to send you and Sonny each a little something to show you how much I love you. I know you like caramel, so I got the special caramel ones for you."

"Thanks, Mom," he said, feeling a sharp stab of emotion in his chest, which he didn't want to concentrate on right now. "But this is hardly a little gift. How much did this cost you?"

"Please, you don't really expect me to tell you that, do you? Besides, it was no big deal, just a little something to tell you that no matter what I'll always be your mom, and I'll always be here for you, just remember that."

"Well, thanks again," he said simply. "I can't wait to eat them."

"You're what makes my whole world go around," she continued, with strained effervescence, and Adam held back a sigh.

"I know, Mom," he said, "you wrote that in the card."

"Oh, that's right. I guess I won't keep you from your work. The job's still going well?"

"Yep."

"Make sure you share the candy with other people at your office," she said, and just for a moment his mom's directive made him
feel about ten years old, which he supposed was kind of sweet, a little sad, and strangely comforting.

Once he got off the phone, he headed down the hallway, cutting a right and meandering over to the one person in the office he
truly *wanted* to share with—even though he'd already given her her
requisite two Blow Pops earlier that day. In fact, he and Peach were
in this nice sort of holding pattern: Adam would bring her lollipops
that he got at CVS on his way to work, and Peach would give him
some mystery treat. Each day it was something different, and he
never knew when it was coming. It would always be something she
picked up on impulse, something she'd seen and thought of him.
That was what she told him anyway.

Peach was his best friend at work by far. Of course, it was only
his fifth day, and she was definitely the most outgoing person in the
company.

Robert's assistant, Grace, was friendly as long as she could assail
you with backhanded remarks about other people in the office,
which was why Adam tried to avoid intersecting with her in the
hallway. Scott seemed like an okay guy . . . though Adam suspected
that he had a thing for Peach, too, which made them unspoken
rivals. Ridiculous, really, considering that Peach seemed oblivious
to either in that way. Which raised another point, one Adam had
thought about numerous times: How could she *not* have a boyfriend
already? He would never have guessed that a girl that beautiful and
confident would be single.

He rounded the bend and ducked his head into Peach's cubicle.
She was on the phone, with her back to him and her legs up and
crossed on her desk. Adam's mouth ran dry as he trailed the shape of
her legs, sleek and sexy, drifting up, disappearing under her short
black skirt. The pale yellow of her sweater contrasted with the
golden bronze of her hair, which was tumbling freely down her
back. He wanted to run his hands through it—then tighten his grip
and pull her toward him, kiss her, push her back, strip her stockings

off, feel the friction of their bodies rubbing against each other, turned on and sheened with sweat.

Inhaling sharply, he tried to reign in his lusty thoughts before he got a full-fledged hard-on right here and now.

"Right, I totally understand," she was saying. "Marty, I think these things take time."

That stopped him short. A shock of jealousy struck him. Who the hell was Marty? Wait, was that a guy or a girl?

"But obviously things weren't as ideal as you remember," Peach added, while Adam lingered shamelessly to listen in. "The very fact that you thought they *were* ideal is at the heart of this." Her voice was soft with compassion and concern. He should go; this conversation was obviously personal. "Right, mmm-hmm," she said, as Adam was edging out. "I'll tell Adam to call you." He froze. "Okay, take care. Call back anytime you want!" Peach finished brightly, then leaned forward to drop her phone back on the hook.

"Hey . . ." Adam said, confused.

Peach spun around in her chair, and smiled when she saw him. A rush of excitement filled his chest, made him smile right back, made him almost forget what he'd been thinking.

"Hey, that was your father on the phone," she said to him, still smiling, though Adam's face had decidedly dropped.

"Huh . . . ?" Adam said, mentally processing that apparently Marty wasn't a girl *or* a guy—it was Martin, his *dad*!

"Omigod, Quin, he's sooo nice!"

"Wait a minute; back up here." *Why is my father calling you? Why are you calling him Marty?*

"Oh, he dialed my line by accident," Peach explained, and hopped up from her desk. She smoothed out her skirt, and momentarily Adam was distracted by the way it wrapped around her hips and showcased her long, sleek legs. "You know, because our phone extensions are so similar. And then we got to talking. . . ."

Adam held back an eye roll; only Peach would "get to talking" with a wrong number.

"He feels like maybe he's really lost Liz for good," Peach added sympathetically. "Quin, I feel so bad for him; he's really sad about your mom. I was chatting with him about it, you know, trying to cheer him up."

"You talked about the *divorce?*" Adam said incredulously, as his face twisted with confusion. Come *on*, this was just too much—too weird. Who was this girl? Who felt comfortable giving advice to a total stranger about a personal situation that was none of her business? And what the hell was wrong with his father—who could always be counted on *not* to express himself—blabbing personal family issues to a faceless voice on the telephone?

Granted, ever since Liz had left, Martin had become increasingly dependent on venting his frustrations to Adam. But now he was unburdening himself on Adam's coworkers, too? Talk about fucked-up! The only person Adam's dad should be unburdening with was Adam's mom, instead of putting his son in an awkward position at work.

Obviously Peach wasn't of like mind. Here she was, as ballsy as could be, commenting on his parents' marriage, and damn it, Adam *really* wanted to be annoyed with her, but . . . she was so sweet it was hard.

"Hey, what's that?" Peach asked now, motioning to the long, thin gold box held flat beneath his arm.

"Oh, right," Adam said, glancing down, suddenly remembering the purpose of his visit. "Candy," he said, holding the box out toward her. "Want some?"

What a day! Peach couldn't be more pleased with her life at the moment. First a fabulous voice mail from Dennis, and now free Godiva. Plus she'd "met" Quin's dad, which indirectly made her feel closer to Quin, more connected to him, which she supposed she'd been angling for, for the past week.

When you talked with someone's family, a little more of the puzzle was completed, a little more dimension added to that supeficial coworker rapport. Quin's dad had introduced himself as Martin, so naturally she'd asked if he preferred Marty. At that, he'd paused and said, "Marty . . . you know, I like that. Marty."

His voice was distinctly different from Adam's; it had a raspy, gravelly quality, while Adam's voice was thick and mellifluous, smooth and richly sweet, like honey.

Now Peach grabbed a piece of chocolate from Quin's outstretched box, and told Quin to sit down. She had much to tell him—like how Dennis's voice mail that morning had left her feeling triumphant. Super Matchmaker Girl, the Problem Solver, Aphrodite for the New Millennium . . . well, she was still playing around with titles. She couldn't remember the last time Dennis had sounded so buoyant, so refreshingly *alive*.

According to his message, Dennis had had a wonderful time with Joan the night before; they'd gone to dinner and a movie, and they must've really clicked, because Dennis mentioned twice that Joan was a "fascinating lady." Not to brag, but if Peach recalled, she was one of the pioneers of this epiphany. How many people would've simply dismissed Joan as hard-edged, without realizing the intrinsic potential she had to be "fascinating"?

Fine, so she was bragging, but not out loud, so it really only half counted.

Dennis had also said that he was going to be a few hours late because of a dentist appointment, which he'd forgotten to tell anyone about. He asked Peach to let people know, if they were looking for him. It was so like Dennis; sharp with numbers and fuzzy with most everything else.

In fact, Peach still recalled the incident several months ago when Dennis had gone on vacation without telling anyone. The whole thing had taken the office by storm; no one could track Dennis down for over a week; they kept calling his house until finally he returned to work with a ripened-tomato sunburn and a peeling scalp. And that was when he'd realized he'd forgotten to mark down his vacation time on the staff calendar.

"Here, take some more," Quin said, sliding the box of chocolates closer to her, which snapped Peach back to the present.

"No, thanks, maybe later. Listen, I have to tell you about my latest coup—oh, but wait, did you want to call your dad back first?"

"No, I'll call him later."

"Are you sure? He could really use some support."

"Peach," Adam said with an edge to his voice. "I'll call him later." *Okay.* Obviously that wasn't up for discussion.

"Well, I guess it's really none of my business. . . ."

"And speaking of none of your business," Adam said, half grinning, "what about Dennis? Did you find out if you set him up with a homicidal maniac or what?"

"No, smartie, that's what I was going to tell you," Peach said, reaching over to grab her phone and punch in the code to her voice mail. "Does this sound like a man who's been shackled to a bedpost?" She played Dennis's message for Adam, who leaned over to listen, and Peach felt his warm breath on her knuckles as she held the phone to his ear.

Her breath quickened and she felt a brief fluttering between her legs. *Ohhh . . .* Was this becoming a full-fledged crush?

Suddenly they heard the jangling of coins. Someone was walking down the hall, and getting closer. "Dennis?" Peach said anxiously, rising out of her chair, moving past Adam to duck her head out into the aisle. It *was* Dennis! He had a lopsided smile—not to mention a brown stain on his shirt, underneath his open trench coat, which looked like it'd been stored for ten years in a wrinkle-compression chamber. Suffice it to say, he also had loose change in his pocket, which accounted for the jangling.

"Sooo?" Peach said, smiling. "Don't keep us in suspense!"

"Us?" Dennis asked, confused, his grayish brows furrowing, and then he glanced over and noticed Adam sitting in her cube. Peach glanced over, too, and noticed the expression on Adam's face—like he didn't want to pry or impose. *Sweet boy.*

"So talk," she told Dennis, pulling him into her roomy cubicle by his arm, feeling something sticky between her fingers; she was willing to bet it was jelly.

There was a sparkle in his world-weary eyes, and could that be the blush of burgeoning affection spreading over his expansive forehead?

Crossing his arms over his chest, he sighed happily. "What can I say? She's absolutely wonderful. I can't remember the last time I felt this good; I can't seem to get this big, dopey grin off my face."

"Well, don't let me keep you guys," Adam said, rising from his chair, looking a little uncomfortable. "I'll see you later—"

"No, Quin, stay," Peach said quickly, as she thought, *Nice try*. She was going to get Adam plugged in with other people, if only just to release him from his cocoon of loneliness, all the way in the far corner of the office. "C'mon, Quin, sit back down," she urged.

So he did, but he wasn't thrilled about it. Jesus, he didn't want to have some sappy conversation about Dennis's love life; he barely knew the guy! Not to mention he had *work* to do. He was beginning to wonder if Peach was remotely familiar with that concept.

Meanwhile Dennis prattled on about how refreshing he found Joan's outspoken manner and bawdy sense of humor. Something about how they both liked warm beer. And some other details Adam missed along the way. In any event, Peach squeaked with delight, clapping her hands together and said, "She sounds perfect, I'm so thrilled for you guys! Quin, isn't this fabulous?"

"Um, yeah . . . it's really nice," he said, shifting a bit in his seat.

"Wow, you're going out again on Saturday? But that's tomorrow!" Peach enthused. "Whoa—two dates, two days apart; this is huge!"

"Well . . . who knows? Maybe we'll end up spending the weekend together if Saturday night goes well," Dennis said, suddenly sounding bashful. (Adam wanted to say, "*Now* you're feeling bashful?")

"The weekend," Peach echoed, eyes wide, mouth curved open.

"Omigod, you guys are totally hot and heavy! Isn't that great, Quin?"

"Yes," Adam replied tightly, "real great."

"Dennis, you definitely have to keep us posted on everything," Peach said—but little did either of them know—Dennis would never get the chance.

Chapter Twelve

"I like him."

Peach practically exhaled the words as her chin sank into her hand and a dreamy little sigh slipped through her lips.

"I know," BeBe said simply.

"No," Peach said, "I mean I *really* like him."

"I *know*." Flashing her a quick smile, BeBe hit the tap to fill a mug of beer. Peach had come to McMurphy's to visit BeBe while she worked; now she had her elbow resting on the bar between her empty glass and a bunch of stray green-and-white napkins.

BeBe handed the beer to a man in his fifties who was waiting alongside the bar in a tan, weathered jacket and skintight blue jeans that were faded almost to white. *Apparently he dresses to the right,* Peach thought with distaste, as she noticed the blatant bulge in the right side of the man's pants. Fine, it wasn't his fault that Peach had looked, but it was honestly hard not to notice. What was *up* with men and tight jeans anyway? The crotches always strangled their balls and made a generally lumpy spectacle that was hard not to ogle.

Men . . . Such simple creatures, yet still baffling. It was amazing how much women were drawn to them in spite of the fact that women were vastly more complex. And honestly, she wasn't being a sexist about this; she was applying a purely psychological perspective. Women had both sides of the brain working together—multitasking, while reason and emotion finished each other's sentences and hummed right along. It was just basic fact that men had a lot less going on upstairs, and it was still about as much as they could handle.

Of course, there were a lot of exceptions. Some of her friends from college, her dad, her brother-in-law . . . and Adam, of course.

Once again, her thoughts were back on Quin. That was how she'd realized that she wasn't dealing with some flitting little crush here—that she didn't just like Quin; she *liked* him. Which didn't answer the question: How did BeBe know?

So she asked her friend just that. "Please, Peach, you talk about him all the time," BeBe said, then quickly amended, "Oh, not that I mind. It's sweet."

With a startled laugh, Peach asked, "How could I talk about him all the time? I've only known him for five days!"

"Exactly," BeBe said, grinning, and handed change back to the middle-aged man with the obscenely tight jeans, who Peach was frankly surprised could even walk. When he left to go watch the football game on the TV set in the far corner of McMurphy's, Peach thought again of Quin—how he played soccer when he was in college, how she'd never asked him his position, and how she honestly couldn't handle how unbelievably cute and sexy he was—and how had she not seen it the second she'd met him? Sure, they'd had a few moments that pushed the envelope of friendly to flirty, like when they'd touched briefly or exchanged lingering eye contact, but her consciousness hadn't fully absorbed it until just now. Suddenly she found herself totally infatuated! It was both bizarre and exhilarating how quickly that could happen, and how impossible it was to recall a time before she'd felt that way.

"Seriously," Peach said now, "do I really talk about Adam that much?"

"Well . . ." BeBe paused. "All the time."

Peach shook her head, her straw poised in her mouth; she couldn't believe she'd been such a bore without even a shred of self-awareness. Gee, it didn't *sound* like her.

"Case in point," BeBe said, "Last night I was eating pizza, and you said, 'Oh, you know who else likes pizza?' and I said, 'The rest of the free world?' and you said, 'Quin.' "

Peach had to laugh—okay, maybe that had been a desperate attempt to bring Quin up. But it had been totally unconscious. Obviously he'd been suffusing her thoughts, working his way from the back of her mind to the front.

"And sometimes you'll be like, 'Oh, you drink water? Hey, you know who else needs water to live? *Quin.*' "

"Oh, come on!" Peach said, giggling.

"Okay, fine, maybe I'm exaggerating," BeBe conceded with a smile. "Anyway, you're lucky; at least you like someone. Mindy's mixed me up with a total horn-dog—though she swears he's harmless."

"You're going out with someone new?" Peach asked.

BeBe shrugged. "Mindy's friend Tony. She gave him my number. Supposedly he's cute and really nice, but he called me earlier today and . . . I don't know."

"Why, what happened?"

"Look, maybe I'm reading into it, but he kept telling me I had a *very* sexy voice. I mean, he just kept emphasizing the word 'sexy'; he said it, like, four times."

"Well, *that* doesn't make him a pervert; it makes him a flirt."

"And when he first called he said something about dialing the wrong number before he got me. He was like, 'I guess I fingered wrong'—*fingered.*"

Peach looked confused—then totally disgusted. Rolling her eyes, she grimaced and said, "*Eww* . . . BeBe, please, you're paranoid! And gross!"

"Okay, fine, maybe. But he really dragged out the word 'fingered.' "

"Well, maybe he has a speech impediment."

"Uh-huh," BeBe mumbled, grinning in spite of her cynicism—or maybe because of it.

"Give it a chance," Peach said.

"Yes, master."

"You forgot 'lord and,' " Peach said glibly.

BeBe just smirked. Then she motioned to the empty glass beside Peach's elbow. "Another Little Princess?"

"No, I'm good for now. So when are you and this Tony guy going out?"

With another shrug, BeBe said, "I'm supposed to call him tomorrow."

Tomorrow was Saturday night. Dennis would be out with Joan for their second date. BeBe might be out with Tony. And Quin . . . he was new to the city. Peach wondered what he'd be doing, and if he'd be lonely.

Just then Mindy flitted behind the bar. Her shoulder-length platinum-blond hair shone nearly white when she stood directly beneath the hanging green-glass light fixture. As she filled two beer mugs, she smiled at Peach. "Hey, what's up?"

"Hey, Mindy, how's it going?"

"Good. Hey, I heard you talking about how you've got the hots for your friend." Mindy had heard that? She'd been halfway across the room! In her hazy state of infatuation, Peach must've been talking way too loudly; probably old Strangled Balls heard it, too. "So what are you gonna do about it—put the moves on?" Mindy asked, wiggling her brows suggestively, like putting the moves on was the only way to live. According to BeBe's accounts of Mindy's overstocked love life, it was.

"I don't know . . . I mean . . . no," Peach replied casually. Her mind was racing, though. Hmm . . . okay, even if she wanted to put the moves on Quin—okay, no "if"; she definitely did—she couldn't.

Could she?

No, no, they were friends. It would be tragically awkward if he didn't like her back in that way. She'd feel so embarrassed. Free spirit or not, jeez, she had her *pride*, after all. "No, he's my friend," she said casually. "I don't want to make it weird." If only it were possible to jump someone, find out if they liked it, and if not, rewind the entire incident, erase it.

Just then two men approached the bar. Mindy tilted her head

and flashed them her perfectly white, sexy-sweet smile, and said, "Hey, boys, what can I get you?"

Restlessly, Peach roved her gaze around the restaurant, then back to the bar, and suddenly she noticed BeBe across from her, talking to a strikingly handsome guy. With slightly rumpled dark hair and icy blue eyes that were piercing even from where Peach sat, he was distinctly, eye-catchingly sexy.

The only thing was . . . wait a minute . . . was that an earring in his left ear? Yes, it was. And it looked kind of glitzy, like a rhinestone or something. *Ewww . . . how lame.*

But then, Peach's opinion wasn't what mattered here. The important thing was, BeBe looked happy. Actually smiling and laughing while they talked, she seemed genuinely charmed and not the least bit cynical or unapproachable.

Suddenly she wrote something on a napkin and slid it over. *Holy shit!* Had she actually just given him her number? Unprecedented!

Five minutes later the guy waved good-bye, and BeBe immediately scampered back to Peach with her face bright red. "I can't believe I did that!" she yelped, and covered her flushed cheeks with her hands.

"Okay, breathe," Peach said slowly. "Tell me what happened."

"All right," she said, inhaling and exhaling, and pressing one hand to her chest. "His name is Luke Vermann. Isn't that such a sexy name, by the way?"

"Sure, yeah," Peach agreed. She supposed Luke was kind of sexy, though to the ear, Vermann left something to be desired.

BeBe went on to explain how Luke had struck up a conversation with her as she was pouring him a Guinness, how his band was playing next door at the Espresso Rocks, a trendy coffee shop known for its thick dessert menu and live music, and how Luke had asked her out for the following night.

"Wow, that's great!" Peach enthused. "Oh, but what about Mindy's friend Tony?"

BeBe's face dropped. "Oh, yeah, I forgot about him."

"What about Tony?" Mindy said, coming closer. Damn, that

girl had great hearing. "You guys are going out tomorrow night, right? He called me before and told me how psyched he is. He thought you were so cool after you guys talked."

"Really?" BeBe said, twisting her face up in disbelief.

Jeez, Peach thought, *could she get a little more confidence?*

"You totally have to tell me how it goes on Monday," Mindy added, then turned to help some customers—male, of course—at the opposite end of the bar.

"Shoot . . ." BeBe said, losing some of the enthusiasm she'd just had, and Peach couldn't bear for that to happen.

"No big deal," she said brightly. "So you'll make plans with Luke for another night. Or ask him to meet you for coffee on Sunday or something. The point is, you met a cute guy tonight and he asked you out in five minutes. Do you know how amazing that is?"

A smile spread across her face again. "He is really hot, huh? And I love his whole look; it's, like, rugged but with style." Which was definitely a step up from John, whose idea of "style" was wearing khakis with black sneakers on special occasions. "He just looks like a *man*, you know?" BeBe continued. "John never really looked like a man; he always looked more like a college guy."

Before Peach got a chance to respond, she saw BeBe's expression fall again. It was like the fizz on her soda had quickly dissipated and left her flat. John again. Peach knew it was scary to be out there, probably nerve-racking to contemplate a date with a drop-dead-handsome guy like Luke Vermann (QVC earring notwithstanding). Of course BeBe would be tempted to reach back—to imagine that a relationship with John could work, to cling to what was familiar and safe. Peach hated to say it, but it was a classic case.

Gently she asked, "BeBe, what's wrong?" even though she knew.

"Nothing . . . it's just . . . I don't know. It's just that talking about John makes me miss him." She held up her hands as if to implore Peach for some patience. "Okay, just hear me out." This was never good. "Ever since John and I have been talking again—I mean, just as friends—it's weird. I know we probably can't be together, but . . ." Now it was "probably" couldn't be together? Peach thought, swallowing the impulse to tell her friend that John was deadweight. "And he listens more these days; he asks about me for a change." Gee, and it only took two and a half years. "And remember he used to make comments sometimes about how my hair was too short, how he wished I would grow it longer?" Yes, all too well—meanwhile it was complete crap. BeBe was a voluptuous and perfect pixie, while John was a chimp without the smarts. (Suffice it to say, Peach swallowed down that comment, too.)

Leaning forward on the bar, BeBe continued, "Well, you know what he told me last night? He said that since we've been apart, he's realized how much he loves my hair. Isn't that funny?"

More like manipulative and transparent, Peach thought, struggling not to butt in.

"I don't know . . . it's like he's finally *accepted* me."

That did it. Clenching her fists, Peach blurted, "Maybe he bought a mirror."

"What?"

"Look, I'm sorry, BeBe, but you can do *so* much better than John. As in—how can I put this delicately?—*sooo* much better."

Jerking her head back, she asked defensively, "What are you saying? That John's ugly?"

"No . . ." Saying it would be rude. "I'm saying, give yourself a chance to meet a better guy. That's all." Was that so wrong? "You're off to a great start. You've already got two possible dates for this weekend."

Just then a cluster of customers approached the bar, and BeBe went to help them. Admittedly, Peach wasn't in the best position to give relationship advice, if advice was supposed to come from actual experience. But then again, her limited boyfriend history probably allowed her some objectivity. It meant she couldn't project her own relationship issues onto others, or obfuscate the truth to make her own reality more comfortable.

The longest relationship she'd had was almost two years ago, with a guy named Justin. It'd lasted only about five months, and it had started going downhill when he began saying "I love you," and Peach wasn't saying it back. No doubt it had been awkward, but hey, she didn't want to lie.

Back in college she'd had little interest in a steady boyfriend, but she'd developed crushes on several different guys she'd met over her four years in New York City. Most of them had been two-dimensional eye candy (she'd only admit this now that her mother and sister were nowhere in sight).

After college, it had been tough to meet guys who excited her—guys for whom she felt that elusive and ever inexplicable "spark."

But she felt it now; there was no denying it. What could she do about it, though? She had to be careful about a little thing called sexual harassment. More than their friendship was at stake—what if she made a move on Quin and he reported her for unseemly advances?

Well, that settled it then. If and when she *did* make advances, she'd be sure to make them seemly.

Chapter Thirteen

Throughout the weekend, Peach thought a lot about Quin—big surprise. She also scantily worked on her mural, and met with the other volunteers from the outreach center, who were helping with the charity singles' dance in January.

On Saturday night, BeBe went out with Mindy's friend Tony, who turned out to be a decent guy with a tragic flaw: the need to pepper his conversations with poorly timed sexual innuendo. What Peach had dismissed as BeBe's paranoia the other night had apparently been dead-on; Tony's horn-dog factor was raging out of control.

On Sunday BeBe had called Luke and left a message on his cell phone. She hadn't heard back yet. Irrationally, she blamed Tony for this. If it hadn't been for him, she could have been out with Luke on Saturday night, rather than stuck at dinner, listening to Tony make tawdry double meanings out of words like "fork" and "strip steak."

Only in BeBe's lamenting did a few more details about elusive Luke come out. For one, he was divorced. The words "damaged goods" came to mind, but of course Peach held her tongue. For two, he was thirty-four years old and still trying to be a rock star. Being a musician on the side was one thing, but drifting from one gig to the next as his sole source of survival . . . well, it didn't bode well for BeBe. Peach was already envisioning a life of weed, groupies, and amps in her living room. BeBe deserved better . . . and what was up with Luke's rhinestone earring? BeBe claimed it was a diamond, but how did that help his case?

Abruptly, Peach caught herself. *Listen to me. Am I getting too judgmental? Too self-righteous? Am I turning into my mother—already?*

If BeBe liked Luke, Peach had to be supportive. Besides, they hadn't even gone out yet; maybe something really special would develop once they did.

Hmm . . . Thinking of new potentials got Peach thinking of Quin. *Again.* Damn it. Why couldn't she stop fixating on him? Sure, she'd had crushes before, but she couldn't recall any nearly as consuming as this one. Adam popped into her mind all the time, which was silly, since they'd known each other such a short time, but she felt unbelievably comfortable with him. Each day she looked forward to seeing him—to hearing his warm, soft voice, watching that reserved expression blanket his face whenever he disagreed with Peach but was trying to hold back from saying so. Actually, he seemed to have that look a lot.

Hmm . . . if only he would talk about the things that bothered him; if only he would tell her more or open up to let her in, maybe she could help him. But he was so damn stubborn. Peach had to keep reminding herself: Even though Adam had a sweet nature, no matter what, he was still a Scorpio.

The weekend had also come and gone without Peach remembering to return her mother's vacuum. *Whoops!* By the way Margot had carried on, you'd think she was a cleaning lady for a living. Of course, there was no excuse for Peach's forgetfulness. She'd tried to explain to her mom that she'd never been good with minutae, but for some reason Margot hadn't appreciated that argument.

Now it was Monday morning.

When Peach arrived at her desk, there were two Blow Pops waiting beside her keyboard. She smiled and sighed. *Adam.* On top of being cute and smart, he was reliable, and she'd never realized what a turn-on "reliable" was until now.

Peach sank down into her chair, leaned back, rapping her fingers on the desk anxiously, and chewing on her lower lip, thinking about Quin and what it would feel like to hug him. What would it be like to kiss him . . . ? Slow and soft . . . ? Wet and *savage* . . . ?

Okay, enough was enough; she needed some advice. She picked up the phone and dialed. Two rings, then Lonnie answered and Peach said hello.

"Hey! I'm so glad you called."

"Why, what's up?"

"Are you going to Aruba for Christmas?" Lonnie asked.

"No."

"Well *I* am," she said excitedly.

"What!"

"Dominick got us tickets—two weeks in Aruba—as a surprise! I love you, sweetie; thank you so much!" she cried out to Dominick, who was obviously in the background. Today was the last day of teaching classes before Lonnie's winter break began, but Peach had recalled her sister complaining that she wouldn't get much of a break because she had to work on her dissertation the whole time. Now Peach wondered what happened with that plan, yet wasn't about to burst her sister's bubble by mentioning the D-word.

"That's awesome! But I was so excited to see you," Peach said, just realizing that this meant Lonnie and Dominick wouldn't be coming home for Christmas.

"I know, that's the only thing that kind of sucks," Lonnie agreed.

"No, but it's great; you're gonna have the best time."

"I hope so. Dominick was saying that we haven't had much time together lately, and . . . well, you know how it is."

"Of course," Peach assured her. "You guys want to reconnect—get your groove on and G-B-two-B." In other words, *fool around* and *get back to basics.*

"Definitely," Lonnie said, bubbling over happily. "But let me check—sweetie, are we gonna get our groove on?" There was a pause. "He's embarrassed now. . . . He said we are—yay, I'm getting kissed by a boy!"

Peach rolled her eyes at her sister's antics, then heard Dominick laugh in the background and say, "Will you stop it?"

Sighing, Lonnie added, "So everything's perfect, except . . ." *Here it comes.* "You know . . ." *The plane.*

"Don't worry about that. You'll be fine; I swear," Peach assured her.

"I know, but I'm afraid I won't be able to go through with it when we get to the airport."

Beyond terrified of flying, Lonnie had been on a plane only twice in her life, once when she was too young to be worried, and the other time several years ago, when she and Peach had gone to Italy. She'd clutched the armrests the entire flight, which Peach wouldn't have minded so much if her arms hadn't been there first. By the time they landed, her wrists were numb. Suffice it to say, all attempts to liquor her sister up before and during the flight hadn't worked.

"When I even think about flying right now, I feel like I can't breathe—"

"No, no, don't worry!" Peach said. "Honestly, I've never heard of a plane crashing on the way to Aruba."

"Really?" Lonnie said hopefully.

Well, it was true; she never *had* heard of that. "Think positive," Peach told her.

"You're right. And hey, even if Dominick and I die, at least we die together."

"That's the spirit."

"Okay—I'm good," Lonnie said, her tone approaching breezy again.

After chatting more about Aruba, and how it didn't exactly mesh with Lonnie's life mission never to own a bathing suit, Peach said, "I have a computer-geek question."

"Oh, sure, hang on. I'll get Dominick—"

"No, wait—not that kind of question. I meant computer geek as in: computer geeks and the women who love them."

"Huh? Oh, *wait*—is this about that guy Adam?"

"Yeah, how did you know?"

"It was just a guess. Why, do you like him?"

"Yes!" Peach blurted.

"That's great!" Lonnie enthused. "What's he like?" Peach gave a testimonial that probably went on too long, and somewhere in there she mentioned Adam's adorable glasses, warm, sexy smile, and low-key humor. She also touched on his deep, honeyed voice and reserved manner before Lonnie said, "Hey, she likes Adam. You know that guy who knows that guy who works for you?"

"Ahem," Peach interjected impatiently. "Could you catch Dominick up to speed later? I need advice here."

"Oh, sorry," Lonnie said. "Hey, why don't you ask if he wants to get dinner sometime?"

Peach gasped. "Dinner? That's so desperate! If he said no, I'd drop dead on the spot."

"O-*kay,*" Lonnie said with a laugh, then called to Dominick, "Hey, hon, is asking a guy to dinner desperate?"

Rolling her eyes impatiently, Peach said, "Lonnie, please, who cares what he thinks? No offense."

"Okay, but Dominick says it's not desperate," Lonnie said.

"Yeah, but Dominick doesn't count."

"Why not?"

"Because . . . he's not your typical guy."

"What do you mean? Hey, baby, Peach says you don't count because you're not a real man!"

"Lonnie!" Peach said, over her sister's giggling and Dominick's muffled voice in the background. "C'mon, stop, it's really annoying."

"Oh, I'm sorry," Lonnie said sincerely. "I was just kidding around."

"No, it's okay," Peach said. She hadn't meant to snap, but she was just so keyed-up over Quin, and she needed help now. "Maybe I could ask him if he wants to get drinks after work. Not *dinner*—just drinks."

"Yeah, that sounds good," Lonnie encouraged.

"Okay, I'll do it," Peach stated resolutely. She hung up the phone and hopped up from her chair, feeling a surge of adrenaline.

When she wanted something, she usually tried to get it, so why should this be any different? She wanted to spend more time with Adam, to get to know him better, definitely to kiss him . . . and hopefully more.

"Oh!" Peach yelped as she bumped into Grace, who was apparently right outside her cube. "Sorry, Grace, I didn't realize you were there."

"Yeah, I was just on my way to copy these files for Robert," she said, pushing up both her arms, which were full of manila folders. Rolling her eyes, she whispered, "The dumb-ass."

Peach couldn't spare the time to indulge Grace's projection of her own low self-esteem—and on a side note, why did Grace always seem to be lurking?

As she approached Quin's cubicle, she heard the tapping of keys. Her heart kicked up. *He's there, he's working, and he has no clue that I'm about to ask him out.*

Her palms began to sweat; restlessly she rubbed them against her wool skirt and ducked her head in. "Hey," she said, smiling.

Adam turned from his monitor and smiled back. "Hey, there," he said, looking so genuinely happy to see her that shivers trembled through her chest, continuing down and fluttering between her legs. *I want him,* she thought, *desperately.* Hungrily, she pictured jumping into his lap, edging up her skirt, and straddling him right here, right now.

Like she'd ever have the nerve. That was fine to recommend to other people, but a whole different story when it came to her own life, and something she wanted this much.

"Here," she said, breaking the ice by reaching into her jacket pocket and pulling out a little white bag. "This is for you."

He smiled and took the bag. Quickly he uncurled it and looked inside. It was a king-size Snickers, his favorite candy bar. "Thanks," he said, "this is great."

"Listen, Adam—"

"Hey, you called me Adam," he said with a grin, and tore open the wrapper.

"Yeah . . . listen, I was wondering—"

Suddenly his phone rang. *Shoot!*

"Hang on a second," he said, leaning back to answer it. "Adam Quinlan. Oh, hi, what's up?" Peach couldn't tell if he didn't feel like talking to the person, or if he just didn't feel like talking in front of *her*. Maybe it was personal family stuff; she knew how sticky Quin could be about that.

First she'd need to get him alone in a nonwork setting, and it wouldn't hurt if he had a drink to help him relax. Peach leaned against the side of his cube entrance; she should probably go and let him talk. That's what she'd do, even though she was impatient to say her piece, but just then she heard Adam say, "Listen, can I call you back?" There was a pause, Peach straightened, and Adam finished, "Listen, get some sleep, okay? I'll call you later."

After he hung up the phone, he sighed and ran his palm over his eyes—as though rubbing away an irritant, or as though tired and coaxing his eyes to stay awake—then he shook himself out of it. Turning his chair toward Peach again, he said, "Sorry about that."

"That's okay," she said. "I hope you didn't get off the phone just because I was standing here being a lurker," she said dryly.

Half grinning, Adam said, "No, no, not at all."

"Who was it, your dad?" *Whoops!* A nosy question—it was none of her business, at least not yet. Not until Quin let her into his life a little more . . .

"No," he said, appearing distracted. "That was my girlfriend."

Chapter Fourteen

Girlfriend! What kind of *bullshit* was that? These were the thoughts still running through Peach's head a few hours later, as she meandered around the office on her way to the kitchen. So his girlfriend's name was Robin, and right now she lived in Europe. Why should it shock her as much as it did? Obviously he was a catch—but couldn't he put a picture on his desk like a normal person, for God's sake?

It was in this frustrated state that Peach headed toward the kitchen and ran into Rachel, who was walking in the opposite direction. Jeez, she liked Rachel, but she was not in the mood for her perkiness. "Hi, Rachel," Peach said, forcing a smile even though she wanted to sulk. *How dare he have a secret girlfriend? Why hasn't he mentioned her before now? Didn't he think it was worth mentioning, even if I was just his friend?* She'd thought she understood men; in fact, there was a lot she'd assumed she'd understood about people in general before she'd met Adam Quinlan.

"Hey, Peach," Rachel said, "see you in the conference room!"

"Huh?"

"The staff meeting," Rachel said, blinking with eyes wide like a doe's. "Remember?"

"Oh . . . I forgot," Peach said, and turned on her heel to fall in step with Rachel. In her lovelorn delirium she'd blanked out the staff meeting.

"Hey, you don't seem like yourself today," Rachel said, as they rounded the bend. "Is it a guy?" she asked with a big, encouraging grin, and Peach almost screamed, *Yes, it's a guy—it's the cutie I have lunch with every day, who buys me lollipops. Yes, it's a stupid goddamn guy!*

"Well, I like someone, but it turns out he has a girlfriend," Peach said finally.

"Really, who?" Rachel asked, sounding rabid with interest.

"Oh . . . you don't know him," Peach lied quickly. Well, she couldn't be honest *every* hour of the day.

"That sucks; I'm sorry. I can totally relate."

"You can?"

"Yes. I like a guy, but I can tell he's not interested, and he doesn't even *have* a girlfriend." She said it with the same upbeat pep with which she said nearly everything, which took Peach by surprise. Could anyone be that cheery? Rachel Latham was so compulsively bright and sunny that she either had no dark side at all, or she had a *huge* dark side and was compensating for it like crazy.

"To be honest," she added with a conspiratorial smile, "it's Scott."

"Omigod, Scott, really?" Peach said, surprised—though why on earth should she be? Scott was cute, funny, and all-around affable, yet it was odd that Peach had never even seen any signs of Rachel's crush. Since when was Peach so oblivious to other people's feelings?

When they reached the conference room, Peach saw Adam's profile through the glass doors, and her breath caught in her throat. He was sitting at the table, looking reserved, unassuming, with that damn unreadable expression of his, tapping his pen on the edge of the table.

"Just look at him," Rachel whispered. "He's adorable."

Exactly. Except that Rachel meant Scott, who was sitting at the table, too. As Peach nudged the glass door open with her hip, her eyes locked with Adam's, and he smiled at her, motioning with his head for her to sit in the chair to his left. Even as her heart pounded heavily in her chest, Peach tried to act casual, approaching Adam as if he were her friend and nothing more, the whole time wishing he didn't have a girlfriend.

Across from Scott sat Grace and Nelson; Peach noticed that someone was missing.

Robert entered and said some pleasant hellos before taking a seat at the head of the table. Then he noticed what Peach had. "Where's Dennis?" he said, looking quizzically around the table. "I just realized he's not with us—is he out sick?"

"He never called in sick," Grace said.

"I haven't seen him, either," Scott added.

"Hey, didn't he have a hot date this weekend?" Nelson said with a suggestive grin. Had Dennis told Nelson about his date with Joan? She supposed he must've, but it was ironic, since Peach had deliberately kept quiet about it out of respect for Dennis's privacy.

"Dennis Emberson—hot date?" Grace echoed with a snort. "Yeah, that'll be the day."

"Hey, who knows?" Scott said teasingly. "Maybe the date turned into one of those long weekends. . . ."

"Scott!" Peach said with a startled laugh.

Chuckling, he held up his hands in mock surrender. "Hey, you never know."

"Yeah, yeah, I think Scott's got the right idea," Nelson joined in eagerly. "I can just see it now—probably Dennis calculated the tip in his head right down to the penny, and his date was like, 'That's it; I've gotta go to bed with *this* guy.' "

The comment hung in the air for a moment, as everyone just kind of half smiled or laughed awkwardly. Somehow flat-out discussing a coworker in bed with someone had crossed the line, creating a pall over the conversation. Swallowing tremulously, Nelson added, "Yeah, can you picture Dennis in bed? He probably cries out, 'Calculator,' in passion!" Now there were only half smiles, and when Peach darted an eye over to Robert, she saw that he was not amused. But Nelson didn't notice—instead he squeezed his eyes shut and started imitating Dennis by moaning, "Expense reports, automatic deposit, oh, yes, *yes!*"

"Nelson, please," Robert interjected, his tone unmistakably firm. "I think that's less than professional."

Quickly, Peach glanced down at the table, feeling too embarrassed for Nelson to look at him. Then she couldn't help herself and stole a peek. His smile was fixed on his face, but his nickel-sized nostrils were quivering. Shamefully, Peach almost laughed, but stopped herself and thought, *Jesus, what kind of person am I?*

With smooth fluidity, Robert resumed the meeting, during which Peach drifted in and out of focus. Mostly she thought about Adam, sitting right beside her. Now that she was fully aware of her attraction to him, it was difficult not to construe every movement he made as sexy, no matter how small. When he shifted his leg under the table, tapped his pen on the table, straightened his glasses . . . or even just the subtle way his chest rose and fell when he breathed . . . Jeez, could she sound more desperate right now?

Needing to take her mind off Adam, Peach looked around the room, almost absently observing her coworkers. Nelson was discreetly picking his nose (if you called "scratching" the inside of his flared nostril with his pen cap discreet), Grace was jotting down everything Robert said, playing the part of the efficient enthusiast. Suffice it to say, Grace would later gripe that Robert was, in fact, a dickhead, shithead, or butthead, who couldn't tell his ass from his elbow. And both Scott's and Rachel's eyes were glazed over. It didn't take long for Peach's gaze to wander back to Adam.

He was already looking at her.

For a moment their eyes locked, and a thick wave of heat washed over her. For the first time she noticed the dark shock of green in his eyes. It must've been the way the light was hitting him. So his eyes weren't brown after all; they were hazel. Almost weakly, she sighed and smiled at him, knowing he was looking back at her only as his friend.

Wait a minute . . . *was* he? She noticed something in his gaze—the way it lingered, flickered down to her mouth, then back up, and the small, self-conscious smile, as though he'd been caught. He looked away.

Peach's heart leaped in her chest. A thick lump of emotion formed in her throat and clogged it like a golf ball. Could Quin feel the same way about her that she felt about him? Her pulse pounded in her ears, as liquid heat stirred between her legs. More than anything right now, she just wanted to kiss him. To ignore this meeting—well, she was doing that anyway—and to climb on top of him. To cover his mouth with hers, kiss him deeply, feel his warm breath against her lips, slide her tongue against his, knock his glasses off his face—to mess him up, ruffle his hair, see those dark tiger eyes drowsy with arousal.

What would Adam look like having an orgasm? What would he sound like? What would he feel like?

Clamping her thighs together, Peach tried to trap the heat in—to savor it and stop it at the same time—and she felt heat creep up her neck, into her face, and suddenly, oddly, Adam looked back at her again. He stared at her with a frustratingly inscrutable expression on his face. Damn it, she just could not read him.

She had to get a grip! It was time for a little self-talk—a little cognitive-behavioral action (sounded vaguely familiar from Psych 101). Adam was her friend. She had to rein in infatuation stuff. She'd always been able to get her emotions in check, and this time would be no different. So he wasn't available for kissing; he was still there for lunches.

Earlier, when he'd first dropped the G-bomb, he'd said that he and Robin were having some problems, but he hadn't gotten into details. Gee, now there was a surprise. Maddeningly introverted—*who, Adam?*—but if they'd been together for five years already, Peach was not holding her breath that they would break up anytime soon. That was how people were—terrified to leave something familiar, anxious about change, frightened of being vulnerable and alone. *Another goddamn classic case.*

As the meeting wrapped up, Robert asked if there was anything else, and Nelson spoke up. "Everyone, don't forget Brenda and I are throwing a dinner party this coming Saturday. I'll e-mail you all directions before then. Adam, I'll make sure you get directions, too."

"Oh, okay, thanks a lot," Adam said, and glanced briefly at Peach. As they pushed out of their chairs their legs brushed up against each other. A jolt of lust struck him, heated his blood. Maybe if she didn't have such sexy legs . . .

He'd met her only a week ago, and he'd spent most of last night picturing her mouthwatering body naked.

Time to go.

Rachel accosted Peach after the meeting, and started whispering to her as they walked down the hall. Adam trailed slowly behind, trying not to ogle Peach's butt or her slim hips swinging as she walked her sassy, confident walk. Even though her outfit wasn't the least bit revealing, it was still sexy. The snug light blue pants poured down her long, shapely legs, and without the matching jacket she'd been wearing earlier, he could see the formfitting sweater underneath. It molded to her soft, delicate-looking curves, and he just wanted to grab her and haul her up against him.

The erotic response he had to her was raw and visceral. It was as if Peach's body emitted a powerful sexual heat, thickening the air between them, trapping him in, and stiffening his cock almost to the point of pain. (It would feel a lot better, of course, if she put her lips on it, ran her tongue over the tip, and sucked the head deep into her mouth.)

If he could just stop fixating on her—on her infectious energy, her warmth, her openness, and most of all, the way she could make him forget about everything else, including his loneliness.

Stop. This wasn't going to happen. What was the point of torturing himself with thoughts of Peach Kelley naked—wet, wanting, rolling around in his bed—if it could never happen? He still had a lot of unfinished business with Robin, but even if he finished it, the last thing he wanted was to jump into another relationship. In fact, he had a feeling he was burned out on relationships for a while. He'd started dating Robin when he was only twenty-four, and before that, he'd been in a six-year relationship, spanning college and beyond. Enough was enough; Christ, even he needed a break from the obligation and stress of having a girlfriend. Not to mention dating someone at work was a bad idea—a terrible idea. Which was why he would forget it.

Chapter Fifteen

"You'll never guess what I found out."

Like a blast of wind Peach blew into Adam's cube and hopped up onto his desk. He swung around in his chair, still taken off guard by her energy, though it continually elevated his mood. The staff meeting had ended only ten minutes ago, and here she was, perched up on his desk like the queen bee. Her sparkly blue eyes had a dark, smoky lining around them today, and her long, sultry lashes were blinking expectantly. She was obviously dying to tell him something.

"What's that?" he asked.

"Omigod, I've been clueless," she said, pressing a hand to her chest for emphasis. The silver rings on her right hand caught a flash of light, gleaming brightly for a just a second. "Completely clueless," she repeated.

"Impossible," Adam said.

As soon as she started talking, he found himself focusing on how adorable she was, eyes wide, hands gesturing, her face expressive and alive. Suddenly his chest tightened. This was more than animal attraction, more than sexual infatuation. Yes, Peach was hot as hell—almost too sexy to touch—but the fact was, he *liked* her. He liked everything about her.

"*Hello?* Quin, you with me?" He snapped back into focus just as his eyes honed in on her lips, darkly stained from the Blow Pop she'd been sucking after the meeting. "Did you miss everything I just said?" she asked with a laugh. "Where were you?"

If only he could show her . . .

"No, no, I caught some of it," he said quickly, sitting up straighter, crossing one leg perpendicularly over the other, and trying to ignore his burgeoning erection. "Uh, something about nuclear proliferation, the state of education, the theory of relativity."

Smirking, Peach said, "Right—and after that I was telling you how Rachel likes Scott. Smart-ass."

"Oh, that's right," Adam said, grinning.

"You're not surprised?"

"Why should I be? I barely know these people. Anyway, define 'likes.'"

"I mean *likes*," Peach reiterated. "You know. As in, he's a *man*, she's a *woman* . . ."

"Okay, I get it," he said, holding up his hand. "But why does that make you clueless?"

"Because I had no idea!"

"Well, why should you? It's not really your business—oh, wait, that argument doesn't apply to you."

Peach laughed and said, "Anyway, you know what I'm gonna do?"

"Um, I'm going to take a stab and say . . . interfere?"

"*Help,*" Peach corrected. "I'm gonna try to get both Rachel and Scott to go to that singles' dance next month. You know, the one you're going to also because it's for charity?" Startled, Adam opened his mouth to protest, but Peach continued before he got the chance. "With a little push, I think Scott might realize what a cute couple they'd make. I mean, think about it—*he's* so cute, and *she's* so cute. It would just be so . . ."

"Cute?"

"*Exactly,*" she said, then tilted her head. "You really *get* me, you know?"

Adam chuckled and rolled his eyes.

"Oh, here," she said, holding out an opened roll of candy. "Want one?"

Adam raised an eyebrow. "Mentos?"

"I found them in my desk," Peach said. "They're kind of weird, but deep down, people like them."

"I like how you talk to me like I'm an alien, with no concept of the customs here on Earth," he remarked before he put one in his mouth and chewed (and chewed).

"Good, huh?"

"Yeah, actually. Thanks. By the way, how do you still have all your own teeth?"

"Who says that I do?" she said seriously.

Startled, Adam's eyes shot to her mouth, and Peach said, "Just joking with you, Quinny," as she reached over to ruffle his hair.

Her hand retracted quickly, and she scolded herself. It was such a silly, innocuous thing to do, yet it was still the kind of touching that could blur the line between friendship and flirtation—between being platonic and making a fool of yourself.

"Quinny," he muttered, quirking the corner of his mouth.

Just then his phone rang, and Adam reached back to snatch the receiver. "Adam Quinlan. Oh, hey, Dad. How are you?" He held up his hand to let her know it would be only a minute, so Peach stayed planted on his desk, waiting patiently. "I don't know, Dad. Well, did you tell her it was really important?" He sighed. "Okay, I'll talk to Mom. Uh-huh, okay."

It sounded like he was hurrying Martin off the phone a little, but Peach just wanted to make sure he was all right, so she said, "Let me talk to him for a second."

"Huh . . . ?" Adam said, as Peach leaned over and took the receiver away from him. Poleaxed and stunned, he sat back, thinking, *What the hell just happened?*

"Marty? Hi, it's Peach. Are you okay?"

Shit, he couldn't believe this. What was his dad, her new best friend now? Or worse, her new project?

"Mmm-hmm. Right, right," she said, nodding, as Adam's father was clearly embarrassing himself, droning on about his marital problems again. Adam suppressed an irritated sigh. "Well, Marty, if

Liz doesn't want to talk, maybe it's not that she really doesn't want to talk, but just that she doesn't want to have the *same* conversation," Peach continued. "Remember, you have to listen not only with your ears, but also with your *mind*."

Oh, Christ, Adam thought, heaving a sigh (not that Peach noticed). That was it—he was finding his dad a therapist—one who actually had a degree and an office, and one who didn't know Adam.

Minutes passed as Peach continued her little pep talk, coiling the phone cord around her finger, crossing her legs, and tapping the backs of her heels against Adam's drawer. Irritation crept into his skin. Maybe it wasn't fair to be annoyed with her, but he couldn't help it; she just made him feel so damn exposed. He didn't want to bring his personal family life into the office, because he'd always been a private person. But it was more than that. It was his friendship with Peach; it was the simple, easy connection they shared at work. He didn't want to complicate it with the other parts of his life. It would be like interlocking circles, and once things started to overlap . . . well, the simple fact was that even though he and Peach were friends, he didn't want her to get too close.

"Okay, Marty, definitely tell me how it goes," Peach said now, finally wrapping up their conversation. "Do you want me to put Adam back on first?" He held his hand out for the phone, but when he pulled it to his ear, there was no one there. "Yeah, he said he'll just call you later," Peach explained simply. More irritation churned in his gut. "So what are you going to do about this whole situation?" she asked—or *probed*—what a surprise. Hell, he *really* didn't like where this was going.

"What situation?" he asked, sure to keep his voice terse and disinterested as he shifted his focus back to his monitor.

"You know, your parents' divorce, that whole thing," she responded, with a broken lilt in her voice that said, *Haven't you been paying attention?* "It's so tough on Marty," she went on. "And I can only imagine what Liz is going through. I wish there were a way to get those two talking again. . . ."

Incredulously, Adam just looked at her, his lips parted, his face twisted. So not only was she on a first-name-basis with his parents, whom she'd never met, but she now she wanted to strategize about getting the two of them back together? What the fuck was this, *The Parent Trap*? He kept his reply short and sour. "Peach, they can handle it, okay?"

"Quin, how can you be so blasé about it?" Peach said, surprised, her blue eyes huge with feeling.

Normally he found that unbelievably adorable; now it was just annoying. Stone-faced, he refocused on his monitor.

"It's so obvious that your dad still loves her. And if she loves him, *too*—"

"Peach, please," Adam said firmly, "they'll handle this. I'm not getting involved."

"But you just told Marty that you'd talk to your mom for him."

"Okay, what I mean to say is that *you're* not getting involved." Peach bristled at his sharp tone, and Adam felt a prickle of guilt because the words had come out much more bluntly than he'd intended. Still, he wasn't going to acquiesce on this one.

"Well, I wasn't trying to get 'involved,' " she said, making quotation marks with her fingers. "I just wanted to help you, you know, to figure out how to deal with all this."

"But I don't *need* help," Adam protested with a frustrated, humorless laugh. Then he started typing something—anything.

"Quin, please, it's obvious this whole separation thing is making you upset. Why can't you talk about it?"

"It's *not* making me upset," he lied, absently punching keys, acting immersed in his work all of a sudden. "I honestly don't think it's that big a deal. Sure, it sucks for them, but it's fine as far as I'm concerned. I mean, I'm an adult; I think I can handle it."

"I'm not saying you can't handle it," Peach said, holding her hands up in surrender—only it didn't feel like surrender; it felt like she wouldn't fucking drop it already. "But I just want to explain the dynamics here. I remember learning about this kind of thing in school. See, when couples go through a divorce, they go through what's called 'grief stages.' Do you know what those are?"

He shot her a glare—the fucking alien thing again.

"Okay, sorry, I'm sure you have," she said quickly. "Anyway, in your family it seems like each member is taking a stage. Liz is representing guilt, Sonny is anger, Marty is denial, and you're acceptance—except that nobody's buying it. Maybe it's because you're carrying the burden of filling Derek's shoes as the oldest child that you're sublimating your feelings . . . ?"

"Whoa," Adam said, swiveling in his chair to look at her dead-on. "Look, Peach, this is really none of your business."

There was no follow-up, no joke about how she should butt in anyway; this time he was angry.

But how can he be angry? Peach wondered. She was only trying to help. Couldn't he see that? "I'm trying to help," she repeated feebly, echoing her own self-justifying thoughts and hoping he would be blown away by them.

It definitely didn't appear that he was.

"I didn't ask for your help," Adam said curtly, then reached over to switch off his computer. Oh, boy, he didn't even wait for Windows to shut down properly—this was serious. Standing up, he avoided looking at her and grabbed his coat, which was hanging in the tall cabinet beside his desk. "Your problem is that you meddle too much," he added, shrugging his jacket on, still not making eye contact with her. "Sometimes you need to just back off."

Suddenly Peach felt irrationally annoyed by Adam's attitude, so dismissive, so damn stubborn—and why was he so threatened by what she was saying? He was too closed-off, unwilling to reveal even a slight chink in his armor. It was a sickness, really. "Well, you know what *your* problem is?" she said hotly.

"Yes. I do." He looked pointedly at her.

Oh.

He moved past her out of the cubicle and, with his back to her, gave a perfunctory wave. "See ya tomorrow."

"What, you're mad at me now?" Peach asked petulantly, trailing behind Adam as he headed down the hallway. She knew she was projecting her own defensiveness, but at the moment . . . *Fuck it.*

"I'm not mad," Adam said, not even glancing back as he continued on his way.

"Then why are you storming off?"

"I'm not storming; I'm going home. In case you haven't noticed, it's quitting time."

"Well, you're all pissy," she retorted, feeling the pull of desperation in her chest, the need to get some reaction, the maddening way that Adam could keep his composure when Peach was making a fool of herself, chasing after him, trying to bait his back.

"Bye," was all he said, before turning the last corner and disappearing out of sight. Peach didn't bother following him any farther—there was her pride, after all.

Chapter Sixteen

On Wednesday, Peach was torn between guilt and anguish—both relatively new emotions, and, as she was discovering, not particularly pleasant ones. The guilt was over Adam, while the anguish was over Dennis—but that would come later.

She hadn't seen Adam since Monday afternoon, when they'd had their ugly squabble—their first fight. He'd been out of the office all day on Tuesday for a software workshop somewhere, and she missed him already. She needed to see him again, to smooth things over, to be best buddies again.

Ever since the incident Peach had been queasy with guilt; in fact, she'd barely been able to enjoy the veggie tacos and peanut-butter pie BeBe had brought her from McMurphy's. They'd hashed it out, and BeBe had been unfailingly supportive, even as she was being mauled by Buster. (Buster was only three pounds, but still—it was kind of hard to have a conversation with your roommate when a dog was attaching its mouth to her leg and latching on like it was a magic carpet ride.)

What right did she have to get so annoyed with Adam when all he was asking her was to be less . . . intrusive? Pushy? Meddling? All loose synonyms for "helpful," by the way, but fine. She'd accept the fact that she'd been wrong to push Adam about his family situation, which was deeply personal to him. After all, he was shyer and more private than she; some people just weren't cut out for Peach's brand of help. In fact, she supposed she often forgot that not everyone was like BeBe—not everyone was going to appreciate constructive criticism and unsolicited advice. *Go figure.*

Of course, when she'd had this revelation, BeBe had muttered, "Who said *I* like it?" but then smiled saccharinely, and said, "Only kidding . . . of course I like it—I *love* it!"

After some soul-searching—most of it while working on her ceiling mural, with Buster growling and dangling from her pant leg, as Peach rocked off balance on her stepladder—she'd realized something else. Maybe in her effort to shift her romantic affection for Adam back to a platonic one, she'd gone into overdrive trying to be his support system—his best friend, his confidante. It made such perfect sense. At least partially, she'd been trying to dwell on something else besides the fact that he was already taken.

Now she sighed as she entered her office building, instantly blanketed by the warmth of the lobby, and comforted by the frenetic movement of all the worker bees buzzing toward the elevators. She said a quick hello to Thomas, the security guard, who was somehow keeping the building secure with his face buried in a crossword puzzle.

Then she hopped on an elevator, just making it inside before the doors sealed shut, and rode to the eighth floor. When she approached the glass doors of Millennium, her stomach knotted. Her breath quickened. Absently, she noted that the zipping wind outside had blown some of her hair out of the sparkly barrettes she wore on each side. But who even cared? She had to get to Quin. Jeez, she actually felt *nervous* to face him—to apologize, which, admittedly, she didn't find herself doing all that often.

She passed Grace, who was on her way to the kitchen. "Morning, Peach," she said, waving with an empty mug in her hand. Then she got the light in her eye—the conspiratorial glint that appeared when she was poised to bad-mouth someone, or to pass on some juicy bit of gossip. *Spare me,* Peach thought, needing to make up with Adam, having no time to humor Grace, whose idea of chitchat included how Nelson's protein shakes had crusted over on the counter, or how Brenda was cheating on Weight Watchers.

"Hey, Grace," Peach said, keeping her tone and stride brisk as they passed each other.

"Still no Dennis," Grace remarked, then *tsk-tsk*ed. That stopped Peach short, several feet in front of her. Turning back, she saw Grace's lips pursed almost smugly as she walked a few steps back to seal the space between them. "Hasn't been here since *Friday*. No call, nothing."

Prickling unease crept into Peach's chest, as she thought back to Friday, when she'd last seen Dennis. *What kind of jackass am I?* She hadn't even stopped to notice that he *still* hadn't come in!

She'd been so damn preoccupied with Quin. And now Grace was telling her that not only had Dennis not come into the office, but nobody had even heard from him! Grace went on to explain that when she and Robert had tried to reach Dennis, there had been no answer at his house; the phone had just kept ringing.

Chest tightening, Peach swallowed hard, trying to make sense of this. With her mind racing frantically, she mentally recapped the little that she knew for a fact: On Friday, Dennis had said that he planned to see Joan that weekend—Joan, the woman *Peach* had set him up with—and now he was missing.

And here was where the anguish came in.

"Oh, Quin!" Peach exclaimed, bursting into his cube, her eyebrows pinched in distress, a troubled expression washing over her soft, beautiful features. In that moment Adam realized how much he'd missed the sultry thrum of her voice, even though it had been only a little over a day since he'd heard it.

"What's wrong?" he said, immediately rising from his chair and coming closer. His chest tightened with concern, and she seemed to realize it, because she quickly reassured him.

"No, no, I'm fine; don't worry. It's just . . . Oh, God, I have this terrible feeling."

"What do you mean?" he asked, then placed his hands gently on her upper arms. "What is it?" His voice was calm and even, and it relaxed her for a second. She expelled a breath, melting into him for a fleeting moment, before his hands slid off her arms, and she explained what Grace had told her about Dennis.

Logically, as always, Adam speculated that maybe Dennis was just running late today, or maybe he'd been home sick for the past couple of days, but had simply forgotten to call in.

Peach wasn't buying it. "Then why wouldn't he answer his phone when Grace and Robert called his house?" she countered. "No—I feel like this whole situation is off."

"Okay, when was the last time you talked to him?"

"Early Friday, remember? You were there, and he stopped at my cube to tell us about his date with Joan." If Adam recalled, Dennis was *yanked* in, while Adam was merely held there against his will, but yes, he remembered. "He mentioned he was going out with Joan the following night," Peach continued. "I remember seeing him leave work before six. Now, according to Grace, that's the last *anyone's* seen or heard from him."

"Hmm . . ." Adam thought for a moment, then said, "Well, you said once that he's not the most responsible guy in the world. You know, absentminded, forgets to check in."

True—Peach had told Adam about the time that Dennis had forgotten to tell the office he'd gone on vacation—but it wasn't like that was a regular occurrence. Well, he'd forgotten to mention his dental appointment last week, too, but . . . no, going all weekend through Wednesday morning with no word was weird. Worry sank into her chest, burning through it like acid—or maybe it was guilt. Adam's remark last week about how Peach didn't know anything about Joan, plus what he said the other day about her meddling too much, kept echoing through her mind. Was there a connection to Dennis's disappearance and his second date with Joan, the woman Peach introduced him to?

"Oh, Quin, what if you were right? What if I *did* set Dennis up with a homicidal maniac?"

"No, no, no," he interjected quickly, placing his hands delicately on her arms again, and when she looked up into his face she felt totally supported. A new feeling again, but this time, a warmly comforting one. "I talk too much; don't listen to me," he said soothingly.

"No, you don't talk too much!" Peach yelped. "You barely talk at all—oh, but in a good way!"

Smiling down at her, Quin strummed his fingers over her upper arms, and she could feel every bit of the affectionate gesture through the thin cotton of her sweater. "Listen, let's just go down to Mackie's Diner later and talk to Joan. We'll go at lunch today, okay?"

"Okay . . ." Peach mumbled, vaguely wondering why she hadn't thought that far ahead yet herself.

"Don't worry," he added, moving his hands up to her shoulders and giving them a gentle shake. "I'm sure Joan will be there, and she'll tell us that Dennis was feeling under the weather after their date, or something like that. Or maybe he mentioned to her a trip he's taking—you know, that he forgot to mention to us, something like that."

Peach thought for a moment before nodding. "Okay. But what if she's not there?"

"Even better," Adam said matter-of-factly.

"Better?"

"Yes. Then we'll know that they hit it off."

"Oh, you mean . . ."

"Maybe Nelson was right; maybe they never even got out of bed," Adam said, half grinning. Abruptly, he seemed to catch the sexuality of his comment, and pulled back from her.

They agreed to meet at Peach's desk at twelve thirty, if Dennis hadn't come in by then, and then head over to Mackie's. Peach prayed there was a happily innocuous explanation for everything. She didn't want Adam to be right about her meddling being excessive, much less dangerous. And call her crazy, but she didn't want to be the one who'd inadvertently sent Dennis to his doom.

Before she left Adam's cube she thanked him for his help, and he said, "Wait. Listen . . . I wanted to apologize for the way I acted on Monday."

"*You* wanted to apologize?" Peach said, her eyes lighting up. Holy shit, she'd forgotten to apologize to *him,* which had been her mission as soon as she'd arrived. "No, no, it was my fault," she insisted. "I'm sorry, Quin, I was pushing way too hard. I mean, it wasn't my place to—"

"No, you were just trying to help and—"

"But still, I should've taken the hint."

"Well . . . maybe," he conceded.

A lump formed in Peach's throat as a tender emotion clutched her heart; in that moment Adam was so boyishly cute, and he was the sweetest guy she'd ever met. Their first fight—thank God that was over.

"It's just . . . I have trouble sometimes . . . talking about what's going on in my head," he said.

More like your heart, she thought, realizing that was cheesy as hell but still true.

"Don't feel bad. I have trouble, too—trouble *not* talking about what's going on in your head," Peach said glibly, then added, "But I'll work on that."

He smiled and said, "So will I."

When Adam and Peach walked into Mackie's that afternoon, they just barely heard the jingle of the bell on the door over the clanging din of the lunchtime crowd. As usual, the overstuffed express line was clogging the whole right side of the restaurant.

"It's always like this," Peach said almost absently, as they struggled to move through the crowd. They didn't get very far, and once they were stalled, Peach stood on tiptoe and let her eyes rove around the diner. "I don't see Joan," she said.

The bell above the door jingled as a boisterous group of women came in together and crammed in at the end of the line. A succession of sighs and eye rolls followed, as other customers got irritably impatient. One lady began singing to herself, "Ch-ch-chaaiiin . . . chain of fooools . . ."

"You know what?" Peach said suddenly, turning to look at

Adam, who had the grimace of someone truly tired of being bumped into. "The express line is complete savagery right now. Let's get a table and wait for someone to help us; when I see Joan, I'll wave her over."

As they made their way through the diner, Adam placed his hand gently on Peach's lower back, leading her down the center aisle until they found an empty booth. It was the only vacant one, two booths from the back.

Someone had put an unfortunate end to the holiday music by selecting "Jesse's Girl" on the jukebox. It wasn't difficult to guess who it had been—the guy leaning against the counter sporting vintage Rick Springfield feathered wings seemed like the most viable suspect. As she watched him bob to the beat, Peach rolled her eyes. Not only did she miss the bubbly Christmas music, but also "Jesse's Girl" was one of those songs that always sounded better when you were with a bunch of girlfriends, and being drunk helped.

As Peach slid into the smooth vinyl of the booth, anxiety frittered along her nerves. She was antsy as hell, and she hated it; she hated relying on other people to tell her things were fine. Several minutes passed, and Peach still didn't spot Joan behind the counter or waiting on customers. Where the hell was she?

Briefly, Peach glanced at her menu; Adam took one, too, from where they were wedged between the plastic salt and pepper shakers. White for salt, pink for pepper. Then Peach scanned the counter again—nothing caught her eye except the rhythmic bobbing of Rick Springfield's head double.

"Don't worry," Adam said, as though reading her mind. "Joan will come out any second."

In the meantime a somewhat burly waitress approached their table. Peach recognized her as someone she saw there a lot, but had never met.

"Hi, I'm Kate. What can I get ya?" she said in a voice that was sternly efficient, and as thick and robust as her body. Adam ordered a roast beef sandwich and a Coke, and Peach ordered a garden burger. "Comes with a salad," Kate said. "What kind of dressing?"

"Oh, no salad, please," Peach said. "Can I just get fries instead? No, make that onion rings. And a Heath-bar sundae for dessert." Nodding, Kate took off just as Peach was about to ask if Joan was working today.

"You know, you're slowly dispelling all my assumptions about vegetarians," Adam commented.

"I am? How?" Peach asked, glancing around the crowded room again.

He shrugged. "I just thought vegetarians were all into eating healthy."

"Yeah . . . I guess that's one way to do it," she said, then pressed her palms on the speckled tabletop. Pushing up on her hands, she lifted her butt off her seat and looked around again. "Well, I still don't see Joan. I'm gonna go take a closer look."

She slid out of the booth and made a lap around the entire place. When she got back to their table, Adam said, "No luck?"

"Nope."

"Okay, when our waitress brings our food, we'll just ask when Joan's working next."

So that was what they did. When Kate returned ten minutes later with their plates, Peach accosted her before she could carry her stern efficiency right out of there. "Wait! Can you tell me if Joan's working today?"

"Joan?" Kate repeated. "Joan quit."

"She did?" Peach asked, surprised. "When?"

Kate shrugged. "Sunday morning. I took the call."

"But . . . how long did she work here?"

"Three years, I think." *Hmm . . .* Three years and then, all of a sudden, she quit?

"Didn't she give any notice?" Adam asked, tapping his straw out of its wrapper.

"Nope. Just quit on the spot. What, you two friends of hers?"

"Um, yes," Peach said quickly. "She's a really good friend of my mother's—um, who's away right now," she added, so Kate wouldn't assume that if Peach's mom was really friends with Joan, then Peach should already have the scoop on her quitting. "Do you know what prompted this? Did she have a better job lined up, or . . . ?"

With a shrug, Kate said, "Hey, I don't know what to tell you. All she said was that she was never stepping foot in *this* place again."

"Well, did she sound upset?" Peach pressed.

"Upset? Hell no," Kate said with a bark of laughter. "She was freaking thrilled! Who knows—maybe it had something to do with that new guy she just started dating."

New guy . . . Peach sat up straighter at the mention of Dennis—or at least, she assumed that Kate meant Dennis—and then said, "Right, right, you mean that man she had a blind date with last week?"

Kate just scrunched up her face suspiciously, as though baffled by Peach's line of questioning, so Adam jumped in. "I'm surprised she'd just quit on the spot. Maybe she had a fight with a manager, or . . . ?"

Glancing at him, Kate remarked, "Look, I've told you all I know. If you ask me, she was acting kind of crazy—like she was being all giddy and stupid. Maybe she got bitten by the love bug or something," Kate finished with a dismissive snicker. But Peach couldn't let this topic be dismissed, not yet. Kate was about to walk away again when Peach yelped, "Wait!"

Turning back, Kate blatantly heaved a sigh of annoyance.

"I'm sorry; it's just that I really need to talk to her," Peach explained, smiling sweetly. "I can't find her anywhere, but I was thinking I'd give her a call."

"So what do you want from me?"

"Well, if I could just get Joan's phone number . . ."

With a grimace, Kate recoiled. "Look, even if I knew her phone number, I'm not about to give it out to strange customers. What the hell is this? Ever hear of a *phone book*?" Her voice was dripping with caustic disgust, indicating that she thought Peach and Adam were complete morons. "For God's sake, just look up *Joan Smith*!"

With that Kate left swiftly, leaving no room for more questions. Clearly she was anxious to serve customers who were bearing tips rather than a barrage of questions about another waitress. *Imagine that.*

"Huh," Peach said to herself, sitting back in her seat, still taking in the information.

"See? I told you not to worry," Adam said comfortingly, and Peach's eyes shot to his.

"What do you mean?"

With a shrug, he replied, "Well, think about it—if Dennis seems to be MIA *and* Joan quit the morning after their date, and was acting all giddy and stupid, then chances are they really hit it off, and are together right now."

"That's true!" Peach said, feeling some of the tension lift in her mind, and her stomach muscles begin to relax.

"Maybe they took off on some romantic jaunt or something, who knows?" he said before taking a bite of his roast beef sandwich. (Disturbingly, he'd said "romantic jaunt" as if the concept itself were synonymous with something frivolous and dumb . . . not that it was any of Peach's business.)

"Yeah," she agreed, and sighed. Relief washed over her, made it much easier to breathe. "Hey, what if they even *eloped*?"

Adam almost choked on his Coke. "Holy shit, could you imagine?"

"Okay, if they eloped, you've got to admit, I'm a matchmaking genius."

Shaking his head, Adam said, "How did all this come back to your brilliance?" The sarcasm in his voice made Peach laugh.

"I can't believe her last name is Smith," she remarked, because it was so simple, yet the last name she'd ever guess. She brought a fat, crunchy onion ring to her mouth and found Adam staring at her. "What?" she said.

"No . . . nothing," he replied, and focused back on his sandwich—which was very hard to do, since it was so damn easy to focus on her mouth.

He supposed he did that often. Had she ever noticed? With each day that passed, Peach seemed to get sexier to him. *Jesus, how is that even possible?* he wondered. Everything about her seemed to turn him on—those full, soft-looking lips that he ached to kiss— right now—except that logistics alone made that an impossibility. There was a wide, food-covered table between them, so if he wanted to lean over and kiss her, he'd have to rise up out of his seat and stretch over their plates, inevitably getting ketchup and other condiments all over his shirt in the process, and he'd probably knock over at least one of their drinks, and Peach would probably ask, "What the hell are you doing?" before their mouths even met.

And second, he was still in a relationship, but even if he weren't, he was definitely not looking to start something up with someone else—and for chrissake, he definitely didn't want to start something with someone he worked with! Their office was way too small for that.

No. Not smart. Personal and professional suicide. Case closed, then. *Forget kissing Peach,* he told himself firmly—and he didn't just mean her mouth.

The walk back to the office was cold and breezy, but still brilliantly sunny. "How's Robin?" Peach asked casually. She knew she was taking a risk by asking him—a risk that he'd tell her how much he loved and missed her, but what the hell? She was dying to know: If Adam was so devoted to his girlfriend, why hadn't he mentioned her sooner? And why didn't he have any pictures of her on his desk?

Looking straight ahead, Adam said, "She's fine, I guess." After a long pause, he added, "To be honest . . ."

What, what? Peach thought eagerly. What was he trying to say? *I've fallen in love with you, Peach. I don't know how to handle it. I've never loved like this before, and it's scaring the hell out of me.*

"I don't think we're gonna be together too much longer," Adam finished.

Peach's heart lurched. It might not have been sweeping melodrama, but it was definitely an excellent start. "Oh, really?" she said, doing more of the casual thing.

"Actually, I know for a fact that we aren't," he added with a sigh of resignation. Now Peach's heart soared. God, what did this mean? Would Adam be a free man soon? Okay, she *detested* that term, but still . . . would he be?

"I'm breaking up with her," he added simply, but a little somberly.

"Really? I'm sorry, Quin," Peach said, crossing her fingers discreetly in her coat pocket.

"Hey, what can you do?" he said with a shrug, and Peach refrained from answering, even as her mind filled with the possibilities—she and Quin together, watching movies, laughing, making out, getting naked. . . . "It's just as well," he said.

"Why do you say that?"

"Because . . . the truth is . . ." Holding her breath, Peach waited. "I *really* don't want to be in a relationship right now," he finished.

A red flag went up and abruptly smacked her right in the face.

"I think I need a total break from dating," Adam continued. "Man, I just want to be *single* for a while. I haven't been single in five years."

What a coincidence—she hadn't been *not* single in twenty-five years. Well, a slight exaggeration, but still. Ech, this was a disaster. The man she wanted was doing the unfathomable—breaking up with a long-term girlfriend, leaving the relationship, throwing himself out into the singles pool—and Peach *still* had no chance with him. Jeez . . . she remembered when she'd actually been lucky. What would BeBe say about her charmed life now?

As they rounded the next street corner and headed toward the revolving doors of their building, Peach glanced quickly over at Adam. She bit her lip, overwhelmed with the desire to kiss him. Or to *be* kissed—that more than anything right now—which was uncharacteristically passive of her. Usually Peach lurched toward what she wanted; she believed that it was when you hesitated that you usually missed out, an oversimplified philosophy that had served her well up until now.

On the elevator ride up to their office, Adam was saying something about how he hoped to get up to Vermont next month for some snowboarding, but Peach was barely listening, focusing instead on his mouth, mesmerized by the way he formed his words, by the contours of his lips. She ran her gaze over his face, struck by how smooth and clean his skin looked, how she yearned to bury her face in the crook of his neck, to inhale his scent, to kiss him right there—gently, softly—with the sweetest, most delicate kind of passion. She'd bet Quin went for it sweetly and gently; it would be just like him.

Then again . . . she thought about still waters, and she wondered if there was a sexually charged animal underneath his tame exterior. She fantasized about letting it out, awakening Quin's raw, primal desire. More than anything, though, she was consumed by her need not only to touch him, but to possess him. The intensity shocked her, even scared her. *God . . . what's happening to me?* she wondered. Was this what love felt like?

Chapter Seventeen

"Can you say disaster?"

"Talk to me," Peach said, waiting for her sister to fill her in on what could've possibly gone so wrong in the short time she and Dominick had been in Aruba. Their plane had landed only two hours ago—how bad could it be?

"Where do I begin?" Lonnie cried. "First of all, the airline lost our luggage; then I had to break it to Dominick that I kept my purse in one of my bags, because it didn't fit in the carry-on, because my dissertation stuff was jamming the carry-on, along with my laptop, and let's just say he was less than thrilled, especially since I was holding all our traveler's checks and information about the hotel, including our confirmation number."

Biting her lower lip, Peach thought, *Okay, so far, pretty bad.*

Lonnie expelled a breath, then continued, "So our plane lands just as a huge monsoon is starting. It was so scary. You could barely see in front of you; I thought our taxi driver was going to crash the whole ride to the hotel. By the time we got to the hotel, we were freezing to death. Also our clothes were soaked, including my sweater, which made me smell like wet dog."

"Maybe it was Dominick who smelled," Peach offered, trying her best to conciliate, as she watched Buster tear through the living room with BeBe's hot-pink underpants in her mouth.

"Trust me—I reeked," Lonnie said. "I was getting looks in the lobby."

"Okay, I trust you," Peach said glibly. "Is the hotel nice, at least?"

"The room's fine, but we haven't been able to step foot outside of it since we got here because we have no clothes. By the way, we only got to check into the room after half an hour of trying to convince the lady who couldn't find our reservation that, A, we actually had a reservation, and, B, we actually had a credit card, but just couldn't give it to her right *now*."

"Doesn't Dominick have his credit cards with him?"

"He just brought his American Express, but this hotel doesn't take that, and all the other cards are in my purse."

"Which is in the lost luggage," Peach supplied, then shook her head. "You're right; this romantic vacation sucks so far."

Lonnie said, "Well, the good news is, we changed out of our wet clothes; the bad news is, we have nothing to change into."

"What, are you both just sitting around stark naked?" Peach asked. Actually the image seemed more funny than tragic, but Peach could tell her sister was not particularly amused.

"No, I'm wearing a bath towel, waiting for my smelly, wet clothes to dry, so we can go buy some stuff at the gift shop downstairs. You know, just some loud tourist garb to tide us over till the airline gets our luggage back to us. Although since the gift shop doesn't take American Express either, we're going to have to beg and barter down there, too. And can I just tell you that this towel is *not* one size fits all."

"Meaning?"

"Meaning that it doesn't even fit all the way around my goddamn chubby body—I hate this stupid fucking towel!"

"Okay, okay," Peach broke in, because when her sister started cursing, it usually meant she was flipping out. "Lon, calm down; you're overreacting."

"I know, I know. I'm sorry—I'm just in a bad mood because, ugh, I am large-and-in-charge right now, and the rain soaked through my carry-on, and now my dissertation stuff is drenched. I don't think I can even read half of my notes. I guess that's what I'm really upset about."

"Where's Dominick now?" Peach asked, as she lifted her feet up in the air so Buster could pass. She'd just started on a bichon buzz, growling and sprinting around the coffee table, picking up speed by the second; any instant she'd be careening and tipping to the side like a motorcycle.

"He's finishing his shower," Lonnie said, and then, "Oh, hi, baby, how was your shower?" Peach didn't hear Dominick's response, but after he mumbled something, Lonnie explained to him that room service didn't start till eight. "Unless you know any good nudist restaurants within walking distance?" Lonnie added sarcastically. "Or maybe cabs that don't mind taking nude passengers?" Lonnie said.

"Ewww," Peach said, as she leaned over and tried to spritz Buster with a water bottle to get her away from the armchair she'd just begun chomping on. (Buster, who'd darted into the kitchen during her buzz, then returned to the living room with an exhausted flop, simply shook the water off her back and kept chewing on the furniture. So much for the water-bottle method that Peach had read about online.) *"Stop it!"* Peach shouted, finally getting Buster's attention. Guiltily, the little white devil dog sprinted from the room. When she ran that fast, she hopped like a bunny. Abruptly she stopped, then turned back to see if Peach was chasing her. She had something in her mouth; must've pulled it out from underneath the armchair. As soon as Peach came toward her, she darted down the hall and out of sight. "Get back here, you little monkey!" Peach called. "You naughty bedbug! You albino candy corn!"

"Hello?" Lonnie said, clearly confused.

With a sigh, Peach turned back to the living room. She just didn't have the energy to chase after Buster right now to try to get back whatever she'd stolen from wherever. Probably a piece of underwear or a dirty sock—sick little weirdo—but whatever.

A few minutes later Peach walked into her bedroom to get a

CD. With the phone tucked under her ear, she turned on her lamp, which had a sheer pink scarf draped over it for a warm, moody effect. Her end tables were really milk crates that were turned upside down and covered with tapestries, and her walls were splattered with blue and green, deep raspberry pink, silver, and more—all remnants of paintings she'd been working on.

Right now she started hanging back up the clothes she'd tossed carelessly on the bed that morning.

"Okay, well, I'll let you get back to your romantic getaway," Peach said.

"No, don't go yet," Lonnie pleaded. "I'm bored. I'm just waiting for my notes to dry so I can make sure they're still readable."

"Who cares about your dumb notes?" Peach said just as she heard Dominick say, "Will you give us a break with the damn dissertation already?" Pursing her lips, Peach thought, *She's blowing this already and it's barely even begun—she definitely needs some help.* "Lonnie, you're in Aruba with the love of your life, and you're both already naked. Wake up, would you?"

"Hmm . . ." Lonnie said thoughtfully, "you have a point. . . ."

Just then Buster ran by Peach's open door, this time with something silky from Peach's floor trailing in her mouth. How had Peach missed her stealing that? She should get it back before Buster ate it—no, that wasn't fair; Buster wouldn't actually eat it. She'd just chew it into Swiss cheese, then unself-consciously spit it back out and bury it under the armchair. "Buster, come! *Come!*"

After a pause, Peach tried again, then sighed. "O-kay. Buster, *don't* come—good girl." Just then Lonnie told Dominick to come closer, and she was using her supersweet voice, which Peach interpreted as her cue to bail out on the conversation. "Hey, I'm hanging up now. Call me tomorrow—no, wait. On second thought, *don't* call me. I mean it, Lonnie. Don't call anyone unless it's an emergency. Now go get busy with your husband." Once they said goodbye and Peach tossed the cordless phone onto her disheveled bed, she realized it was quiet in her apartment . . . *too* quiet.

"Buster?" she called, and ducked out of her bedroom. She turned her head both ways, checking for signs of the puppy as she walked down the hall into the living room. Nothing. Next she rounded the bend to the kitchen and flipped on the light. At first she didn't see Buster anywhere. But then she spotted a ball of fluff—Buster's small round booty—hunkered down in the corner of the room. "Buster, come here, please," Peach said politely, but the puppy didn't even turn to look up.

"Buster," she said again, stepping closer, but Buster was busy. Chewing something again. "What have you got there?" she asked, coming even closer.

Just as she got within a few inches, Buster darted through her legs and all but slid across the tile floor. Peach sprang into action. She lurched to catch her, but missed. Damn, she was fast! Once Buster was out of the kitchen she started laps around the coffee table, then outran Peach down the hall, and into BeBe's room. "Come here!" Peach called, flying across BeBe's bed to grab Buster before she slipped by again, and then—

"I *got* you!" she yelped as half her body spilled onto the floor. Dangling off the bed, she caught Buster by the waist—did dogs have waists?—and brought one hand to the dog's mouth. "Give it up, girl," she said, as she pried open Buster's jaws. "Oh, my God!" Peach nearly shrieked as she pulled a small plastic cylinder of orange paint out. *Holy shit!* Buster had had the whole thing in her mouth!

Thank *God* it was unopened and still tightly sealed! "Oh, my God . . ." Peach said again, as tears stung the backs of her eyes and a turbulent wave of emotions washed over her, hard and fast. Profound relief and tenderness flooded her chest at once as she scooped Buster all the way up off the floor and onto the bed. She hugged her so tightly that Buster mewled softly, and Peach relaxed her embrace. *Dear God, if she'd eaten that paint, would she have died?*

How could Peach be so careless as not to be watching her better? How could she be so self-absorbed? Acute guilt and disgust mingled with regret as two tears spilled over and striped her cheeks.

Surprisingly, Buster didn't resist being held, as she usually did, and simply sagged in Peach's arms. Nearly giving Peach a heart attack must've tired the little puppy out.

In a matter of moments Buster snuggled her face into the crook of Peach's elbow and sighed. More tears burned Peach's eyes. Dogs *sighed*? Why hadn't she known that? And why did that simple fact amaze her? Fill her with wonder?

Buster began snoring, and the light, wheezy sound tugged at Peach's heart. Hugging her more tightly, but also tenderly, she rocked her in her arms. "Oh, sweetheart," she said softly, "I *promise*—I promise I'll take better care of you from now on."

There was a hard knock on the door.

It startled her; then she remembered she'd ordered pizza over thirty minutes ago. "Who is it?" Peach said, carrying Buster, who dug her nose even deeper into Peach's elbow as they both approached the door.

"Pizza here," a man with a foreign accent said through the door. Okay, she could smell pizza on the other side, so she would believe him, and when she looked through the peephole she saw that the box said, *Mama Giada*—it all checked out. Sliding one hand off Buster, she opened up and said, "Thanks, you can just set it on the floor." He gave her an odd look, which she ignored, and handed him some money from the front pocket of her paint-stained overalls. Once she pushed the pizza box all the way inside with her foot, she started to close the door, when another knock on it startled her.

"Hey, Peach . . ." It was BeBe's ex-boyfriend, John, nudging the ajar door all the way open with his hairy fingers. Oh, *please*. Not to be a bitch, but Peach and Buster were having a moment here, and John was a major third wheel. Also, his presence only confirmed that he was starting his pathetically predictable pattern all over again—getting BeBe confused, then punking out when it came to being an actual man.

Swallowing a sigh, Peach forced herself to be pleasant. "Hi, John, how are you? Actually, BeBe's not here right now."

"Oh?" he said with a slight edge of panic in his voice. "Where is she?"

Peach wanted to say, *Out on a hot date with someone who's not you.* In fact, it even would've thrilled her to fib and say, *Out with a sexy musician named Luke who's a lot older than you.* But she didn't want to take a chance that it would jinx BeBe's chances with the V-man, who still hadn't called her back. Instead, Peach opted for the simple truth. "She's at work, I think."

John made exaggerated sniffing motions with his nose. Each one caused his unibrow to crease, like a caterpillar doing ab crunches. Finally he said, "Is that a pizza you got there?"

"No, it's a rack of lamb."

"Huh? Ohh, right. Good one," he said, then used one finger to lift the box lid up an inch or two. "Hey, what do you got on that—are those 'shrooms?"

Peach barely held back a grimace. *What a dork!* Yet . . . for BeBe's sake, she'd be nice. "Yeah, mushrooms and onions. So anyway—"

"Man, that looks awesome. I love pizza."

Welcome to the human race; you're still not getting any. He waited a few more seconds, and Peach had the sincere feeling he was waiting for a pity slice. *Not gonna happen, Unibrow Boy.* "Well, so, like I said, I think BeBe's at work," Peach said to break the stalemate.

"Oh. Well. Maybe I'll go stop by McMurphy's and say hi," he said noncommittally.

"Mmm-hmm, okay," Peach replied, nodding, staying planted at the open front door so John wouldn't come farther inside and try to flip on ESPN. When John kept lingering around the pizza, Peach threw in, "They have *'shrooms* there, too," as encouragement.

Finally John left.

Peach couldn't believe that Buster was actually too zonked to lift her head for pizza, but then, it had been a busy night. She'd walked her earlier; Buster had let loose on her buzzes; then the dog had had a brush with death—plus she'd forged a newfound bond with Peach, who was still reeling with guilt.

Twenty minutes later, when she was on the sofa, the pizza box open on the coffee table, a can of soda in hand, and Buster sleeping beside her on the couch, Peach thought about how lucky she'd been that Buster hadn't gotten into that paint tube. How lucky she was to have Buster, *period*. And how close she'd come to having to share her dinner with John.

Life was truly blessed.

Now if only BeBe would find someone worthy of her . . . someone who could be mature, and loving, and see what a total gem she was. If only she could move on, once and for all, and forget about something that was never going to work. . . .

Come to think of it, that was excellent advice for Peach to take, too.

Chapter Eighteen

By Friday morning Millennium was buzzing with theories about Dennis. He still hadn't come in to work, and he wasn't answering his home phone. Since Dennis wasn't part of the cell phone revolution, there didn't seem to be any other way to contact him—especially with his daughter and ex-wife still away on their trip. The most popular consensus was that Dennis had taken a vacation himself and forgotten to mention it, just as he had done several months back.

Of course, Peach and Adam had concluded something along those lines, too—except they were pretty certain that whatever trip Dennis had taken, it had been of an impulsive, romantic nature, and that Joan had gone with him.

When Peach recalled how infatuated Dennis had been after his first date with Joan, and what that other waitress at Mackie's had said about Joan's goofy behavior on Sunday morning, it all seemed to fit. But Peach hadn't shared her conclusions with the rest of the staff, because it just seemed too personal a speculation to spread around the office. What she really wanted was for Dennis to return soon so that *he* could share the news, so that he could explain things for himself and assure everyone that he was fine.

Late that afternoon, Peach took Dennis's mail over to his desk to keep his mail bin from completely overflowing. As she set the stack down on his blotter, Dennis's phone rang. Her heart jumped. Startled at first, Peach looked at the phone and blinked. But then she realized: It might be Dennis! Leave it to him not to remember anyone's phone number at work but his own.

Eagerly, she snatched up the receiver. "Hello?"

"Yes, hello, I'm looking for Mr. Dennis Emberson," a female voice said, sounding polite but tentative, and Peach thought, *Hell, who* isn't *looking for Dennis Emberson?*

"Um, he's not here; can I take a message?" Peach asked, hiding her palpable disappointment as she reached for a pink slip from the message pad beside his phone. Damn it, she'd really hoped it was Dennis so she could confirm that everything was fine—that he and Joan had eloped in Vegas or whatever they'd done—and then she could go back and tell the rest of the staff not to worry.

"My name's Patty," the woman said. "I found Mr. Emberson's wallet on the street on Monday, and his business card was inside of it. I'm so sorry I'm just getting a chance to call now; it's been such a crazy week, and I kept forgetting."

His wallet? Peach thought, confused. He'd lost his wallet?

But wait. . . . Like a shot of fear, her heart kicked up. Unease slithered into her skin, skittered along her nerves. If Dennis had lost his wallet, and Patty had found it Monday, then that meant Dennis had lost it at least five days ago. Where could he have been between Monday and now that didn't require a wallet? Or at least some of its contents? Credit cards, bank cards, driver's license . . .

With some trepidation, Peach asked, "Where did you find it?"

"Right on the corner of Boylston and Arlington," Patty said.

Oh, this was definitely not good—especially considering that Dennis lived outside the city, so if Patty had found his wallet that far from his home, chances were he'd never even gotten home. And considering that she'd found it five whole days ago . . .

Oh, no . . . oh, no . . .

Now she was panicking. A thick, hard lump lodged in her throat as her heart banged feverishly against her ribs. Twisting the phone cord around her fingers, gnarling it and not even noticing, Peach tried to think what possible *good* explanation there could be for all this.

"Hello?" Patty said. "Are you still there?"

"Yes, I'm here," Peach replied, and swallowed hard, almost painfully.

"I can mail the wallet to the address on his driver's license, but I figured since I'm going to be downtown today, I'd just drop it off to him."

"Yes, that's good," she improvised quickly. "Um, just leave it with the security guard in the lobby—he'll make sure Dennis gets it." What good would it do to send Dennis's wallet to his house if he wasn't even there to get it? And anyway, she wanted to get more information herself. Maybe there would be something in the wallet—some appointment he'd scribbled, some receipt from purchasing an airline ticket—*something*.

Yet Peach couldn't shake the feeling that there was no way Dennis could go on a jaunt—romantic or otherwise—without his wallet. In fact, the only thing she knew for sure at this point was that she needed to talk to Adam.

Twenty minutes later Peach was using the phone at Adam's desk, perched on top of it beside his printer, rolling her eyes and making gagging gestures as she talked to an unhelpful detective on the other end. When she spoke, she kept her voice low, because she didn't want to worry her coworkers about Dennis any more than they might already be.

Okay—fine. She also didn't relish reminding everyone that possibly the last person to see Dennis Emberson (*alive?*) was the same woman Peach had fixed him up with. The same woman whom Peach basically knew zilch about. On the one hand, Kate had said Joan sounded happy and in love, but on the other, what if she was happy because she'd just made a fresh kill? Shutting her eyes, she tried to block out the frightening pictures her imagination was conjuring, and she told herself to calm down—*please calm down*—but "herself" wasn't interested.

Her stomach churned queasily, roiling with anxiety and guilt, even though there was always the possibility that Joan had had nothing to do with the fact that Dennis Emberson had disappeared. In fact, why on earth was Peach assuming there was a connection? There was absolutely no proof of one.

And yet . . .

If Joan liked Dennis, and she hadn't seen him or talked to him since their last date, wouldn't she get in touch with Peach to ask her what was going on? After all, Peach had been the matchmaker. No, but then again . . . since Peach and Joan barely knew each other, it stood to reason that if Joan didn't hear from Dennis, she'd just assume he was blowing her off—case closed.

Still, it was a disturbingly odd coincidence that Joan had picked that particular weekend to quit her job at Mackie's.

Basically, Peach had no clue what to think. And she'd been desperately hoping that if she called the police, she'd get some reassurance—that all her questions would be answered. But Detective Harry Mays was clearly not from that particular school of civil service; he was apparently more partial to the enigmatic-asshole school.

"We'll look into it; the department thanks you for the information," he repeated flatly.

"But what does that *mean*?" Peach nearly wailed, because he'd been trying to pacify her with that "the department thanks you" crap for the last fifteen minutes. "You're gonna send a search party out, aren't you?"

"A search party?" Mays echoed incredulously, then snickered.

"Well, he's been missing more than forty-eight hours; isn't that the drill?"

"Normally, yes, but nobody's filed an official complaint."

"What do you think *I'm* doing right now?" she asked, getting even more frustrated.

"And what did you say was your relation to this person?"

"We're coworkers," she said; then to give herself more credibility, she added, "And I'm his friend!"

"I see. Well, there's no missing-persons report here from his family."

"He lives alone," Peach protested, "and his daughter and ex-wife are away right now on a trip." Damn it, why hadn't she asked Dennis exactly where his flaky ex was taking their daughter, Nan? Then she would have something a little more specific to offer than "the wilderness."

Was it possible that Rachel's sister, Alice, might know? Before their falling-out, she and Nan had been best friends. The notion popped out of Peach's head as fast as it had popped in, because Detective Asshole was asking her a question.

"Do you spend a lot of time with him outside of work?"

"Well . . . no," Peach conceded. She could hardly fudge "a lot" when the truth was none at all. Still . . . what was his point?

"Then I suppose you're not really in a position to judge if he's legitimately missing or has simply gone away on a trip. Maybe he just quit the job but didn't have the guts to tell anyone."

"No way," Peach said with a scoff, and shook her head at Adam, who was sitting in his chair, looking on quietly and supportively.

"It's possible," Detective Mays said calmly, clearly unimpressed. "But don't worry. We'll check it out. Why don't you give me his address and phone number, and we'll have an officer go down there and see if everything's all right? We wouldn't want him lying on the floor dead or something."

Peach's mouth dropped in horror. Was this how they comforted someone who was worried? Or was this all part of the infamous "black humor" cops used to cope with morbidly depressing fatalities?

Okay—that wasn't helping, either. *Oh, Dennis,* she prayed, *please, please be okay. . . .*

After she told the police officer everything she could think of about Dennis, though he seemed interested only in his name and address at the moment, she mentioned the blind date he'd gone on, and the fact that she couldn't locate *that* woman, either. "And what's her name?" he asked.

"Joan Smith."

He paused, then said, "John Smith? You serious?"

"Joan," Peach emphasized, thinking, *Yeah, the woman's name is John—where do they find these people?*

"Joan Smith," he echoed. "For real?"

"Yes—believe it or not, some people are actually named Smith."

"Okay, okay," he said. "And what's her address?"

"Well . . . I don't know exactly. But she lives either in Boston or the greater Boston area . . . or somewhere in Massachusetts, anyway." Then he asked for Joan's phone number, not sounding too impressed by the address info. "I'm not exactly sure about that, either," Peach admitted, biting her lower lip as warm color drifted to her cheeks. Boy, she'd really fucked up this time, setting Dennis up with a woman she knew nothing about. "I mean, I tried to look her up in the phone book," Peach explained feebly, "but there was no listing for 'Joan'—there were some for 'John,' of course, and some other male names. Also, there were a bunch for 'J. Smith,' but only a few of those answered, and there was no Joan there, so—"

"And where does she work?" he asked impatiently.

"Let's see . . . well, she used to work at Mackie's Diner, downtown, but then she quit." Expelling a sigh, she finished, "To be honest, I have no idea."

After a short pause he grunted and said, "I'll see what I can do. But they're both adults, and so far no family or next of kin have filed missing-persons reports. You know, there's no law against taking off on a vacation or something without telling your coworkers."

Placing a palm to her forehead, she swallowed a scream of frustration. "But Officer—*without his wallet?* And don't you think it's odd that he lost his wallet and didn't even report it?"

"Most people don't; they just cancel their credit cards. But like I said, the department thanks you for the information."

"Can I talk to someone else?" she blurted, suddenly remembering the homicide detective who'd worked with Lonnie to solve a murder three years ago. "Joe Montgomery," she finished. "I'll wait."

"You know Joe?" Mays said, sounding surprised.

"Yes, I do." *Sort of . . .*

"Well, how about that? But actually, Joe's not here. He's away on his honeymoon till next week."

"What? Who goes on their honeymoon in the beginning of December?" Peach yelped with frustration.

"People who get married at the end of November?" Mays answered flatly. He was so goddamn smug, and worst of all, he was right. Logic and reason had abandoned Peach at the moment; she'd officially gone around the bend, sick with worry, expecting the National Guard to go find Dennis so *she* could feel better.

After she hung up with Detective Harry Mays, Peach rubbed the heels of her hands over her eyes. "Oh, Adam," she said plaintively, "I don't have a good feeling about this."

"What happened?" he asked evenly. As always his smooth, honeyed voice was calm, reasonable—it was so comforting.

After relaying the details of her conversation with Mays, she said, "But we can't just sit here and do nothing!" Then she hit her palm on her thigh and hopped off Adam's desk, bursting with resolve. "That's it. I'm going to Dennis's house to look around. Right now."

"But wait," Adam said, rising from his chair to follow her out of his cubicle and down the hall. "You just said the police are going to go over."

"Oh, please, they don't know what they're doing," she said with a wave of her hand.

"And what if there's no answer?" Adam said, still following her as she hurried down the hall and around the bend to her desk. "What, are you gonna break the door down?"

"I don't know what I'm gonna do," she said truthfully, and snatched her coat and scarf off her partition wall, almost dragging the string of chili-pepper lights down, too.

"Wait, Peach, I think you should just let the police handle this," Adam warned, reaching out to cup her shoulder. She froze at the contact and glanced up into his hazel eyes. "And what about work? It's only eleven A.M."

"Oh, right . . . well, just tell Robert that I'm out brainstorming on a new concept—you know, tell him I'm wandering around the city, part of my 'artistic process.' That ought to work."

"Peach, wait," he said as he followed her out of the Millennium doors and to the elevators. The hall overlooked the lobby below like a balcony, and vaguely Adam heard the chattering of people crossing to and from the Daily Grind and Au Bon Pain. He told himself that he shouldn't be so worried about her . . . but he was. He didn't want her getting hurt, or going alone, and also he felt guilty. Why did he have to make that joke about Joan being a homicidal maniac? Why did he have to blow up at Peach for her meddling? Right now she was worried that he'd been right on both counts, and he knew she was blaming herself for whatever had happened to Dennis.

"I *can't* wait," she said now. "And can you go online and try to find out where Joan lives? You know, just work your magic!"

"What magic—*Google?*" he asked, scrunching his face with incredulity. "I don't know anything about her!" He could hardly do much more than that under those circumstances.

"Just do whatever you can, okay—please?" She tilted her head and leveled him with the sweetest look of entreaty, her big blue eyes blinking with feeling, her mouth pursed in concern, and then she offered him a conciliatory smile and gave his biceps a soft, friendly shake. Her touch was warm and gentle, and he savored the contact, though it was fleeting. Then she said, "Thanks," and turned to go.

Adam was left standing there, wishing she'd stayed, feeling the weight of her absence, like the air had been sucked out of the room.

Chapter Nineteen

Adam's so-called magic was a bust. Through his Internet searches, he hadn't been able to find out anything about Joan, but had learned quite a bit about many *other* people named Joan Smith. There was a Joan M. Smith who appeared often for her bobsledding record, and a Joan Q. Smith who was working toward a degree in geophysics, but something told Adam that neither was Joan, the ex-waitress from Mackie's.

Meanwhile, Peach had called him about half an hour ago from her cell phone to tell him that he was right—Dennis's house had been locked and had appeared deserted. One thing that gave her a glimmer of hope was the fact that his car was missing. She said it wasn't parked in the driveway, and she didn't see it when she stood on tiptoe to look inside his garage windows. So maybe Dennis *had* gone somewhere, totally of his own accord.

However without his wallet, his driver's license, or a word to anyone, Peach still wasn't buying it.

Adam hated that Peach felt responsible. The fact was, even if something bad had happened to Dennis, it probably had nothing to do with his date with Joan—and even if it *had*, he didn't want Peach to blame herself. Her heart was in the right place, but since she'd mentioned once that she hated trite platitudes, he wasn't about to console her with that one.

Now she was on her way back to the office. There was something Adam could do that might help them figure this out, but damn, he *really* wasn't a big fan of the idea. It would put him in a precarious position, since it would involve using his network access in a way that wasn't technically ethical.

Yet . . . all he could think about was how important all of this was to Peach, and how much better she would feel if they had some answers—preferably some uplifting ones.

That settled it then. It might cross his personal sense of ethics, but for Peach he'd do it.

"I hope nobody catches me doing this," he remarked a few hours later, when he and Peach were accessing Dennis's e-mail account from Adam's computer.

"Don't worry; most people have gone home," Peach said, checking her watch, though she already knew it was after five. "I'm so glad you thought of this!" she said, smiling and looking more radiantly herself than she had all day. He was sitting at his desk while she stood beside him, resting her hand on the back of his chair. "What would I do without you?" she added, and leaned down to give him a quick, one-armed hug.

Sweat broke out on his neck. Suddenly his tie felt too tight, and his palms itched to touch her, to grab her, to haul her over the arm of the chair and into his lap. *No, not now,* he thought, trying to command his mind not to think of these things. He was trying like hell not to get blatantly aroused by her closeness—that distinctive scent of hers didn't help matters, or the thick, choking heat that always seemed to billow and sweat between their bodies.

Glancing up at her as she stood over him didn't do anything to break the spell. He could tell she'd been licking one of the blue-raspberry Blow Pops he'd left on her desk that morning, because her lips had an almost violet stain on them now. Inexplicably, the bluish effect was dark and smoldering; all he wanted right now was to kiss her, lick inside her mouth, to have her open those violet lips wide for him.

As his eyes traveled up to her pale blue eyes, he found her looking back at him—*watching* him. She was studying his mouth, her eyes a little glazed as if she were deep in thought. As she bit her full bottom lip, Adam swallowed hard.

Abruptly he turned his face to focus back on his monitor.

He inhaled a deep breath through his nostrils, then let it out. *Focus, asshole. Peach needs you to figure this out.*

"Okay . . . let's see here," he said as he accessed Dennis's e-mail in box, scanning the list of messages from the past week. "Well, there's been no activity on his e-mail account since that last Friday afternoon that he was here. But this is just his work e-mail; I don't know what he uses at home."

"No, Dennis doesn't strike me as the e-mail type. This is probably the only one he uses. Open the most recent message."

He did. It was from Grace, reminding Dennis that he had a budget meeting scheduled with Robert for the following week. "Hmm . . . what about the other messages that Friday?" Peach asked, as Adam opened them one by one. They all appeared to be standard business fare, including several brief e-mails from Brenda pertaining to invoices, both new and outstanding.

Next Adam checked Dennis's sent mail. His replies to Brenda consisted of a few words each, simply providing answers to her questions. "Here's something that was sent to Scott," Adam remarked, opening an e-mail from last Friday with the subject heading "stock info." Both he and Peach scanned the message quickly—it was a brief note apologizing for the stock tips Dennis had given Scott, which had subsequently backfired. In the e-mail, Dennis mentioned that his cousin, the stockbroker in New York City, had given him some truly terrible advice and he really hoped there were no hard feelings. "Sucks for Scott," Adam mentioned offhandedly.

With a nod, Peach said, "So much for e-mail. Now what?" Sighing, she shut her eyes for a second to think, and moved over to lean against Adam's desk. She accidentally knocked over his stack of mail, which had been lined up exactly with the edge of the desk. Envelopes and fliers swept onto the floor and fanned out on the dark golden carpet. "Oh, I'm sorry!"

"Don't worry—just my mail," Adam said.

They both bent down to get it at the same time. With her head close to his, he could smell her hair. He wanted to bury his face in it, run his fingers through it; in fact, for the first time, he really came close to kissing her. . . .

"Oh, my God!" Peach said, picking up a fluorescent-yellow piece of paper. "This is it!"

"What's it?" Adam said, shaking himself out of his aroused trance—yet again.

"Look!" she said, handing him the flier. "Monkeyville, the new comedy club on Arlington Street." She took the flier from him and smacked it with the back of her hand. "I'll bet anything this is where Dennis went with Joan on Saturday night!"

"Where do you get that?" Adam asked skeptically.

"Because these fliers have been flooding this office since we moved here. We all get them in with our mail—like three or four a day—and let's face it, Dennis is an accountant; he's not that creative. Plus, it isn't far from the corner of Boylston and Arlington, where he lost his wallet sometime last weekend. It just stands to reason that *this* is where he took Joan."

"Okay . . ." Adam said, thinking it over. "Even if he did go there, what now?"

She shrugged. "I don't know. Maybe somebody there will remember him; maybe they can tell us if he and Joan were getting along or if they left together—just anything to help us piece together his whereabouts. It's a start, anyway," she added, maybe a little defensively, because her plan did sound kind of threadbare—but hey, she was desperate. Checking her watch again, she said, "Okay, the flier says they open at seven. So that gives us over an hour to kill before we head over."

Adam stopped short, jarred by that "we" part.

Then Peach tilted her head and said, "What's wrong, Quinny? Better plans?"

A laugh slipped out—he couldn't help it—and he shook his head. "No, no, nothing better to do."

"Oh, I'm touched," she said glibly, and patted his cheek. For the first time that day he saw that saucy attitude, that confident smile, that fierce lioness she liked to think she was.

Monkeyville was a zoo. After work Peach and Adam had grabbed dinner at the Pru, then scooted down to Boylston Street, which was lined with cute restaurants, bars, and shops. At this hour, sidewalks were filled mostly with young professionals mingling after work, as well as the requisite segment of any urban population: thirty-nine-year-old men still trying to live the dream.

"I think Scott lives around here," Peach remarked casually, recalling that Scott had mentioned getting a new apartment nearby about a month or so ago.

Meanwhile, Adam tensed up. *How the hell does she know where Scott lives?* he thought with an edge of jealousy.

When they finally got inside, Adam noticed right away that half the guys there were checking Peach out. She acted oblivious to it, didn't even smile or pay any attention, and then he realized . . . she *wasn't* acting. Jesus, couldn't she see how guys stared at her? Looked twice on the street sometimes? She honestly seemed to have no clue.

"Now I see why it's so crowded!" she said, nearly yelling to be heard over the loud music that blared through the club, and pointed to the banner that hung above the stage toward the back. It read, *Amateur Night—Tonight!*

Surprisingly bright inside, Monkeyville had a stage set back from the rest of the floor. A fat metallic railing formed a dome around the seating area, which was filled with tables and chairs. Strips of neon-pink lights crisscrossed across the entire ceiling; the bar stretched along the far right wall, and behind it was a huge mirror engraved with an outline of a huge monkey head. Kind of *Planet of the Apes* meets *The Jetsons* meets a motel vacancy sign.

"Amateur night, what a treat," Adam said flatly as he surveyed the place. "Maybe if we're lucky we'll catch some prop comics while we're here."

With a giggle, Peach agreed. "Good point; let's make this quick."

Adam watched as it took less than two seconds for Peach to get the bartender's attention. He was a huge, ugly guy who smiled sleepily at her. "Hey, there, what can I get ya?"

"Hi," Peach said, then held up the photo of Dennis and Nan that she'd taken off Dennis's desk. "Can you tell us if you remember this man? I think he might've been here last Saturday night, and now he's missing."

"Oh, man, I'm sorry; I wasn't working on Saturday," he said apologetically. "But let me go get Eddie; he might've been here then. I'll be right back, just one second, okay?" he added—more like groveled, Adam thought as he rolled his eyes. Then he leaned his lower arm on the bar.

"Thanks," Peach said, and began rapping her fingers on the bar while she waited. Soon the bartender returned with another guy. Smiling broadly, he asked Peach how he could help her. Once she explained the situation and showed Dennis's picture, she said, "If he was here, he was probably with a woman." Then she described Joan's appearance in detail.

The part about the high-top Reeboks clicked with Eddie, who snapped his fingers and pointed, and said, "Yeah, yeah, I remember now! Right, they got drinks here and went to sit down over there." He pointed toward the left side of the club.

"Oh, great!" Peach said, eyes lighting up as she turned to Adam. "We're finally getting somewhere!"

Smiling back, he touched her lower back supportively, then asked Eddie, "Do you remember anything else?"

"Yeah, now that you mention it . . . I remember that they seemed pretty into each other. In fact, I remember thinking that they were kinda old, but it was kinda cool."

"Did they leave together?" Adam asked, wanting the information, but selfishly also wanting to remind Peach that he was helping, wanting her to remember that he was there.

"Crap, I don't know," Eddie said with a shrug.

"Think," Peach urged. "Did you notice anything bizarre or deviant?"

"Huh?"

"What she means is, did anything strike you as unusual?" Adam spoke up. "Or did you notice if they left together?"

"Yeah, what he said," Peach agreed.

With another shrug, Eddie replied, "To tell you the truth, there was kind of a lotta commotion at one point—one of the comedians really bombed, and it was chaotic. I wish I could tell you more, but I wasn't paying that much attention. But like I said, they looked into each other. You know, like, sexy."

Peach had the feeling that was going to be as good as it got. Next Eddie tracked down Bethany, the waitress for the left-side seating on Saturday night, and she concurred that Dennis and Joan had seemed happy together. Like Eddie, what made Dennis and Joan memorable to Bethany was their age; they'd stood out a bit in a crowd of mostly twenty-somethings.

And there was something else. Bethany recalled Dennis reaching right for the bill when she'd brought it to their table. If Dennis had paid, that meant that he'd definitely lost his wallet sometime after the show.

When they finally left Monkeyville, the night felt quiet. It wasn't really, because it was Friday night and the streets were overrun with clunky taxicabs, chatty people, and laughter—yet somehow, when Peach and Adam stood across from it all, beside the Public Gardens, looking at each other, it truly felt as if it were just the two of them out tonight.

The moon glowed hazily against the misty, blue-black sky. A bristling wind cut sharply across their faces, and Peach shivered. Hugging herself, she wished she could hug Adam for warmth instead, wished it were all as simple as that.

"So we're back to square one," Peach commented.

"Yes—square one is getting very comfortable," Adam said dryly.

"I know, right. This is so frustrating! But I'm not giving up yet. I'll figure out our next scheme soon, I promise."

"Can't wait," he said with a lopsided grin.

She smiled at him. "So what are you doing for Christmas?" she asked, partly from curiosity, partly as a ploy to drag out the evening a little longer. Now that their errand was done, she knew that Adam had no real reason to linger.

"Jesus, I don't even know," he said with a sigh. "Normally—" He stopped himself because, of course, normally his family was together at their house in Manchester. "I don't know. I guess I'll go see my mom, who's at my aunt's, and then go to my dad's. Or the other way around, whichever," he said briefly, and let it drop at that, even though Peach could see his face darken. She hadn't meant to upset him again, so she switched gears.

"Well, you're welcome to come to my house if you get bored. Oh—not that your family is boring!" she said with a laugh. "I just meant—"

"No, no, thanks for the offer," he said, smiling, and then reached out affectionately to touch her arm. "Really, I appreciate it."

They just looked at each other, only a foot away, and Peach found herself almost swaying forward. She wasn't sure if she really was or if she was only imagining it, but Adam's mouth seemed to be getting closer . . . and closer. . . . Her lips parted—

A cab careened past them, nearly coming up onto the curb. Startled, they both jumped to the side, and a litany of beeps followed as the taxi straddled two lanes. Protectively Adam brought his right arm across Peach's shoulders. "You okay?" he asked, looking down at her, his eyes searching hers.

"I'm fine," she replied, still a little dazed, thinking, *I almost kissed him!* Slowly Adam's hand slid down her back, and then back to his side. She blew out a breath she didn't realize she'd been holding, still shaken by the cab and by the reality of what she'd almost done. In that moment it might have seemed like no one else existed but the two of them—and that nothing else existed beyond this darkened street—but the fact of the matter was: Robin *did* exist. She was real. And, Peach promised herself, she wouldn't forget again.

Chapter Twenty

"Can we go yet?"

"We've been here for two minutes!" Peach said with a laugh as she and BeBe stepped through the heavy oak door of Ellen Weinberg's house and wiped their feet on the mat. It was Saturday afternoon—or as BeBe called it, day six of V-man watch—because Luke Vermann still hadn't called, but she was clinging to her last scraps of hope.

BeBe hadn't planned to come to Ellen Weinberg's birthday party, despite her mom's relentless guilt trips about how Ellen was "practically a godmother," but she had something important to discuss with her. She'd asked Peach to come, too, and Peach had borrowed her dad's car so they wouldn't have to take the T, then walk through the fresh layer of snow that had covered the ground that morning.

And now BeBe, who'd begged Peach to go, already wanted to leave.

But she truly couldn't leave, because she'd come with a purpose. A tragic and terrible purpose. BeBe intended to take the Weinster up on her offer for a trial period, and ask her to find Buster another home. As much as she cared for the puppy, BeBe felt overwhelmed by Buster's—*ahem*—spunk. God, it killed Peach even to contemplate, especially after how much closer she'd felt to the puppy over the last week, but technically Buster *was* BeBe's dog.

They'd thought they'd puppy-proofed the apartment before Buster's arrival, but after the incident with the paint tube, Peach had worked double-time to make sure there was nothing toxic or dangerous within reach of the dog. Plus, Buster had been coming around. Now when the dog would drift off to sleep, she would curl onto Peach's lap, and when she wanted to pee, she'd make a mewling sound and look up with her big black raisin eyes, rather than just going on the hardwood floor. It was funny the things in life you came to appreciate. . . .

And now, whenever Peach took Buster for a walk around the block, Buster pranced alongside, while Peach sang quietly to her the little song she'd made up: "She's a powdered munchkin / She looks like a doughnut 'cause she *is* one." Yes, they definitely had a nice rhythm going.

Of course, none of this changed the fact that she was still a hellion. And she'd gnawed the whole bottom of the red-silk-covered armchair into strips of fabric and white, pulled cotton. She'd even scratched the legs of BeBe's dark-brass night stand until they were streaked with shimmery gold lines, which sounded kind of pretty, but actually wasn't so hot.

Naturally, Peach had cried and pleaded with BeBe not to give Buster back, but BeBe insisted she was just too much of a handful. And ultimately, BeBe had the final say, because Ellen Weinberg had given the dog to her—this had been BeBe's wish. Peach could help, but working 9-5 everyday, she couldn't do it alone.

Besides, there was little doubt that the Weinster could find a puppy a better home than a shelter or the pound ever could. At least, that was what Peach had to keep reminding herself, because the neighbors had been grumbling, basically threatening to complain to the landlord if Buster didn't cut out the late-night barking and stop latching on to the ankles of every tenant that passed by. But apparently BeBe had decided that Buster was beyond help, and that was that.

So she'd practiced her spiel in the car ride over today. BeBe planned to make it clear: *My mother was not right; this has nothing to do with irresponsibility.* That it was just this particular puppy BeBe couldn't handle—and that few people *could* handle.

Nice knowing you, Buster. . . .

"You haven't even said hi to your mom yet," Peach pointed out. "Or chatted it up with the Weinster."

"Perfect—I'll go start the car."

"Get real," Peach said, grinning, then touched BeBe's shoulder and said, "Seriously—you know you don't have to do this. You can still change your mind."

After a thoughtful pause, BeBe said, "No, let's go. But don't be mad at me, okay?"

Peach said nothing.

Mrs. Weinberg's pad was palatial, yet for all its elegant opulence, it needed some sprucing up, in Peach's opinion. The ceilings were high, the entry foyer was huge and airy, the walls were barebones white, the artwork was sparse and flat. Peach thought it all could use some splash, some color, some joie de vivre . . . but she supposed it wasn't her place to say.

The butler, or "manservant," as he introduced himself, was disappointingly named Cliff, instead of Jeeves or Giles or Lynn (as in *Belvedere*). *Oh, well* . . . But it was just . . . how many manservants was Peach going to meet in her life?

Cliff led them through the foyer, around a steep white staircase, and into a large room filled with people. Everyone was chatting, walking around with plates of food and flutes of champagne, while tingling Muzak strummed faintly overhead. Kids were running around, too, a bunch of six-year-olds with cell phones, the usual.

As far as Peach knew, most of the Lydecker clan would be there today: BeBe's older sister, Yvonne (a bland academic who looked more like Ellen Weinberg's progeny than Ramona's), Yvonne's husband, Simon (infamous mooch, slippery eel, and Hugh Grant wannabe), and their young daughter, Kimberly (whom BeBe adored, but she worried that Yvonne and Simon were turning her "weird"). And BeBe's mom, Ramona, would be at the party stag, since BeBe's parents were divorced.

BeBe's dad lived in California with his second wife, and kept in only sporadic touch with his daughters, but mailed them money fairly often. This was a big part of how BeBe could afford to live in a beautiful Back Bay apartment working as a bartender.

"Oh, Bee, over here!"

Peach looked around and spotted Ramona about twenty feet away, waving over the heads of other guests. The Weinster was right beside her, with her usual cordial smile and stiff posture. Both women were in their late fifties. While Ramona was short and round with a helmet-head of hair dyed the color of Cinnamon Toast Crunch, the Weinster was tall and slim, with a cornsilk blond pageboy that never seemed to fall flat.

"Oh, good, you're finally here!" Ramona said, giving BeBe and Peach brief air kisses. "People have been asking about you, wondering where you've been."

"What people?" BeBe questioned, her gaze roving around the room. "I barely recognize anyone. Oh, happy birthday, Mrs. Weinberg!" she added, smiling at Ellen.

"Yeah, happy birthday," Peach said brightly. "Thanks for inviting me."

The Weinster was all smiles, and Ramona spoke again. "Bee, Yvonne was asking about you. She said she hasn't talked to you since Thanksgiving."

"Oh, yeah—where is Yvonne, anyway?"

"Upstairs using the restroom. Apparently she's been very busy at school lately." This was another thing BeBe and Peach had bonded about early on: Both their older sisters were ensconced in academia. While Lonnie taught freshman English and women's studies at Maine Bay, Yvonne taught math and statistics at a small private college in western Massachusetts. The kick of it was, as BeBe was fond of mentioning, Yvonne's husband, Simon, whom Yvonne had met while traveling through England and married within six months of knowing him, was now a full-time student there, getting his diploma for free, because he was married to a professor. It irritated BeBe to no end that Simon got not only U.S. citizenship and a free college education through Yvonne, but also got spending money to use "as needed" (assuming it was ever an imperative to go to Foxwoods).

"Yvonne said she tried calling you last week," Ramona remarked to BeBe. "Simon has a friend visiting from England, and Yvonne thought you two might hit it off."

"Oh, really?" BeBe replied with the deadpan enthusiasm that was usually reserved for things like car inspections or vacuuming behind the refrigerator. "Thanks but one dog's enough," she added sarcastically.

Conveniently, Ramona didn't seem to hear. "You should consider going," she urged. "If he's half as charming as Simon . . ." As her voice drifted off, BeBe grimaced and shot Peach a look. Peach had to stifle a laugh. It killed BeBe that after nearly ten years, Ramona was still taken in by Simon's suave, debonair, I'm-Pierce-Brosnan's-cousin routine.

"How are you girls enjoying motherhood?" Ellen Weinberg said, tipping her champagne flute to her artfully lined, rose-colored lips.

"Oh, yeah . . ." BeBe floundered. "About that . . ." *That* being the real reason for coming to the Weinster's party in the first place. *Buster.*

Peach's heart squeezed in her chest. *Don't say it; please don't say it. . . .*

Peach could tell that BeBe desperately wanted to have this talk without her mother looking on. She wanted to ask the Weinster to take Buster back, but she didn't want to come off as incapable—just ill equipped at the present time. *Good luck with that.* In the presence of maternal scrutiny, most people couldn't help but regress to self-conscious children, seeking both approval and rebellion in the same breath. "Well, first of all, let me tell you that we love her," BeBe said. "She's an absolute doll. Right, Peach?"

"Yeah, we call her Chuckie," Peach said glibly. BeBe twisted her lips and shot her a look. Her glare seemed to say, *Always the wiseass . . .*

"It was hard for me to give her up," the Weinster remarked,

waving one of her fine, delicate hands through the air. "Rochelle was so cute, you could just melt, even if her ears *were* too long."

According to whom? Peach thought irritably, but knew the answer anyway, so she held her tongue. But she did say, "Actually, we changed her name."

"Oh?" the Weinster said, arching a penciled-on eyebrow in surprise.

BeBe smiled. "Yeah, we named her Buster."

Ramona let out a short, incredulous laugh. "Bee, you can't be serious!"

"Why not?" BeBe said a little defensively.

"You can't name a girl *Buster*."

"This is 2005," Peach said breezily. "You can name a girl Lettucehead, if you want."

"I like the name Buster," BeBe added. "It reminded me of the imaginary dog I had when I was little, remember?"

"Vaguely . . . but wasn't that a male dog?"

"Mom, it wasn't *real*," BeBe said, rolling her eyes.

"Ramona, please, don't make a fuss," Ellen Weinberg said, tapping her friend on the arm. "If they didn't like my name, that's fine." Then she turned back to BeBe and Peach. "So this means you're keeping her? Not going to take me up on my offer for a trial period?"

"Oh, well . . . actually, about that . . ." BeBe stumbled. "Um, funny you should ask . . ."

"I knew it!" Ramona interrupted, as a smug smile creased the pudgy apples of her cheeks. "It's too much responsibility for you, right? I *told* you, you wouldn't be able to handle something like that, Bee."

"No, of course she's not too much responsibility," BeBe said quickly. "It's nothing like that. It's just—"

"I knew it," Ramona repeated, shaking her head, still smiling. Then she elbowed the Weinster and muttered, "Ellen, didn't I tell you?"

"Tell her *what*?" BeBe snapped, and Ramona dismissively replied, "Nothing, nothing." Peach held her tongue, but it took a mammoth effort—she wanted to tell Ramona to shove her self-righteous comments, even if, in this particular case, she happened to be right.

Glancing at BeBe, Peach saw her friend tightening her mouth in a way that said, *My mom is so goddamn annoying, I wish I could slap her—and why can't she just be proud of me?* So regression and maturity were presently battling for BeBe's soul.

For as long as Peach had known BeBe, she'd had a push-pull relationship with her mom; Ramona often told BeBe that she wasn't responsible enough to live on her own in the city, that she couldn't handle the dangers of working as a bartender (even at a family-style chain restaurant like McMurphy's). But to Peach it seemed obvious that Ramona was really just afraid—fearful that BeBe *was* capable enough, was okay and, in many ways, no longer needed her. A very alarming notion to someone as self-important as Ramona Lydecker. You didn't need to be a shrink to see that. And, predictably, the more Ramona tried to undercut BeBe's independence, the farther she seemed to drive her away.

"Bee, *there* you are."

They all turned to see BeBe's older sister, Yvonne, approaching the circle of women. She had her usual bored expression fixed on her face. (It wasn't bored as in, *This party is boring;* it was more like, *God, the plebeian masses bore me,* which was why it was her usual expression—it really fit all occasions). As she came closer, she offered a cursory smile with lips so thin they were barely perceptible. Her fine brown hair hung securely in a low ponytail, which only accentuated her angular jawline. From Peach's perspective, Yvonne was a fierce contrast to BeBe, who was round and full and vibrantly alive—even when she was still sulking.

"Hey, Yvonne. How are you?" BeBe said with a short wave.

"Fine, and you? Hi, Peach."

Peach said hello just as a little girl with long brown hair and big dark eyes came up behind Yvonne and tugged on the sleeve of her starchy blouse. This had to be BeBe's niece, Kimberly, whom Peach had heard about but never met.

"Hi, sweetie!" BeBe jumped in, smiling brightly.

"Hi, Aunt BeBe," she said softly, shyly eyeing Peach—a new face, a stranger.

Peach said hello, too, thinking, *Don't people hug in this family?* The Lydeckers' standoffish body language was surprising, especially when Peach compared it with the open, affectionate way her family interacted with each other. In that moment she realized how lucky she was. As for BeBe . . . it must be regression again, because take her out of this setting, and she was the cuddliest little bundle.

Kimberly tugged on her mother's sleeve again, then held up her empty paper cup and whispered something in Yvonne's ear. "Just put that in the rubbish bin," Yvonne said to her. "It's over there. . . . Pardon? Yes, the water closet is upstairs. Turn right at the top of the steps."

She motioned toward the distant entry foyer, where there was a steep, massive staircase, if Peach recalled. But obviously Yvonne didn't plan to escort her daughter there. She was apparently into self-reliance, also known as making your kid feel neglected at a party she was dragged to. Feeling a stab of pity for the little girl, Peach said, "Kimberly, I can show you—"

"Oh, no, Peach, you stay and talk," Ramona said, and took her granddaughter by the hand. "I'll take her. Come on, Kimberly. We'll be right back."

Ellen Weinberg also excused herself, and went to go mingle with her other guests.

After they left, Yvonne said, "Hey, Bee, did Mum tell you about Simon's friend, Fielding?"

Fielding? Peach thought, surprised, but hey, whatever. She grabbed a potato puff from an hors d'oeuvres tray that was making the rounds.

Yvonne continued, "Fielding's only in the States for another few weeks before his visa runs out. He told me he'd really like to meet you. I would've set this up sooner, but he just mentioned it out of the blue."

"Yeah, I'll bet," BeBe muttered, and a laugh burst from Peach's throat. Quickly she turned it into a cough to cover it up, then ordered a Shirley Temple from the next waiter she saw. She knew how BeBe's mind worked: Cynical already about men and their motives, BeBe wasn't likely to trust the sincerity of a guy whose visa was about to run out—*especially* if he was friends with Simon.

"Seriously, Bee," Yvonne said, continuing her pitch when BeBe failed to salivate at the prospect of Fielding, "he's quite an interesting bloke; you should really go out with him."

"No, thanks."

"I think you'd probably have a smashing time," Yvonne pressed.

"Why is it so important to you? I don't understand," BeBe said.

"Well, you don't have to get all *bristly*."

"So, Yvonne, Kimberly's really adorable!" Peach interjected, trying to break the tension and deflect Yvonne's focus. "Um, how old is she, again?"

"Ten," Yvonne answered, shifting her attention to Peach. "Actually, she has a birthday coming up next month. By the way, how's your flat? Are you two managing all right?"

Nice—successfully deflected.

"It's awesome," Peach said, chewing some of her crunchy potato puff. Instantly it left a salty taste in her mouth, so she looked around to see if her Shirley Temple was en route yet.

"Well, I'm just glad everything with the flat worked out in the end," Yvonne remarked, as she fiddled with her ponytail holder at the nape of her neck. "I mean, after John rather screwed you over, Bee. By the way, how is old John anyway—do you two still talk?"

"Sometimes," BeBe admitted with a shrug. "We're still friends . . . kind of."

"Really?"

"Yeah, what's wrong with that?" BeBe asked a little petulantly, and Peach shut her eyes, willing her friend to take the defensiveness down a notch. It seemed she got her back up at everything Yvonne and Ramona said to her. But then again . . . these were the Lydeckers. The way they communicated could probably put anyone in the mood to fight.

"I'm just surprised," Yvonne replied simply. "I mean that you're still friends. He was kind of a dim bulb—no offense."

"Now why would I be offended by that?" BeBe said sarcastically.

Just then Ramona returned from the bathroom with Kimberly, who exuded a bashful shyness that touched Peach's heart. She looked like she could use a friend.

"I like your dress," Peach said, smiling down at her.

"Oh . . . thanks," Kimberly mumbled, then smiled that awkward, crooked smile kids had when they ventured out of their comfort zone, even for a moment.

Finally, Peach's Shirley Temple arrived. "Thanks," she said, flashing an appreciative smile at the waiter, who smiled back and kept on going.

"Are you Aunt BeBe's friend?" Kimberly asked her.

"Yes, I'm her roommate, too," Peach said. "Hey, you should come visit us sometime!"

"Yeah . . . I wanted to go see her new apartment one time; then Mum said she couldn't take me that day."

"Oh. Well . . . you should definitely come by soon," Peach encouraged. When Kimberly nodded and turned her face toward her mother's hip, Peach tuned back to the grown-ups' conversation ("grown-ups" being a technicality, at best).

"Mum, I was just telling Bee about how John was all wrong for her," Yvonne said to Ramona.

"I agree; I never really saw that going anywhere. It seemed like more of a physical thing."

"What?" BeBe said, clearly confused. Casting a sideways look at Peach, she whispered, "What world am I in?"

Peach grinned—and not just because of Ramona's presumptuous conclusion, but also because the notion of using John purely for sex seemed laughable. Especially considering that BeBe had often complained about their sex life, saying John was too stingy with foreplay and too *efficient* with the main event. Plus he was so obsessed with sports, BeBe used to say the only way to get his attention during a game was to show up at his apartment wearing nothing but a foam finger and a smile.

John—a physical thing? Not likely.

"You know, Bee, sex is really not that important in a relationship," Yvonne said with a touch of self-righteousness (and the implicit admission that whatever action she was getting between the sheets with Simon was less than stellar).

BeBe just gritted her teeth and said, "Can we please change the subject?"

Just then a slim, well-dressed man with a pale complexion and short black hair came up behind Yvonne, ran his hand around her waist, and dropped a barely-there peck on her cheek. "Oh!" she said, surprised. "Simon, you startled me."

"Sorry about that, love," he said, ruffling his daughter's hair, then flashing a confident smile at Ramona, Peach, and BeBe. "Pardon me, ladies."

BeBe muttered a half-assed hello, and introduced Simon and Peach. Upon inspection, Peach noticed that Simon's hair didn't have a part. Literally. Not one hint of a part *anywhere*. How was that possible? With no discernible direction that his hair went in, it just lay atop his head like a perfectly tailored jet-black piece of sod. For some reason it seemed noteworthy . . . like his teeth, which were unique, at best. All the ones in front were varying degrees of yellow, and seemed to be vying for the position of most perpendicular to the gums.

Yet Peach had to admit there was something kind of charming about him. Something suave, cool, collected. It had to be the accent.

"Could you spot me a fifty, love?" Simon asked Yvonne now. "I want to meet up with Fielding for a bit."

Obviously disappointed, Yvonne said, "Oh, you're leaving already? Well, where are you two going?"

"Dunno, love. A pub or two."

Discreetly, Peach checked her watch. It was barely two in the afternoon. *Hmm . . . liar or lush?*

Yvonne slipped her hand into the pocketbook that hung at her side and handed him several bills. Then Simon asked for her car keys, too, reminding her that she and Kimberly could always get a ride back to the house with Ramona.

Meanwhile, Peach could feel the irritation vibrating off BeBe's body, but BeBe elbowed her in the side, in case she didn't catch the point.

Peach chatted a little more with Kimberly before she left with her mom and grandma, presumably to go circulate. Now it was just Peach and BeBe. Suddenly BeBe pointed and said, "There's the Weinster! I gotta go grab her before I lose my nerve."

You already have, Peach thought, waiting for her friend to realize it herself.

"Mrs. Weinberg!" BeBe called, and met her halfway with Peach trailing along.

"Yes? What is it, BeBe?" Ellen Weinberg asked, her thickly coated eyelashes blinking expectantly.

"Um . . ." BeBe began. "Listen . . . about Buster . . ."

"Oh, you know, that really is the most precious name," she said. "Now that I think about it, it's just so . . . eccentric."

"It is?" BeBe said. "Oh, well, thanks . . . but, um . . ."

"And I'm so glad you both bonded with her. You know, between you and me, I had the feeling your mother was wrong about this one. I just knew that once you laid eyes on Rochelle—oh, I mean Buster—you would fall in love with her. She really is so cute. And she has a little bit of fire in her, too," she added with a light-hearted laugh.

Biting her lower lip, Peach glanced at BeBe, watching her expression falter, seeing her swallow.

Finally BeBe sucked in a breath and let it out with a sigh. "Me, too," she said, profound relief infusing her tone and relaxing the tightness in her face. It hadn't been a surrender; it had been a conscious choice.

A smile curved Peach's cheeks as she put her hand on BeBe's shoulder and gave her a supportive squeeze. "Please, we love Buster to pieces," she told the Weinster. "We just can't imagine life without her. Right, BeBe?"

"Right," BeBe said, and exhaled with a smile.

Chapter Twenty-one

The following night Peach hopped up the steps of their apartment building, on her way home from the outreach center, where she'd met with Tim, the program coordinator, and some other volunteers working on next month's singles' dance. They'd gone over several details, and Peach had offered to provide some Millennium gift baskets for the door prizes.

Now she entered her apartment to find all the lights on, but Bebe nowhere in sight. "Hello? BeBe?"

"In here," BeBe called from the bathroom. "You can come in."

When Peach opened the door, she found her roommate sitting cross-legged on top of the toilet lid, eating a candy bar and flipping through one of the dog-training books she'd gotten earlier that afternoon. This one was titled *Bichon Frise: The Misunderstood Genius*.

"What are you doing in here?" Peach asked.

"Hiding from the dog. By the way, what's she doing now?"

"Uh, I don't know; let me go check."

BeBe climbed off the toilet lid and followed Peach out into the kitchen, then the living room. "Buster?" BeBe called out very tentatively. "Here, girl."

"Could you sound more desperate?" Peach said, angling her head back.

"What do you mean?"

"Nothing," Peach said, because why explain the obvious—that BeBe's idea of "calling" sounded a lot like begging? "There she is!"

Peach whispered suddenly, spotting the puffy white puppy curled up on the area rug, peacefully sleeping beside the sofa. She was probably dreaming of human carnage, but still . . . she looked so sweet when she wasn't baring teeth.

"Ugh, she was driving me crazy before," BeBe whispered, putting her palm on her forehead. "She wouldn't listen to anything I said. And I was just reading a book, *Birth of a Bichon Nation,* that said in the seventeenth century bichon frises were the little darlings of the French royal court. Apparently they would just sit by the king's feet and be all deferential and well behaved. I mean, what am I doing wrong here?"

Squinting, Peach said, "Um, trying to relate to the king of France is probably your first mistake. But don't worry; we'll get there." Ever since Ellen Weinberg's party, BeBe had a new resolve not only to keep Buster, but also to train her: to face the challenge, to put the time in, to take on the responsibility—fine, and also to prove her mother wrong. Extra incentive was that if Buster learned to take direction and be less of a maniac, the other tenants in the building wouldn't form a mini lynch mob to get BeBe and her dog evicted.

"I downloaded a bunch of articles to my laptop before," Peach added. "And this thing about obedience school. It's called Puppy Preschool, I think."

"Great, I'll read them tonight. Thanks for helping me," BeBe said, and flopped onto the sofa, exhausted; Buster looked tired, too, now lying on her back with her paws curled up to the sky.

The phone rang and Peach grabbed it. "Hello?" she said, shrugging out of her patchwork coat and tossing it onto one of the armchairs. Twisting her lips, she handed the phone to BeBe. "It's John," she said.

As Peach headed to the kitchen, she found herself thinking about Adam. *That's different.* She'd been thinking about him all weekend. But what could she do? She really, truly cared about him . . . she just wanted to get closer to him.

And when she wasn't thinking about Adam she was worrying

about Dennis, and figuring out her next scheme to uncover what had happened to him and where the hell he was.

As she entered the kitchen, she winced at the mess she'd made of it that morning. Paint rollers and brushes (all on top of the cabinets, out of Buster's reach), scraps of paper sectioning off the "do not touch" areas, and the window open to keep the fumes at bay, even though it was freezing cold outside. Meanwhile the wind had obviously blown BeBe's lovely, expensive kitchen towels all over the floor. Her roommate was a saint.

"Listen, *asshole*," she heard the saint saying now, and Peach ducked her head out of the kitchen to find BeBe standing with one hand on the phone, the other on her hip. "I don't *have* to tell you where I was on Saturday. Where were you on Thursday when I text-messaged you?" Then BeBe scoffed. "Playing PlayStation—*all* day? You expect me to believe that?"

Why not? Peach believed it with every fiber of her being.

"Oh, quit trying to be the alpha male," BeBe continued. "It's *not* working. . . ."

Peach retreated back to the kitchen, laughing softly to herself; her roommate had spunk, even if she was a soft touch. She grabbed a rubber band from the kitchen drawer and pulled her hair into a high ponytail as she heard BeBe slam the phone down and yell, "He's so goddamn annoying!" The phone rang again, and BeBe snatched it up. "*Hello?* Oh. Sorry. Who's calling, please?" Figuring it was for her, Peach went back into the living room as BeBe said, "Oh, okay, hang on—wait a second . . . Kimberly? Is that *you*? I thought that voice sounded familiar. Sweetie, it's Aunt BeBe!" There must not have been much fanfare on the other end, because after BeBe exchanged quizzical looks with Peach, she said, "Okay, okay, here she is." Handing the phone over, she whispered, "My niece called to talk to *you*."

Scrunching her face in bewilderment, Peach shrugged and brought the receiver to her ear. "Hello?"

"Hi," Kimberly said in a voice that was both small and distinct.

"Hi, there. How are you?" Peach asked, again shrugging at

BeBe, who just shook her head and laughed to herself. Then she went to the bathroom to start running her bathwater.

"I'm fine," Kimberly said.

"Did you just call to say hello?" Peach asked lamely.

"Yes."

"Oh, well, it's great to hear from you. Um . . . so how's school?"

"Fine."

"Uh-huh . . . that's nice."

BeBe came back out in her tightly cinched terry-cloth robe, clearly waiting for the water to heat up. Confused, she whispered, "What does she want?"

To say hi, Peach mouthed, then scraped for more small talk. "How's school going? Do you like your teachers?"

"Yes."

Okay . . . what did a twenty-five-year-old say to a ten-year-old anyway? Kimberly was a sweet, smart little cookie, but Peach was at a loss at the moment. Then again, she supposed she could always dumb it down and talk about boys.

"Do you like any boys in your class?" she asked.

"No," Kimberly said.

BeBe leaned over to speak into the phone. "Boys are stupid, Kimberly. Repeat after me: Boys are stupid—"

"Would you please . . ." Peach said, shifting the phone over to her other ear, rolling her eyes, and thinking, *Who's the ten-year-old?*

"My birthday's in three weeks," Kimberly said then.

"Oh, yeah?" Peach said, smiling into the phone, because she just sounded so tiny, so precious, so unspoiled by the vicissitudes of turning eleven. "Are you gonna have a birthday party?"

"No," Kimberly said.

"How come?"

"Mummy said next year." Jeez, Yvonne made her daughter call her *Mummy?* Didn't she remember that word meant something different in America? And more important, why the hell did Kimberly have to wait till next year? Eleven was a major milestone!

"Why next year?" Peach asked gently.

"Because she says the new house isn't ready yet," Kimberly said glumly. "But it's okay, 'cause I don't have anyone to invite anyway."

"What do you mean?"

"I don't have any friends."

"*What?*"

"I just moved to a new school last month, but I have one friend named Meg."

"Oh . . . well, she must be nice," Peach threw in as her mind worked overtime. That tinny, resigned little voice was breaking her heart. Yes, fine. *Technically* it was "wrong" to go against a parent's wishes for their child, but in fairness . . . it didn't sound like *Mummy* had any reason not to want the party other than that her new house wasn't ready. Well, hell, the best parties were never in people's houses anyway; they were in respectable establishments like Chuck E. Cheese or Roller World. "Listen, I don't want you to worry, Kimberly. Let me think on this, okay? I promise your birthday's gonna be a good one this year."

When Monday afternoon came with still no sign of Dennis at the office, Peach got another idea, one that involved Adam's using his network access to hack into Dennis's hard drive, so they could comb through his personal files for clues. Hey, she never said Adam would *like* it . . . but these were desperate times.

"Okay, like I said, I don't know if we'll find anything, but—"

"I know, Quin, I know; just do it," Peach commanded, then softened her dictatorial tone by smiling sweetly and adding, "Pretty please?"

Adam just smirked and went to work on his keyboard. Peach didn't want anyone in the office to know she was investigating Dennis's disappearance—especially Grace, who would blab it to *everyone*. Peach wanted to know more before she got the rest of the staff in her business, or rather, in Dennis's business. As it was, they seemed ready to assume that Dennis had simply left work because he didn't have the balls to quit.

Just that morning Robert had officially addressed the Dennis situation during the staff meeting. He'd said that he didn't know what was going on, but he was going to make his best efforts to look into it and resolve the matter. It was all pretty vague, but then, what else could Robert say to his staff? That he had no fucking clue, and probably suspected that Dennis hadn't had the balls to quit, either?

Peach had called the police department again, and they'd said they were "looking into the matter." Period. What the hell kind of update was that? She hadn't even gotten the "the department thanks you" crap this time. She had the distinct feeling that due to some pesky privacy laws, the police had no intention of keeping Peach abreast of any and all developments with the case. Unbelievable! But she planned to contact Detective Joe Montgomery when he returned from his honeymoon anyway. He'd bent the rules for Lonnie a few years ago; maybe he'd bend them for Peach now.

Now it was two thirty and the office was quiet. It always got like this after lunch, when people seemed to descend into an enervating mix of sluggishness and food coma. It was a perfect time to be hovering over Adam at his desk, doing some covert sleuthing.

"Let's be quick about this," Adam said. "In case someone comes over to me for something, I don't want to have to explain myself."

"You're such a straight arrow," Peach said, then nudged his shoulder. "Come on, Quinny; take a risk."

Smirking, he replied, "I feel like that's pretty much all I do in your company."

"What do you mean—this?" Peach scoffed. "Please, this is nothing."

"Right, right, I forgot," he said. "The lioness."

He used his master password to access Dennis's desktop, which appeared before them on Adam's monitor. Which made Peach wonder . . .

"Hey," she said, "how come you didn't just use that when I locked myself out of my PC a couple weeks ago?"

"I did eventually. I wanted to do it right away, but you kept trying to make me stay and guess your password, remember?"

The corners of her mouth quirked up. "You liked it," she said. "Admit it, you liked hanging out with me a little."

"I admit it," he said, then shifted his attention immediately back to the computer screen. "So what am I looking for?" he said again.

"You tell me—you're the computer expert. I'm thinking we troll the hard drive for anything interesting."

"Peach, can you be a little more specific? Unlike you, people might actually notice if I'm not at my desk for two hours. Unlike you, I actually work for a living."

"Touchy, touchy," she said teasingly.

As Adam combed through Dennis's hard drive, looking through the files in his folder named "Personal," he came across some school pictures of his daughter, Nan. "Hey, isn't that Rachel with her?" Adam asked, when he opened a digital photo of Nan with two of her friends at some kind of school dance.

"No, that's Rachel's sister, Alice," Peach explained. "She's four years younger than Rachel. I know, they look so much alike, don't they?"

Adam studied the picture for another few seconds. "Wow, there's such a strong resemblance, they could honestly be twins."

"Actually, Alice is friends with Dennis's daughter, Nan—or they *used* to be friends, anyway."

Next Adam checked Dennis's "Letters" folder, but the last letter was at least a month old, and all the ones from the past few months seemed to relate to pretty generic business matters—and on a side note, were filled with some pretty pathetic typos. Come on, who spelled "whom" with two Os? Again, Peach marveled at how Dennis could be so good with numbers but so bad with . . . well, communication and other human things.

"Hey, what about his planner?" Adam suggested. "Everyone has one on their M drive."

"No," Peach shook her head. "Dennis was way too disorganized to keep a planner." Then she tilted her head and said, "We have an M drive?"

With a chuckle, Adam opened up Dennis's planner. To Peach's surprise there were a lot of entries in it. So Dennis *had* kept information in his planner. Who knew how up-to-date it was, or how well he adhered to it, but the point was, there was info, even up to the Friday before he disappeared.

"What's this?" Adam said now, leaning farther forward, studying the screen. The glare off the computer monitor cast a blue glow over the lenses of his glasses, which distracted Peach momentarily. Then she looked back at the computer. On the screen Adam highlighted the entries in Dennis's planner—not only for that last Friday, but also the Wednesday and Thursday leading up to it. All three days had some of the same cryptic, abbreviated notations in common. On Wednesday, Dennis had entered: CNSLT R ABOUT N? Thursday's entry read: CHK TM-SH / COMP. S. 4 N/R.

"Consult R about N," Peach said, decoding the more obvious abbreviations. "Check . . . I don't know what that that's supposed to be."

"Maybe the next part is 'compare' something for N and R?"

"You think the S stands for 'something'?" Peach said a little skeptically.

"No, no, I just meant 'something' as in I don't know what S stands for," Adam said.

"Oh. So Dennis wanted to compare something for N and R," Peach mused out loud.

"But with that slash there, we really don't know if N and R are connected, or if they refer to two totally separate tasks," Adam remarked. Damn, he was right. What kind of entries were these? Didn't Dennis know that they didn't make sense to other people?

Finally they checked the entry for Friday, the last day Dennis had come to work. It read—

"Adam?"

Both he and Peach jumped.

Robert had ducked his head into Adam's cube, and now was arching a questioning eyebrow. "Hello, Peach. Are you two working on something? I can come back."

Even though Robert's tone was pleasantly cordial, it still made Peach fumble. "Oh . . . well . . . I was just checking on something."

She glanced back at Adam's monitor; he'd minimized Dennis's planner so Robert wouldn't see. *Fast work,* she thought, relieved, and then realized: Why not just tell Robert the truth? She'd just say she was worried about Dennis and checking his computer for any possible clues to where he might've gone.

"I was just cleaning up a virus that Peach brought to my attention," Adam said quickly. "Uh, it came in an e-mail to her and threatened to corrupt the network, but don't worry; I've got the situation handled."

"Oh. I see," Robert said after a pause. "Well, whenever you finish, will you stop by my office? I wanted you to take a look at my USB port. I seem to be having trouble with it."

"Sure, sure, no problem," Adam said, nodding.

Overzealously, Peach nodded, too, for no particular reason, and when Robert left she said, "Hey, why don't we just tell him the truth? What we're doing is for a good cause."

"Because I'd rather not say I'm breaking into someone else's personal files without permission or direct orders from the company. It's not exactly something I want to broadcast my third week on the job—call me crazy."

"Ohh, I see," Peach said, then tapped his arm. "Don't worry, crazy is the *last* thing anyone would call you, Quinny. So open up the thing again," Peach ordered, and reached over to do it herself. They were on Friday now, the last time anyone at work had seen Dennis, the last time anyone had heard from him, though after visiting Monkeyville last week, at least Peach knew for a fact that Dennis had made his date with Joan on Saturday night. Unfortunately, Peach still had no clue how to contact Joan, and the police were clearly not interested in facilitating her efforts—though hopefully they had located Joan on their own and asked her about Dennis.

The entry for Friday read: TAKE ACTION, RE-WORK CONTRACT, N.

"Huh?" Peach mumbled, studying it with frustration. "Why

does he have to abbreviate everything? Unless he's afraid of someone here seeing it . . . And what contract is he talking about?"

"And why would he have to rework them?" Adam added, shaking his head. "So far the only thing that's certain is that in the days leading up to Friday, he consistently mentions N and R. What that stands for, though, who knows?"

"Initials?" Peach suggested. "N could stand for Nan, Dennis's daughter. But then . . . I don't know what kind of contracts that would have to do with."

"Rachel?" Adam said, venturing a guess. Nodding, Peach thought about how Dennis had wanted to talk with Rachel the week before he'd disappeared. He'd mentioned it a couple of times, but Rachel had been dodging him. But why on earth dodge Dennis? What could that have been about?

Until now, Peach hadn't given it much thought, but she supposed it had been odd, especially since neither Dennis nor Rachel had divulged what it was about.

After refreshing Adam's memory on all this, she said, "I don't know; they were just both acting kind of cagey."

"Cagey?" he repeated skeptically. "This is the first I'm hearing about anything 'cagey.' "

"No, really."

"Are you sure you're not reading into it now, trying to make something of nothing?"

"No," she insisted, thinking, *Men—they're only logical when it's inconvenient for me.*

Rhythmically, Adam tapped his pencil against the arm of his chair. "Okay, so Rachel and Nan are two viable possibilities."

Viable possibilities—could he be more formal? She nearly ruffled his hair, he was so cute sometimes, but stopped herself. It seemed less innocent every time she contemplated it.

"You know what? Let's walk and talk," Adam said, rising from his seat. "I don't want Robert to think something weird's going on over here."

"What's he gonna think, that we're having hot sex on the desk or something?" she said. It had just burst out of her, sarcasm uncensored, but the statement had been too blatant, the image too vivid, and now an awkward silence stretched between them, one that was charged with unspoken tension.

Hot blood rushed to her cheeks, and she swallowed hard. She and her big mouth . . . She'd made a lame joke, but in doing so, had brought the image of the two of them having sex to the forefront of both their minds. And moreover, everyone knew a basic psychological fact: When you were around someone you wanted to have sex with, you brought sex into the conversation like crazy. Had she just tipped her hand? Did Adam realize yet how much Peach wanted to sleep with him? To shag his brains out, as Yvonne would probably say?

If he did, he didn't let on, but just said, "Let's go," and stepped out into the aisle.

Peach followed, then realized: "Wait. We need a copy of those entries. Can we print them?"

"Oh, right—no, I got it," he said, coming back to the desk, opening up to the planner again, copying the selected entries, and e-mailing them to himself, all in less than five seconds. "Let's go," he said again, and they both headed down the hallway.

They'd barely gone five feet when Nelson appeared beside a narrow shoji screen in a nearby corner. "Hey, did I hear you guys mention Dennis?"

Peach was surprised by the question. She had thought she and Adam were keeping their voices quiet, and she had to wonder how much Nelson had heard. It wasn't really like him to be particularly nosy; he was usually busy trying to be funny and/or scratching at something.

Then it hit her: did the N in Dennis's planner refer to Nelson? It was possible—maybe a leap, but then, what *wasn't* at this point? All Peach had was a gut feeling that the letters in the planner might be initials, as well as the fact that the entries seemed to lead up with more urgency to something—up to "Take action," which was written on the Friday before Dennis had vanished.

"We were just saying that it's not the same without Dennis around here," Peach said casually, then switched topics. "How's Brenda, by the way?"

"Great," Nelson replied with a nod. "She really likes working at home with the baby there. I said to her, 'Hey if you like creamed corn and doody on your spreadsheets, more power to you!' "

Peach offered a pleasant smile. Adam just nodded, looking nonplussed. After Nelson continued past them down the hall, Peach tugged on Adam's sleeve. "Come on," she said, pulling him around the bend and into the kitchen, which was now deserted.

"What are we doing?" he asked as he allowed her to drag him around (he liked her touching him).

"Too many prying ears out there," she said quietly. "Let's talk in here. Okay . . . what about Nelson as the N in Dennis's planner? And if the N stands for Nelson, then maybe R stands for Robert—you saw the tension between them that time in the conference room when Nelson was making those sexual comments about Dennis. Plus, Grace has mentioned a few times that Nelson might be on his way out."

"True," Adam said, pondering that.

Squinting, Peach added, "Of course . . . I suppose technically R could stand for Scott."

"Huh?"

"Scott's first name is Richard," Peach said, remembering when she'd gotten a piece of mail addressed to "Richard West," and that Scott told her he preferred to go by his middle name. "Oh, but that wouldn't make sense," she added, dismissing the thought. "How would Dennis even know that Richard was his name?"

"Well, probably Scott's paychecks are made out to his legal name, right?" Adam said.

"Oh, right, I hadn't thought of that. And I know there was a little tension because of some stock investment that went sour. But still . . . Scott just seems like too big a leap."

"So who else?"

"I don't know. At this point, I'm just grasping at anything—can you tell?"

With a short laugh, Adam said, "Actually I can, but it's cute." Color drifted to her cheeks, which was uncharacteristically bashful behavior for her. Adam cleared his throat and said, "Well, as much as I want to help, I don't want to keep Robert waiting much longer."

Oh. Well, that took the wind out of her sails. He'd just been being really sweet, and now he was ditching her. She knew he was right, he had work to do, but she supposed she was just disappointed that he'd picked that moment to pull back from her.

Damn Scorpio, she thought . . . but humored him anyway. "All right, no problem—how about I'll go talk to Rachel, see if I can find out what exactly Dennis wanted to talk to her about last week, what the big thing was. Maybe I can even find out more about Nan. At least it's a place to start."

"Are you abandoning the Nelson theory then?" Adam asked.

"No, not at all. Just putting it on the shelf," she replied, and they both went in opposite directions.

Chapter Twenty-two

Luck could hardly compete with the fact that Rachel had already left early for a doctor's appointment. So Peach decided to approach Grace and see what she could learn. If R referred to Robert, Grace was a great place to start—hell, she was such a busybody, even if R stood for "renaissance" or "rotated tires," she still might know something.

Peach waited until she saw Robert milling around the office before she headed over to Grace's desk, figuring Grace would talk much more freely if Robert wasn't right in his office.

When Peach got within five feet from Grace's desk, she was overwhelmed by a pungent stench. Glancing down, she quickly found the source. Grace had left some boiled eggs peeled, sitting next to her other snacking staples—a thick pepperoni log, a neon-orange block of cheese, and some plastic knives for cutting, or lopping off, as the case might be. On the other side of the peeled eggs were some slices of bologna, loosely covered by plastic wrap. If it weren't for the box of Saltines beside her desk lamp, you'd think Grace was on Atkins.

"Hi, Peach, how's it going?" Grace said, returning to her desk with photocopies in her hand. After she plopped down in her chair, she set her papers on her blotter and reached for a hunk of cheese.

"You know, same old, same old," Peach said, trying to position herself casually, as though she'd come all the way to the far reaches of the office just for small talk. "I was just looking for Rachel, but Scott said that she left early for a doctor's appointment."

"Mmm-hmm," Grace said, nodding with a full mouth.

"Um . . . I know Dennis wanted to talk to Rachel about something last week. I wonder if he ever did?" Could she be more the queen of the unsuave non sequitur right now?

Lifting her eyebrows at that, Grace leaned forward, waiting for more. She must have figured that Peach had brought it up so she could reveal some interesting, juicy gossip. But she didn't. That was it. Nothing else. *Peach* was the one waiting for gossip, but it seemed Grace was too preoccupied with her lunch at the moment to jump on board with some unsolicited commentary. Still determined to get somewhere, Peach switched gears. "Is Robert in?"

"No. Why, you need him for something?"

"No, I, uh . . . I was gonna ask him about something—a new basket idea," she improvised.

"Why don't you just call Brenda?" Grace suggested.

"Oh, well, I wouldn't want to bother her at home."

"Bother her? That's a hot one. She's *supposed* to be working from home," Grace said huffily, and used her plastic knife to saw off a few more hunks of meat and dairy. "Anyway, Robert's not here—the asshole has left the building!" she said in a mock announcer voice. "Took that Easterbrook clown out to lunch, said he wouldn't be back for at least an hour."

Peach remembered Grace saying at lunch last week that Robert was hiring Easterbrook for some consulting work, to help streamline the company as it embarked on expansion. Grace had also included Nelson among the possible list of "expendables" once the transition was made.

"It's so weird," Peach said, leaning her hip against Grace's desk and crossing her arms over her chest. "Robert's our boss but we barely interact with him. I mean, he's not really the hands-on type, I guess." She doubted she could fish harder than this, but she was desperate to find out if the R in Dennis's planner stood for Robert, or if the N stood for Nelson.

"Speak for yourself," Grace said with a snort. "He's in my face twenty-four/seven. The man doesn't know his ass from his elbow—I'm surprised he doesn't have me wipe his nose, too."

Tilting her head, Peach probed, "Grace, how come you hate him so much? Is it just because he's your boss, or did he do something in particular?"

"I don't *hate* him," Grace replied. Then she cupped her hand over her mouth and whispered loudly, "He's just a royal pain in my *ass!*"

Okay—so basically just because he was her boss.

"Yeah, I guess it's different when you're someone's direct assistant," Peach said, humoring her. "Because everyone else seems to like him—even Nelson, right?"

Pruning her face up, Grace reared her head back. "You think *Nelson* likes Robert?" She snorted. "More like he's scared shitless of him! Of course, maybe if Nelson paid more attention to what he's supposed to do around here, instead of trying to be the funny man, he might have a prayer." At this point Grace picked up her pepperoni log and bit a piece off the end. Peach couldn't help but picture the slicked surface of Grace's palm as it clutched the greasy processed meat. "And Nelson *claims* he worked over the weekend last week—yeah, right, I don't buy it. In fact, I heard . . . Oh, I shouldn't say anything."

Oh, please, so what else was new? Ordinarily Peach wouldn't push, but this might be important. "No, really, what is it, Grace?"

"Well . . ." Grace paused, obviously still debating whether or not to blab, as Peach leaned forward with keen interest, having the feeling that pro-blabbing would win out. "I heard a rumor that Nelson wants to be a professional comedian," she said finally. Heard or *over*heard while her head was superglued to someone else's partition? Well, either way, it hardly seemed relevant to Dennis's whereabouts. "He's such a kook anyway," Grace went on. "When Dennis didn't show up for work last week, right away Nelson was in my face, asking if he'd called in, if anyone had heard from him. I mean, he just kept at me and at me—'Where's Dennis? Has anyone talked to Dennis?' He was practically foaming at the mouth. I had no idea the two of them were such close friends."

Shaking her head, she reached for a crumbly Saltine from inside its battered box. "Strange bird," she said, and Peach had to agree.

The rest of the week crawled by because Adam was out of the office at a software trade show in New York City. Peach missed him terribly, and she'd thought about calling his cell a hundred times, just to say hello, but always stopped herself. They weren't at that kind of comfort level yet, she supposed. They'd never even been to each other's apartments, or seen any real parts of each other's lives outside of work.

In his absence, one mission had been accomplished anyway: Peach finally got to ask Rachel why she'd been dodging Dennis two weeks ago. She'd hoped Rachel would start babbling, stuttering, getting an eye tic, something—anything that might point to her being the mysterious R in Dennis's planner. But again, it seemed to be a dead end. Rachel claimed it was all about some supply order forms she'd filled out incorrectly, and Millennium had ended up paying for the supplies twice. According to Rachel, Dennis wanted to straighten out the mix-up with her, but she stupidly thought that if she avoided him, they could both just forget about it. When Peach had asked why Dennis hadn't mentioned any of this to anyone, Rachel had shrugged and speculated that Dennis probably hadn't wanted to embarrass her—especially in front of her idol.

Honest to God, that was Rachel's word, not Peach's, though Peach was infinitely flattered by it. Still . . . she knew that Rachel had had a good two weeks to come up with this story. And without Dennis around, there was no one to refute it. But when it came down to it, Peach supposed she believed her.

Now it was Friday morning. Or at least it was to the rest of the world. To BeBe it was day fourteen of V-man watch. It was getting pretty hard to remain hopeful for Luke Vermann's call, but BeBe was still keeping her fingers crossed.

As they walked Buster through Boston Common, Peach

breathed deeply, taking the brisk air into her lungs. It was one of those beautifully bipolar mornings; snowflakes fluttered down from an electric-blue sky, as cold bursts of wind broke through bright yellow sunshine.

BeBe shivered and said, "It's fucking *freezing* out." Another way to look at it.

"Don't change the subject," Peach said.

"What's the subject again?" BeBe used her free hand to run over her coat to warm herself up, and the other to tug on Buster's leash. At the moment all Peach and BeBe could see was a white fluffy ball peeking out from behind a thick tree. "Come on, come on, Buster."

"The subject is you and your men. Give me the rundown." So far all Peach knew was that Ken, the tightfisted doctor, had left another message on their answering machine, and Mindy said her friend Tony was wondering why he hadn't heard from BeBe again. With their erratic schedules lately, they hadn't had a chance to catch up.

"Please, I have no men," BeBe said, and blew on both hands, which reined in Buster's leash. Looking back, Peach saw Buster standing there panting with a big smile on her face—literally.

"Come on, what else am I clinging to? I'm crazy about a guy who already has a girlfriend, and who thinks of me as his best buddy. I need to live through you."

BeBe scoffed. "When *you* need to live through *me*, it's not only a sad day, it's also a lot of pressure."

"First let's talk about Ken. What's the story? You gonna call him back or destroy his life instead?"

"Well, I'm not calling him back," BeBe said.

"The cheap thing?"

"Yeah. I just didn't feel like working on that. Besides which, no spark."

With a nod, Peach said, "Fair enough. Drop him. Next."

"Who? Tony? I told you, too sex-starved for me. I mean, I'm sex-starved, too, but I keep it to myself." Peach laughed, and BeBe added, "Speaking of starved, last night I dreamed about an ice-cream sandwich. How sad is that?"

"I've dreamed about cake a few times," Peach said with a shrug.

"*Really?*" BeBe said, obviously astounded that Peach, who pretty much ate what she wanted, would still dream about food.

"Yeah, definitely. It's all just a metaphor for sex anyway."

"Hmm . . . maybe sex is really just a metaphor for food," BeBe suggested.

That stalled Peach in her tracks. Pressing a palm to her forehead as her mouth curved curiously, she looked at BeBe, her eyes wide, and said, "That is brilliant. I never thought of that!"

"See? I have ideas," BeBe said kiddingly, then jerked back when Buster pulled hard on her leash, trying to chase after a withered leaf that was blowing in front of them. Then Buster stopped, and was chewing on a mysterious something.

"Sweetie, this is a walk, not a buffet," Peach said, crossing over to try to take the object out of Buster's mouth. Buster's head reared wildly, and Peach had to pry her mouth open to remove a gum wrapper; then she rubbed the puppy's fluffy white head. "Good girl," she said, and very shockingly, Buster angled her head to give Peach's wrist a gentle lick. "Oh, my God! BeBe, she licked me!"

"She *did*?" BeBe said, sounding stunned, as her scarf whipped and ribboned in the wind. "Wait, wait, I want to get a lick, too!" That should've sounded weird, but of course it didn't. Buster had yet to lick; she'd only been into nipping.

"Anyway, I have an announcement to make," BeBe said. "I'm officially ending the V-man watch."

Slanting her a look, Peach said, "Thank you."

"Also, I'm taking a break from dating for a while. After we go out with Simon's friends, I'll officially be out of the game."

"Whoa . . . since when are you going out with Simon's friend? And I know you didn't just say 'we.' "

"Oh, please, please, please," BeBe begged. "Simon's friend Fielding has a cousin visiting, and he needs a date, too."

"Needs a date? Nobody *needs* a date," Peach argued. After a thoughtful pause, she spoke more seriously. "BeBe, normally you know I'd help you out, but . . . I honestly don't feel like going out with anyone right now."

With a knowing sigh, BeBe said, "All right. I understand. It's because of Quin."

"No, no, not because of Quin," Peach said, then added, "Yeah, because of Quin. What made you decide to go out with Fielding?"

BeBe shrugged and seemed a little evasive when she said, "I don't know. Yvonne convinced me."

As they turned to look straight ahead, Peach suddenly spotted someone familiar in the distance. Holy shit—it was Joan!

"Joan?" Peach called out, then started jogging toward her, without stopping to explain to BeBe. She had to catch up with her before she slipped away again! "Joan! Wait up—*please*!"

"Where are you going?" BeBe called to her, as Peach kept scurrying, her coat flying open behind her in the icy wind. Joan was about two hundred yards away, but Peach knew it was her—the same long-dress-with-sneakers look, the same frizzy knot of hair on top of her head—it was *her*. This might be Peach's only chance to get some information about Dennis. Just after she'd convinced herself that Joan had suffered the same cruel fate that Dennis had, whatever that was, now here she was.

"Wait up, Joan!" she cried again, as onlookers practically gawked. Peach sprinted past them, too anxious about her mission to be the least bit self-conscious. Joan was wearing earmuffs. *Can she not hear me calling her name? Or is she just ignoring me?*

After another try, finally Peach got Joan's attention and she turned around. "Peach?" she said, squinting, and Peach jogged the last few yards to close the space between them.

"Oh, my God, where have you been?" Peach exclaimed, her breath coming up in short, quick puffs. "I went to Mackie's and they told me you quit. Then I tried to find your number and address, but I couldn't." (*Way to sound like a major stalker, but who really cares at this point?*)

"You did?" Joan said, clearly shocked. "What on earth for? Is something wrong?"

Knitting her brows, Peach asked, "When was the last time you talked to Dennis?"

"Oh, I haven't talked to him since we went out . . . a couple weeks ago, was it? I was kind of wondering what happened there. . . ." Her voice trailed off, as Peach's heart kicked up.

Panic seized her chest; her last hope of finding out where Dennis might be was quickly evaporating.

"But what happened after your date?"

Joan shrugged. "Nothing. He drove me home, said he had a nice time. I thought he was gonna call me after that. But then he never did."

"Joan, Dennis is missing!" Peach blurted. "He left work on the Friday before your date, and never came back again. Now, I need you to think—did he say anything to you about his plans for the rest of that weekend? Or about any problems he was having with anyone—his ex-wife, someone from work, anything?"

Joan shook her head, looking appropriately stunned. "Missing . . ." she mumbled, shaking her head. "I can't believe it."

"Did anything unusual happen when you guys were out?" Peach was feeling increasingly anxious. Here Joan was finally right in front of her, and she was still coming up empty.

Joan shrugged, still shaking her head. "No, I mean, we went to Monkeyville, the new comedy club over on Arlington, we had a nice time, and— Oh, wait. There was one thing, but it was no big deal."

"What?" Peach persisted. "What, Joan? Anything at all might help."

"Well, there was someone at the club he knew. Performing, I mean. Some short guy with a nose like a bull." Hey, wait—that sounded like Nelson. "He was there for open-mike night, and Dennis was like, 'Hey, I work with that guy!' "

"And then what?" Peach asked, rabid for details.

With another shrug, Joan said, "Then I went to use the bathroom. There was such a long line I ended up missing the guy's whole act. Ladies' rooms, you know how that goes."

"Right, but did Dennis talk to this guy afterward? Maybe approach him after the show, or . . . ?"

Joan shook her head. "Not that I saw. Look, like I said, we had a great time, we said good-night, he told me he'd call me. That's all I know. Oh, except that Dennis did mention he might go into the office the following day." She finished with a shrug.

"Do you have any idea when he lost his wallet?" Peach asked, just as a city bus wobbled up Tremont Street and abruptly stopped.

"Oh, shit! That's my bus; I've gotta go!" Joan said, and hurriedly crossed the busy street.

"Wait, Joan!" Peach called. "Why haven't you answered your phone—and how come you quit Mackie's?"

Squinting in the bright morning sun, Joan looked back at the bus; it was obvious the only thing on her mind was hopping it. Quickly, she replied, "Oh, I haven't paid my phone bill; they cut me off—sorry. Anyway, I've been staying with a friend in Wayland for a while," she added, which would certainly explain why she seemed clueless; obviously the police hadn't been able to contact her, either. If they'd even tried.

But she still hadn't said why she'd quit. "Wait!" Peach called out. "What about Mackie's? Joan, please wait!"

"Mackie's blows!" was all she said before she darted to catch a city bus that soon disappeared.

When Adam got home from the computer trade show, his only thought was seeing Peach, and he would finally get to tonight at Nelson and Brenda Perhune's dinner party. No, it wasn't true about Peach being his only thought. His other thought was of Robin.

He had to end it with her; he couldn't let their relationship—or what was left of it—die on the vine for one more day. Before he even began to unpack, he grabbed his phone and called her. The extremely long number he had to dial was a tart, if blatant metaphor for the profound distance between them.

The phone rang. It was a low-pitched, almost baritone thrumming in his ear. He waited, then—*click*.

"Hello?"

"Robin," he said, feeling his chest start to tighten.

"Oh. Hi." Still sulking about the fact that he wasn't dropping everything to come spend Christmas with her. Good, if she was bratty, it might make this easier for him.

Stop stalling. Maybe he should make small talk first? Ask her about her day? No, small talk was bullshit. *Just get to it.* "Listen, Robin . . . we have to talk." To her credit, she didn't try to interrupt, to guess what he was thinking, to fill in the next sentence. She was always more the strong, simmering type, and there were times, like now, when he sincerely appreciated that about her. Damn, this was going to be harder than he thought. "We have to end this," he stated bluntly. Instantly he felt a sharp stab of guilt at the words—for how they had to make her feel—but he didn't retract them. Instead he softened his voice and continued much more gently, "You know it hasn't been working out for a long time. It's been . . . well, obviously it's not doing us much good to keep dragging this out."

Pause.

Strained silence.

Another beat of brutally strained silence. Then she spoke; her words were steely calm, her tone cool and brisk. "Thanks, Adam. Thanks a lot."

"I'm sorry, Robin," he said, meaning it. "I don't want to hurt you, but—"

"You're just going to pull this out of nowhere," she said icily.

"Nowhere?" he repeated, feeling irritation claw its way past his guilt. Suddenly he felt sorry *and* annoyed. Damn, breakups were the worst. "Robin, come on, we haven't seen each other for over a month—what kind of relationship is this?"

"Who's fault is that? I asked you to come for Christmas, didn't I?" she argued.

"Look, we were already having problems before you left, but when you took that job . . . Look, you moved away—you left me. I mean, you *chose* to move away; they didn't tell you that you had to.

It wasn't a promotion, but you chose it anyway. Everything just went to hell after that."

"You know, you have a real talent for blaming me for everything that's gone wrong in our entire relationship," she said. Her voice might be frosty, but he had to admit he admired her control, as frustration, anger, hurt, and guilt roiled inside him, threatening to bubble over.

"That's not what I meant," he said. "I don't mean it's your fault. I . . ." He expelled a deep sigh. "Look, Robin, we both haven't been happy in this relationship for a while; we both know it—"

"So you're just ending it—five years together and right before Christmas? Thanks a lot. Really, Adam—thanks."

Shit! Christmas, holiday blues . . . he hadn't factored that in. He had to be the biggest asshole of all time. But then . . . how could he keep the relationship going with Robin when he'd been tortured by less-than-platonic feelings toward Peach, which were growing more intense every day? Each time he saw her . . . well, it was getting impossible to be in Peach's company and not think about tearing her clothes off, about feeling her hands slide down his pants, or fantasizing about her tongue on his cock. . . .

Jesus, he was crazy about another girl; this was the only decision he could make. "I'm really sorry," he said, of course leaving out any mention of Peach, because it would hurt Robin too much if she thought there was someone else.

"Good-bye, Adam," she said crisply. *Good-bye,* he thought a little sadly, but didn't get a chance to say it, because she slammed the phone down so hard it reverberated against his eardrum, even as it set him free.

Chapter Twenty-three

Normally Peach wasn't early to a party, but this time she made an exception. Tonight was Brenda and Nelson's dinner party, and here Peach was, too keyed up to wait, even though she had to. Where was Adam? When would he get there? She was bursting to tell him what she'd discovered about Joan and Nelson and Dennis, and *damn it*, where was he already? She hadn't seen him all week because of his software conference, and now she was more desperate than ever to catch him up to speed on everything . . . to look into his adorable face . . . to feel his presence, really there, up close to her.

She was sitting in the Perhunes' living room, making small talk with Brenda while waiting for Nelson to come downstairs—Nelson who'd withheld that he'd seen Dennis before he'd disappeared. The question was why. What else was he hiding?

"Yew shuch a pwetty widdle baby, aren't you?" Brenda said, turning her focus to Annie, who looked adorable in her pink-and-white-checkered pajamas. "My pwetty widdle monkey face," Brenda continued cooing, as Peach looked off to the side to keep from blatantly rolling her eyes. The only other guest who'd arrived so far was Grace, who was over at the table with the appetizers spread out, presently filling her plate with ham, cheese, and any other gratis cold cuts that had been set out.

The doorbell rang. Peach jumped in her seat, rising from the love seat, trying not to look so utterly desperate for it to be Adam at the door. It wasn't. "Robert!" Brenda said, holding Annie in one arm. "I'm so happy you came after all!"

"Hello," he said, leaning down to give her a polite kiss on the cheek. "I'm glad I could make it, too." Then he handed her an expensive-looking bottle of wine. "This is for you." Suddenly Peach felt like the most self-absorbed loser on the planet; she'd forgotten to bring something to the dinner party. Her mother would be horrified; where was her head lately?

Yet, as ashamed as she was, she was still mostly preoccupied with another issue—where was Adam?

"Hello, Peach," Robert said, smiling casually. "And Grace—you look lovely as always."

Lovely for what? Herman Munster's twin sister? Whatever. Peach was getting antsy. "Um, I'm just gonna step outside for some air," she said, and went onto the front steps to watch for Adam. The crisp night air blew coldly against her cheeks.

Headlights shone in the distance, flooding the sidewalk as the car careened up the street and closer. It stopped a couple of houses down from Brenda and Nelson's place, and Peach had to lean over the porch railing and angle to get a look at the driver before he cut the lights. *Finally!* Even in the dark, she could tell it was Adam. Her heart sped up. She hopped down the front steps to go to him, when a yellow taxicab came speeding to a sharp, swerving stop in front of the Perhunes' mailbox. *Damn!* It was Rachel. Obviously Peach was in no mood for chitchat, and if Rachel knew Adam had just arrived, too, she'd probably accost both of them to be all bubbly and friendly. Nobody needed it.

Time to think fast—or maybe not at all—as Peach jumped behind the thick shrubbery surrounding the front steps. Rachel didn't see her, but trotted upstairs to knock on Brenda's door. Peach hunkered lower in the bushes and waited until Brenda opened the door and exchanged pleasantries with Rachel—who, by the way, had brought a cake—as Peach continued to feel like the most classless freeloader in the world.

Hopefully no one would ask Rachel if she'd seen Peach outside, or question where Peach had gone. The front door swung closed just as Adam hit the walkway. "Quin!" she called, whispering from the bushes. *"Quin!"*

Abruptly he stopped and looked around. God, he was cute. She'd forgotten how acutely he could steal her breath—his glasses, his serious expression, his shirt and tie, even after work. He was so fucking adorable—not to mention confused, as Peach whispered his name again. Finally, as he went to climb the steps, she reached out to grab his pant leg. "What the hell . . ." he began, as Peach shifted her grasp to his elbow and tugged on him.

"Come *here*!" she whispered as he ducked into the bushes with her.

"Peach! What the hell are you doing down here?" he asked, not sounding mad, just totally perplexed.

"I'm sorry. I wanted to get you alone so I could talk to you for a couple minutes." He just looked at her; then the corners of his mouth angled up. He thought she was a weirdo; she knew it. But, oh, well, it could be worse, she figured, and took a deep breath.

Then she exploded in prose, telling him all about how Nelson had done a comedy act at the very same club where Dennis had gone with Joan, how Joan hadn't heard from Dennis since that night, but how he'd mentioned that he planned to go into the office the following day—and finally, how *Nelson* had told Grace that he'd come into work that same weekend.

After she was done rambling, Adam just shook his head, taking it all in. "I don't know, Peach. . . ."

"Oh, come on; don't be cynical—this is bizarre; you can't deny it!"

"You're absolutely right—this *is* bizarre," he said, eyeing their foliage surroundings and making it clear they weren't talking about the same "this."

Peach crossed her arms and tilted her head, obviously waiting for him to be serious, and Adam just grinned at her. He couldn't help it. The absurd seemed to follow her around like a colorful cloud. "Okay, okay. You're right. I admit, I don't know what to make of all this stuff with Nelson. But I don't know how doing an improv act at the same club Dennis had gone to would play into what happened to him."

"Why is he hiding that he saw Dennis on that Saturday night? Adam, don't you see? Maybe he's hiding it because he was the last person to see Dennis *alive!*"

Adam turned more serious. Damn, she was really upset about this; her soft features were stricken, her forehead creased with worry. Trying to be supportive, he said, "Okay, but if what you're saying is that somehow something happened between Dennis and Nelson on Sunday, when they both supposedly worked, what would losing his wallet on the street have to do with anything? How does that fit in?"

"Well, that part is a little fuzzy."

"And if something *did* happen at the office on Sunday, what could it have been? I mean, what possibly could've happened to Dennis—where *is* he?"

"That part's kind of fuzzy, too," Peach admitted.

Still, Adam assessed the facts, as she'd given them: Ever since Joan had told Peach that Dennis was planning to go into the office that Sunday after their date, it seemed likely that whatever had happened to him had to do directly with Millennium. Beyond that, everything was blurry.

Peach sighed. "Okay. Come on." She turned to step out from behind the shrubbery and back onto the steps.

As she climbed up, Adam watched one slim, shapely leg pulling up the rest of her sexy body, and he expelled a breath. He wanted to run his hands down the sleek outline of her body, grab her butt, feel her push back against him. . . .

Abruptly, he shook the thoughts off. It was bad enough being in that tight space between the shrubs with her so close and shivery, and him wanting to pull her close and warm her, hold her, snuggle up against her. When she turned back and saw him dawdling, she sighed impatiently and said, "Come *on.*" Adam quirked his mouth again—on top of everything else, she was bossy.

. . .

A few hours later, Peach was feeling thoroughly unsatisfied. The dinner party was nothing to do cartwheels over. The highlight was probably when Annie barfed at the table, and Nelson announced, "Baby vomit overboard!"

Meanwhile, while Brenda had cleaned it up, she'd switched gears from smart, competent woman with a good head on her shoulders, to cutesy nursery-school lady—with Nelson joining right in, morphing from class clown to keeper of the lisping flame.

First of all, sorry, but Peach didn't care if it was adult barf or newborn barf—it wasn't cute no matter how you looked at it. Second—and more important—she was not getting any closer to learning about Dennis. To quote her late grandma Deborah, this was for the birds.

Every time she'd tried to steer the conversation around to Dennis so she could gauge her coworkers' reactions, they all just exchanged tired, pat sentiments about how they hoped for the best, hoped there was a logical explanation, yadda yadda.

Time to do some real investigating.

But how?

Throughout the evening Peach kept her eye on Nelson. A couple of times she spotted him going upstairs, and when she'd stood at the foot of the steps, craning her neck with abandon, she'd seen him going in and out of a locked closet. He always shut the door behind him, locked the door, and pocketed the key in his sport coat—which was now hanging loosely on his chair, as everyone sat back with full bellies, yet awaiting dessert.

But first Nelson said he wanted to make another toast. Sure, why not? He'd been giving aimless, rambling "toasts" all night. "Hey, what's the deal with earwax?" he said now. "Have you ever noticed it smells a lot better than it tastes?"

Adam nearly choked on his drink, while Peach rolled her eyes and thought, *Maybe he's just drunk, and the sad part is, that's giving him the benefit of the doubt.*

"Not that I would *know*, of course . . ." he continued.

Abruptly, Peach pushed her chair away from the dinner table. Adam slanted her a questioning look. She just looked at Brenda and said, "Um, may I use the bathroom?"

"Of course, it's on the second floor—third door to your right," Brenda said.

Peach made a note to go to the second floor, third door to her *left*. The bathroom wasn't going to tell her anything, but Nelson's private closet might.

Improvising, she dropped down to her knee, right beside Nelson's chair. "Oh, sorry . . . I dropped my contact lens," she said, pretending to feel around for it.

"Really?" Rachel said innocently. "It just fell out of your eye?" Okay, Peach supposed that sounded kind of weird, but did Rachel have to pick now to get interpersonal?

"Yeah, well, I guess it was loose . . ." Peach floundered. "Got it! Um, anyway, I'll be right back; I'm going to use the restroom," she said, as she stood up swiftly, palming the key to the closet before rising to her feet. Nobody seemed able to see her very well, crouched down on the floor, and Nelson didn't even spare a look downward.

Peach disappeared up the stairs and looked back over the railing to make sure no one was coming; then she went straight for that closet. With her luck, it was just some linen closet where he kept his *Playboy*s . . . but then, why would he keep slipping upstairs to duck into it all evening? No, something wasn't right—with Nelson, his closet, his whole bit. Actually, she'd never contemplated a more devious side to him, until she'd found out that he'd lied about the last time he'd seen Dennis.

Feverishly, Peach jammed the key into the lock. But her hands were nervous; she had to make this fast, and she didn't even know what she was looking for. So of course she fumbled and missed aligning the key and the lock twice before she steadied herself, took a breath, and told herself to get her head straight and just *do* this.

She clicked the key in the lock and turned. Then she opened

first one of the narrow double doors, then the next. It was hard to tell how deep the closet was because it was pitch-black inside, and before she found a light switch she felt a hand on her back. Startled, she jumped farther inside, and her heart almost stopped as the doors closed behind her.

Chapter Twenty-four

"Quin, what the hell are you *doing*?" Peach whispered after he placed his hands gently on her upper arms and told her to be quiet.

"Trying to save you from making a fool of yourself," he said bluntly, "not to mention getting fired."

"Getting fired?" Peach repeated, then scoffed. "Nelson couldn't fire me if he wanted to."

"No, but Brenda could." *Oh. Good point.* She supposed she'd walked into that one. "Now what the hell are *you* doing?"

She tried to explain, but out loud it sounded stupid.

"Look, Peach, everyone's downstairs having dessert. Just go back before anyone comes looking for you."

"Probably no one's even noticed that I'm gone," she said.

"Yeah, right. Nelson just said, 'Hope she didn't fall in!' I'd say they're starting to notice."

"Already?" Peach half whined, and sighed like a martyr in the blackness of the closet. "This sucks. Well, we'd better look fast."

Adam almost laughed at the overconfident, presumptuous way she'd said "we" before implicitly putting him to work. But he figured two people would go faster than one, and then Peach would have to relent and go back down to join the party. "Do we even know what we're looking for?" he said. "Or is that a stupid question?"

"Just feel around on your side, and I'll feel around on mine, okay?" she suggested.

"Okay," Adam said, turning in the squished, small space to face the shelves that lined his side of the closet. For a walk-in closet, it was pretty tiny, definitely hard to maneuver in, and it didn't help to have two bodies inside at once, because it was impossible for them not to be tightly pressed together.

Damn . . . Every move they made knocked their backsides together, or their elbows, their hips. . . . With intense effort, Adam resisted the overpowering urge to turn around and press himself against her—to rub his cock against her perfect heart-shaped ass. Swallowing a sigh of frustration, he gripped the edge of the shelf in front of him and tried to focus on anything else but touching her.

The closet was tight, but Peach's chest was tighter. She'd known it was Adam because of his scent; she'd recognized that before he'd even spoken. In the utter darkness they could barely see each other—the only light was the narrow strip cutting through the scant space between the top of the doors and the doorjamb. Standing so close to him in this confined space was nearly suffocating . . . sweltering. . . . She gulped hard, feeling the shallow intakes of her breath, and her heart banging hard and fast against her ribs. He was just so close. . . .

Desire overwhelmed her with every touch of his body against hers, no matter how fleeting, but still, she focused her attention on the row of shelves on her side of the closet. So far she'd felt cool, soft fabrics, probably pillowcases and sheets, and some clunky objects, like an iron and an unused shoe tree. Her hands climbed up to the highest shelf—she had to stand on tiptoe to reach it—and in her stretching up to feel around, her butt knocked into Adam again.

"I feel something," she whispered.

"So do I," he muttered, almost under his breath.

"But I can't get it," she finished. *Damn it!* Her fingertips kept grazing what felt like a fat book with a small box of some sort on top it.

"What is it?" Adam said, turning to face her, his chest practically pressed against her back, and he added, "Here, I'll get it. But then we've got to get out of here." He reached over her. It happened so quickly Peach didn't have time to try to duck or squirm out of the way, not that there was anywhere to go, and suddenly she felt

Adam's whole body flush up against hers. She gave a sharp intake of breath as another jolt of erotic sensation hit her; just then she became aware of Adam's breathing, the feeling of being enveloped and held securely within his arms. His left was braced on the high shelf; the other was pulling down the mystery items.

Peach swallowed and said, "Thanks," as she turned in his arms. How could two people be in a dark closet and *this* close to embracing, and still act natural? And had she really felt what she thought she'd felt pressed against her lower back a moment ago?

She bit her lip at the possibility of feeling it again. . . .

"What is it?" she whispered.

"I don't know," Adam replied, his voice husky and low. Peach nearly shuddered as she savored the sensation of her legs barely touching his. She ached to push up closer, to rub herself against him. She ached to break the silence between them, not with friendly conversation, not even with speculations about the case. No, the case was on hold right now, which was insane, since their snooping was on borrowed time, but . . . *Fuck it.*

All she wanted right now was to kiss him. A long, smoldering kiss . . . a wet, sexy kiss . . . a steamy, forbidden moment with Adam—*Quin*—her *friend.*

"It's some kind of book, and a tape recorder, it feels like," he said now.

"Here, let me see," she said softly, but when she reached for it she touched his hand instead. She froze. Her hand stayed right where it was, and she released a shallow, shaky breath. The air in the closet was stiflingly humid. They were just kidding themselves to deny it, but a thick, gauzy blanket was wrapping tightly around them, and then she heard him whisper her name.

His voice, usually so smooth and fluid, sounded rough and gravelly. Then, as though it were instinct, they both seemed to meld into each other, magnetically pulled together, sealing the space between them where the heat rose urgently and demanded a reaction from their bodies. "Peach . . ." he whispered hoarsely.

Soon her body was snugly up against his. She felt the hard

strength of his legs, the warmth of his stomach pressed against hers, closer to her chest, and, most of all, she was acutely aware of the alignment of his pelvis with hers. "*Peach . . .*" he said again, and it almost sounded like a question or an entreaty, and then she felt his hand slowly snake up her back, and his other hand crawl under her hair to cup her neck, and she let out a thready moan of barely contained arousal. The hot spot between her legs was wet, burning. She felt almost sticky, tender, ready. . . .

He kissed her.

It happened so quickly, and it was the gentlest, most provocative kiss she could've ever imagined. Adam's soft lips cushioned hers, moving slowly, tentatively, coaxing hers to open . . . which they did, and abruptly—sharply—desire inflamed her, set her off like a shot, and she clutched his shoulders, tilted her head, and slid her tongue deep inside his mouth.

He groaned, tangling his hand in her hair while the other slid down to her butt. He clutched her there, brought her up harder against him, and kissed her back with barely restrained hunger, as the big hard bulge in his pants nudged against her pelvis, taunting her.

Frantically Peach gripped fistfuls of his shirt as she moaned, crushed her lips harder against his, licked into his mouth, and snaked her tongue against his.

All she wanted was to pull him closer—to drown him in her. To consume him. "Oh . . ." Peach whispered, and pulled back just enough to drag air into her lungs. She was short of breath, not from the kissing, but from the intensity of her emotions maybe, and Adam brought one hand up to run his warm palm gently over her cheek. His hands were so strong and gentle at the same time. Unwittingly she tilted her head to press against his hand, and then she remembered something crucial. "What about Robin?" she whispered. Instantly, fear fluttered across her chest; she was afraid of the answer.

"We broke up," he said, his voice low and husky.

"*What?*" That wasn't what she was expecting. Sure, Adam had said that his relationship wasn't working out, but people often said those kinds of things. In fact, it had taken BeBe and John a few tries before their breakup stuck, and even that relationship was still clinging to its last futile, minuscule scrap of hope. "When?" Peach asked.

"Today," he said, and leaned down to kiss her again, but she reared her head back enough to stop him. "What happened?" she whispered brokenly.

Kissing her again, feverishly devouring her mouth, squeezing her butt in his hands, flattening her body against his, he whispered, "You . . . you . . ." That was the only answer he gave her, and then he ran his tongue down her neck, making Peach's knees buckle.

"Oh, *God* . . ." she moaned, as he trailed his tongue back up and over the rim of her ear. Hot puffs of his breath washed across her skin—inflaming her between her legs, making her breasts and crotch nearly ache with longing.

His mouth captured hers one last time before their lips pulled apart and Adam stopped, still nearly panting. So was Peach, and the only sound in the closet was the choppiness of their breath, until Adam spoke. "Peach . . . *wow*."

He brought both hands up to cup her face and hold her cheeks lovingly in his palms. She still felt his rock-hard erection pulsing against her, and the raw eroticism of that should've been at odds with the sweet tenderness of the moment, but instead—coming from Adam—it all seemed to fit.

Suddenly they heard Brenda calling from downstairs: "Adam! Peach! Are you both up there?"

They jumped apart. The sweatiness of her body inside her clothes, the humidity between her legs, and the perspiration gathering on the back of her neck were probably a combination of feral sexual urges and sudden panic. What if Brenda found them in here? Or worse . . . what if Nelson did? He was the one who seemed to be hiding something.

"Shit," Adam muttered, and took Peach's hand. "Come on, before they find us in here." They should've moved faster, though. It was so weird the way people often froze in terror at moments like that, thereby sabotaging their own escape. And so it was now.

They flung the doors open a moment too late; Nelson was already in the hallway, standing there looking shocked and a little scary. Peach squeezed Adam's hand tightly as she swallowed down a swollen lump of fear that had formed in her throat.

"What are you *doing* in there?" Nelson barked. He was clearly seething, and his nostrils were dilated to the size of quarters. "And what are you doing with *that!*" he exclaimed, snatching the tape player up off the floor, where it had fallen when Adam and Peach had started making out. Glancing down, Peach noticed the title of the book that had fallen, too: *The Beginner's Guide to Stand-up Comedy*. It was fat and instructional, and reminded her of one of those Idiot's Guides, which sounded about right.

As Nelson held his tape player tightly, cradling it like his baby, he accidentally pressed play, and they heard Nelson's recorded voice. "Hey, I just had a baby," Nelson said on the tape. "It's crazy—hey, raise your hands out there, anyone's who's ever been a baby. Can I get a show of hands . . . ?" Flustered, Nelson punched on the buttons to stop it, but he ended up fast-forwarding the tape a little; then they all heard: "What's the deal with earwax? Ever notice it smells better than it tastes?" Hey, he'd done that joke tonight, Peach recalled. Using the term "joke" liberally, of course. *Wait a minute. . . .*

Finally Nelson got the tape player to stop, just as Brenda called up from downstairs, "Babe? Is everything okay?"

"Uh . . . oh, yeah, babe, everything's fine!" Nelson called back. "We'll be down in a minute!" Then he turned back to Peach and Adam, who were standing, guilty as hell, caught in the proverbial act, but in the act of *what* exactly? Foreplay . . . raw animal lust . . . finally giving in to the steamy physical attraction they'd been fighting for weeks?

"I record jokes as I think of them, okay?" he snapped. "I don't want to forget them." *Why the hell not?* Peach wanted to ask, but then, that fell way at the bottom of her list of questions for Nelson.

Although she supposed that would explain why Nelson kept going in and out of his closet that night; every time he'd thought of a one-liner or new bit, he must've rushed to record it before it was lost for all time.

None of this got to the heart of the real matter, though—*Dennis.*

Then they heard Brenda saying good-night to Rachel, Robert, and Grace downstairs. *Shit!* Now it was just Peach, Adam, and the Perhunes. And their secrets—whatever those were. "How did you even get in there?" Nelson asked, motioning toward the closet, his eyes glittering wildly with rage. Peach had never seen him like this. And his voice . . . it was cold and menacing . . . dangerous even. "Answer me, goddamn it!"

"Sorry," Adam said, "I, uh . . ."

Oh, come on! Peach thought. How were they supposed to bull-shit their way out of this one? Adam had his palm comfortingly on her back, and she appreciated his attempt to reassure her that he would take charge of the situation, that he would take care of this somehow—take care of *her.* It was sweet as hell. Unfortunately, it was also a waste of time. Might as well lay it all on the table and confront Nelson—it was the only way they might get some answers.

"Look, Nelson, we *know* you saw Dennis on the Saturday night before he disappeared," Peach piped up. "You were both at Monkeyville on amateur night—ring a bell?"

Nelson's voice faltered when he said, "H-how did you know about that?"

"What's the difference how we know?" Peach said. "The point is, why were you lying about it? Why haven't you told the police that you saw him that night? Did you talk to him? What did he say? Did you see him on Sunday, too? You told Grace you were working over the weekend, and Dennis told Joan that *he* was working over the weekend. Now come on—"

"Stop!" Nelson yelled, clearly irritated by Peach's ferocious bar-rage of questions. (Hey, she had to try.) Just then Brenda appeared at the top of the stairs. Peach nudged a little closer to Adam for support, suddenly having a scary thought—what if Brenda was the brains behind whatever Nelson had done? *Dear God* . . .

Brenda walked closer, no baby Annie in hands, and as she did, she asked, "Babe . . . is everything okay?"

With a sigh of resignation, Nelson looked at his wife and shook his head. Somberly, he said, "They know."

Chapter Twenty-five

"Know *what*?" Peach asked, not nearly as aggressive as she'd been a moment ago, feeling prickling panic crawl up her neck, and fear grip her chest. *God, please let Dennis be okay. Please let my worst fears be unfounded.*

"You mean they saw?" Brenda said to Nelson, arching one of her thin black eyebrows in concern.

"No, I would've noticed," Nelson said.

"Saw what?" Adam asked.

"The act," Brenda said, coming closer to stand by her husband and tower over him for support.

"Dennis must've told them about it, before I had the chance to—"

"To *what*?" Peach yelped with alarm. "To hurt him? To kill him? Dear God, Nelson, what did you do to Dennis?"

"Kill him?" Brenda echoed, clearly confused. She exchanged glances with Nelson, who looked equally flummoxed.

"Why would I kill him?" he asked, wrinkling his face up as if Peach were crazy. (Jeez, why did it seem like she got that look often?) "Sure, I was mortified, and yes, I was afraid he would tell someone at work what happened, but—"

"What did happen?" Adam pressed, sounding composed but determined. It was hard to believe that just a few moments ago Adam had also shown a totally different side to himself . . . the passionate side, the fiercely uninhibited side, driven purely by sexual hunger.

Swallowing hard, she refocused quickly.

"What happened? I'll tell you what happened. I bombed," Nelson stated plainly. "It was the worst night of my entire life, if you want to know the truth. The audience heckled me, yelling, 'Get off the stage! You suck! A malignant tumor is funnier!' " Tightly pressing her lips together, Brenda touched her husband's shoulder sympathetically. "I don't even know where it all went wrong," he continued, looking up to the inert ceiling fan for answers. "I was doing some really good new material—at least, *I* thought it was good." (On a side note, if his latest observations on earwax were part of his new material, it would certainly explain a lot.)

"But what about Dennis?" Peach asked ardently. "What's the connection to that night at Monkeyville and his disappearance?" She barely refrained from adding: *Let's fucking* get *to it, already, you neurotic tool!*

"Nothing!" Nelson said defensively. "I have no idea what happened to Dennis! Look, when I saw him in the audience that night, I panicked. I just froze—maybe that's why I couldn't deliver my punch lines that well; I was too self-conscious."

"I *see*," Peach said, extrapolating. "So then you blamed *him* for your failure? And you decided to get him back somehow—"

"No," he insisted. "For chrissake, I didn't do *anything* to Dennis, okay? All I wanted was to go beg him after the show not to tell anyone at work that he'd seen me perform and how badly I'd done. But when I went to try to find him after the show, he'd already left. It all happened so quickly, I . . ." When Nelson's voice drifted off, Brenda patted his shoulder and looked solemnly at Peach and Adam.

"I was home with Annie that night," she said, then gazed down at her husband again. "But I wish I could've been there for you, babe."

"Thanks, babe," he said, reaching up to cup her face and look soulfully into her eyes.

Hello—Twilight Zone alert—what about Dennis?

So Peach asked if Nelson had seen him at the office the next day, Sunday. Nelson shook his head. "No, I never went in; I just told Grace that. I was hoping she'd tell Robert so he'd think I was working really hard."

"But—"

"Look, I didn't tell anyone about seeing Dennis that weekend because I just wanted to forget the whole night. I was so scared he'd tell people at the office the next week—at the very least, I figured he'd tell you. But I have no clue what happened to him, why he disappeared or left the company or whatever." Nelson let out a short, humorless laugh and added, "Hell, maybe he couldn't stand working in the same office as a no-good hack like me!"

Brenda crouched down to encircle him in a bear hug, and crooned, "Babe, oh, babe . . ."

"Babe," Nelson mumbled into her shoulder, letting her rock him from side to side, "this city is one tough room."

That seemed like a particularly good time to exit. Peach and Adam slipped past Brenda and Nelson, hurried down the stairs, and grabbed their coats before fleeing outside into the cold. Faintly, Peach could smell rain in the air—hovering in the clouds, waiting to pour over the chilly night, to pummel the blacktop like a frenzied baptism. It was only fitting; tonight was a new beginning.

"Here, I'll drive you home," Adam said after they'd walked almost two houses down to his car.

"Thanks," Peach managed, as her heart beat frantically beneath her breasts. Everything was catching up with her, the adrenaline from her confrontation with Nelson, the feverish way she and Adam had been clutching each other, melding their open mouths together, the way his tongue had slid against hers, the way he'd sucked on her bottom lip and cupped the back of her neck with his strong, warm hand.

Adam stopped to open the passenger-side door for Peach. He turned the key, but before he pulled the handle he paused . . . and looked at her. She was looking up at him, blinking with uncertainty, not sure where they went from here. God, he was only a few inches away from her, and so breathtakingly handsome under the muted pink glow of the street lamp.

At the exact same time, Peach reached up and Adam leaned down, and their lips met for a long, lingering kiss. Lightly Adam stroked her cheek with his fingers while he kissed her, strumming over her skin as rain began to fall. There was something so tender yet so erotic about that moment, and when they broke the kiss and she looked dazedly into his eyes, she smiled at the wet streaks across his glasses, the ardent expression on his face—at *everything* about that one moment. Then her smile faded, and suddenly passion took over.

He pulled her to him. One hand ran around the back of her neck; the other held tightly to her waist, crushing the velvet of her patchwork coat with his fingers. She plowed her fingers through his wet hair and gripped his head to her as she kissed him hungrily.

Rain spilled in fat drops over their faces, drenching their hair, yet doing nothing to cool them off. Perspiration broke out on Peach's neck, her stomach, between her legs, and with a push of his hips Adam aligned their bodies and pressed his erection against her. He rocked against her, and she pushed back just as hard, just as frantically, her butt up against the car, feverishly turned on by the sensation of Adam's cock grinding against her, and then, suddenly, he pulled her arms off of him. Hands encircling her wrists, he pushed her arms back, pressing them down against the cold metal of his car. She let out a sharp cry, unable to comprehend the fierce jolt of arousal she got from his restraining her—the thrill of being dominated like that—but it must have been because, no matter what, she knew he would never hurt her. And he would never truly dominate her, because she was the lioness and he was a sweetie pie, albeit a Scorpio, and there was something so exciting about bringing out the lion in the lamb.

In fact, where did he even get that move? Robin? Suddenly she was insanely jealous. The image of Adam making love with anyone else infuriated her and filled her with a fierce sense of possession. She'd never thought of herself as the jealous type, but she now knew that when it came to Adam she absolutely, unequivocally *was* the jealous type. If any other woman even touched him, she'd rise up fighting—first with her, then with him. He was *hers*. *That's it; it's been decided.*

All these bizarre thoughts were swirling in her mind as Adam kissed her deeply. His mouth possessed hers with hot intensity, and she yielded to him completely. She kissed him, opening her mouth on his, just as frantic for more as he was, hearing her own short breaths and broken moans, and she finally turned her head just to drag some air into her lungs—to regain her sanity, to slow it down, to unscramble her mind till it was coherent again. But as soon as her chin fell against his shoulder, she felt his hands in her hair. His fingers tunneled through it, then gripped tightly, pulling just enough to arch her neck.

Her head fell back as he kissed her throat and then licked her pulse point with deft pressure. *"Ohh . . ."* she moaned, grappling to hold on to his arms, to keep her balance when her legs felt weak enough to let her sink onto the rain-soaked street.

His cock was huge and hard and buried between her legs, which were awkwardly parted and trembling. Her skirt was plastered to her body, and her coat was probably ruined, but she couldn't stop.

"Jesus," Adam whispered hoarsely barely pulling back. He expelled a heavy breath, and looked into her eyes. Then he kissed her again—gently at first, then roughly, more of the pendulum— frantic then slow, hot then *unbearably* hot, stop then start, pushing and pulling—

Moaning eagerly, Peach claimed his open mouth, stroked his tongue with hers, and suddenly Adam grabbed onto the lapels of her coat. With a grunt he yanked them open and dropped his head to bury his face between her breasts. Her stretchy blouse was wet and clinging and might as well have been paper-thin, because the sensation of Adam's open mouth running over the curves of her breasts was like liquid fire shooting straight to her G-spot, burning her panties onto her skin.

When he sucked her nipple hard through her shirt, Peach cried out, almost losing it—oh, right; she already had—and now she tightened her grip on his head to stop him. "Wait," she said brokenly. "This is too weird. We have to stop."

He expelled a breath, and rested his face in the crook of her neck for a moment before chuckling against her skin. Just then she realized that the rain had turned to snow. Both of them looked up at the sky at the same time . . . then back at each other. A smile broke across Peach's face as a snowflake landed on Adam's glasses, and he smiled back at her, warmly but still looking dazed.

A car veered down the darkened street, splashing water up in the air, reminding Peach and Adam how public a place this really was, and Adam said, "We should go."

He stepped back, opened the door for her, and she untwisted her skirt before sliding into the passenger seat. She looked through the streaky, wet windshield at Quin as he walked quickly around the front of his car, and her stomach knotted.

The snow was floating straight toward her, dancing and sparkling on the glass—it looked so beautiful, so ethereal—and when Adam got in the car, her heart lurched. "You're right; we should go," she whispered now. "To your place."

As soon as they got to Adam's apartment, Peach felt nervous. Her senses had been rattled ever since she'd realized how much she liked him, and the effect he had on her was frustrating, but invigorating. It was something new and overwhelming to sink her teeth into. And speaking of sinking her teeth into something . . . his naked flesh seemed like a good place to start.

Ever since she'd met Adam her days were more vibrant; she woke up with more enthusiasm and less certainty, if that made any sense . . . but who could be sensible in the unlit foyer of Adam Quinlan's apartment, after he had just shut the door and sealed the two of them inside? Alone in the quiet darkness. Peach turned around and found him right behind her. He shrugged off his coat, and she bit her lip. "Would you like the tour?" he asked. Saying yes didn't cross her mind. Unless he meant a tour of his bed, his naked body, his—

She threw her arms around him. Groaning, he pulled her coat off, let it drop to the floor, then slipped his hands under her knees and scooped her up. Her lips crushed his as her legs straddled his body, and he carried her to his bedroom. When he set her down on his bed, he quickly climbed on top of her. She slid her palms up around his neck and ran her fingers through his hair. Then she pulled his face down for another kiss—a slower, more sensual one, one that began with her running the tip of her tongue along the seam of his lips and ended with him restraining her arms again, pressing them back, deep into the pillow.

They rolled over and she was on top. His hands slid up under her skirt and gripped her butt, massaged it, pulled her down hard against his swollen cock. They rolled again, and he was on top, grinding his erection against her as she cried out with each thrust of his hips.

She almost pulled back and blurted that she loved him. *Almost.* But it would've been crazy. So instead she kept kissing him, pulling his shirt from his pants, coaxing it off of him.

Following her lead, he unbuttoned her blouse, whipped it off her, and pulled her bra down. Cupping her breasts in his hands, he rubbed his thumbs over her nipples, and Peach's eyes slid closed. She'd never been particularly self-conscious about her small breasts, and she certainly wasn't now, since Adam was literally panting as he squeezed her, buried his face in between them, and sucked her nipple into his mouth.

The heat was seeping through their clothes, through her skin, into her bones. His body felt hard and powerful on top of hers. She could hear his breathing, shallow and choppy—just like hers. She ached to touch more of him, so she flattened both palms against his chest and pushed; they rolled again. Once she sat on top of him, she stroked his chest and undulated her hips, grinding the damp center of her stockings against his impressive erection. He tightened his grip on her hips and pushed up against her over and over. "Oh, *Christ*," he groaned, and she trembled at the deep, potent sound of him so intensely turned on, and the thickly masculine quality of his voice.

In her lusty haze, for some inexplicable reason, she thought back to the day they'd first met. How strange it was that at one time she hadn't known him. She never would've guessed when she'd first walked into his cubicle that she'd someday be sitting on top of him. That she'd be in his bed, she'd feel him hard—*make* him hard—she'd hear him pant, she'd see his face when he was aroused, and that she would care so deeply for him.

When she'd introduced herself to him, knocked over his cup of pens, watched his face tighten up when she'd asked him too many questions, she'd never dreamed they would be so close. But they were. The depth to which she needed him in her life terrified her . . . but exhilarated her, too. She'd never experienced this powerful a re-action to any other guy. But she supposed there was one thing she'd always sensed about Adam . . . he was special.

"Are you okay?" he whispered now, rolling them over and set-tling on top of her, fitting their bodies together snugly—like puzzle pieces, of course they fit so perfectly—and Peach felt a sleepy smile spread across her face.

"I'm great," she said simply, and pulled him down for an-other kiss.

Within moments they were spiraling out of control. They stripped each other completely naked. Adam licked his way down her body, then between her legs, slid his fingers inside her. Rubbing against her walls, he sent rippling vibrations through her, nearly making her climax. Still shaking, she touched him everywhere, stroked his thick, hard cock, circled her thumb around the tip, made him cry out harshly, gutturally, until neither of them could hold back any longer.

Truly Peach felt out of control—as savage as it might sound, her body was raging, feeling as though it *needed* to have sex with Adam. Right then, right there. She was so wet, so dazed, so inflamed by what he was doing to her, she thought she'd die if he didn't thrust inside her over and over, if he didn't come inside her, and if he didn't do it soon.

"Do you have condoms?" she whispered.

"Yeah, yeah," he said quickly. "Um . . . somewhere." He rolled off her and frantically looked through his nightstand drawer. Obviously there was nothing there. "Shit," he whispered, and raced to his bathroom. Peach had to laugh as she heard him opening and closing drawers and cabinets frantically. Actually, it was very endearing. He must not have needed to have condoms handy in a while—or at least since he'd moved to Boston.

Smiling to herself, she thought, *Even if we don't have sex tonight, maybe I'll die of frustration, but there's no way I could be happier. . . .*

"Oh, yes!" she heard him say in the other room, and then he hurried back to bed.

"Found some?"

"Yeah, in this duffel bag I never unpacked," he explained, then smiled boyishly at her. "As you can tell, it's been a while."

"For me, too," she said.

He didn't seem to want to think about her making love with anyone else either, because he quickly silenced her with a kiss. Rubbing her clitoris, he sheathed himself, then worked her up into another hot, sweaty frenzy with his fingers before he slid inside her. Her neck arched, her eyes squeezed shut, and her body tightened, because he was pretty big and she was very tight; then Adam groaned with near anguish as he withdrew and thrust again.

Peach felt totally swept away by the sexual energy scorching between them, yet at the same time it was so unbelievably wonderful, she almost felt as though she were watching this happen. She'd never felt so acutely aware of another person and what he might be thinking and feeling. She usually assumed that she knew what people were about, but with Adam, who didn't wear his emotions openly, it was often hard to tell.

But she'd psychoanalyze later. Right now she wanted sex.

"So you think Scott's cute, huh?"

"*What?*" Peach laughed, pulling her head up off the pillow. "Where did that come from?"

"You said it the other day."

"I did?" she said, not remembering that, but grinning because he sounded jealous.

"When you were talking about him and Rachel getting together. You mentioned that he was cute."

"Oh, *right,*" she said, nodding. Slanting him a look, she added, "I think I said that Rachel was cute, too." She was trying to remind him that her comment had been purely platonic all around.

"Yeah, it's not Rachel I'm concerned about," he said with a slight edge to his voice. So he wasn't convinced, and he *was* jealous! "And actually what you really said was, 'Scott's soo cute,' " he said, imitating her voice in a way that was so overly effusive, Peach had to laugh.

Now she felt how thrilling it could be to have the person you wanted and cared about worried that other people wanted you, or that you might want other people. Granted, it was a little twisted. Lonnie had that with Dominick. In the back of Peach's mind, she'd always held out hope that she'd find what her sister had, and now it was starting to seem possible. The friendship that they shared, and now the fireworks . . . what was left?

But would Adam fall in love with her, too? And if he didn't . . . what would she do?

Sudden tears stung her eyes because she was so overwhelmed by this emotion, the intensity and how quickly it rushed through her, over her, overwhelming, drowning, and filling her up all at once. *Please don't let this moment end.*

She remembered the night they'd gone to Monkeyville, when Adam had mentioned that he wasn't looking to get into a relationship right now. But surely he would change his mind. Even if he didn't know it yet . . . She'd never been good at accepting defeat, and somehow the stakes had never seemed this high.

"What's going on in that swirly brain of yours?" Adam asked. He was propped up on his elbow, studying her.

"Nothing . . . just thinking about"—*what will happen next*—"Rachel and Scott," she lied. "You just reminded me; I should really try to do something to get those two together."

"Oh, Jesus," he said with a laugh, then rolled his eyes and fell onto his back.

"What?" Peach said, propping herself up, searching his face, and smiling.

"Nothing, nothing," he said, grinning, and threw his forearm over his eyes. Postsexual sleepiness, Peach could tell, though she was feeling wide-awake. "You just have this compulsive need to help people or something."

"Hey, can I help it if I care deeply about the people I come in contact with?"

"Yeah, you know what *I* think?" Adam said, now slipping both hands behind his head and looking up into her eyes. He was equally sexy with or without his glasses. "I think you just like to perch yourself up on your desk, looking down at all your pupils."

"What?" Peach said with a burst of laughter. "That's crazy!"

"Uh-uh," Adam murmured, and rolled over on top of her; she murmured as their bodies aligned and crushed together again. He dragged his soft, warm lips over the sensitive spot on Peach's neck, then flicked his tongue over it, and her eyes slid closed. Then he brought his hand to her tousled hair, and she exhaled a breathy, aroused sigh. As she arched her neck, he said, "It's true. You've always got some scheme cooking."

He licked a hot, wet line from her neck up to the rim of her ear as he ran his hand down her bare side to her inner thigh, massaging her hot, tender flesh gently.

"Oh, Adam . . ." she whispered, overwhelmed by the intensity of her reaction to his touch. She rocked her hips on the bed, waiting for his fingers to touch her more intimately—between her legs, to slide inside her. Instead his hand went the opposite way, running down her thighs toward her knees with torturous slowness.

Faintly she heard him say, "When you're near me, it's hard to concentrate on anything except . . ." He took a tiny bite of flesh between his teeth, then pressed his scalding-hot tongue against it, lapped the spot, made her shiver, and finished, ". . . your legs." Running his hand along her hip bone, then back down to her thigh, he added, "God, you've got great legs."

"Really?" she said, flattered but too turned-on to absorb the compliment fully.

"Is this news to you?" he said, pulling his head back and grinning boyishly. Then he kissed her before she could answer. It was unbelievable the way he looked so tame, yet oozed sensuality. The way he kissed her, the slow, deeply drugging suctioning of his lips on hers, and on her skin . . . the gentle way he aroused her, licked her breasts, touched her. His caress was loving and affectionate, but potent, electrifying. "You're so beautiful," he murmured now, rolling all the way on top of her, covering her body with his, and rubbing his erection suggestively against her lower body. With a soft, yielding moan, Peach slid her eyes closed and wrapped her legs around him.

He started to slip inside her, and for the first time in Peach's life she almost didn't stop him. Almost didn't *think* to stop him. Then she got a semblance of a hold on her senses. "Wait . . ." she said softly, trying to find her voice, to bring herself up for air, for reason. "I guess now we should discuss, you know, our histories," she said, though she didn't want to hear anything sordid about Adam's sexual past.

"*Now* we should discuss our histories?" he said flippantly. "No, seriously . . . okay. Do you want to start?"

"I've been with two people," she said. "My ex-boyfriend, Justin, and this guy Chris I dated right after college."

"No details," he said quickly, before she could give him any (as if she would!). "I've been with two people, too," he added.

Suddenly Peach felt fiercely jealous, but at the same time relieved. "Really?" she said, surprised—though she didn't know why she should be, except maybe because he was twenty-nine, not to mention terrific in bed. "Robin and who else?"

"I had a serious girlfriend all through college and a little after. We were together for about six years."

"What!" she yelped. "Six years with her, and five with Robin?"

"About. What?"

"What, what?"

"You have that look on your face—the alien thing again."

"No, it's nothing . . ." she said, grinning. "It's just that you're, you know, one of *those*. . . ."

"One of what?" he asked, pulling back curiously.

Those guys who only go for long-term relationships, no flings, no meaningless hookups. She smiled inside, because this only confirmed that things were gonna work with them after all. But she didn't want to tip her hand or scare him off yet, so she kissed him softly and sighed against his lips.

"You're my misty sea-green angel," she murmured as she ran her fingers through his hair, holding his face close to hers.

His eyes searched hers quizzically. "What does that mean?"

"It means . . . I like you." As they kissed, he entered her with maddening slowness, and her body went up in flames. Her hips rocked on and off the bed. She dug her fingers into his shoulder, then thought, *Jesus, what am I doing!* "Wait—a condom," she said.

Adam said, "Oh, Christ, I'm sorry . . ." and grabbed another one from his nightstand.

His thrusts were slow and deep, and they went on and on, making her arch her back, tangle her hands in his hair, beg him to go even faster, even deeper, and so he did. Panting, he brought his hands under arms, holding tightly to her shoulders as he rocked his body frantically against hers. And she rocked back, drawing up her knees, her feet resting flat on the twisted sheets, and she rotated her hips, shuddering with each thrust.

Breathing hard, clinging to his back as sweat broke out on the back of her neck, Peach cried out, and her legs nearly shook from her muscles that were pulled achingly tight. And then she felt the burst of a thrillingly hot, vibrating climax. It rolled through her lower body fast and hard, making her tremble and finally, Adam began to come. He groaned deeply—like it was the best feeling he'd ever had—and immediately after, Peach collapsed flat on the bed and fell dead asleep.

Chapter Twenty-six

On Monday morning Peach got back to reality. After the weekend she'd spent with Adam—laughing, talking, watching movies, snuggling, and having hot, relentless sex—she supposed it was past time she came back to earth. They hadn't talked about what their newfound romance meant, or where it was headed. Peach knew that Adam didn't think he wanted a relationship, but that was pretty much what this was. He wasn't ready to call it that yet . . . but she was sure he'd come around.

Now she got off the phone with Detective Joe Montgomery of the Boston Police Department. The good news was, he was finally back from his honeymoon, and was much more considerate of Peach's feelings than Detective Mays had been. The bad news was, he couldn't tell her much, even if he wanted to, because Dennis Emberson's disappearance wasn't his case, and he had little idea what was going on with it.

He did tell her something interesting about Dennis's car, which Peach remembered had not been in the driveway or garage when she'd gone to Dennis's house. According to Joe, the police tracked it down to an impound lot, where it had apparently been towed. Here was the thing: the car had been towed on Sunday afternoon, from a metered spot near Monkeyville. But that didn't make sense. If Dennis had driven Joan home after their date, then when and why had he parked his car near Monkeyville again?

With a sigh Peach hunched over her keyboard and rubbed her balled-up fists over her eyes. *What now?*

. . .

"I thought of something we can try."

Peach whipped around at the sound of Adam's voice. He was standing in the entrance of her cube, looking adorable in his white shirt, red tie, and khakis, with his glasses a little crooked on his face, which was unshaven. She knew he hadn't had time to shave today; they'd spent the weekend together, and she'd left his place early that morning. When she'd left to go shower and change at her own apartment, Adam had still been sprawled naked on the bed, completely zonked out. And *that* had been adorable, too.

"Peach," he said, and whistled to get her attention.

"Right, go on . . . you thought of something we can try?" She assumed he meant something to help them find Dennis, and any ideas were welcome; she'd been fresh out since she'd busted into Nelson's closet.

"I can check his computer's history of activity on the network. In other words, see a listing of all the documents and files he accessed before he disappeared, how many times they were opened, and if he made changes to any. It's all archived in the database; you just have to know how to get there."

"What will that tell us?" she asked, confused.

He shrugged. "Maybe nothing. But since you're convinced that whatever happened to him had something to do with his work here, it might give us a clue."

"Oh, right! And then we'll know if he came in to work that weekend, like he'd planned to, after all," Peach said, then relayed to Adam what Joe had told her about Dennis's car being towed and impounded two weeks ago. Obviously the fact that Dennis still hadn't come to get his car was a very bad sign. But Peach couldn't let herself get defeated with negative thinking—not now. Adam had an idea, and she was going to latch onto it hopefully.

The fact that the police were looking into the matter at all provided her with some relief, though she wondered how driven they were to stay on the case. It wasn't like Dennis was a helpless child or someone famous or a criminal on the run. Then his disappearance would make headlines. And to be fair, without any evidence of a crime, the police had no overt reason to suspect foul play, and no reason to suspect anyone at Millennium of wrongdoing because, to the naked eye, Dennis got along well with everyone. According to Grace, Robert had even volunteered to show the police Dennis's performance evaluations, all of which indicated what a competent accountant and well-liked employee he'd been.

Nevertheless . . . Peach couldn't shake the feeling that this all had something to do with Dennis's last entry in his planner—the one that read, *Take action.*

"We can do it at my desk," Adam said now. Then, realizing how it sounded, he grinned. "I mean, I can access it at my desk. Actually, I can just tell you what I find—you don't have to come."

"Of course I'm coming!" Peach said, hopping up from her chair.

"Nice skirt," he said as she walked toward him.

She glanced down; it was her tea-length zebra-striped skirt, which today she'd worn with black stockings and heels. "Thanks," she said, and kept going, until he grabbed her hand and pulled her back.

"What, no kiss?" he said softly, touching her body with his.

Instantly Peach melted into him, moving her lips softly over his while she used her tongue seductively. Then he quickly pulled back. "That's enough," he said gruffly. "Don't get me all excited."

"Who, me?" she said, blinking innocently.

"We probably shouldn't even be doing this at all," he said. "An office romance is something that's generally frowned upon."

Peach rolled her eyes. *What a straight arrow,* she thought, and not for the first time. Then she tugged on his sleeve. "C'mon, let's go, you," she said, and led the way.

Once they were at Adam's desk he got to work accessing Dennis's info. After a few minutes he said, "Well, this is interesting."

"What, what?" Peach said, leaning over him, almost rabid with interest.

Still scanning the screen, Adam explained, "The last time Dennis logged onto his PC was Friday morning, three weeks ago." The last day Peach had seen him.

"Then he never came into the office that weekend, like he'd told Joan he planned to?"

"Or if he did, it wasn't long enough to boot up his computer," Adam remarked.

"Hmm . . . what else?"

Adam scrolled with his mouse. "The last activity archived was on that last Friday. Apparently he opened several documents related to personnel."

"Personnel?" Peach echoed, surprised. "But that's Brenda's area." Up until recent developments, Millennium had been way too small to require a full-fledged HR department; Brenda did all the hiring and firing.

"Well, all the documents he opened are saved in the personnel folder on the H drive," Adam said. "I guess it's possible, then, that the contract Dennis mentions in his planner is an employee contract."

"Yes!" Peach said quickly. "Wait, we need to look at his entries again. You e-mailed a copy to yourself, right?"

"Yeah, let me open it up. . . . Here it is," Adam said.

Quickly Peach reread the cryptic abbreviated notations in Dennis's planner from the last few days he'd been in the office. She honed in again on "re-work contract," wondering *whose* contract Dennis was referring to, and why on earth would *he* be reworking it? He was the accountant, so the legalese of a contract would hardly be his turf, and in terms of individual perks or stipulations, that would be Robert Walsh's job as Millennium's president.

No, on second thought, it would be *Claire* Walsh's job, since she was the owner and CEO of the company.

When Peach posed this to Adam, he shook his head in shared bafflement. "I don't know . . . maybe Dennis was referring strictly to a salary or raise issue. You know, something that involved his crunching some numbers for Robert . . . ?"

Peach looked at the entry that read, COMP. S. 4 N/R. Compare salaries? Could that be what the S stood for? Compare salaries for N and Robert? Then she glanced back at Friday's entry. TAKE ACTION, RE-WORK CONTRACT, N.

Hmm . . . wait a second. Suddenly a thought occurred to her. It was the *way* she'd been reading it. "Hey, wait," she said, leaning closer to the screen, "maybe we've been looking at this wrong."

"What do you mean?"

"Maybe it's not 're-work contract'—maybe it's *regarding* work contract."

"Work contract?" Adam echoed. "Is that different from employee contract?"

"Yes!" Peach said, just realizing, "yes, of *course*!"

"Wait. I'm lost," Adam said.

That was right—she'd forgotten for a moment that he was new to the company. "Work contracts are for consultants," she explained. "You know, it's a short-term contract—it's a whole separate thing from a permanent employee's contract. In fact, I remember Grace and Robert talking about that the day we were having cake in the conference room." Nodding her head, she added, "N must stand for Nicholas Easterbrook, the consultant Robert hired recently to do some streamlining, or whatever the hell consultants do." Eagerly, she scanned the three entries from Dennis's planner again.

CNSLT R ABOUT N?
CHK TM-SH / COMP. S. 4 N/R
TAKE ACTION, RE-WORK CONTRACT, N

"Consult Robert about Nicholas?" she read out loud, plugging in her new theory. "Check . . . something . . . and compare . . . something . . . for Nicholas and Robert. Take action regarding work contract for Nicholas."

"Wow," Adam said, his hazel eyes widening behind his glasses, "this is starting to come together . . . sort of."

"Yeah . . . we just have to figure out why Dennis was concerned with Easterbrook's work contract. Why would he even get involved in anything Easterbrook was doing?"

After thinking for a moment, Adam speculated, "Maybe Easterbrook was charging too much to the company, fudging his expenses, something like that. You know, corporate accountants have that whole ethical code they're supposed to follow."

"What's that?" Peach asked.

"You know, that ethical obligation they're supposed to adhere to, to look into any spending in the company that's suspicious."

"You're asking if I know about that? I didn't even know we had an M drive," she said glibly. Then, tilting her head, she said, "I wonder what Dennis meant by 'take action'? What was he gonna do?" The other question was left unsaid: *And what was done to him?*

Picking up Adam's phone, Peach hopped up onto his desk. "Here—check the personnel folder for a spreadsheet called 'contact information' or something like that," she said, pointing to his computer screen like a teacher. "Get me Easterbrook's cell phone."

"Wait, you're just going to call him? What are you going to say?" Typical Adam—he wanted a clear, cogent plan of action when there was no time to spare.

"I don't know. I guess I'm just going to wing it."

"Wing it?" he repeated incredulously. "That sounds like a terrible idea."

"Quin, sometimes life is messy."

He grumbled something under his breath, and read the phone number off his screen once he found it. Easterbrook's cell rang three times before he picked up. "Hello?"

"Um, hi . . . I'm calling from Millennium Gift Baskets," Peach said, her eyes shifting as she scrambled to come up with something brilliant. "I was wondering . . . um . . ."

"Yes?" Easterbrook said, a little impatiently. (Jeez, didn't he realize that brilliance took time?)

"Oh, is this a bad time?" Peach asked, stalling.

"For what? I'm working at the moment."

"Oh—working on streamlining our company, or on something else?"

Adam gave her a thumbs-up and mouthed the word "smooth" before covering his eyes with his hand. Peach swatted him on the arm.

"No, I'm working for another company right now, if you don't mind. I was under the impression that Robert wouldn't need my consulting services until May, at the earliest."

May? That was six months away. So why had Robert told Grace to get him a work contract for Nicholas ASAP? Peach distinctly remembered that from a few weeks back, when they were having cake in the conference room for Brenda's birthday.

And why had Grace said that Robert bought Nicholas Easterbrook a laptop so he could work at home, and taken him out for lunch several times recently? It didn't make sense.

"I thought you were working for us right now," Peach said.

"Look, I don't know what all this is about. There must have been some sort of miscommunication between Dennis and Robert, because Dennis called me about this matter, as well. In fact, I told him the same thing I'm telling you."

"Which is what, exactly?" she pressed.

But Nicholas wasn't taking the bait. "Who is this again?" he asked suspiciously.

"Peach . . . Peach Kelley," she said tentatively.

"Well, Ms. Kelley, as I mentioned, I'm busy at the moment. I've already discussed all this with Dennis, so please direct your questions to him."

I would love to! Peach felt like screaming in frustration, but considering that Easterbrook had already hung up on her, there was probably little point.

Chucking the phone down on its cradle, Peach sighed and said, "I remember when the name Peach Kelley actually meant something in this town."

With a laugh, Adam shook his head and said, "No, you don't."

"Okay, fine," she admitted, grinning in spite of her frustration.

Once Peach relayed the gist of her brief conversation with Nicholas Easterbrook, Adam did the same search through Robert's e-mails, hard drive, and archived activity on the network that he'd done with Dennis. Unfortunately, he found no link whatsoever to the personnel files that Dennis had been looking into. "But Robert has to be up to something shady. It's the only thing that makes sense," Peach insisted. "I mean, if he never really hired Nicholas, but he's claiming that he did and charging laptops and lunches to the company—"

"And *paying* him," Adam finished, then hit ALT and TAB to bring up the planner entries again. The second one, which they couldn't understand before, now seemed to make some sort of sense. "What about 'check time sheets'?" he proposed.

Peach finished, "Compare *signatures*—holy shit!"

Robert Walsh had been embezzling from his wife's company! By pretending he'd hired Nicholas Easterbrook for some consulting work, he must've been signing Nicholas's time sheets and what? Signing over his paychecks, too?

"There must be some P.O. box he has the checks sent to."

"But wouldn't it be automatic deposit?" Peach said, then realized, "Oh, right, but you have the option of not doing automatic deposit if you want."

"Right. Hmm . . ." Adam looked at the contact information spreadsheet again. "No P.O. box listed here, just Easterbrook's street address."

"Maybe that was one of the things Dennis noticed? That the address where Nicholas's checks were being sent was different from the one in the system?"

"Or maybe he only noticed that after he started digging— maybe he noticed that Robert's and Nicholas's signatures were too similar," Adam said, shaking his head. "Who knows? But I guess the point is, he was looking into all this, and he even called Nicholas about it. Hey, if Robert forged a work contract, signing Nicholas's name, there should be a few office copies."

Peach shook her head. "All the personnel files are confidential and locked in Grace's filing cabinet. We'll never get in there without her blabbing to anyone who'll listen."

"True . . ."

"But if we sneak into Robert's office after everyone's left for the day . . . Think about it. Right now this is all just theory, but if we find a P.O. box number written down somewhere, or maybe an expense account with Easterbrook's signature forged at the bottom, anything like that . . . Hey, we might even find out if Dennis ever confronted him." Or *took action*, as he'd planned to . . . right before he disappeared.

Chapter Twenty-seven

They didn't get their opportunity until Wednesday night. Robert left the office at six thirty, which was early for him, and it gave Peach and Adam a chance to sneak into his office.

"Okay, the coast is clear," she said as she ducked her head inside his cube. They'd both been lingering at Adam's desk, but when they'd heard the office go quiet, Peach had gone to make rounds to be sure everyone was gone.

Now they crept through the elaborate maze of cubicles and headed toward Robert's office. Only a few feet from his door they heard footsteps.

"What was that?" Peach whispered.

"Someone's coming," Adam said quickly, and nudged her into a small conference room to the right. The room was pitch-black, especially since the view from the windows was a skyscraper that blocked the stars and the streetlight. Both huddled by the closed door, they waited.

"Do you think it's Robert?" Peach asked.

"I don't know."

"But—"

"*Shh.*"

Peach, who was flattened closest to the doorknob, turned it slowly and cracked the door. Through the scant space she saw Grace at her desk, which was sandwiched between the conference room and Robert's office. She was rooting around for something, then finally muttered, "Oh, here it is," as she snatched up the Tupperware container of mayonnaise and tossed it into her tote bag. (God forbid it stay out all night—it might smell in the morning, and have to compete with the stinky brick of cheese that Grace was apparently still aging at her desk.)

As she slung her tote bag over her shoulder and turned to go, her phone rang. "Hello? Oh, hi, Midge! How're you doing—how's Florida?"

"Who's Midge?" Adam whispered. Peach felt his warm breath against her temple, and realized just how close he was to her in the darkness (not that it could ever truly be close enough).

"Her sister," Peach replied, just as they heard Grace say, "Yeah, nothing much here, same old bullcrap. You should've seen the mess that was left in the kitchen today. Nelson—el Slobbo—was at it again. . . ."

Rolling her eyes, Peach said, "Great, this could be a while."

They both sighed and waited. Vaguely Peach could hear Grace still yammering to her sister, indulging in the usual sparkling repartee about how everyone at work was a stupid asshole and they could all kiss her ass, etc., etc. Then she said something about how some bar up the street from her, Old Smokey's, was going out of business, and she couldn't wait for that. None of this was the least bit distracting to Peach, though, who felt physically overpowered by the magnetic and seductive pull toward Adam in these close quarters.

Standing so close to him, she could smell his clean, masculine scent, faintly hear him breathing, and acutely *feel* his presence. Hot, vivid images flashed through her mind. They'd just made love the night before, and already she was breathless and needy for more.

They'd spent every night together since this weekend, when they'd first made love. Being with each other was so passionate but comfortable at the same time, and even though there hadn't been any official talk that evoked the word "relationship" yet, it seemed like it was just a technicality.

Now she felt him moving closer. With a shaky sigh she shifted over, too, brushing her hip against him. His breath quickened and soon he was directly behind her, snaking his arms around her stomach and pulling her closer. He whispered her name just before he closed his mouth over the curve of her neck, kissed her warmly, wetly, and then sucked some of her flesh between his teeth. Heat poured through her veins, flushing her face and inflaming every part of her. He spun her around, and when his mouth descended on hers, they kissed deeply.

Peach's fingers climbed up Adam's shirt, clutching the cotton in her hands, gripping him to hold him as close as she possibly could—to possess him completely—and Adam groaned as he pressed her up against the door, nudging it all the way closed.

"I could kiss you for hours," he whispered hoarsely, and the words weren't original, but couldn't have sounded more sincere. She smiled softly at him, looking dazedly into his face, barely visible in the darkness. "Peach," he murmured as he slid his strong, warm palm to the back of her neck.

Tenderly he pulled her toward him until their lips met, and as Adam's tongue slicked inside her mouth, Peach moaned. She rocked her body against his, nearly trembling when he kept one hand on her neck, but crept the other down beneath the waistband of her skirt, outside her silk panties. Her breath caught as his fingers stroked over her crotch—so gently, almost not at all—it was such a tease, but so incredible. And then his thumb pressed up against her opening, rubbing the fabric of her underwear against her, almost inside her. She held back a moan, but only because Grace was out there and bit Adam's shoulder instead. When he started circling his thumb, applying more pressure, Peach nearly cried out. "Deeper," she whispered in his ear. *"Please."*

With a growl he pushed the elastic of her panties over and slid his finger inside her. The pleasure was so acute, her knees wobbled and her eyes squeezed shut. "Oh, God," he said gruffly. "You turn me on so much." Right now she was torn between letting him continue touching her, or sinking to her knees to slick her tongue over the tip of his penis—to suck the head into her mouth and hear him groan. Damn—both options were so unbelievably arousing to her, it was hard to choose. And who could think straight when Adam was touching her like this, anyway?

Suddenly they heard a loud thud.

Both froze.

Peach figured that Adam might feel a little ridiculous frozen with his hand where it was, so she pushed on his wrist, and he moved his hand to rest on her hip. "What was that?" he said, his voice still thick with lust.

"I think it was Grace hanging up the phone," Peach replied. They listened for a few more seconds. Total silence on the other side of the door—Grace had left.

"She's gone," Peach said, stating the obvious and pulling up her skirt, which Adam had pushed down to midthigh. She didn't know why she suddenly felt embarrassed. But in any event, the moment had been broken, though she knew it would take less than a kiss to get it going again. Yet that wasn't going to get them anywhere with the Dennis Emberson case, especially when this might be their only chance to sneak into Robert's office.

They slipped out of the conference room, crossed past Grace's desk, and pulled on Robert's door. Locked. "Well, it was worth a try," Peach said, then crossed back to Grace's desk. Odds were excellent that his assistant would have a set of keys, too. And lucky for Peach, Grace demonstrated her disrespect for her employer by not even bothering to hide them. As soon as she opened the top drawer—besides pens, paper clips, Scotch tape, and some assorted condiment packets—Peach also found a key that was brightly tagged with orange marker: ROBERT'S OFFICE.

"Well, that was easy," she said snatching it up and hip-checking the top drawer shut. Once inside Robert's office, she turned on his desk lamp and they scoured his desk, trying not to make even the slightest mess. They dug through his in box, his out box, his desk drawers, looking for something that might connect Robert to Easterbrook, or indicate that Robert had fudged Easterbrook's employment and expenses.

Peach was in the middle of snooping through the loose papers still on the tray of Robert's printer when they heard the jangle of keys outside the door. *Oh, shit!* "Hide!" Peach whispered frantically, and quickly yanked the chain of the desk lamp to turn it off.

Adam grabbed her hand and ducked into Robert's executive bathroom just as Robert opened the door. Breathing hard, crouched next to Adam behind the open bathroom door, Peach realized they'd left the light on in Robert's office. Luckily, he didn't seem to notice.

Through the crack between the hinges and the doorjamb, they watched him. He was looking frantically for something; hastily, he lifted up folders and papers, lifted up the trash can, looked around the bookcase, then bent to check under his desk. "Oh, thank God!" he said aloud as he got on all fours and stretched his arm to reach something.

He pulled out what appeared to be a mitten, though it was hard to tell at this angle. It was bright red with balls and tassels hanging down from it. And it was . . . familiar. Quickly Robert slipped it into his coat pocket and left his office, hitting the light switch on his way out.

Adam heaved a sigh and relaxed back against the bathroom wall. "Oh, man, that was close," he muttered.

Absently, Peach agreed. At the moment she was still preoccupied, trying to remember where she'd seen that mitten before.

Chapter Twenty-eight

Christmas came that weekend, and as usual it went too quickly. The festivities at Peach's parents' town house in Brookline were hardly the same without Lonnie there.

Hopefully her sister had worked out her issues with Dominick; hopefully they were romantically entwined right now, enjoying the last moments of their trip to Aruba. If Peach knew her sister, though, Lonnie would definitely call tonight, before Christmas night was through, to wish her family happy holidays and to tell them she loved them.

The holidays were missing more than her sister—Peach missed Adam, too.

He'd gone to New Hampshire to juggle his dad in Manchester and his mom in Portsmouth. Apparently Sonny was meeting him at their dad's, but refusing to see their mom as some sort of statement. Peach felt sorry for Adam, because he kept all his frustrations inside: frustration over his sister's immaturity, and the fact that his brother couldn't be bothered to call, both of which hurt their mother very deeply. Peach knew Adam better than he thought; beneath his reserved, efficient veneer, he had a huge heart.

That was why she loved him. She was dying to say it to him— just to say it out loud. Right now this thing between them didn't have a name, but of course it was a relationship. They ate lunch together every day, brought each other treats every morning—well, they'd done that as friends, too—but now they kissed, they held hands, they made passionate love with each other, they snuggled in the morning. What more was there to a relationship?

"Peach," Margot called from upstairs, "your sister's on the phone!"

"Oh! Let me get it," Peach said, and hopped off the kitchen counter, where she'd been eating leftover Christmas cookies and thinking about Adam—apparently so intently that she hadn't even heard the phone ring. She picked up the extension in the family room. "Hey! How's it going?"

"Hi, Merry Christmas!" Lonnie said cheerily. "Everything's going great—except that we don't want to leave yet."

"So you guys worked things out?" Peach asked as she flopped onto the thick suede sofa and coiled the phone cord around her fingers.

"Yes," Lonnie said, lowering her voice, "you were right."

"About which part?"

"All of it—especially the part about slipping it into the conversation that Dan's unappealing—you know, short, bald. Oh, and I threw in some acne."

"Nice touch," Peach said with an approving nod.

"Pathetically immature, but it *worked*," Lonnie said. "I'll never doubt you again."

"Don't lie on Christmas," Peach said, and Lonnie laughed. They chatted for several more minutes, and Lonnie asked about her job. Peach shrugged. "It's okay; I'm kind of bored there," she admitted. Seeing Adam was really the most exhilarating part of every day. "I've been there over a year now already," Peach added. "Enough is enough."

"But what about the Ethan Eckers doll?" Lonnie asked. "Doesn't Millennium have all those plans for spinoff characters and everything? They're definitely not going to want you to leave."

Peach shrugged. "Yeah, I guess. I don't know; we'll see." The truth was, lately Peach had wondered if she was suited to the corporate world. How great it would be to find a place where a person was supposed to strip down facades, rather than erect them.

Next Lonnie asked about Adam. "What's happening there—are you two still friends or what?"

"Oh, my God, I didn't tell you!" Peach said, realizing just how long it had been since she'd talked to her sister. "We're involved now." Immediately, a blissful smile spread across her lips, and a gush of warmth pooled heavily in her chest.

After she filled her sister in on the latest developments (including how good the sex was), Lonnie said, "This is *great!*"

"I think I love him!" Peach blurted.

"Oh, my God—this is huge!" Lonnie said enthusiastically, then called to Dominick in the background, "Sweetie, she and Adam are in love!"

"Well, I don't know how he feels yet," Peach qualified.

"Still, this is great," Lonnie repeated. "I can't wait to meet him!"

"I know," Peach said, smiling. "I can't wait for everyone to meet him. Actually, I mentioned to him that if he finished his family stuff early, he should come by . . . so we'll see."

"So Mom hasn't met him yet, either?"

"Nope. No one has." In the back of her mind, Peach knew that Adam was gun-shy about moving too fast, and undoubtedly meeting the 'rents represented just that. But she was patient (at select times), so she could wait until he was ready.

"Mom must be dying with the suspense," Lonnie said—and a little gleefully, Peach noticed.

"Please, she's just thrilled she got a vacuum cleaner for Christmas."

"Eww," Lonnie said, clearly appalled at such a miserable, housewifeish gift. "Who gave her *that?*"

"I did," Peach admitted, "but it's not what you think. It was hers; I borrowed it over a month ago."

With a burst of laughter, Lonnie said, "Omigod, you're a savage! You gave Mom her own vacuum for her Christmas present?"

"No, of *course* not. I gave her several things, in addition to the vacuum."

"Uh-huh."

"And hey . . . I put a bow on it," Peach added in her own defense. Her sister just laughed again, still not overly impressed.

Adam was on his way to his apartment, after two days in New Hampshire, when he suddenly did a U-turn. Peach had told him he was welcome to stop by her parents' place in Brookline. He'd thought he wasn't ready for that—that it would make him feel uncomfortable meeting her mom, that it just seemed too . . . serious.

But now he felt desperate to see her, missing her with an urgency that clutched his chest and twisted his gut into a big, aggravating knot.

Goddamn it . . . what was he going to do about her?

Nothing, he told himself. Everything didn't have to be labeled; they could just keep going with the flow and having fun. Yet it was shockingly hard to instruct himself to do the opposite of his usual tendencies. To ignore his impulse, which was to *claim* her. Not to ignore his growing affection for her, but to act on it. To make her only his. The idea was sharply thrilling—but also scary as hell. And smothering . . . he couldn't help it. The thought of another relationship, a ready-made girlfriend, all the obligation that came with that, it just made him feel pressured, claustrophobic.

But still, he needed to see her. Christmas had vanished quickly this year. Christmas Eve had been spent helping his mom look for apartments in Portsmouth. Then he'd driven to Manchester, where his dad had been helpless with dinner and played it up for as much sympathy as he could. Sonny had asked when she was going to get the new car she'd been "promised," and Martin kept saying, "Ask your mother; she's the one tying everything up. I don't understand why she's doing this."

Adam hated blurred lines, ambiguity, and yet that was exactly where he found himself. On the one hand, he felt fiercely protective of his mom, defensive of her, but on the other, he couldn't help it, but he *was* annoyed with her. Why couldn't she have skipped all this drama and just told Martin to change?

Maybe because Martin wouldn't have listened; he would've continued tinkering with his electronics, dismissing her frustration as "her time of the month"—despite the fact that she'd already been through menopause. As she had informed Adam, which brought him back to his annoyance: He was a twenty-nine-year-old guy who did *not* want to know about his mother's menopause! *Jesus.*

But after her terrifying health scare, could Adam really fault her for any of this? Was it even any of his business?

As he neared Peach's parents' street, Adam's pulsed kicked up. Inhaling deeply, his chest filled with anticipation, excitement . . . longing. Sex with Peach had been unbelievably *hot*. It had more than measured up to his fantasies; in fact, when he thought about it, he honestly couldn't believe the intensity of what sparked between them when they touched each other. Just thinking about how she licked her lollipops turned him on.

He pulled into the narrow driveway of the town house marked 18. A brightly lit wreath with fat colored bulbs hung on the door. Adam cut the engine and sighed. God, how he missed holding her—he needed to crush her to him, to feel her hair against his lips, to breathe in her tangy, sweet scent. Most of all he needed to hear her sultry voice when she moaned, whispered, or just when she spoke to him. Whether she was teasing him or trying to be intensely serious, she was so damn cute.

Hiding her gift behind his back, he climbed the brick steps to the front door and rang the bell. A few moments passed before the door swung open.

"I can't believe you're here!" Peach yelped.

Instantly a smile broke across his face. She always had that effect; she always had him smiling. "You didn't think I'd come?" he said softly, and leaned down to hug her, thinking that he hadn't intended to come, which now seemed ludicrous.

"I wasn't sure," she replied, hugging him back, clutching the fabric of his coat in her fingers, pressing her cheek against his chest. Closing his eyes for a moment, Adam buried his nose in her hair and let out a breath he didn't know he'd been holding. Everything seemed so unimportant except this moment; it was such a relief to be with her.

When they finally pulled back, he got a look at her. Again—adorable. She had on tight blue track pants, furry gold socks, and a sweater with a million colors in it that all collided into one headache-inducing mess. "You look really cute," he said, grinning.

"I do?" Peach said, sounding a little surprised as she looked down at herself.

"Here," Adam said, handing her the wrapped present he'd been concealing from her.

Pressing a hand to her heart, Peach smiled enthusiastically. "Oh, thank you, that's so sweet! I've got something for you, too. Come in, come in."

He closed the door behind him before Peach hustled him into the family room. "You sit there," she said, pointing to a spot on the floor beside the Kelleys' towering Christmas tree. Its thick, full branches reached out, sparkled, and commanded all of the attention in the room. She ran upstairs, and soon returned with a foil-wrapped box in her hand, and a little something tucked under her arm. "My parents really want to meet you," she commented as she flopped down on the floor, cross-legged and facing him. "But they left about ten minutes ago; went to take some cranberry bread and Christmas cookies to Mrs. Marashino down the block. They'll probably be there for a while. Okay, you first," she said, pushing the box into his hands.

"Okay . . ." he said, smiling, and tore open his gift. Well, actually he didn't tear—he peeled the paper off with methodical care, with patience, with dignity, while Peach shook her head in bemusement, thinking, *Doesn't he know this is Christmas?* He pulled out the first item in the box—a navy-blue button-down shirt—and thanked her. Then he pulled out the second item, which was a crazily loud T-shirt that made Hawaiian prints look understated. Adam had to laugh. "What occasion is this for?"

"I don't know; I just thought it was kind of funny," Peach said with a smile.

"I see; so we're doing gag gifts now?" he said, grinning.

"No . . . but I thought it wouldn't hurt to shake up your wardrobe a little. Besides, you only have to wear that shirt around me, okay?"

He nodded. Then he tilted his head and reached over to stroke her cheek. "Thanks. I love both of them," he said, and leaned over to kiss her. As his lips pressed softly against hers, Peach lifted up off her butt to get closer, holding on to his collar to anchor herself, to hold Adam tightly, to savor the kiss and make it last.

"Okay, your turn now," Adam said thickly, when they finally pulled apart. With no further encouragement, Peach went to town on her gift. Inside the wrapped square box was a sleek, silver watch with a slim wristband and a pale-green face.

"I know you like silver," he explained, leaning over to look at it with her and pointing, "but it's smaller than the one you wear, and it has your birthstone crystals inside, see?"

"It's gorgeous, thank you; I love it!" she said, and hugged him. Then she pressed her lips to his ear and whispered, "I have something else for you, too." Instinctively, Adam's groin tightened. Peach reached behind her back and pulled out a small bunch of mistletoe. So that was what she'd had tucked beneath her arm when she'd come down the stairs. "I took it off my parents' bedroom doorway," she said.

"Oh"—Adam pulled back a little warily—"won't they mind?" He hadn't met her parents yet, but he wanted them to like him when he did.

"No, they won't even notice it's gone. I'm the one who put it there in the first place." Then she rose up off her butt again, onto her knees, with her face just inches from his. Dangling the mistletoe above them, she said softly, "C'mon, what are you waiting for?"

Twenty minutes later, Peach and Adam were snuggling together on the family room couch, looking at the fire. They'd spent the last hour kissing passionately, deeply, and running their hands over each other's body slowly. Now Peach combed her fingers through Adam's hair, while Adam gently stroked her spine.

Briefly they had talked about what they'd been like back in high school, and it had been pretty predictable: Peach had multitasked in school clubs, and helped paint scenery for the school plays and concerts, while Adam had been on the soccer team, the math club, and read a lot of Tolkien. It was odd how, fundamentally, everyone was a type.

"Sometimes I wish things could be like they were when I was younger," Adam said now.

Peach thought, *Sure, who doesn't?* but kept it to herself. Instead she combed her fingers through his hair and asked, "What do you mean?"

After a pause, he said, "Like Christmas, for instance. When I was younger, it just used to be such a big deal. It was so exciting, and . . ."

"Carefree?" Peach said when Adam's voice drifted off.

"Yeah," he said quietly, pensively, and Peach realized for the first time that he was lonely. Wetness pooled in her eyes at the thought. She quickly tucked her head into his chest so he wouldn't see her get upset. She couldn't explain it, and as Grandma Deborah used to say, *Life's tough all over, kid*—but still, her heart ached to take all of Adam's loneliness away. To erase any sadness he might feel, now or ever. Right now his hand caressed her breast through her shirt, his open palm rubbing against her nipple. With a soft sigh, she continued stroking his erection through his pants, pressing against it with the flat of her hand, hearing his breath quicken. *Hmm . . .* So maybe he wasn't such a sad case after all. . . .

There was something subtle and seductive about their slow, languorous touches; something infinitely special about this cozy, heated moment. With a faint smile, she shut her eyes and sighed. "I love you, Adam," she murmured sleepily.

It felt like a huge release to finally say the words, and she never even realized that Adam had tensed up and frozen beneath her hands.

Chapter Twenty-nine

The following week Peach tried not to notice that Adam was different. It wasn't something she could pin down specifically, but she could tell . . . he was distant, not quite as open or affectionate; rather than getting closer to her, he felt farther and farther away.

They hadn't spent the night together since Christmas, when he'd left her parents' place soon after cuddling, before her parents had returned, and suddenly feeling tired after his drive.

It seemed like every night Adam had too much work to do on Millennium's new network to hang out—or so he claimed. Not that Peach was usually prone to cynicism, but she knew moodiness when she saw it.

Goddamn Scorpio.

Meanwhile, she was starting to believe that she'd never see Dennis Emberson again. Occasionally she convinced herself there was some positive explanation for his disappearance—like he'd slipped through a hole in the fabric of space-time and entered a parallel universe where unkempt accountants and jelly doughnuts ruled.

Now Peach sighed and pushed around her McMurphy's takeout that she'd brought home after visiting BeBe earlier. Talk about a depressing night. She needed Adam to help brighten things, to give her a sense of hope, but *noo.* . . . Why did he have to pick now to be working all the time? She missed him.

Had she moved too fast by telling him she loved him? Scared him off? Now, how could she? She was just being honest about her feelings—and surely she hadn't been telling him anything he didn't already know. That settled it then. Adam's funk—whatever it was—would pass. Leaning back against the sofa, she stretched her legs out in front of her, shifting Buster in her lap. In turn, Buster rolled over onto her back and pointed her nose to the ceiling as Peach watched TV. She hadn't realized the news had come on; the last thing she needed right now was maudlin revelations about the state of humankind.

Too late. Just as she reached for the remote control to switch the station, she heard the newscaster say something about how a body was found in a Dumpster, apparently someone killed by a blow to the head, and yet to be identified.

Thoroughly depressing, Peach thought sadly, poising to change the channel just as a picture of the victim appeared on the screen. "Oh, my God!" Peach exclaimed, dropping her jaw as the remote slipped from her hand and clattered against the coffee table. "Oh, my God!" Peach said, barely croaking out the words. Seconds passed, as she sat bug-eyed looking at the screen, frozen in place, with her heart thudding hard and fast in her chest.

She knew the victim's face all too well. Dear God . . . Joan Smith had been *murdered*? But when? And why?

The newscaster went on to describe the crime, and said it looked like a mugging, but Peach passed right over his conclusions, and instead honed in on something else he said—the dead woman had been found with one red crocheted mitten on her limp, lifeless hand.

Frantic knocking rattled Adam's door. Who could it be? He'd just gotten into bed. God knew he hadn't had time to make new friends in Boston yet, except for Peach— *Maybe it's Peach!* His heart jumped; he leaped out of bed, and then he remembered . . . he needed space. Strange the way you could need something and thoroughly hate it at the same time.

The knocking persisted. When he finally opened the door, his chest tightened. Breath stalled in his throat. It *was* Peach. And she looked unbelievably beautiful, angelic, vibrant, sexy as hell. Her blue eyes were huge with emotion, her cheeks were flushed from the cold, her bronze hair and long velvet coat were dusted with snow. Hell, she must've walked all the way from the T stop. "Hi . . ." he said, still at a loss for words as she hurried past him inside, shivering. He shut his door and turned to face her.

"What took you so long?" she said, blowing on her fists. Instinctively Adam rubbed his hands over her arms to warm her up. "You'll never believe it!" she said as soon as she pulled back. "Joan Smith has been murdered!"

"*What?*" Adam said, stunned by the words.

Peach explained about the news broadcast—how the news anchor had said the "unidentified woman" had been dead for several days, how *that* was why the red mitten in Robert's office had been so familiar to Peach—she'd seen it on Joan at Mackie's—and how Robert must've killed her, God knew why. When she finally finished she was out of breath. She plopped down on his sofa and said, "So what should we do? I mean, we can go to the police tonight, of course, but then what? There's got to be *something* we can do to figure this out! I mean, how did Robert and Joan know each other? And what the hell did it have to do with Dennis? But obviously it has to, right?" Throwing her head back against the couch cushions, she pressed her palms to her forehead and said, "Adam, this whole thing is *killing* me!"

After a long moment he sighed and said, "Well, we should definitely call the police, but beyond that . . ."

"What?" she said, curious where he'd been going with that sentence.

He shrugged, not really looking at her, kind of looking past her, and said, "Beyond that . . . I don't know. I really don't want to get too involved," he said.

Peach's face fell. "Since when?" she asked, scrunching her face in confusion.

"Sorry, but . . . look, I can't keep playing amateur detective. I think it's time to let the police handle it," Adam explained casually, and turned to go sit at his desk, which was over by the window. Then he fiddled with his mouse, while Peach swallowed a sigh, counted to five in her head, and forced herself to remain calm.

"What are you talking about? Adam, what is with you lately?"

He shrugged again, still not looking at her, but supposedly at his monitor, and now she just snapped. "Okay, that's *it!*" she said, hopping up from the couch. "What is your problem?"

After letting out a baffled laugh that sounded artificial, Adam replied, "What do you mean? I don't have a problem."

"Yes, you do; you've been acting so *weird* the last couple days— hey, can you stop pretending to work on your computer and have a freaking conversation, please?"

"About *what?*" he said with blatant annoyance. "You're telling me I have a problem and I don't."

"Don't play stupid!" she said. "Is this because I told you I loved you?"

Adam stiffened as silence fell over them. Swallowing, he averted his eyes, looking down for a long moment, then finally back at her, and when their eyes met, his gaze was cooler and more detached than she'd ever seen. So now she had her answer.

"Is this because of Robin or something?" Peach asked. "Have you talked to her recently, or . . . ?"

"Robin has nothing to do with this," he replied curtly. But now that she'd mentioned it . . . bringing up Robin only reminded Adam why he did not want another relationship right now. Jesus, he wanted space, freedom, breathing room. He didn't want to lose Peach, and he definitely didn't want to hurt her, but this was moving too fast, and he suddenly felt out of control, like there was no way out.

"Answer my question," Peach demanded, her watery eyes cutting through him like ice picks. "Have you talked to Robin lately?"

"Please stop talking about Robin, okay? *Jesus.*"

"Why can't I talk about her?" Peach asked hotly.

"Look, Peach," Adam said, cutting off any further discussion, "I was with Robin for five years—I've been with you for, what, five *minutes?*" As he said the words, he saw hurt wash over Peach's face, darken her pale blue eyes, and instantly he felt a sharp stab of guilt. He wanted to take it back, but he couldn't bring himself to say anything else.

Tears filled her eyes as she headed for the front door. Adam winced, wanting to punch himself. Instead, he spoke with feeble contrition. "Peach . . . wait. . . ."

"Just leave me alone," she said, and didn't bother looking back.

Once she'd left his apartment, Adam stood in his doorway, nearly paralyzed by his own indecision. He should go after her; he knew that. But he couldn't get his feet to move. This was for the best . . . wasn't it? The relief of having his freedom back would probably hit him any second. Or in several seconds. He'd just keep waiting.

And in the meantime, he was more certain than ever that he didn't deserve her.

Later that night, Peach called the police to identify Joan Smith as the murder victim. It hadn't been necessary, since someone at Mackie's who'd seen the broadcast had already called the police. However, when Peach called, she demanded to talk to Joe. After telling him about seeing Joan's other red mitten in Robert Walsh's office—and then in his possession—plus Joan's connection to Dennis, who was still missing, Joe was astounded. He thanked her for the information, promised to keep her name out of the investigation, and warned her to stay out of it from this point on, that the cops would handle it.

She hadn't known what that would mean until a few days later, when two homicide detectives showed up at Millennium to talk to Robert.

Peach caught the word from Grace, who had no idea why the police wanted to speak with Robert—and she had no clue that Peach knew why—but she merely speculated that he'd dodged his taxes, or maybe it had something to do with Dennis. Nodding casually, it had taken every ounce of restraint for Peach not to say that

Dennis was *exactly* what this had to do with—Dennis and Joan—if only Peach knew how the hell it was all connected.

Clearly, that was what the cops were there to find out, too; Peach lingered around Robert's office, pretending to be busy at one of the filing cabinets, waiting for Robert to be taken away in handcuffs and maybe one of those foot chains with a big lead ball at the end.

But five minutes after they'd stepped in Robert's office, the policemen stepped out. There were no cuffs, no tearstained cheeks from a flogging-induced confession. What the hell kind of justice was this? In all likelihood Robert Walsh had killed Joan Smith and done God knew what to Dennis, and there he was, saying cordial good-byes to the cops and wishing them luck with their investigation. "As I said, I wish I could be more help," he said now, shaking both of their hands. Once they left, Robert smiled briefly at Grace and Peach and coolly returned to his office. Jeez, did *nothing* rattle this guy?

She supposed she shouldn't be too surprised, though, since Joe had told her that without that red mitten, the police would need a lot more to go on if they wanted to get a search warrant for Robert's office and apartment. They'd first have to dig around and see what developed as they investigated. This implied waiting, which was probably why Peach had temporarily blocked it out. Joe had also told her she'd have to lie low and be patient, which translated to synonyms of waiting, so they got filtered out, too.

Now she could see how hard this was going to be; Robert was going to be tough to break. As Peach watched him walk calmly back into his office and close the door, Peach exhaled a deep, shaky breath, just realizing how crucial it was that Joe had left her name out of the investigation entirely. It was hard to be patient when you might be working for a murderer, but next to impossible when you were the girl who turned him in.

"I can't remember how you convinced me to do this."

"Moral support," BeBe reminded Peach as they turned the corner, rapidly encroaching upon their destination. They were meeting Simon's friends from England, Fielding and Lindley, at Sonsie, a self-consciously swanky restaurant on Newbury Street.

Of course, moral support had been only part of it. After diligently avoiding Adam at work for the past couple days, Peach had been psyched for Saturday. The insulation of the weekend, the safety and solitude of her bedroom, huddled in a swirl of blankets, watching TV, with a big bowl of microwave popcorn and peanut M&M's . . . it all sounded perfect. Yet after four hours of it, it became morbidly depressing. Cabin fever began encroaching, making her feel trapped, like she'd never dig herself out.

All of this made BeBe's last-ditch effort to coax her into a double date with Simon's friends sound a little more appealing. Besides, how could Peach say no when going out seemed the only way to take her mind off Adam tonight?

And if Adam couldn't appreciate her love—if he couldn't accept it, couldn't reciprocate it—then he couldn't possibly be her soul mate. *He's not even good enough for me,* she thought glumly as she and BeBe approached the restaurant.

Peach's cell phone rang. Instinctively her heart lurched—*maybe it's Adam!* Then she regained her senses—*forget that asshole*—and then she glanced at the number and realized that it wasn't him anyway. "Hello?"

"Hi."

"Hi, Kimberly!" Peach said, recognizing the small, soft voice right away. "How's it going?"

"Fine."

"Are you getting excited for your birthday party?"

"Yes."

"That's good." The slumber party would be at Peach and BeBe's apartment, and would be just the three of them. They'd invited Yvonne, too, but she'd declined—mentioning that the deal she'd struck with BeBe was sufficient, which was how it had come out: The reason for BeBe's sudden change of heart about going out with Simon's friend Fielding was bribery. If she did that, Yvonne would let them throw Kimberly a little birthday party at their place in the city. "Hey, what kind of cake do you want?" Peach asked Kimberly now, as she followed BeBe through the warmly lit restaurant over to the bar.

"I don't know. Mummy doesn't let me eat cake at home."

Peach rolled her eyes. "Okay, well, then, I'll surprise you. Listen, I've gotta go right now, but your aunt BeBe and I will see you soon, okay?"

" 'Kay," Kimberly said. "I can barely wait."

Peach slipped her cell into her coat pocket as BeBe snagged a small high table across from the bar. Taking a seat, they both surveyed the restaurant. They were supposed to look for a blond guy wearing gingham—already off to a platonic start, if you asked Peach. But as of now, no checkered shirts in sight.

"I can't believe I'm actually going out with a guy named *Lindley*," Peach mused out loud, still bemused by the idea. Shaking her head, she repeated to herself, "Lindley. Huh." Tonight Peach wore a stretchy black blouse with tight, hot-red bootleg pants and glittery black heels, while BeBe kept it cute in simple black pants and a lilac-colored sweater.

"I've decided to do what you said, and go into this with a positive attitude," BeBe said.

"Hey, that's great," Peach said, nodding, though not fully believing. Not that she could blame her friend in this case; she'd been manipulated into being here in the first place.

"I'm not going to assume just because this guy's friends with Simon that he's lame . . . or a mooch . . . or pale and devious with sod hair—oh, wait, but he's supposed to be Simon's *friend*, not his twin."

"Are you *done*?" Peach said with a laugh.

Giggling, BeBe nodded. Just then a tall, slim guy with blond hair, an angular jaw, and a green checked shirt came toward the bar. Trailing behind him was a stronger-looking guy with a shaved head, black pants, and a black sweater. Peach waved them over. The bald one was Lindley, Peach's date. It turned out he wasn't Fielding's friend so much as he was his second cousin. He had bright green eyes and a shy smile; there was an endearing and huggable quality about him, what Peach's mom would call "the teddy bear type." Fielding, on the other hand, had a bit of an attitude. Then again, it also seemed like he'd knocked back a few before he came. His crisp British accent was a little slurred when he said to BeBe, "Sorry, we're late, love—the tube here is *ghastly* slow."

"No problem," BeBe said brightly.

After a waitress took their drink orders, Peach said, "So . . . how are you guys enjoying your visit to the States?"

"Rather enjoying it a lot," Lindley said, smiling.

"It's been interesting," Fielding added, "even though Americans are insufferable, for the most part." Hmm, he forgot to add "no offense"—an acutely American touch to insulting people to their face.

"Are you two both from England originally?" BeBe asked conversationally.

"I'm from Yorkshire," Lindley replied, then motioned to Fielding, who was sliding off his chair. "And this one's from Ireland originally." Wordlessly, Fielding crossed over to the bar for another beer, and Lindley joked, "In case you couldn't tell."

A laugh slipped from Peach's lips, and BeBe muttered under her breath, "Oh, no, nothing for me, thank you," because Fielding hadn't asked.

As the night went on, the chemistry didn't burn any hotter between BeBe and Fielding, who turned out to be something of a drunken fish, who apparently hated America, yet was dying to stay longer. As for his cousin, he seemed like a sweetheart, but while Peach was with him, she could think only of Adam. Now, as she leaned back in her chair, her gaze drifting around the bar, she suddenly stopped short. *Shit!* Luke Vermann was leaning against the bar, draping an arm around a blond girl who easily could've been in college. Peach had seen him only once in her life, but she recognized him right away, and of course his big diamond earring played a critical role in that.

How was she going to keep BeBe from spotting him all over another woman? Not only would it set back her progress of late with her self-diagnosed skinny-blonde envy, but it would sink her confidence in her own judgment, and be an express train back to John. Peach didn't want that to happen. "You know what?" she said quickly. "I've got the worst migraine. I'm sorry," she said, smiling weakly and bringing her hand to her forehead to go along with her lament. "I didn't want to say anything, but ... it's really bad."

BeBe studied her through squinted eyes for a moment, then nodded and said, "Oh, no, one of your migraines again? We should go." Peach didn't get migraines, so that meant that BeBe was definitely on board with ditching these guys, though Peach felt a little guilty about Lindley. But, on the other hand, why give him false hope? She knew she wasn't even close to contemplating romance with any man other than Adam at this point. "We should go then," BeBe added, offering a small, apologetic smile.

Peach rapped her fingers nervously on the tabletop. Any minute BeBe could turn around and see the V-man. If only the waitress would come over with the check. *Come on, come on* . . . Finally she came, and Peach reached inside her coat pocket, where she kept a small drawstring pouch for her license, cash, and keys. Since Fielding and Lindley had asked them out, they would probably pay for the round of drinks, but just in case, Peach figured she'd have her money ready. The quicker they settled the bill, the more likely Peach would be able to scoot BeBe out before she spotted Luke and then obsessed about what she'd done to make him not call again.

"Now we can tally up the check to figure out what you owe, love," Fielding said, heavily slurring his words.

"What *I* owe?" BeBe said, sounding appalled. Apparently she hadn't been preparing to pay; she probably felt picking up the tab was the least Fielding could do after indirectly insulting her all night. She snatched the bill from his hand. "Okay," she said crisply, "let's see here. . . ." She made a show of roving her eyes over the check and calculating in her head. "Okay, hmm, add this up, plus

tax and tip . . . carry the one . . . and . . . *zero*," she finished pointedly, and dropped the check on the table.

Peach darted a glance over her shoulder to see if maybe the
V-man had left or spontaneously combusted by now, but no such
luck. Meanwhile, Fielding looked flummoxed by BeBe's calcula-
tions. "Zero?" he echoed. "Come again, love?"

"Zero," she repeated with emphasis. "As in, I don't owe *anything*
for this shlocky night. God, you're as big a freeloader as Simon." His
face was screwed up and his shoulders arched, and Peach wondered
if it was BeBe's caustic tone that put him off. Or was he merely trying to decipher the underrated yet apropos term "shlocky"?

Turning her head toward Peach, BeBe said, "Are you ready to go?"

"Um, *yeah*." *More than ready.* BeBe went first, and Peach
quickly stepped to the side to block her view of the bar; then, a few
feet behind BeBe, Peach handed Lindley a ten. But he wouldn't take
it. What a sweetie . . . too bad he wasn't Adam.

As they scooted out of the restaurant, Peach turned back at
Lindley, who was watching her with his bright green eyes and a look
of silent apology for how the night had turned out.

Sorry, she mouthed, because he seemed like a nice guy, and she
wished that made a difference. Once they hit the street, Peach exhaled a sigh of relief.

Later that night, shit hit the fan. "What the hell are you doing?"
Peach said, her eyes still droopy, barely open at all actually, as she
followed the blare of light and the sound of BeBe's voice saying,
"Down, down," into the living room. Three dog-training books
were sprawled across the sofa, and BeBe had a pained look on her
face as she hastily flipped through a fourth one.

"She's just not *getting* it!" she said with a frustrated sigh. Well,
hell—even demon dogs needed their rest—and from the bleary-
eyed look of Buster, BeBe must have gotten her out of a sound sleep
to teach her these commands. With Buster there were two basic
modes, hyperactive and collapse, so Peach doubted that Buster
could fake much zeal for this little four A.M. lesson on "down."

"Come on; who cares if she gets it?" Peach said, yawning and cinching her kimono belt tighter. "She doesn't get anything half the time, except the mauling-everyone-in-sight command."

"I know! Maybe I should call John," BeBe said, lurching toward the phone. "He'll know what to do—"

"What?" Peach yelped, coming more awake and snatching up the cordless phone before BeBe could get it. "Nice try!"

BeBe held up her hands in a desperate gesture of entreaty, her eyes alive with the fiery need to rationalize. "Only because he's good with dogs!" she insisted. Twisting her lips, Peach tilted her head and set her hand on her hip. "It's true: His family has two dogs, and he's always been good with them!"

With a roll of her eyes, Peach refrained from adding that if John was good with dogs it was probably because he was about as clean-cut as Teen Wolf. Anyway, that was hardly the point. This was all just an excuse for BeBe to slip back into the John vortex—and the question was, *why?*

"BeBe, you're not calling John."

"But I have a good reason this time. . . ."

Peach shook her head firmly. "You told me last week that you wanted to break the cycle. That you didn't want to keep talking to him."

"I know but just one quick call to ask about dogs . . ." Her voice trailed off; even she probably sensed how lame it sounded.

"No," Peach said firmly.

"What do you mean, 'no'?"

"I mean *no*, you're not calling John. It's never gonna happen, so just forget the whole idea."

"So I should think about it?"

Peach expelled a tired laugh before setting the phone back in its cradle. "Sit down, please." BeBe did what she said, sinking onto the sofa and inadvertently crushing one of her bichon books. "Now, what's really going on? What's wrong with you?"

Suddenly BeBe's face pruned up, and she looked on the verge of tears. Covering her eyes with balled-up fists, BeBe said, "I think I made a big mistake." Then she started to cry.

"What do you mean?" Peach asked, dragging out the word "mean" with soft, nurturing concern, as she sat beside her friend and put an arm around her shoulder.

"About John . . ."

"You didn't make a mistake," Peach insisted, reminding her, "You guys broke up for reasons—a lot of reasons—you know that."

BeBe sniffled and wiped more tears with her round little fists. "I know, but after going out with what's-his-face tonight, it just made me realize all the great things that John had. Like, he wasn't pretentious, you know? Plus he was already a U.S. citizen."

Short list, Peach thought sardonically, while she squeezed her friend's shoulder supportively.

"Listen, I know it's hard to say good-bye to someone," Peach said gently, thinking, *Boy, do I know.* Which should've sounded ridiculous echoing in her mind, since she'd known Adam Quinlan for only a month, but she truly did understand the choking pain of heartbreak and disappointment. "But you're forgetting all the reasons that John and you could never work."

"Like what?" BeBe mumbled through congested sniffling.

"Okay, first of all, there was the religion thing. If you ever married him, you'd have to convert, remember?"

"I know, but I think I've changed my mind about that. It's not such a big deal—I'll even wear the beanie and everything."

Suppressing a grin, Peach said, "Um, as much as I'm sure John would appreciate your calling it a *beanie*, I think only guys have to wear those."

"Even better!" BeBe exclaimed, smiling feebly with dark, watery eyes that were puffy and pink in the corners.

"Next point: You were all set to live with him, and he totally freaked out on you." Before BeBe could debate the point, Peach added, "It's a question of maturity, BeBe. He's twenty-eight years old, you'd been dating for two and a half years, and he just bailed on you." BeBe sat silently, clearly mulling that point over (and by no means for the first time). "And what about that whole crooked-smiling thing of his?" Peach asked. "That used to drive you crazy!"

"No, wait," BeBe said, scrunching her eyebrows together, "that drove *you* crazy."

"Fine . . . well . . . still."

BeBe let out a laugh. It sprang out of her throat, even as she fought back a new welling of tears, and then she started really laughing. Turning to hug Peach, she wrapped her arms tightly around her, sighed, and said, "Thanks, Peach. You're the best friend I ever had."

"I'm glad," Peach said, starting to feel chokingly emotional herself.

"My life would be so empty without you," BeBe threw in, and now Peach started to cry, too, but only a little bit before she got her shit together.

Afterward, the mood in the room was distinctly lifted, like the calm *after* the storm, and Peach said, "Hey, to get your mind off everything, how about you help me with Kimberly's party?"

"Why, what's left to do? You've already stocked the kitchen to oblivion—we could open a Doritos stand on the corner."

"I know, but find a balloon guy for me, will ya?"

"Huh? We're hiring a balloon guy?" BeBe said, surprised.

"Yeah, it came to me in a dream I was just having," Peach explained, then slanted BeBe a knowing look. "A dream I never got to finish, I might add."

"Sorry," BeBe said with a grin. "If it's any consolation, she wasn't too thrilled either," she added, motioning with her head to Buster, who was completely zonked out on the living room floor, lying on her back, curved up toward heaven like the angel she wasn't . . . but might be someday.

"So what do you say?"

"Okay, I'll surf the Web for a balloon guy."

"Great—but no weirdos."

"Oh, you take away all my fun—but I'll do it anyway." After

sniffling again, she hugged Peach tightly and said, "Thanks for being there."

Once BeBe had gone back to bed, Peach lingered on the sofa, thinking that no matter what BeBe thought, this had been a turning point. She'd backslid but stopped herself in time. Whether she realized it or not, she was getting a little more okay with being by herself.

Which got Peach thinking . . . even though she'd lost her sort-of boyfriend and her new best friend all at the same time, it was *Adam's* loss, too.

And funny enough, Adam was on the other side of the city right then, thinking the exact same thing.

Chapter Thirty

By Monday morning, Adam had built up his resolve. He walked toward Peach's cube, intent on breaking the ice with her. He'd been so overwhelmed with work last week, it had made it a little easier not to approach her, and to ignore the cold shoulder she'd so clearly been giving him. But when he was home alone at night, it was killing him. He missed her so much; there was an aching emptiness in his life without her. And it wasn't just because he was in a new city with no friends. Honestly, he couldn't care less about that. He didn't want to talk to anyone but her—and in the predictable irony of life, she was the one person who hated him with a passion. But it couldn't be that simple. Hell, only a week before she'd told him she *loved* him. She had to still feel something for him, didn't she?

And though he'd been dying for his freedom—whatever that meant—when he'd broken up with Robin, it all seemed like such bullshit now. Without Peach his life felt bleak, lonely; his chest felt hollow almost to the point of pain.

With his gut churning, he went to her cubicle. She was sitting at her desk. All he saw was her back. He swallowed hard at the sight of her shoulders, her hair, her— Oh, who the hell was he kidding? He was scared shitless of her. Terrified she'd tell him she'd already moved on.

But he knocked anyway. "Come in," Peach said, spinning around in her seat, and just like that, her face fell. "Oh. It's you."

Not exactly an effusive greeting, but he supposed it was more than he deserved. "Hi, there," he said, barely stepping over the threshold, barely able to bring himself closer to her. But God, it wasn't his fault—he was speechless looking at her, her casual elegance, her natural sexiness, her sassy innocence. It was like she was a mass of contradictions, spicy but sweet, and he couldn't remember, though he knew there actually had been a time when he'd felt comfortable with her. Now he was intimidated and tongue-tied. "Um . . ."

Peach just glared at him. Christ, how could he have blown it like this? No, it couldn't be too late. There had to be a way to win her trust, and to get back to the place where they'd been building something.

"*Yes?*" she said expectantly. Her voice wasn't so much angry as it was flat and devoid of emotion. That, in and of itself, was so unlike her.

"You busy?" he asked, coming more into her space, tentatively but with determination. She would not ignore him until he left. He was determined to get her to talk to him, if not about what happened, then about whatever she wanted—so that he could be her friend again . . . so they could be more than friends again.

"Yeah, kind of," she replied.

"Oh, well . . ." He paused, slipped his hands in his pocket, and nodded to convince himself he was brimming with oblivious casualness and confidence, and it didn't matter if she believed it, because she wasn't even looking. "So I talked to my dad earlier. He called me pretty upset," he said.

She looked up at that. "Is he okay?"

"Oh, yeah, he's fine," Adam assured her quickly, then grinned. "He wanted to talk to you, actually."

"Me?" she said, surprised. "Why me?"

Adam shrugged. "I guess he wanted your advice. Yeah, apparently he convinced my mom to come over for dinner so they could talk about how he really understands what she was saying about not being appreciated. And then he said if she just tells him what she needs from the grocery store, he'll pick it up for her on his way home from work. Then she flipped out, saying how he invites her over for dinner and then expects *her* to cook it."

Shaking her head, Peach winced and said, "Oh, Marty . . . no . . ."

"That's what I told him. Except I called him Dad, I think." Peach chewed on her lower lip for another second before turning back to face her desk, and Adam cleared his throat. "Listen, Peach . . . I'm really sorry."

"Sorry for what?" she said, all but ignoring him as she flipped through a gift catalog, marking it with a pen, yet whipping through the pages so fast it was hard to believe she was being very discriminating.

"For being an asshole," he said simply—and honestly. Might as well come clean. After all, this was *Peach*—he wasn't about to bullshit her with excuses, because not only would she get even more annoyed, but she also deserved better.

"I see. Well, thank you. Apology accepted. But I need to get back to work."

"Since when?" he asked jokingly, trying to get her to crack a smile, but instead she shot her head up just long enough to glare at him.

"If I could just try to explain," he said, cursing himself for not just spitting it out—for being such an overly cautious bastard.

But it hardly mattered now; it was moot, because Peach cut him off, spinning around in her chair. When she looked at him her eyes were the coolest blue he'd ever seen. She was totally detached from him right now; he could tell. It was like a sharp object stabbing into his heart and then twisting.

"Let's just forget it," she said crisply. "I'm really not interested in dealing with a lot of baggage anyway; honestly, I think this all worked out for the best. I hope you find what you're looking for."

"I *did*," he said, then stepped closer, close enough to set his hands lightly on her shoulders. Immediately she swung back around and poised a high heel to kick him in the shin.

"Just back away," she warned, grimacing at him as if he were some creepy pervert. She could be so overdramatic sometimes.

Still, he complied, and stepped back. But he wasn't letting up yet. Instead he paused, obviously swallowing a sigh—*ever restrained*, Peach thought with annoyance—and then said, "I wish I'd acted differently. I mean that night when you—"

"I *don't* want to talk about it," she interrupted.

Peach was losing what was left of her patience. She didn't want him to see her cry; once was enough. Turning away from him again, as a clogging lump of emotion formed in her throat, she said, "Just for*get* it already, Adam—*jeez*."

When he finally left her alone, she was shaking. With her insides trembling and her knees clamped tensely together, she thought, *God, I'm a wreck.*

She wished she could've had the maturity or the dignity to listen to his so-called explanation, but then again, why did he deserve that? She wished for a lot of things. She wished he hadn't ruined the purity and perfection of what they'd shared and the trust that they'd been building. But the weirdest part—which she truly couldn't figure out—was that even as aching sadness crushed her chest, roiled in her stomach nearly to the point of sickness, she still wasn't sorry that she had fallen in love with him.

Thursday night Peach was at McMurphy's chatting with Scott, who'd convinced her to go for a drink after work. But her mind was back on Dennis Emberson. And Joan Smith. And Robert Walsh and that red mitten. And, of course, on Nicholas Easterbrook. Over a week ago she'd told Joe Montgomery to let her know everything that was happening with the case, but he still hadn't called.

"So when do you think Robert will hire a new accountant?" Scott said now, drinking his Sam Adams from the bottle. "It's been weeks and still no Dennis."

Excellent point, but who knew with Robert? Maybe it had

something to do with stealing from the company, murdering a waitress, and waiting till the old accountant's bones were interred? *No.*
She shook off the thought. But not because she didn't believe it.
The truth was, she no longer held out much hope that Dennis was
alive. The only way she could picture him healthy and alive was per-
haps if he'd confronted Robert about his embezzling, and in turn,
accepted a payoff to keep quiet and disappear. Technically, Peach
supposed, that was possible. But then why would Robert kill Joan?
Not that Peach had any proof Robert had done it, but the red mitten in his office, and the fact that her dead body had been found
only half a block from their building, cinched it as far as she was
concerned. One of the mittens had obviously fallen off when he was
carrying the body out. Or maybe he'd killed her on a deserted
street—but the mere fact that she'd been to his office at all made
Robert the number one suspect.

Earlier that day, when Scott had asked Peach to go for drinks after work, she'd told him she was planning to visit BeBe at McMurphy's, but that he was welcome to come along. Then she'd extended
the same invitation to Rachel Latham, who declined, saying she had
plans with her younger sister, Alice—prompting Peach to ask Rachel
if Alice had talked to Nan about Dennis's disappearance. Rachel
said yes, but claimed she didn't know the details; basically, she'd been
vague. Peppy and smiling while doing it, of course, but still vague.

Nan and her mom had contacted Millennium, asking that
should anyone think of anything that might help to locate Dennis,
to please contact them. It was breaking Peach's heart not to go to
them, to share her whole winding search for Dennis, to tell them
about Robert, but she couldn't. The police wanted her to keep
quiet. (Didn't they realize what they were asking?)

Now BeBe came scurrying out from the restaurant kitchen,
back to the bar, all apologies. This was the first chance she'd had to
stop and chat. "Sorry, I just can't seem to get a spare minute tonight.
It's crazy."

"No problem," Peach said casually, still mulling over Joan

Smith's murder and how it might be tied to Dennis's disappearance. She'd known that Robert had been questioned, but his demeanor outwardly didn't change to the staff. He didn't even discuss it, except to mention at the meeting that the police had asked him routine questions about Dennis and his work habits, any problems or enemies, the usual questions. Peach, of course, wasn't buying that. She knew full well that the reason the police had made a beeline for Robert was because *she* had tipped them off about his connection to Joan and his possible embezzlement. Surely, they'd asked him questions about Joan and Dennis. Of course, by now Robert had obviously gotten rid of the incriminating mitten, and at this point the police didn't have enough to justify a search warrant.

As for the embezzlement, Peach couldn't care less about Robert's financial shenanigans anyway—who cared if he wanted to steal from his wife's company? All she wanted to know was what had happened to Dennis, and what had happened to Joan, before Robert skipped the country.

"Peach? Hello?"

It was BeBe waving her hand in front of Peach's face. "Oh, sorry. What did you say?"

"Well, I said many things, but most of it was lame small talk, so I won't bother repeating it."

"It wasn't lame," Scott said casually, then looked over at Peach. "She was telling you about some guy named Feeman . . . ?"

With a bashful laugh, BeBe qualified, "The *V-man.* And I didn't realize you were listening."

"Right, she was saying something about this V-man dude. How she realized he was probably gay. 'Cause he wore some big emerald earring or something."

Grinning, BeBe said, "Diamond, and it wasn't that big. He said he got it because it represents love—and I never said he was gay. Who are you, anyway?"

"Oh, BeBe, sorry—this is Scott from work. Scott, this is my roommate, BeBe," Peach said, making belated introductions.

"Nice to meet you," Scott said, smiling, and reached across the bar to shake BeBe's hand. "Represents love?" he continued, grimacing with disgust. "He actually said that? Man, that line is *cheesy*. Hey, I know I don't know you, but you can do way better."

"Thank you," BeBe said, grinning, then leaned on the bar with her elbows. "You're probably right. And if a guy can't even call a girl back he's obviously a deadbeat."

"Exactly," Scott said.

"Peach, another Fish House Punch?" BeBe asked, throwing a dishtowel over her shoulder and motioning to Peach's empty glass.

"No, I'm good. Actually . . . give me a Clover Leaf."

BeBe nodded and turned to make it. Since Peach had helped BeBe study for her bartending exam a while back, she often had obscure drinks in the forefront of her mind.

Meanwhile, Peach remained vaguely aware that she was being the biggest drag tonight, but she just couldn't help it. How could she relax with all of these loose ends? "Hey, will you guys excuse me?" she said suddenly, and slid off her bar stool. "I'll be right back."

"Sure," he said; then she heard BeBe say, "Where is she going?" and Scott said, "I don't know . . . but you can keep me company with your lame small talk. Really, I don't mind."

Peach moved through the crowded restaurant outside to where it was quiet. The sky was blanketed in navy blue and glittering with silvery-white stars. She needed to clear her head—to figure out her plan of action. *Now what?* she asked herself. There had to be *something* she could do. Robert still had no idea that she was the one who'd gone to the police, which gave her some leeway at work with her snooping. She would have to look more closely around the office, around Robert; she would have to be crafty, stealthy like a cat burglar. Hell, Robert probably figured she was just some flaky young artist type; he probably wouldn't notice her lurking around. One thing was clear: She needed to get back into his office. She and Quin had barely had a chance to look around that first time. And hey, nobody had to know. Maybe she should slip something into one of Grace's meat logs to make her dopey. Okay, of course she would never do something like that.

Ten minutes later she returned to the bar and found Scott, BeBe, and Mindy all chatting (apparently still mocking the V-man, which was becoming more than a coping strategy for BeBe, but a staple of conversation). Nobody seemed to notice Peach's absence or return, but could she really blame them? She'd been a major dud all night.

"The V-man's a pussy," Mindy declared bluntly.

"I agree," Peach piped in—not that she would *ever* put it that way herself.

"The sexy ones are always trouble," Mindy added with a knowing twist of her lips.

Scott smiled casually and said, "I take issue with that." BeBe grinned at him.

"Look, the point is, you can do waaay better than the V-man," Peach stated. "You could dance circles around him—you could dance circles wearing a lei, while he lies there with an apple in his mouth. In other words, he's a pig." Not that she truly knew if he was a pig or not, but she had her loyalties, after all.

"I agree with Peach," Scott said, nodding, then held up his hands before anyone could protest. "Hey, I'm a guy; I can sense these things."

When BeBe smiled at him, it was almost flirty, which was particularly notable because she didn't flirt very often. BeBe was from the straightforward, uncoy school of femininity that was so underappreciated by men of their generation—or *any* generation thus far.

"By the way . . . can I ask, how old are you?" Scott said.

"Twenty-six," BeBe replied. "Why? Do I look older?"

"No, no, you look young. I was just curious. But I hate asking women that. You can get eaten alive," he joked.

With a laugh, BeBe asked, "Why? It's just my age; it's not like you asked my weight." Hastily she amended, "Not that you should."

Soon Peach zoned out of the conversation, thinking instead about her plan of action. She would call Joe again and see if there were any developments he felt like sharing. Then she'd wait for an opportunity to slip into Robert's office and do her own little search-and-seizure. After all, as long as the police had no search warrant, what chance did they have?

Chapter Thirty-one

Skipping all pleasantries the next day, Peach called Detective Joe Montgomery and yelped into the phone, "Why the hell haven't you called me!"

"Nice greeting," Joe said. "Hey, I told you I'd keep you posted. I didn't say it would be on a daily basis."

"Well, just tell me now, what the hell is going on over there? Is anyone doing *anything*?"

Joe released a sigh. "You know I'm only humoring you as a favor to your sister, but don't push it."

Rolling her eyes, Peach relented. "Fine, fine . . . please just tell me: Are the cops gonna arrest Robert or what?" Then she realized that even though her desk was far away from everyone, she should really lower her voice.

"Or what," Joe said.

"But *why*?" she whined with frustration, slapping her palm on her desktop. Abruptly she realized she wasn't being nearly quiet enough. Honestly, she'd intended to whisper, but emotion was getting the best of her. Fortunately, though, Robert's office was all the way on the other side of the floor. Lowering her voice, she continued, "I told you all about the mitten. I know the one in Robert's office has to have been the match for the one that Joan was wearing when they found her dead. I mean, what are you all waiting for—a woman on Pluto?"

"Kid, give me a break here. Look, we've talked to Walsh. According to him, not only didn't he know this woman, Joan, but he says he's never even been to Mackie's, so we can't establish any connection at the present time. Meanwhile, Robert assures us there was simply a miscommunication and that Nicholas was contracted for this coming summer—Easterbrook confirms that."

"Well, I know *that*," she mumbled. "Robert's just trying to cover himself—"

"I'm not gonna tell you again," Joe warned. "Stay out of this."

"But you believe me, don't you?" Peach said, hearing a thread of desperation in her own voice. "I mean about Robert and the mittens, and Dennis and—"

"Hey, kid, of course I believe you," he said, "but there are procedures here you know nothing about. So the best thing you can do is to keep a low profile. Don't let anyone know your suspicions, or anything, please. Just do what I'm telling you."

"But I can't just do nothing! Asking me to do nothing is like asking me to gouge my eyes out."

"That bad, huh? Jesus," Joe muttered. "Why don't women ever listen to me? What am I doing wrong?"

After Peach hung up with Joe, getting as much (or as little) feedback as she was going to, she prepared for phase two of her plan: sneaking into Robert's office at her nearest opportunity. Unfortunately, what she didn't realize was that Robert had been standing right outside her cubicle for all of phase one.

The next day Peach lucked out at lunch—or so she thought. Brenda visited the office and took everyone out for pizza. Peach passed, claiming she had one of her mythological migraines again, and waited until the office cleared out before she headed to Robert's side of the floor. He hadn't gone for pizza, either, but apparently had a lunch meeting scheduled with some toy store reps.

She knew Adam had gone to another software convention in New York City, so he wasn't there, either. After she took the key from Grace's top drawer, she slipped inside Robert's office, unsure of where to start and exactly what to look for. She thought back to the last time she'd been here, when she'd seen Robert stick Joan's mitten into his coat pocket—

Coat pocket! Looking around, Peach found several sport coats hanging in the supply closet across from Robert's desk. Maybe he'd left the mitten in one of them and forgotten?

After rifling through the pockets of all his sport jackets and finding nothing inside—literally *nothing*, not even a gum wrapper or receipt. She was obviously dealing with a major sicko here— Peach heard the office door open. Then it slammed shut.

She whipped around, still inside Robert's closet, as her heart lurched into her throat. Then she heard maddeningly slow steps move across the carpet—there was no way that was Grace. Only one person was so deliberate, so calculating, so controlled. *Oh, God, I'm going to die,* she thought, as her heart banged frantically against her ribs and her pulse pounded hard in her ears. As terror choked her, she stayed frozen in place, not sure if she should come out or duck further into the closet and try to bury herself behind the coats.

But there wasn't time to make a decision.

"Peach, why don't you come out now?" Robert Walsh said coaxingly. Then he appeared in front of her, facing her as the closet door remained mostly open.

Her mouth ran dry as words stalled in her throat. Her breath was short and shaky as she kept hearing the news caster's voice echoing in her head—reciting the details of Joan Smith's murder. A blow to the head then left to rot in a Dumpster. Days had gone by before she was found. . . . *Oh, dear God.* As her chest constricted with fear, like a giant fist squeezing her heart and lungs, she struggled to recall the Hail Mary, but predictably her rebellion against her mother's nagging about church would came back to haunt her at the most inconvenient time.

"Now, Peach, this is silly," Robert said calmly, tilting his head at her with amused condescension. "What did you think you'd find in here? Did you really think you'd find that red mitten?"

Braving a glance into Robert's dark, cold eyes, Peach watched him come even closer, until he was standing only inches away from her. She had to think fast—something to get him off the track, to buy her time. She had to fish. "How could you do it?" she said, just barely finding her voice. "To Joan who . . . meant so much to you?"

"Really?" he said with a laugh, and arched an eyebrow at her as he grabbed a belt from the rack on the closet door. "That's funny— a woman I'd never met in my life calls me up to blackmail me and it turns out she *meant a lot* me? How interesting." As he wrapped the belt menacingly around his hands, he sneered; he knew Peach was full of shit, but she latched onto something he'd just said to buy even more time.

"Joan was blackmailing you . . . about what, embezzlement? How did *she* know about it?"

"An inside source told her," he explained, and stepped closer. "Now I realize it must've been Dennis, of course, but at the time I had no idea they even knew each other. She called me up claiming she had evidence, which, frankly, I thought was a lie, but I couldn't very well take the chance. Anyway, it was a big mistake for her to try to blackmail me."

That was an understatement, Peach managed to note, even as her body nearly trembled with abject terror and pulse-pounding nervousness. So Dennis had uncovered that his boss, Robert Walsh, had been falsely billing for Easterbrook's work, and mentioned it to Joan. It all made sense. His note in his planner had said, *Take action.* He was probably planning to take action, like going to the authorities, or at the very least confronting Robert, but Joan had beaten him to it by trying to shake Robert down first.

But that still begged the question: What had happened to Dennis? Had he confronted Robert after all? Had Robert killed him, too?

But why would the cops have found Joan's body and not Dennis's?

Or had *Joan* offed Dennis so she could get all the spoils? It made a twisted kind of sense. If Dennis did what was ethical, and went to the proper authorities about Robert's embezzlement, what would that do for Joan? But if she could use the information to extort money from Dennis's boss, then she could profit, even quit her job—so *that* must've been why she'd left Mackie's so abruptly! And why, according to the waitress she'd spoken to, Joan had sounded so giddy and happy. She had probably figured that she'd stumbled onto a major score. Everyone knew that blackmail was often an endless means of income.

Dear God, what kind of monster had Peach mixed Dennis up with?

Peach gulped as Robert took another step forward. He raised up his hands and snapped the leather belt tautly between them. Abruptly he lurched for her.

"Aaah!" she screamed, and kneed him hard in the groin before she'd had a chance to even realize she'd done it. He faltered only slightly, and then she did something pretty gross, but necessary: She hurled a big phlegm globber right in his eye.

"Uck! Goddamn it!" he exclaimed, squinting, rearing his head back, and Peach took advantage of the opportunity by kicking his kneecap, a move she'd seen in a few self-defense films in college.

Robert let out a sharp cry as his leg buckled, and Peach sprinted past him, hurling his door open so hard it hit the wall with a slam, and she bolted from his office.

She ran, looking back as she circled by Grace's desk, then went around the bend of empty cubicles heading toward the exit. She heard Robert inching in on her—God, he was close! Fear prickled around her neck, and sweat broke out on her back, face, everywhere, as she heard him call out, "Get back here, you little bitch!" He was close enough that she could hear his change jingling in his pants pocket as he chased her, but now she didn't look back.

She could see the fire exit that led to the stairs—quicker than the elevator anyway—and she pounded the door open with her elbow and hip. The alarm sounded. And she darted down the steps the door opened again, and within seconds—it all happened so fast—her head was jerked back hard. She screamed again, not sure if it was shock or pain or bloodcurdling fear. He pulled her hair so hard she fell brutally against the stairs in the stairwell, feeling a blast of hot, seeping pain spread over her back, and as she was losing consciousness, she heard a woman scream, a woman who wasn't her, and a man shout, "What the fuck are you doing?!" It sounded vaguely like Scott . . . then everything else blanked out.

When Peach woke up she was in a hospital bed, and Adam was standing over her. As her eyes fluttered open, she felt his warm palm slide over her cheek. "You're awake," he said softly, and blew out a sigh.

"What happened?" she asked groggily.

"You hit your head really hard, sweetie," a jovial nurse said from the corner of the room, where she was pulling down the window blinds. "You had a bad concussion, but you're gonna be fine. Oh, whoops!" she yelped suddenly, covering her mouth with a plump, dark brown hand. "I'm not supposed to tell patients about their condition—only the doctor is supposed to say anything."

"Oh, thank you, though," Peach said, smiling feebly, as she recalled everything that had happened in the office earlier. It all flooded back to her, hurting her head even more. Looking up at Adam, she said, "Pet peeve: doctors on power trips." Her voice sounded a little gravelly, as though her head had awakened but her vocal cords weren't quite there yet, and Adam smiled at her and strummed his fingers over her cheek.

"Don't get all worked up on pet peeves now; you need to relax," he said, sounding serious and concerned.

"I am relaxed," Peach replied. "Besides, my nurse said I'm okay. What's your name?" she called to the nurse who was now unfolding a fresh blanket and bringing it over.

"Rita," she answered, smiling.

"Hi, I'm Peach," she said, then turned to Adam again. "If Rita says I'm good, that's enough for me. By the way, what's *your* name?"

Adam's face dropped in alarm, and Peach giggled, which came out a little broken and wheezy. "Just teasing you, Quin."

Rita laughed, and after covering Peach with the blanket, she left. When the door swung closed it was just Adam and Peach in the small, sterile room. Hospital rooms in movies always looked more

inviting and spacious than the ones in real life. And the smell . . .
urine.

Oh, shoot. Maybe she'd wet herself! After a quick peek under
the covers, she relaxed. *Whew.* Okay, she wasn't a complete savage yet.

"Your mom's here; she stopped in the shop to get you flowers.
She called your dad at work and told him that you're fine; it's just a
really bad bump. No internal damage. And I'm happy to see no
amnesia . . . I think," he teased, but there was still considerable tension in his face. And . . . expectation? But what was he expecting
from her?

"So you finally met my parents," she said. It wasn't a question,
more of a casual observation. Then she asked, "What happened
with Robert? And who called you? You're supposed to be in New
York City today and tomorrow."

"Your mom called me." That stung—it was such a boyfriendy
thing for her to do, and Adam was definitely not her boyfriend.
"When Brenda called to tell her what happened to you, she asked
for my number," he went on. "I guess she figured I would know
more about what was going on." Lonnie must've told Margot how
close Peach and Adam had become—how embarrassing, when she
thought about it now. "When I called to check my messages at
home and I got the one from your mom, I came back to Boston as
soon as I could." She swallowed a hard lump in her throat, and
winced a little from the stabbing pain of it.

Adam finished, "I guess what happened was, Brenda heard the
commotion in the stairwell as everyone was coming back from
lunch, and she and Scott ran to check it out. Rachel called the police, I think. They arrested Robert."

"Oh, thank God," Peach said with palpable relief. Maybe if
they had Robert in custody, he would be inclined to talk, to spill the
beans about what happened to Dennis. She was sure that he knew.
It was just a matter of beating—*ahem, coaxing*—it out of him.

Silence fell over them then. It was a charged, loaded kind of
silence—filled with things they needed to say, yet neither knew how

to start. Adam was looking at her as if he were about to try to win her over, try to get her to care about him the way she had. No, she couldn't take that. She'd just started getting used to giving him the cold shoulder, cutting him out of her life. "I was so worried about you," he said softly, his eyes searching hers.

"Thanks," she mumbled, and looked down at her hands, which were folded across her stomach.

"Peach, I'm sorry for how I acted. Can we just start over?"

"Start over? You mean like, 'Hi, how are you, nice to meet you?' Or like, 'Let's have sex so you can turn into a cold, distant prick'?"

Adam winced. "I'm really sorry," he said again. "I didn't know how to handle everything—I mean, I just got out of a relationship, and—"

"Please," she said, cutting him off abruptly. "Stop. If you want to be friends again, that's fine. But I don't want to talk about you and me." She was being rigid to the point of insanity, completely unyielding and unforgiving, but she couldn't seem to stop herself. She'd been so crushed by his rejection, so destroyed, and he'd made such a goddamn fool of her! She wasn't ready to get sucked back into such helpless emotions—she was not willing to be so nakedly vulnerable again. *No way.*

"Jesus, I'm trying to make amends here," he said, frustrated. "What do I have to do? Just tell me."

"Nothing."

"Peach, I love you."

This was too much. Instead of crying or throwing her arms around him, she looked away. "Stop, please. I don't want to hear this," she said.

"Goddamn it!" Adam said, and plowed his hand through his hair. "Why are you being so stubborn?"

Just then Margot walked into the room with a big bouquet of flowers. Peruvian lilies—Peach's favorite. In that moment she craved the safety of someone who loved her the way her mom did, someone who truly knew her, and who unfailingly would be there.

"Hi, Mom," she said. "I'm awake."

With a quiet sigh, Adam said good-bye to both of them, then left.

"Well, he was sure in a hurry," Margot remarked. "Did something happen?"

"No."

"Oh, something's wrong, I can tell."

"I *don't* want to talk about it," Peach said firmly, as acid tears burned her eyes.

The next two weeks were a blur. Robert had been arrested for the murder of Joan Smith, and was under investigation for fraud and embezzlement. His estranged wife, Claire, returned to Boston to take care of business. She also confirmed that she'd mentioned divorce to Robert back in November, which was probably when he'd cooked up his scheme to steal as much as he could from her company before he was fired. He hadn't made a confession, but the police had found traces of Joan's blood on Robert's desk lamp, and some fibers from his jacket in the Dumpster where her body was found. Now that they knew his motive was blackmail, everything was coming together.

Except for Dennis. What the hell had happened to him? If Robert knew, he wasn't talking.

In the meantime, Peach had taken a week away from Millennium just to decompress from all that had happened. It had given her a chance to take a bus trip to Maine to visit Lonnie and Dominick, and to work on a new painting. It had been relaxing, but at the same time, watching Lonnie and her husband interact with each other made Peach's heart ache. It wasn't that she begrudged her sister that kind of love with someone; it was just that Peach wished so much to have it, too. She hadn't even realized she was ready for a serious, meaningful relationship until she'd met Adam, and now it all seemed like a passing chance. Had she made a mistake by not trying again?

The charity dance for singles had been a success. *Finally* Peach had played a role in a charitable event that actually made some money. Interestingly, she had convinced both Scott and Rachel to go, thinking sparks might fly between them, but at the actual dance, sparks flew between Scott and BeBe instead. Thank goodness BeBe had acquiesced at the last minute and agreed to come to the dance. Meanwhile, Rachel spent most of the night talking to Tim, the program coordinator at the outreach center—and why hadn't Peach envisioned that match herself? Both fountains of optimism, Rachel and Tim were simple, smiling creatures, bursting with a love of life. Hell, they were *perfect* for each other.

And Peach had missed it, but these days that was hardly news. After her whole experience setting up Joan and Dennis, Peach's view of herself as an astute matchmaker was considerably jaded. Well, *obviously*—Joan had turned out to be an extortionist, who for all they knew might have left Dennis for dead somewhere to protect her own blackmail scheme.

Heavily, Peach sighed. BeBe kept telling her that whatever happened to Dennis wasn't Peach's fault, but come on—of course it was, and the guilt was like a barbell sitting on her chest every day.

In fact, the more Peach thought about her so-called savvy with people—her supposed perceptiveness, her purportedly keen insight—the more she realized it needed a lot of work. What the hell did *she* know, anyway? There was something to be said for being more like Adam—for refraining from jumping into the mix of someone's life and trying to stir it up.

At least she'd done one thing right: Kimberly's birthday party, which had been tons of fun, even if Peach and BeBe had come painfully close to needing their stomachs pumped. (Who knew that when you hit a certain age, s'mores, Doritos, cherry Coke, and ricotta pizzas didn't sit that well together, especially when they were followed by virgin Piña Coladas?)

But seeing Kimberly so happy helped restore Peach's faith—or hope anyway—that maybe she could do a little bit of good. And it was in that spirit that she contemplated one more attempt at butting in to something that wasn't technically her business. Lately she'd been thinking a lot about Nan Emberson and what she was going through. Peach wished she could find out what happened to Dennis, if nothing else, to give his daughter some closure.

Now it was Saturday night, and Peach was in the kitchen, finishing up her angels mural with a rich golden trim. BeBe was in the living room, practicing some basic commands with Buster; apparently they were starting Puppy Preschool in a few days, so BeBe had begged off on plans with Scott to work on Buster's "behavioral difficulty," as she was calling it these days.

She heard her say, "Buster, why don't you go gnaw on Peach's limbs for a change?"

"Thank yoouuu," Peach sang from the kitchen, and BeBe giggled as she came into the kitchen and Buster doggy-heeled her to the fridge, anxious for a handout.

"No, you eat your own food," BeBe said, as Buster continued to yelp and whine. "Down," BeBe commanded firmly, and then there was silence. The puppy dropped down to a sitting position, which BeBe had trained her to do. It was most definitely a start.

Peach was dabbing paint in the far left corner of her mural, while her mind swam with sad reflections. She was thinking about Adam again, and how much she still missed him. It was crazy how even though she'd only known him a short time, she really felt like she *knew* him.

Had she been unreasonable not letting him explain? Had she been too cold, too relentless when Adam had tried to profess his feelings for her in the hospital? Was she really so certain that revenge for being spurned was more important than being with the man she loved? Her mom used to tell her and Lonnie that their Irish blood could make them stubborn, and to be forgiving—not to hold on to grudges, not to simmer in anger—and Peach had always dismissed all this as her mother's usual prattle. But now she had to wonder: Had her mother been right?

Absently she painted the trim as the same questions kept running through her mind. Had she been too hard on Adam—too stubborn? Had she pushed him away because of her pride? Was she fulfilling her mother's prophecy?

"Hey, did you know Old Smokey's is closing down tonight?" BeBe remarked offhandedly, as she entered the kitchen again to grab a peanut-butter cookie from the jar. Buster was on her heels.

Jarred back to the present, Peach thought for a second, then replied, "I don't even know what Old Smokey's *is*." Stepping down from the stepladder, she used one hand to balance herself and the other to chuck her brush into its paint-splattered ceramic holder.

"It's some old run-down bar near the Charles River—Lee Street, I think they said," BeBe explained, bending down to pet Buster, who was rolling around on the floor, looking to have her pink belly rubbed. "They were just mentioning it on the news before," she added. "Apparently it's been around for over thirty years or something."

Peach wiped her hands off on a towel, and suddenly she remembered something. Old Smokey's . . . she'd heard that before. But where . . . where. . . ? *Oh, right.* Grace had been talking about it to her sister, Midge, a few weeks ago, when Peach and Adam had been hiding in the conference room, waiting to sneak into Robert's office. That was right! Grace had said something about how she lived right down the street from it, and she couldn't wait until it closed.

Instantly Peach's mind started racing; connections zapped and splintered, and she realized something that should've been obvious. Here she'd just been thinking how well she knew Adam, even though they hadn't dated long. Well, couldn't the same be true for Grace and Dennis? A few years ago, Brenda had told her, they'd been on a couple of dates. Didn't seem like much, but what if there was some tiny tidbit of information shared, some insight into Dennis that only a woman who'd dated him, who knew him outside of the office, might have? Maybe in her short time of dating him, three years back, she'd learned things that could help Peach figure out where he was now. A long shot, yes, but certainly no crazier than anything else Peach had done since Dennis disappeared.

"I've gotta go," she said abruptly, buzzing out of the kitchen and into the living room, where she'd left her coat and scarf.

"Go where?" BeBe asked, following her.

"I've gotta talk to Grace," Peach explained.

"Who's Grace? Wait, you mean that lady from your office?"

"Yes," Peach said, shoving her feet into her still-tied silver Nikes and coiling her knit scarf around her neck. Her hair was uncomfortably stuck in it, but she didn't even care. "It's this whole Dennis thing again—I'm sorry. I just can't let it go yet. I just realized . . . maybe there's something Grace might know that would help. I know, I know—if she knew she would've said something by now, but I'm thinking it could be something that she doesn't even *know* that she knows—ya know?"

"Huh?" BeBe scooped Buster up in her arms and cradled her the way Buster liked to be held, then pressed a cheek against the white fur on the back of her neck. Buster relaxed and blinked, her little paws now hanging loosely over BeBe's forearm, watching Peach throw her coat on over her scarf.

"Bye, cutie pie," Peach said to Buster, then looked at BeBe. "It's hard to explain. I've just gotta see if there's something—*anything*—that Dennis might've told Grace back when they were dating that might shed some light on all this."

"They dated?" BeBe repeated incredulously.

"Yeah, and I always forget that, too, because it was so nothing, Brenda said. Just a handful of dates, like, three years ago, but still, if there's any chance Grace might remember something—even something he liked to do for fun, or a place he mentioned going, or *wanting* to go—even somewhere they might've gone together—maybe something will jump out. If I just get her thinking back and talking . . . who knows?"

"Peach," BeBe said gently, "I'm sorry, but . . . Dennis is gone. You have to accept it." With a resigned shrug, she added, "He was probably killed by that Robert guy. And if his ex-wife and daughter couldn't think of anything helpful to tell the police, why would this woman who dated him for, like, a second have anything to bring to the table? I just don't want you to keep obsessing on this."

"I know, you're right," Peach conceded, but headed for the door anyway. "But I've gotta try this," she said over her shoulder. "It's my last hope!"

"Well . . . be careful!" BeBe said to her back. "And call me when you get there! Actually, wait—shouldn't you call Grace first to let her know you're coming?"

Flitting past the gold-and-white pin-striped wallpaper that lined the hallway, Peach called back, "I don't know the number."

"Then how do you know her address?" BeBe cried out, but Peach was already on her way down the stairs.

When Peach's sneakers hit the pavement, cold snow pelted her in the face, and a biting shiver racked her body. Bundling up, she hurried quickly toward the T stop. She *hated* to wait, and she couldn't do it one more second.

Adam knocked hard on Peach's door. Damn this—he was not going to let her go so easily. He knew she must still feel something for him. The question was, how could he show her how much she really meant to him?

But then, he'd figure that out after he saw her. Adam had always been logistical, good at planning and strategy, but when it came to Peach, all planning and logistics were besides the point; the only thing she'd accept was something spontaneous and straight from his heart, no bullshit. And it might even be too late for that.

The girl who answered the door was not Peach. As she looked through the small space, the chain bisected her face, and she asked, "Yes?"

"Hi, I'm Adam . . . a friend of Peach's. Is she here?"

Her eyes widened, and she released the chain and opened the door. "Hi, it's nice to finally meet you," she said. "Peach isn't here, and, um, to be honest, I'm kind of worried about her."

"What do you mean?" he asked, immediately on alert.

"Well, she left over an hour ago. I told her to call when she got there and still haven't heard anything."

"Where did she go?"

"Um, to some lady from work's house—Grace?"

Furrowing his eyebrows, Adam asked, "Why would she go there?"

"Something about Dennis's disappearance again," she said with a hapless shrug. "The thing is, I don't even think she knew where she was going."

Shit! Adam thought, filled with blinding mix of frustration and concern. Why couldn't she drop the whole goddamn thing already, and leave it to the police? Her sleuthing had almost gotten her killed once, and now, even though Robert wasn't out on bail, Adam didn't want to contemplate Peach's putting herself in more danger. Who knew how deep Robert's shit ran? Maybe he knew people who could—

"Goddamn it," he muttered, then caught himself. "Sorry. Listen, I'm gonna go try to find her. I have my car. Here's my cell phone number," he said, scribbling it down on a receipt from his pocket. "If you hear from her in the meantime, will you please call me and let me know where she is?"

"Yeah, definitely," the girl said, nodding. "I mean, I'm sure I'm just overreacting."

"Yeah, we both probably are," he said lightly, forcing himself to calm down and soften his tone. He didn't want to alarm her friend just because he was panicked. And the fact was, he *was* jumping to conclusions. But it was kind of hard not to when you knew Peach and how impulsive she could be, definitely to a fault, and you knew she was in over her head, and more than anything, you knew how much you needed her.

"Thanks," he said, smiling briefly at her roommate, then hurried down the hall.

Chapter Thirty-two

Damn that T sometimes. With the fare up to the cost of a drugstore Snapple, Peach was less than patient with the trains that randomly broke down on the tracks, in the underground tunnels, and left passengers stuck in stagnant blackness for half an hour. Call her a diva, but if one more person elbowed her or coughed in her direction, she was going to get violent. (Fine, fine, she'd just get sulky.)

Now she was rounding the corner of Hamilton Road, onto Lee Street. *Perfect!* There stood Old Smokey's, an almost buried wooden pit stop with a small sign on the door that read: *Old Smokey's Gin Joint, Est. 1972, A Boston Tradition.* Peach supposed it was kind of sad that it was going, yet apparently it had descended into a brawlish kind of place over the past decade.

Continuing down Lee Street, Peach saw narrow box houses lining the road, all nearly overlapping one another. *Hmm . . .* Which one was Grace's house? She'd been so impetuous when she'd left her apartment on a mission, and now she was wondering how exactly to go about this. She supposed she could call BeBe at home and have her do a quick Internet search, try to find the number of Grace's house. Oh, that reminded her! She was supposed to call BeBe anyway to tell her she was okay.

Just as she was reaching inside her coat pocket for her cell, Peach spotted the name Gomez on the mailbox right in front of her. *Fabulous!* Some good luck and timing for a change. Hooking a right, Peach walked up the skinny, winding walkway that led to the front door. She felt awkward showing up unannounced like this, but it was for a good cause, and hopefully that would count for something.

It was weird, though. As Peach approached the front steps she had the eerie feeling that someone was following her. She turned quickly . . . but there was nothing there except the chill of the night and the low whistle of the wind.

She hopped up the steps, checking over her shoulder again. Still nothing. Boy, this was one creepy neighborhood. Just as she was poised to knock on the door, Peach heard voices inside the house. Jeez, Peach didn't want to interrupt Grace if she was having company—and how were they supposed to have an all-night brainstorming session about Dennis's whereabouts if Grace was entertaining?

Glancing over, Peach noticed that Grace's front blinds were open just a few inches. Shamelessly, Peach bent down to see if she could peek inside and see what the deal was before she knocked. That was when she noticed that the window itself had been crookedly closed. Maybe it was jammed, but there was a slanted inch of open space, which was probably why she could hear inside the house.

Peering through the slit in the blinds, Peach saw Grace sitting in an armchair, directly across from the window. She had her head thrown back, and her eyes were closed—shoot, was she asleep?

Then Peach heard a low moan. Where had that come from?

"Oh, yeah . . . right *there* . . ." Whoa, it had come from Grace! Lolling her head against the back of the chair, Grace added, "Don't stop—I *need* it. . . ."

Squinting, Peach bent even lower to get a better look through the partially open blinds. Maybe Grace was just having a really good dream.

But then her eyes opened, and she lifted her head forward a little to talk to someone who must've been kneeling on the floor in front of her. With drowsy eyes, she said, "Why'd you stop?" and a man answered, "My hands are tired." And then he stood up, his side profile coming into view, and Peach's jaw dropped.

Dennis Emberson!

Peach literally did not believe what she was seeing—after weeks of wondering about Dennis, after finally accepting that he was probably dead, but still needing to know—now to see him standing there in Grace Gomez's apartment, with Grace reaching up for him, and pulling him down again by his wrists . . .

With her heart slamming against her ribs, Peach swallowed hard and tried to process the wealth of conflicting emotions coursing through her. An indescribable rush of relief and euphoria washed over her, flooding her chest, sucking the breath right out of her. *Dennis is alive!* And at the same time, confusion and suspicion gnawed at her stomach, rocking her insides to the point of sweeping nausea. *What kind of fucking sick joke is this?*

Leaning down, Peach ducked into the shrubbery to get a better look. Brushing thick, prickly leaves aside, she scanned the limited view of Grace's living room, and now she could see what Dennis was doing. He was back on the floor, kneeling beside Grace, rubbing her bare feet with a pained expression on his face. "Are you sure I do this *every* night?" Peach heard him say as he dug his fingers into her arches and she moaned again.

"Yeah, that's right," she said, "just like that."

"Okay . . . is that good?" he asked, stopping and waiting.

"No, don't stop. More . . . I need it," she said. "And after this, if you could just sand my calluses, that would be heaven."

"*More* calluses?" Dennis asked incredulously, his face looking weary and exhausted. Then he wiped his brow and kept digging his fingers into her naked arches. He was dressed in a sweater and sweatpants, both of which looked way too big for him.

"What do you mean?" Grace asked, tipping her head up again and looking at him.

Sounding apologetic, Dennis said, "I'm sorry, it's just . . . it seems like there's always so many *more*."

"Well, I work to support us, and then Saturdays I go grocery shopping for us," she said defensively, and then added a little haughtily, "I can't help it that I'm on my feet all week." Pulling back her left foot, Dennis relaxed his shoulders, as though heaving a sigh of relief.

Then Grace stuck her bare right foot toward his face and wiggled her toes, as though to say, *Hello, don't forget this good stuff over here.*

Shaking her head, still stunned by the confounding spectacle in front of her, Peach put her hand over her open mouth, just trying to take it all in.

"I know, I know," Dennis was saying, sounding resigned as he went to work on her right one. "I rub your feet every night, and on Sundays we do the corn pads."

"Right," Grace said, nodding, then slanted a look down at him and added, "You know, none of this ever bothered you *before*."

Before? Before *what*? Before his olfactory glands had fully developed?

Suddenly a blast of light lit up the window from behind, and instinctively Peach ducked deeply into the bushes. Turning around, she peered through the leaves. Oh, it was just a car . . . but it was now swerving toward the curb right by Grace's mailbox. And it looked a hell of a lot like *Adam's* car.

Her pulse kicked up even more. What on earth was *he* doing here?

He slammed the car door and headed up the walkway. *Great, could he draw more attention?* Peach looked back through Grace's window, but she and Dennis didn't seem too distracted from their previous business.

As soon as he got to the top of the stairs, he spotted Peach cowering down by the window, and just as he was about to open his big fat mouth, Peach yanked him hard by the hem of his jacket, with her finger pressed to her lips. His mouth dropped open to say something, but she silenced him immediately with, "Shhh."

But it didn't last long. "Jesus," he whispered, hunkering down, too, but since he was considerably taller than she was, he looked less at home with the whole thing. "What the hell are you doing hiding? What, is this your new thing?"

"What the hell am *I* doing?" Peach said with her eyes widening. "Why are *you* here?"

"Because BeBe said you were on your way to see Grace, so I found out her address and—"

"Omigod, you're the reason I was getting the feeling that someone was following me!" Peach whispered.

"I drove here; I wasn't following you."

"No, I mean I must've just *sensed* it." He brushed right over that and asked again what she was doing there. "Looking for Dennis," she answered, then motioned toward Grace's window. "And I finally found him."

When Adam saw Dennis, his mouth fell open, and Peach covered it quickly with her palm to make sure he didn't shout anything. But the instant her palm touched his warm, semiwet, open lips, she felt a jolt of electricity at the contact. She suppressed the urge to kiss him right then.

Peeling her hand from his mouth, Adam leaned in closer to the window, as if getting a closer, sharper look would make it make sense when it didn't.

"What the hell is Dennis doing here?" he whispered.

"Rubbing Grace's feet, and that's not even the weird part." Peach explained how Dennis seemed a little disoriented, and how Grace had recounted what their "normal" routine was, making it sound like they'd been doing this for years. "Adam, she made it sound like they were a couple. None of this makes sense."

"Holy shit!" Adam said, as he glanced up into the window again. "They're kissing!"

"What!" Peach yelped a little more loudly than she should have, and looked inside. It was true. Grace had Dennis's face cupped in her hands and she was really planting one on him. He appeared to be acquiescing, yet not bowled over with passion. And then Grace pulled back and said, "Come on, say it. Please. You never say it to me."

Dennis said, "Um . . . it just feels strange to say; I don't know why."

She sighed haughtily. "It never felt strange before. Come on, *say* it."

After a moment, Dennis said something, but it was muffled. Adam and Peach just exchanged questioning looks; then Grace said, "Again . . ."

And he repeated it. This time they heard it. He called her "sweetums." And then she went in for another juicy kiss, and that's when Peach lost her balance and, steadying herself, accidentally crushed a twig beneath her feet. "Shoot!" she whispered, but Grace and Dennis didn't seem to notice. Grace pulled Dennis up again and coaxed him to straddle her on the chair. Grace's greedy hands slid down his back and over his butt to cop a feel—then she squeezed.

"That's it!" Peach said, rising to her feet, and pushing past Adam. "I'm going in."

"What! What do you mean, you're going in?"

"Use your imagination," Peach said dryly, though admittedly she was being bitchy, because she'd deliberately been avoiding Adam to keep from getting sucked back into all those feelings for him again. Yet here she was . . . pining for him, loving that he was here with her, missing him so much, so palpably, all over again. *Damn him!*

She banged on the front door. Adam shook his head, then rose to stand beside her. "I'm coming, too," he said. "Someone's gotta keep an eye on you."

"Whatever," Peach said, acting like she didn't care (key word "acting"). But putting her feelings for Adam aside, she had to make sense of this whole thing with Dennis.

Within minutes there was scuffling, and then Grace came to the door. She peeked her head out and said, "Peach! Adam? What are you doing here?"

"Well, I'm *not* here to rub your feet," Peach said, and pushed the door open a little more. "Dennis! Dennis, come out here!"

"What are you talking about?" Grace said, trying to sound shocked and baffled while she blockaded the door. "I want you both to leave—*now!*"

"I'm sure you do, Grace!" Peach said, annoyed. "But in the

meantime I want to talk to Dennis. Dennis, come out!" she cried out again.

"Hello . . . ?"

They all turned and saw Dennis emerge from the other room, looking questioningly at all three of them. "Damn it! I told you to stay in the other room!" Grace shouted.

"Is everything okay?" he asked, looking thoroughly bewildered. "Who are these people?"

"Dennis!" Peach exclaimed, and pushed past Grace, barreling over her, and threw her arms around him. "You're alive; you're okay!"

Befuddled, he slipped his arms loosely around her and exchanged a questioning look with Adam, and Adam was more than a little perplexed himself. He said to Grace, "How come you didn't tell the authorities that Dennis was here? How long have you known where he was?"

"Authorities?" Dennis echoed, confused, then looked to Grace. "Sweetums?" He sounded uncomfortable saying it, but also uncertain, as though using the endearment would give him Grace's protection somehow.

"No, no," Grace said, grappling quickly, "ignore them; they're trying to put you away again. You can only trust me; I'm the only one you can trust!"

"Dennis, what's going on?" Peach said, and looked into his eyes, giving him a shake. "What ever happened to you after your date with Joan?"

"Who's Joan?"

Peach looked flummoxed by that question, and glanced back at Adam. Grace was not trying to keep him at bay; she'd focused her attention on Peach and Dennis, as though silently acknowledging that right now Peach was a force that simply wouldn't be stopped, so there was little point in trying. Adam had realized that in general about her; it was only one of the many reasons he'd fallen in love with her: her will, her determination, her guts. And now she was interrogating Dennis, and Adam said to Grace, "Why don't you just explain what's going on?"

"Dennis, you don't remember Joan?" Peach asked now.

He shrugged. "I'm sorry; I don't remember much of anything since the accident. I don't remember you, either, so I'm really sorry if I should," he said weakly.

"You don't remember *me*?" Peach said, as though *that* were truly ludicrous, and Adam couldn't help but grin to himself. "Adam, do something," she said, looking back at him, her blue eyes searching his with entreaty.

He felt a primal need to swoop in and help, to alleviate her worries, to make her trust him again. "Grace, what did you do to him?"

"Nothing!" she wailed. "I didn't do anything! I just tried to build a life with the man I love! Please don't ruin it all—not now—not after three years of waiting and wishing desperately!" She threw her blockish head in her hands and sank to her knees, bawling hysterically, tears riveting through her fingers, down her arms, splashing lightly on the entry foyer's linoleum floor. "Please, oh, *God*!" she howled.

"Grace, what's going on?" Dennis said, alarmed, confused, and now looking suspicious. "Please tell me what's going on!" Grace kept crying, muttering something about loving Dennis for so long, and he turned to Peach and said, "Ever since I woke up from the accident, I couldn't remember my name or anything, and Grace took me home again. She said my memory would come back once I got settled in our home and back to our routine. She said it's happened to me before. See, apparently I have a mental condition, and if I don't keep it in check I'll be hospitalized. So Grace takes care of us, supports us, while I stay home with her. And apparently we're in love." He said that last part as though *that* were the suspicious part of Grace's whole ludicrous tale.

"Dennis, *what* accident?" Peach asked him now; then she looked back at Grace. "Grace, what happened to him?"

"I didn't plan it, okay?" she explained. "It's just that when I overheard how excited he was about that bitch, Joan, and how he was going out with her again on Saturday, I was so upset. I was so afraid it would actually turn into something real. With Dennis, I didn't believe he was capable of getting excited about anything or anyone like that. He sure never got excited about me," she remarked bitterly. Aha. When they'd dated a few times three years back and Dennis had stopped being interested. But surely Grace didn't care about that? Surely if she ever cared, it was long since water under the bridge . . . wasn't it?

"Come on, Grace, tell us what happened," Adam said to her calmly, looking at her intently through his glasses, his voice cool and collected, his eyes logical and waiting. And in that second Peach realized that they'd inadvertently set up a good cop bad cop kind of thing—Peach's was the overbearing, ballsy, do-or-die approach to getting a full explanation, while Adam's calm, logical method exuded a more comforting sense of encouragement—eliciting responses, apparently, because Grace slumped down and rested her forehead against the banister of the stairs.

"I followed him that night. I waited for him outside that comedy club, Monkeyville. I watched him through the window, laughing, having fun with that skinny little bitch," she explained, and it hit Peach like a thunderbolt: So that was how Grace had known about Nelson's goal of becoming a professional comedian! She'd seen him going to Monkeyville for amateur night—or maybe she'd even been milling in the background of the club when she was spying on Dennis and Joan.

"So what happened to him?" Peach demanded. "Did you hurt him? Did you cause him to . . . be this way?" she said, meaning slow in the head or whatever one would call it. Then she gave Dennis a quick, supportive smile, and he just looked bewildered, more so than usual.

"No, I didn't hurt him!" Grace said. "I just took advantage of an opportunity. See, he and Joan left Monkeyville and went for a walk—and I followed. I was so jealous, I was boiling with rage. It wasn't fair! That should've been me walking down the street with him! That should've been me holding his hand!

"Then out of nowhere, a mugger jumped out, took them by surprise. It all happened so quickly. I was twenty feet behind anyway, and the guy jumped in front of Dennis, demanding his wallet. When he took it he knocked him down." So that was how Dennis lost his wallet. The mugger must have discarded it on the street after cleaning it out, then ran.

"What about Joan?"

"She managed to run off as soon as the mugger attacked. Like I said, it all happened so fast . . ." Grace mumbled, then turned to Adam, whom, in some weird way, she seemed to view as her redeemer. "I just went over to help him up, to make sure he was okay, but . . . when he didn't remember his name or anything, I realized he'd been clocked pretty hard on the head. And I realized I could take him to the hospital, or . . ."

She could take him to her lair! Peach thought, still reeling with shock, outrage, and a frenzied sense of relief that hadn't yet sunk in. Jeez, all this time Dennis Emberson was alive, clueless to the fact people were looking for him, clueless to the fact that before he'd lost his memory, he'd uncovered Robert Walsh's embezzlement, and by telling Joan, he'd set a blackmail and murder scheme in motion. Even now he looked pretty clueless. His receding hairline was bisected by some errant strands that descended and hung down his forehead. His pound-puppy eyes were more drawn than usual.

"So you told him that what? You and he had a relationship?" Adam asked her now, and Grace nodded. And apparently she'd concocted some ludicrous story that he had recurring mental slips and would end up in a loony bin again if he didn't lie low in their house and let her take care of him. Where the foot rubs and callus treatments came in, Peach wasn't quite sure. This was too crazy! So Grace had been in love with Dennis all these years, had been carrying this total obsession, and Peach had missed the boat on that one, too. She was not nearly as astute about people as she'd thought; she would have to rectify that.

Now Grace wiped her nose on the sleeve of her puffy chenille robe and continued, as tears streamed down her cheeks. "I loved you so much, Dennis. I just wanted it to be like it was that first time you asked me out . . . and then you just lost interest for no reason."

Welcome to being a woman, Peach thought. It was the ultimate classic case of all time: Guy likes girl, girl likes guy, guy decides he can't stand girl for no discernible reason, girl gets hurt. (And on a side note, what the fuck was *up* with that, anyway?)

"Grace, I'm taking Dennis home," Peach said.

"But first we're taking him to the hospital," Adam added, and swiftly opened the door wide for Peach and Dennis to walk through.

"I'm still so confused," Dennis said. "I feel like such a fool."

Peach smiled softly at him as she led him out the door and said, "But at least you're alive."

After Dennis was admitted to the hospital for observation, and the police arrested Grace for kidnapping, Adam drove Peach home. Now they were parked outside her building. Apparently Grace had told the same thing to the cops that she'd confessed to them, but she'd also mentioned that she'd had tons of pictures of her and Dennis in her apartment. In reality they'd all been from one of their dates a long time ago that she duplicated and cropped and enlarged in a bunch of different ways, but when he'd come back, he'd had no reason to question their life together. While he'd slept that first night, she'd sneaked out early in the morning, bought some male clothes from the Salvation Army, and slipped them into the closet to further continue the illusion that not only did they have a relationship, but that he was totally dependent on it and her.

Peach had spent the entire ride in Adam's car processing all that had happened, and her mind kept going back to the fact that Adam had been there—literally her partner in crime—the whole time. And it had felt so natural; even after the total lapse in their friendship, it seemed they fell back into it so easily. God, he was just so special to her. She wondered how she could tell him that she'd been stubborn, unforgiving, unyielding . . . terrified of getting hurt again. But if the offer was still open to give it another try . . .

No, no, she couldn't say *that,* exactly. Talk about desperate. If only he would say something. Instead, though, he cut the engine and just looked at her.

"Well . . ." she said lamely. "What a night." Even lamer! But so what; it was only Adam, the man she loved. And, in fact, if she was going to go *this* far with the lameness, why not go for that whole other bit about taking her back?

There was no need, though. Adam studied her for another second, then reached his hands up, slid his burning hot palms on her neck, and pulled her toward him. Smoldering heat nearly consumed her, stole her breath. His lips met hers, gentle for only a second, and then, like a burst of fire, the kiss turned hot, fast—wet. Peach immediately kissed him back passionately, desperately, clutched his coat to pull him closer. She couldn't deny this anymore; she wanted him, all of him, always, and she crushed her mouth on his, feeling his skillful tongue snake inside her mouth and his lips suck and pull at hers, tasting him, feeling the hot, quick pants of his breathing when their lips parted. He tilted his head and kissed her again. Hungrily, their mouths fused, and they held each other tightly. Peach felt arousal stir between her legs, hotly, wetly, and the tangible reality of Adam's mouth on hers, his hands possessing her, claiming her, was barely registering. It was all so electrifying it was almost surreal, and finally he pulled back, breathing heavily, his eyes glazed beneath his glasses, and she could feel hers slitted half-closed, too.

"I love you," he whispered, his voice a thick rasp. "Please believe me. I love you so much. . . ."

"I love *you*!" she blurted. God, she'd never thought she'd say those words again, especially not to Adam—to Quin—who'd broken her heart once already. But here she was in his car, after the craziest night of her life, after she'd been so sure they'd lost each other forever. Her mouth descended on his again; then she murmured, "I missed you so much . . . I missed you . . ."

He pulled her tightly against him and buried his head in her hair. "I'm sorry for everything."

"I know; so am I," she said quickly. "Let's just forget it all."

"But—"

She put her palm over his mouth and pulled back to look into his eyes. "Do you think you know me?"

He took her hand off his mouth.

"What do you mean?"

"Just answer the question."

"Yeah, I think so."

"Then you should know when I say something, that's it. It's law. It's done."

"Oh, really?" he challenged, grinning.

"And furthermore," she continued, "you should know that I believe deeply in instant gratification."

"Well, hell, of course I know that," he said.

"Good, glad we agree," she said, and climbed on top of him, straddled him in the car, and kissed him again.

He groaned and tangled his fingers in her hair as she began undulating her hips against his, grinding against him, bringing his erection to an aching state of arousal. When she slammed her hips down hard on him, the sensation was unreal. She moaned, and he let out a husky growl. She pulled his glasses off his face and tossed them on the passenger's seat.

She noticed that the windows had actually fogged up in those few moments, and she smiled.

"What are you grinning at?" he asked, looking dazed, almost pained with arousal. His hands came down to clutch her waist, his fingers digging into the denim of her jeans as he pulled her flush up against his cock again.

She could feel it hard and full beneath his pants, and against her. "Nothing," she whispered. Then she started rocking against him again, and moved her head so he was kissing her neck, sucking it, dragging his open mouth and warm lips, his scalding-hot tongue licking its way down. Before she knew it, he'd worked his hand inside her pants, underneath her underwear, and he was stroking her bare flesh.

"You're wet," he whispered.

"That's an understatement," she said brokenly, and moaned deeply when he slid his middle finger deep inside her. "Ohh . . . God . . . don't stop."

"Mnm . . . bossy . . ." he said, but it didn't sound like he minded. Then he used two of his fingers to stroke the inner walls of her vagina, making her sexual nerves vibrate and explode with sensations.

Within seconds both were lost to frantic moans and the sweaty, heated moments in the fogged-up car. He stroked her until she climaxed; then he put his car in reverse, did a frantic and illegal K-turn, and peeled down the street, hard as a rock. She stroked him with her hand as he drove to his apartment.

The rest of the night was something of a blur—the sultry, erotic kind that was steaming with sensations, and without recriminations, and when they woke up the next morning, neither made any move to pull away. Instead Peach told him, "You mean so much to me."

"I feel so lucky," Adam said on a sigh. "And happy . . . which is inevitable, I guess."

"Why?"

"Because," he said, seriously, studying her as he held her close underneath him and sun spilled through the crack in the blinds, "you have that effect on people."

It was the most wonderful thing anyone had ever said to her; the words wrapped around her heart as her arms wrapped around Adam—her new best friend and so much more. Snuggling against his warm, strong chest, she sighed and thought, *So this is love.*

Epilogue

six months later

"So how's the dissertation coming?" Peach asked her sister, who was sitting beside her on the bleachers. Her long black hair was flying crazily in the summer wind, while Peach had hers tied up in a ponytail.

"It's going a lot better," Lonnie said, nodding. "I'm almost halfway there."

"Hey, that's great," Peach said, though she always knew her sister would pull the thesis off, even if it were at the last minute.

"Well, maybe not *half*way, exactly," she amended, "but I'd say that I'm at the point now where I feel it could be really good. Someday. If I had a lot more time . . . and maybe if someone else were writing it."

Peach just laughed.

Visiting Boston for the next two weeks, Lonnie and Dominick had joined Peach and Adam today at the Annual Summer Canine Agility Competition. BeBe and Buster had entered, which was their new thing now—agility competitions, which kept Buster healthy, in shape, and most of all, quasi-obedient. It gave BeBe a real focus, a passion. And some of the proceeds of each competition went to a dog rescue fund.

At the moment, Adam and Dominick were pulling the cars around, because the last event of the day had just ended. Lined up on the bleachers below Peach and Lonnie were Ramona, Kimberly, and Scott, of course. This was a first for BeBe's mom, who'd come today to show support and, inevitably, to try to stay connected to

BeBe, but by going into her world, instead of trying to pull her back into Ramona's.

As for Peach, she no longer worked at Millennium. Almost getting killed by the company president had kind of soured her on the place. Meanwhile Claire Walsh had returned to Boston to clean up Robert's mess and to get the business in order. Focused solely on the bottom line, Claire offered Peach a twenty-five-thousand-dollar, onetime flat payment for all the rights to the Ethan Eckers doll and his subsidiaries. Peach had snatched it up. Ethan Eckers was Millennium's property now, and soon to have knockoffs in toy stores across the country, but Peach had no interest in the franchising of her little brainchild. She adored him, but it was time to move on already—though she still couldn't believe sometimes how one bored night of fiddling around with fabrics and buttons had changed her life.

As for Dennis Emberson, he'd recovered most of his memory, though there were still a few gaps here and there. The doctor had explained that because of the nature of Dennis's contusion, his brain was, for all intents and purposes, bruised. But as the bruise healed, and as Dennis was thrown back into his normal life, surrounded by people he knew, things would come back to him. His daughter, Nan, had been devoted to helping her dad recover. In fact, the whole traumatic episode had also gotten Nan to reconcile with Rachel's sister, Alice. Apparently they'd both realized that life was too precious to waste fighting over a guy. A guy had come between them—*that* had been what the whole mysterious falling out was about—something so silly should have been obvious.

Meanwhile, Grace Gomez had pleaded "no contest" to charges of kidnapping and obstructing justice in return for a small sentence, some psychiatric care, and several thousand hours of community service. Maybe it was twisted, but Peach felt sorry for her.

On the love front: Adam's parents, Liz and Martin, were reconciling. Liz had moved back into their house, on the condition that Martin went to marriage counseling. Both still called Peach occasionally—usually for advice about something they thought was too petty to bring up to their counselor. It was probably a pretty dysfunctional arrangement, but hey, whatever worked, and Peach was happy to listen. It was great practice, too, since she would be going back to school in the fall to get her degree in psychology. The whole Dennis debacle had made her realize that she was in no position to help others until she honed her craft.

"Here they come!" she said now, standing up and leading the way down the bleachers. Scott followed and went to hug BeBe first. They walked out toward the open field, away from the manicured grounds, which were flooded with participants and spectators. "Hey, you did great," Scott said, hugging her.

"Oh, thanks!" BeBe said brightly, her face pink and vibrant from the competition, and squeezed him back. They made an adorable snapshot: BeBe short, round, and cute, and Scott tall, lean, and cute. It was just so . . . cute. "Thanks, you guys, for coming," BeBe added.

Ramona held Kimberly's hand as they approached, just catching up because Ramona was crossing the soft grass very gingerly in her Ann Taylor heels. "Yes, it was really enjoyable," she said when she got there.

"Thanks, Mom," BeBe said. Buster was jumping up on everyone, frantically overstimulated by all the attention. She darted off on her own, then circled around and broke into a frenzied bichon buzz—though they would expect nothing less. When she finally calmed down, BeBe called her over. And she came. Then she dug her nose in the grass, apparently rooting for truffles.

"Oh, no, BeBe, she's eating something!" Ramona said, pointing at Buster and looking horrified at what it could be.

"Oh." Peach looked down and then told Buster to "give," and abruptly she dropped what was in her mouth—a gnarled, discarded cigarette. "Oh, jeez," BeBe said, grinning with exasperation as she bent down to scoop Buster up. "Come on, sweetie; don't eat that stuff. No cigs when you're on the patch."

Ramona reared her head back, pressing a plump, manicured hand to her chest, and BeBe rolled her eyes. "It was a joke, Mom."

"Oh. I . . . see," Ramona said, clearly not bowled over by the humor.

Just then Dominick and Adam emerged, and Dominick pointed toward the street. "Hey, the cars are parked out front."

As soon as Adam saw Peach, his face broke into a smile, and hers did, too, as always. She wondered when she would stop feeling so filled with love for him, when it would get uninteresting, when he would become simply ordinary to her. She couldn't even fathom that.

He came right to her, and she was pulled toward him, and automatically they grabbed hands. Then Peach turned back to everyone and said, "Let's go celebrate."

As they headed toward their cars, Adam lagged half a step behind Peach, looking at her in near amazement, still not fully believing that she was his. That he really *had* her in his life.

Often he thought about that first day she'd burst into his cube and interrogated him—blew into his life and splashed color into it as if it were one of her blank walls. And it seemed so long ago, because he'd learned so much more about her since then, yet he remembered that one moment with startling clarity. Something had passed between them—a zing, a spark—one of those things you never fully absorb until you're looking back on it.

That day she had invited him in and little had he known . . . it would change everything.

Photo by L. Winters

Jill Winters discovered her love for writing fiction while she was procrastinating on her master's thesis at Boston's many bookstores and coffee shops. A Phi Beta Kappa, summa cum laude graduate of Boston College, she has taught women's studies and is the author of three previous novels, *Plum Girl, Blushing Pink,* and *Raspberry Crush.*

Jill loves to hear from her readers. Visit her online at: www.jillwinters.com.